A
Stolen
Child

A
Stolen
Child

Sarah Stewart Taylor

Minotaur Books
New York

First published in the United States by Minotaur Books, an imprint of St. Martin's Publishing Group

A STOLEN CHILD. Copyright © 2023 by Sarah Stewart Taylor. All rights reserved. Printed in the United States of America. For information, address St. Martin's Publishing Group, 120 Broadway, New York, NY 10271.

www.minotaurbooks.com

Library of Congress Cataloging-in-Publication Data

Names: Taylor, Sarah Stewart, author.
Title: A stolen child / Sarah Stewart Taylor.
Description: First edition. | New York: Minotaur Books, 2023. | Series: Maggie D'Arcy mysteries; 4
Identifiers: LCCN 2023004462 | ISBN 9781250826688 (hardcover) | ISBN 9781250826695 (ebook)
Subjects: LCGFT: Detective and mystery fiction. | Novels.
Classification: LCC PS3620.A97 S76 2023 | DDC 813/.6—dc23/eng/20230208
LC record available at https://lccn.loc.gov/2023004462

Our books may be purchased in bulk for promotional, educational, or business use. Please contact your local bookseller or the Macmillan Corporate and Premium Sales Department at 1-800-221-7945, extension 5442, or by email at MacmillanSpecialMarkets@macmillan.com.

First Edition: 2023

10 9 8 7 6 5 4 3 2 1

To Lisa, with gratitude for your friendship—and your readership

Come away, O human child!

To the waters and the wild

With a faery, hand in hand,

For the world's more full of weeping than you can
understand.

—from "The Stolen Child" by W. B. Yeats

A
Stolen
Child

One

....

"Guards! Guard and American Guard! Guard and American Guard!"

My partner, Garda Jason Savage, and I are just finishing up our community patrol when we see two boys beckoning to us along the South Circular Road. Jason rolls his eyes at me. We've tried to get to know this little gang of kids who live and go to school in the neighborhood so that we'll come to seem as familiar as the houses and shops they pass by every day. But they picked up on my accent right away and now when they address me, it's always qualified by my nationality.

The younger one, a runty blond-haired kid named Luke, calls again, "Guards, guards! American Guard and Guard!"

"What is it, Luke?" Jason asks when the boys reach us. "Are you all right, so?"

Luke, all baggy school uniform and spindly limbs, looks up at us, his eyes wide. "Guards, you've got to come, Donald's in the drain!"

Jason and I exchange a skeptical glance. Are they playing a prank? It wouldn't be the first time the kids have tried to trick us. Our first week on the beat, they put a large doll in a baby stroller and rolled it along the sidewalk, yelling, "The baby! The baby!" and laughed when we raced to retrieve it.

But Luke seems genuinely upset, so we follow him to the end of

Carlisle Street, almost running to keep up with him. Up ahead, I can see a crowd of kids clustered in front of a house that's under construction. In a perfect little microcosm of the flavor of the neighborhood, the house next to it is already sleekly renovated, with a tasteful glossy charcoal front door and two planters filled with topiary. The house on the other side has a peeling facade, a rampantly growing rose garden overtaking the iron fence, and row upon row of small animal figurines in the dusty windows. FOR SALE signs are posted in front of a third of the houses in the neighborhood.

"Let's see now," Jason says soothingly as we get close. "What's the trouble?"

The kids shuffle aside, and we step into the small front garden. It's been completely dug up and there's a pile of gravel and debris to one side. Luke points to a large, half-covered drain hole, from which we can hear loud and insistent quacking.

"Donald's a duck?" I ask stupidly.

"Yeah, he's going to starve down there. We've got to get him out," Luke is saying, hopping around excitedly and getting in the way of us seeing anything. Most of the kids in the little gang are Luke's age, ten or eleven, but there are three teenagers, two girls and a boy, watching from the sidewalk. Their younger counterparts seem to generally trust us, but I've seen these three around, and they exude waves of teenage resentment and skepticism about law enforcement. One of the girls has dyed black hair in a severe bob-and-bangs cut, her school uniform too big on her thin frame, paired with black tights and heavy black shoes. Her friend has stringy dark blond hair worn long and straight, a smear of too-bright pink lipstick on her mouth, and small eyes surrounded by dark eyeliner. The boy just looks furious with the world. He's tall, broad-shouldered, his face troubled by acne, and he looks like he'd rather be doing anything than participating in the duck rescue mission.

"Now then," Jason says. "Youse all step aside and I'll see what the situation is here." The kids move to the edge of the sidewalk as he looks down into the darkness. "Hello there, Donald. Have you gotten yourself into a fix?"

A loud battery of quacking comes from the drain.

"He's got a wife down by the canal," one of the kids says. "I'd say he's worried about whether she thinks he's run off." Jason and I exchange a glance and try not to smile.

"Can you get him out, guards?" Luke asks, his voice high and a little hysterical.

"Of course we can," Jason tells him in a calm, soothing voice. "Now, I'll just move the cover away. Garda D'arcy, will you help me?"

The two of us drag the heavy metal cover to the side. "He must be pretty far down," I say quietly. Jason takes the flashlight from his vest and shines it into the hole. There's more quacking and then, out of the blackness, we see the head of a duck, his iridescent head-feathers set off by the flashlight. "I think I can reach him," Jason tells me. "You'll have to hold my feet."

"No problem. I didn't start lifting at the gym for nothing."

I turn to the kids. "Does anyone have a jumper or a coat we can put on the ground so Garda Savage can lie down?"

"Tina," Luke calls out. "Give us your jumper." The blond girl tosses him her fleece jacket—now I can see a family resemblance between them, which explains the girl's presence here—and he rushes over to lay it down.

Jason rolls up his shirtsleeves and gets down on his belly. Once I've got a good grip on his feet, he inches over the drain and I start lowering him down. The quacking becomes louder the lower he goes, and I can feel all the kids waiting behind me. Jason's voice drifts back up to me. "Come on, Donald. I'm trying to help you here. The sooner you let me get you, the sooner you'll be back to your wife in the canal."

"Come on, Donald," Luke blurts out. "Let him catch ya!"

"I've got you," I call down to Jason. "If you need another few inches."

"C'mere to me, Donald," I hear him say. "C'mere, you." I feel him swinging his arms around and then he yells out, "Got him!"

"Give me a hand," I say to the kids, and they all help me pull Jason back up to the edge of the drain and onto the sidewalk. He's tucked the duck under one arm and as soon as they're back in the light, Donald starts quacking wildly again and trying to break free.

"You got 'im!" Luke shouts.

I help Jason stand up. "Now, let's take him back to his wife," he says and gives an indignant Donald a pat on his head. Making a noisy but triumphant procession, we all follow Jason along the little side streets and back down toward the canal as passersby stop to find the source of the commotion. Amid lots of quacking and flapping on Donald's part, Jason stoops at the water's edge to release him. There's already a small group of waterfowl there, three swans and a half dozen mallard ducks, and Donald gives a few final quacks and then goes to join them, propelling his feathery body smoothly beneath an overhanging willow tree, the wispy pale green branches reflected on the surface of the water.

"There, now, I think he was saying thanks a million," Jason tells the kids. "He'll be all right. Job well done."

"Thanks, guard," Luke says.

There are a few more *Thanks, guards* and then they all melt away, the teens, still looking bored, bringing up the rear. The dark-haired girl hangs back a bit to walk with the boy and I watch them go, a little thread of worry tugging at me. I'd guess they're about fifteen, and I remember what a tough age that was for my own daughter, Lilly, and her friends. Jason and I have learned a bit about some of these kids' home lives, and they're not very stable. The neighborhood is gentrifying quickly and from what Jason's said, it's lost some of the community watchfulness that existed for children when he was growing up here; there are smoothie shops and fancy coffee and million-euro-houses, but the neighborhood is full of danger for kids on their own in the afternoons.

As if to drive the point home, a familiar figure comes around the corner. I recognize him as a low-level drug dealer named Cameron Murphy whom Jason and I have interacted with before. He's spent a few months here and there in jail for minor offenses, but he doesn't have the air of a hardened criminal. He's not much taller than I am, but he's pumped up every muscle he's got, and he keeps his hair longer and gelled on top to give him an extra couple of inches. He has a Sylvester and Tweety Bird tattoo on his neck and when he turns his head, his skin wrinkles and Tweety takes on a demonic attitude.

Cameron is sucking furiously at a cigarette, keeping his eyes down while still scanning the street for someone he's either looking for or trying to avoid. He slows when he spots us along the canal bank, but he's too smooth to stop or change direction. His body goes rigid, but he keeps coming, still surreptitiously checking for whoever it is in his sights.

"Hiya, Cameron," I call out to him. "How are you today?"

"Ah, good, very good, now," he says. "What's the story yourselves, guards?"

Jason says, "Fine, thanks. Anything going on we should know about?"

"Ah, I wouldn't say so, now. I'm just out for bit of a stroll meself." He nods and walks past us, heading in the same direction as the kids, which makes me nervous. I'm seen him talking to Tina and her friend a few times, and I'm pretty sure nothing good is going to come of any friendship between them.

"Well now," Jason says once Cameron's gone, straightening his high visibility vest and patting his chest in a self-satisfied way. "That feels like a good day's work. Though we'll have to keep it quiet. The lads hear about this and we'll never get out from under it. You'll be Donald Duck D'arcy for the rest of your life. And I'll be responding to fake calls for injured waterfowl until the day I retire. Yeah, I'd say best not to spread this one around."

"My bill is sealed." I gaze up at the blue sky and sunshine and the green dome of St. Mary Immaculate across the canal in Rathmines, hardly a cloud in sight. "I thought it was supposed to rain today."

"Ah, sure, it'll be coming later," Jason says wisely, reaching up to scratch his forehead. "I'd say about four o'clock." He's only thirty, with thinning hair he's started rearranging over his scalp in a way that makes him look older. Contemplating the upper atmosphere, patting the beginnings of a belly under his uniform, he could be an ancient country farmer, gauging his chances of getting the hay in today. Jason is a city boy, born and bred only a few streets from where we're standing, but his first posting was as a guard in a small-ish town in County Offaly and he seems to have incorporated a rural sensibility into his personality even though he's back in Dublin. His blunt, kindly face inspires trust and he's physically imposing enough to make people think twice before misbehaving.

"I wore my fleece because it was supposed to be cold and now I'm sweating," I grumble.

Jason just nods and looks upward again as if things might have shifted in the last thirty seconds. They haven't. The sky is still clear, reflected in the calm ribbon of water. I tug at the collar of my dress shirt and too-warm jacket.

My uniform still feels strange, too heavy, too conspicuous after so many years in plain clothes as a detective. I resigned from my job on Long Island a year and a half ago and then finished at the Garda Training College in Templemore in August. My friend Roly Byrne, a detective inspector with the Garda's criminal investigation bureau, pulled some strings to get me posted to Dublin, where my boyfriend, Conor, and his son live and where my daughter, Lilly, is going to school. It feels like I'm right back where I started when I was twenty-five and a new officer with the Suffolk County Police Department, patrolling the streets, arresting drunks, driving by beaches and parking lots and high schools to make sure nobody was up to anything they shouldn't be, spending enough time on the beat so when something really bad happened, people wouldn't hesitate to let you know.

Jason's and my scheduled community patrol has already brought us all the way down Clanbrassil Street to the Grand Canal. We'll keep walking along the canal until we reach Portobello Bridge and then head north again up Richmond Street as it turns into Camden Street and then back to the newly finished Garda Station on Kevin Street. The skinnier-at-the-top rectangle—on the south side of the Liffey and not far from Dublin's city center—that we'll have described once we're done is loosely our patrol area. For the past two months, since I finished the training I need to work as a Garda officer in Ireland and was paired up with Jason, it's been our job to get to know it, to get to know the people, the businesses, the houses that are empty, the ones that are under construction, the ones that are occupied by families who have been in the Portobello neighborhood for generations, the ones that have sold to young couples flush with cash from the red-hot Dublin real estate market, and the ones where suspected drug dealers or gang members or pedophiles live.

It's taken time to figure it out, to understand how the roads and lanes and alleys all flow together, the networks of streets between the canal and the South Circular Road, once called Little Jerusalem because of the Jewish community that settled there in the early twentieth century, and the quiet residential neighborhoods above that that run parallel to Synge Street and up toward Camden Row. I'm just figuring out where the good coffee and lunch places are off Camden Street Lower, the hipster espresso places and health food cafés within easy walking distance of the increasing number of tech-related start-ups and creative industry offices in the neighborhood. Our patch is gentrifying quickly, though there's still plenty of street crime, robberies and drug dealers bleeding east from Rialto and Dolphin's Barn, and many of the kids we come across in the course of our work live in one of two older social housing complexes at the northern end of our beat.

I worried about how Jason would adjust to being partnered with a middle-aged American woman with twenty years of police work already under her belt, but he seems to take it all with a relaxed acceptance that will stand him in good stead his whole career. He doesn't have the kind of edgy, multilayered intelligence that gets you into the specialist bureaus or promotes you to detective, but he has street smarts and an overwhelming sense of calm about him. He's expert at defusing tensions—in particular talking down belligerent drunks, which I've seen him do quite a few times now—and he has the look of an Irish grandfather from a photograph of the 1950s. People think they know him, even when they don't, and he works it to his advantage. He also has a good rapport with the kids; kind, but a little stern.

We're passing the neighborhood pub just off the canal when my radio unit crackles and the dispatcher gives our call signs.

I respond and a voice comes through with a bit of static. "You near the canal?"

"Roger that."

The dispatcher says there's been a report of a possible homicide at an apartment complex called Canal Landing. "You know where it is? Unit 201." Jason is listening and his head snaps up.

"Roger that," I say.

"Bureau is on the way," the dispatcher says.

I tell him we'll head right over.

"Shite," Jason says. "That's where we responded to that possible domestic Saturday night."

Dread sweeps through me. "Yeah, I know."

We were on a four-to-midnight patrol Saturday night, talking to a neighborhood resident about some graffiti on the South Circular Road, when we got a call about a possible domestic violence situation in an apartment complex right on the canal; someone had heard screaming and fighting and called in to the emergency number.

I'd walked by the gated development of apartments many times, one of a pair next to a vacant lot on that section of the canal. Canal Landing is the shabbier one, built on the cheap in the late '90s, with twenty duplex units, four to a block, wrapped around a parking lot and small courtyard. The development next to it, called Harbour Quay, is more solid, newer, higher end. On Saturday night, we waited for Canal Landing's property manager to let us in through the gate, and when we asked him if he'd heard the screaming himself, he said, "I didn't hear anything," shrugging as he led us through the quiet parking area, dodging a child's bike lying on the ground and two plastic trucks. "I've got a place there on the first floor by the gate and one of the tenants knocked on my door, said there was screaming in one of the apartments, and to call the guards."

When we knocked at 201 though, a young woman answered the door, dressed in a bathrobe and looking confused when she saw our uniforms. She struck me as legitimately surprised to see us and when we said we'd received a call about a disturbance, she apologized for the noise, explaining she was watching a loud movie. She gestured to the large-screen television, where a now-muted action film was playing, and she seemed fine to us, with no visible injuries on her lovely, fine-boned face. We looked past her into the apartment, which seemed to be otherwise unoccupied, gave her the usual spiel about feeling comfortable reaching out for help and even left her a card with the number of the domestic violence prevention hotline. We felt fine about leaving and filed a report indicating that we hadn't located the caller but that the sound was likely the movie the woman in 201 was watching. That was it. I can't even remember her name, though we took it down for the report.

When you've responded to a possible domestic and left without arresting anyone, a follow-up call to the address is bad news. A possible homicide at the address is pretty much your worst nightmare.

Jason's normally placid face is twisted in worry now. "I guess we'd better get down there and see what's going on," he says, casting a final glance at the canal, at Donald and his wife and the other birds carving rippling channels through the water. The skies are darkening now, and I think he must be right. It's going to rain tonight.

Two

....

The same property manager who was here on Saturday meets us at the gate and says, "It's 201, same as the other night." He's dressed in a sweatshirt and work pants and his hands have spatters of white on them. "I was painting the trim around back," he says when he sees me notice it.

"Tell us what happened," I say as he leads us past the parking area and lets us through the outside door of Block Two to the small lobby. It looks the same as the other night, though now there's a folded stroller propped up against the wall and a stack of cardboard for recycling next to it.

"I was painting around on the canal side and I noticed the sliding door to her terrace there was wide open. We've had some break-ins and we've asked tenants not to leave the doors to their terraces open unless they're out there. They're practically on the street, so it's a bit tempting for anyone walking by. I knocked a few times at her door and didn't get an answer. Rang her mobile. Nothing. I have a master key, so I started to open it—I figured she was out and I'd just latch the terrace door for her—but it was already unlocked. I opened the door and called out. I had a bad feeling, like. It was so quiet and . . . I don't know . . . I stood at the base of the stairs and called up to her, but something made me go up a ways and . . . I saw her foot. I thought maybe she'd fallen down or . . . but she was really still. It was pretty clear she was . . . dead, like. And, well, you'll see. So I rang you lot."

His face has a gaunt, grayish look and he's clutching an unlit cigarette between the paint-splattered fingers of his right hand. He's very shaken, I think, and I can feel how much he wants to light it.

There are four doors arranged around the lobby. Number 201 is to our left. "What's her name again?" I ask as we pause in front of the door. "The resident? I've forgotten."

"Jade." The young woman's face flashes before me. *Green eyes, fine-boned face, sharp cheekbones, a curtain of pale blond hair falling over her face. Jade.* Now I remember being grateful that Jason wasn't the kind of male partner who would sneak in a little aside later about how uncommonly hot she was, the comment forcing its way up like a burp.

"Wait here." I slowly push the door open, calling out, "Garda officers. Is anyone here?"

Silence.

The small, open first floor of the apartment is very cold and a bit messy. There are piles of laundry lying around, and a stack of dishes teeters in the sink in the small kitchen. A wide bank of windows and a sliding glass door open to a small, enclosed terrace that's practically on the street. I see what he means. The low railing around the terrace would be easily scalable. You could almost just step over it. You'd want to be very careful about security.

But the sliding glass door is wide open, just like he said. That's why it's so cold in here.

"She's upstairs." From the hallway, the property manager points to the staircase leading to a loftlike second floor.

"Garda officers," I call again. Jason slips past me and takes the stairs quickly. I follow him and when I reach the landing, he says, "In there, Maggie," pointing to the doorway of a bedroom. I see a bare foot and bare lower leg on the threshold and then the rest of her and I watch as Jason slips on a single latex glove from his jacket pocket. He puts a finger to the woman's neck to check for a pulse. I meet his eyes and he shakes his head. I already know from the stiffness of her body, the vacant glaze of her green eyes. Her long blond hair is arrayed like a halo above her on the floor. She's wearing a black T-shirt and a pair of red bikini underpants. Her eyes are open, the skin around them speckled with petechiae, the whites bright with more petechial hemorrhaging, and her neck is obviously bruised, a collar of red and purple on her pale skin. *Manual strangulation.*

Shit. Shit. Shit. We should have followed up after Saturday, should have asked more questions. I can feel regret spread through my body, making me nauseous. Jason's guilty look tells me he's feeling it, too.

We radio in the new details, clear the bathroom opposite the bedroom, then check the terrace downstairs. There's no one out there, just two folding chairs and an upside-down wooden milk crate with a bowl filled with cigarette butts on it.

I think about the beautiful young woman who answered the door to me and Jason Saturday night, who told us she was fine and the screaming her neighbor heard was just a movie, the woman who's now lying dead on the floor of her bedroom, strangled by someone—probably a boyfriend or lover—who wanted to be absolutely sure she wasn't going to get up off the floor of this once-modern, now-depreciating piece of Celtic Tiger real estate. Her mouth is hanging slightly open, as though she's about to talk. A heavy weariness sweeps over me. Everything that is going to come, all the effort, all the manpower, all the expense, could be avoided if she could just sit up and tell us who did this to her.

But, of course, she won't. She won't ever talk again.

I feel my brain shift into gear. *When it has been established that there is no hope of resuscitation, the responding officer moves quickly to preserve any and all evidence at the crime scene.*

Checking my phone, I write down the time we arrived on the scene and the details I've got so far. Then I tell Jason to stand outside the door to make sure no one comes anywhere near to the apartment until the crime scene techs and the divisional detectives and the Bureau of Criminal Investigation detectives arrive.

Inside the apartment, I take off my boots and stand close to the front door to look around. I want to get a sense of her, of her space, before they make me go outside to direct traffic while the professionals do their work.

I failed her once. Maybe I can find something now that will help us get her killer. I only have a few minutes with her and I'm going to make them count.

There's a narrow table to my right next to the door. It's where she puts her keys, in a white ceramic bowl shaped like a cat; three or four sets of them, all house keys it looks like, and I confirm her name from the envelope on the top of a pile of mail: Jade Elliott.

I climb the stairs in as few steps as possible to take another quick look at her. First, her clothes. Simple black T-shirt, underpants. She was having a quiet evening at home. Except, the underpants are red and lacy. And she's got on mascara and lipstick. A date then, or somebody dropping by for sex. I'm betting there's more evidence under her body, but there's not much else I can see without contaminating the scene.

Downstairs, I check the kitchen. Sure enough, there's an open bottle of red wine, three-quarters empty, on the counter. I can't see into the sink without treading all over the floor, but I'm hoping there are two glasses somewhere. Glasses means we can get prints and maybe DNA from whoever was drinking with her.

Then I scan the small living room. There's a charger and cord plugged into an outlet but no phone. There's a stack of fashion and lifestyle magazines and Irish and UK tabloids on the coffee table, the headlines screaming about celebrities having babies or going into rehab. One of the headlines references a high-profile murder a couple of neighborhoods away in Inchicore that a few of the Garda detectives I know are working on, the stabbing of a businessman with ties to organized crime.

The big television we saw the other night is silent now. Next to the coffee table is a low blue couch and two blue chairs with pink pillows and a colorful rug that looks relatively new. That's good, too. It's probably shedding a lot of fibers. They'll be on anyone who was in the room. The walls are mostly bare, but there are two large framed photographs above the couch. They're both of Jade Elliott, black and whites of her wearing a long, satin gown, her face heavily made up, her body and face contorted into high fashion poses. She must have been some kind of model, which makes her fine-boned face, her extreme thinness, her out-of-the-ordinary beauty make sense to me now.

I close my eyes and inhale the air. I can smell perfume, something light and floral, maybe not perfume at all but a scented candle, covering the whisper of stale cigarette smoke from the terrace. There's a whiff of garbage from the kitchen with a familiar note that I can't quite place. Then I have it: dirty diapers. When I open my eyes again, they settle on a small pink blanket draped over one of the chairs. I quickly scan the rest of the room. There's another colorful blanket laid out in one corner and a few plastic toys and stuffed animals in a small basket.

I feel my heart rate speed as I start to pick up on the details that are everywhere now that I'm looking. The baby gate folded discreetly to the side at the bottom of the stairs. A package of baby wipes in a corner of the living room. Three pink sippy cups drying at the edge of the kitchen counter.

And then, the refrigerator.

Trapped under a magnet, partially obscured by a ripped-out magazine advertisement, is a casual, unposed photograph of Jade Elliott. She's holding a baby with blond curls, round cheeks, and wide green eyes that match her own. The baby wears a pink dress, laughing, her smile wide and joyous, and Jade is gazing down at her with an expression of love, total devotion. It's a gorgeous picture of a gorgeous woman and a gorgeous baby.

Her gorgeous baby.

It takes me three steps, as big and far apart as I can make them, to cross the room. I grab the photograph off the refrigerator and the magnet clatters to the floor. I fling open the door, startling Jason and the manager out in the lobby. "Did she have a baby?" I demand. "Is there a baby?"

The manager looks sick now, still processing the sight of the body. His eyes widen as he realizes he forgot about the baby. "Yeah, little girl. That's her pram." He nods toward the stroller leaning against the wall between Jade's apartment and the apartment next to it.

Fuck. I resist the urge to yell at him. Why didn't he say anything? "I've got to check the apartment for her," I tell Jason. "Radio it in."

He looks away. He's glad I'm doing it. He doesn't want to be the one to find a dead baby.

I shut the door behind me and climb the stairs again in as few steps as I can to check the bedroom, my whole body buzzing with dread. Stepping carefully over the body, I do a quick search of the closet, the bureau, under the bed. I make note of the iPhone on the bedside table so I can tell the techs. There's a small crib in one corner that we missed before because it's draped with clothes, but no baby anywhere. Then I check the bathroom cupboards and the hamper, just to be sure. No baby, though there's baby shampoo and diaper cream—Natural Life Nappy Rash Balm—under the sink.

When I check the downstairs again, I see a few more toys placed neatly on a low set of shelves. I look carefully, behind the drapes, the couch cushions, in the narrow closet next to the front door. No baby. I can't help but feel relief flood through me. I've only seen dead babies a handful of times in my career. Car accidents mostly. A drowning. And then, once, a little boy accidentally smothered on the couch by his older brother. I've never gotten that one out of my head, the peace and stillness of his tiny face, the mother's wails in the background.

I turn to the open sliding doors and the terrace. It's not far to the street. Could the baby have crawled out there and climbed over the barrier? It seems unlikely. Wouldn't someone have seen her? Even now, people outside are passing by constantly, six of them as I slowly count to ten in my head. Then I catch sight of a shimmer of water through the trees.

"She's not here," I tell Jason and the manager out in the hallway. "We need to check the canal. Where else could she be? Could she be with someone else?" I'm trying not to shout at the property manager. He should have said something about the baby first thing.

He looks terrified. "I don't know," he says. "I think there's an ex-husband or something. I saw him with the baby once. I think he takes her fairly regularly."

A tiny flash of hope pushes out the panic. "What's his name?"

"I've only been working here a couple months. I don't really know the tenants yet."

I resist the urge to slap him. "You go check the canal," I tell Jason. "The sliding glass doors are open. She could have crawled away. We may want the Water Unit. Or someone could have come in and abducted her. If the baby's not out there or with the father, if she's been abducted, then they'll need to send out an alert as soon as possible." Ireland's version of an Amber Alert is a Child Rescue Ireland Alert. I know time is of the essence. If someone's killed Jade Elliott and taken her daughter, we need to be looking for them as soon as possible.

And, of course, chances are that person is the ex-husband. That's just numbers and probability. We need to remember it, but we can't let it box us in.

We need his name. We need to know where he is.

Three

....

Jason goes outside to radio it in and then check the street and the canal.

I try to decide which door to knock on first. There are four apartments, the doors in a rectangle around the lobby. Jade's is to the left, looking out over the vacant lot through the windows in the kitchen and over the canal through the living room windows and sliding glass door. Number 202 shares a wall with her on the canal side, 203 is directly opposite Jade's, and 204 is behind us, on the parking lot side of the building. No one answers my knock at 203, but when I try 204, a woman of about my age with short gray hair flings the door open and says, "What's happened? Is everything okay with Jade? Where's Laurel?" She's in medical scrubs, light blue.

I take in her fearful eyes. She must have been watching through the peephole in the door. "Laurel? Is that the baby?" I ask her.

She nods. "What's happened?" A man is standing behind her, looking equally terrified.

"Laurel's father doesn't live here, is that correct?"

"No, but—What's happened? Is Laurel okay?" She's caught the scent of tragedy. She knows something awful is going on out here.

"I'm sorry, I just need you to answer my questions. Do you know his name or where he lives?"

"His name is Dylan. He used to live here but I don't know where he lives now." Her eyes are big. I realize I'm scaring her and I make an effort to slow down, lower my voice.

"Okay, Dylan. Any idea where he works, how we could reach him?"

"I think he does something with computers. His office isn't far from here. I think he owns the place. It's Maguire. Dylan Maguire." She turns to the man standing behind her and says, "Do you know, love?" But he shakes his head, and she says, "Is she, is she . . . okay?"

I ignore her question. "Computers? No idea of the company name?"

"No, but hang on." She leaves the door open and goes inside, coming back with a piece of paper. As she hands it to me, I hear sirens. The reinforcements are here. "That's his number," she says. "We minded Laurel for her a few times and she gave me that, for emergencies."

I look down at the piece of pink paper, torn from a pad. Some-one's written *Jade's mobile, Dylan Maguire, Nicola,* and *Eileen,* each with a number next to the name.

"Nicola's her sister and Eileen's her mam," the woman says help-fully.

"Thank you . . ."

"Gail," she says. "Gail Roden. Is there anything we can . . ."

I turn away from her and dial Dylan Maguire's number on my cell phone. *Answer, answer,* I pray.

He does. "Dylan Maguire." All business.

"Mr. Maguire, my name is Garda Maggie D'arcy. I need to know if you are the father of a baby named Laurel."

"What? Yes, is she okay? Why are you calling? What's happened? Where is she?"

I feel my heart sink. She's not with him. Or at least he's not admitting it. "Mr. Maguire, I need to confirm that Laurel is not with you."

"No, she's with her mother, Jade. What's happened? Where's Jade?" I can't help it: I find myself judging the quality of the concern in his voice. It feels authentic, but it's hard to tell over the phone.

I hesitate. How much to reveal at this point is for the investigators to decide, but I have to tell him something. "Mr. Maguire, how soon can you get to the Kevin Street Garda Station?"

"I can't . . . I'm in Lyon. On business. But where is my daughter? What's going on?" I feel my heart sink again. Depending on how long he's been in France, he's probably not our killer. Thinking of the report of a possible domestic disturbance, I want to ask him if he was in France on Saturday night, but I need to let the investigators do it.

"There's been an accident," I say, falling back on a cop's noncommittal euphemism, as Jason comes up the stairs and shakes his head at me. *No sign of her.* "Jade has been badly hurt. Your daughter isn't here. Is there anywhere else she could be? Anyone Jade might have left her with? I have a number here for Jade's sister and mother. What about your family?"

"What? I don't understand. Jade's mother didn't . . . I would be very surprised if she'd brought Laurel up there. She wouldn't have brought her to my family." He sounds panicked now. I hear noise behind him, traffic, voices. He's somewhere public. "Where is Jade? Where is my daughter?"

Three uniformed guards appear in the lobby and Jason briefs them in a low voice. Gail Roden and the man I assume is her husband or partner are listening from their doorway. Suddenly, I'm panicking. I should have waited to call. I need to tell him something. His daughter is missing.

"Mr. Maguire, we don't know. I need you to call around to your relatives and make sure there isn't anywhere else she could be. And you're going to need to come back to Dublin," I say. "A Garda detective will call you back as quickly as possible to explain more. Please stay by the phone." I hang up before he can ask any more questions.

The new uniforms are waiting for instructions. "Is someone from the bureau coming?" I ask, referring to the Garda Síochána's Bureau of Criminal Investigation, which provides investigative and forensic services and coordination for the divisional Garda detectives, especially for serious crimes like homicides. They nod and look toward the door, and I hear Roly Byrne before I see him.

"Who called it in?" he's asking someone. "Get the name of the person who called it in right now."

Roly's pushing fifty, the third-most senior investigator on his team, but he moves like a twenty-year-old, full of energy, his perfectly shined dress shoes reflecting the light in the lobby. We've been friends for a long time now and seeing him under happier circumstances always makes me smile.

"D'arcy," Roly calls out when he sees me. "They told me you responded. What's the story here?"

"We've got a female vic in there, young woman named Jade Elliott, but Roly, we've got a missing baby, too." I tell him about responding and finding Jade and then smelling diapers and noticing all the baby things. "I searched the apartment and she's not there. My partner checked the canal bank and the street outside—the door was open—but she's not there either. I should have waited for you, but I called the baby's father. I don't think he and the mother were together and he says he's in France on a business trip. In any case, he says the baby's not with him and thinks it's unlikely she's with family. Someone needs to ring him back right now. You'll probably need to have the French police meet him and escort him home. I've got a number for the victim's mother. I can ring her or you can. If the baby's not there, you'll probably want to get the Water Unit in and activate the Child Rescue Alert."

He nods. "What's the relationship with the father like? You know?"

I glance away, embarrassed, then say quietly, "Seems like they're not currently together, but Roly, Garda Savage and I responded to a disturbance here Saturday night. Neighbor reported hearing a woman screaming and the property manager over there rang 999. She seemed fine, confused about the noise, no one with her, and we didn't take it any further. Obviously, we should have."

He studies me for a moment. "Maybe, maybe not. Let's see where this goes. You know where the mother lives?" I shake my head. "Anybody know where the mother lives?" Roly calls out.

We all look at Gail Roden. "Navan, I think," she says. Navan's a town about an hour to the north, in County Meath.

"Her name is Eileen," I tell him. "We've got a number. One for her sister, too."

Gail Roden starts speaking, then stops before saying, "She's not really a baby anymore, Laurel. I think she's almost two."

Roly nods at her, then turns to one of the uniforms and says, "Get on to the Garda station in Navan. Someone needs to get to her place and see if the baby's there. Only . . ." I know what he's struggling with. We need to make sure the baby's not with her, but he also needs to make the notification of her daughter's death. He thinks for a minute. "Do it," he says. "Get a FLO over there, too. It makes sense to get everything in place for the alert. Go find the new fella from my team—he's outside, can't miss him, he fancies himself G.I. Joe—and give him all of this." The FLO is the family liaison officer who will help get Jade's mother through the hours and days that come after what's likely to be the worst moment of her life.

I hand the uniform the piece of paper with the names of Jade Elliott's mother and sister on it, and he goes off to find Roly's guy so he can make the call.

I've investigated a few missing children cases in my time, mostly noncustodial parents taking kids out of town or out of state for a few days in anger about how their lives have ended up. Then there were a few teenage runaways, kids who got fed up with their parents and decided to take off and spend a few nights with friends. I've only worked on one true abduction and murder in my career, a ten-year-old girl taken from a playground by a sex offender. She was abused and then smothered, and we found her body a week later in a dumpster. She was wearing a tie-dyed sweatshirt, one she'd made herself, and she'd written her name on the back in puffy fabric paint.

With a shiver, I remember that little girl's name was Lauren, one letter off, and hope it's not a bad omen.

Four

....

Roly introduces me to the divisional detectives from Kevin Street who will be overseeing the investigation and working it with him and then gives me his thumb and pointer finger at a right angle, like a gun. "Tell me," he says. "Who found her?"

I nod and gesture toward the property manager. "Emergency call was placed by this gentleman here. He's the property manager."

We both look at him and he says, "Bobby Egan. Robert Egan."

"These units are duplexes," I continue. "They have first-floor ter-races on the canal side. He noticed the door to the terrace was open and knocked on the door. Door was unlocked and he went in and found the body—body's up at the top of the staircase—and rang us. Right?"

Bobby Egan nods.

Roly fixes his pale blue eyes on the guy. "How'd you know to look upstairs?"

"Something was . . . weird, like. I called out her name and the silence was . . . I went halfway up the stairs and I guess I saw her foot. That part's kind of a blur."

Roly's phone rings and he takes it while Jason and I stand around for a bit, guarding the door. While we're waiting, the scene of crime technicians come in, already dressed in their white boiler suits. Behind them is a tall guy in a black canvas army jacket. He's got his chest out, his arms loose at his sides like he's been jogging. His silver-gray hair is cut short in a pseudo military buzz cut and he looks like he's been on a beach, little white lines in the tanned skin of his face around his pale blue eyes. If he could be wearing sunglasses indoors, he would be. I recognize him immediately.

"Pat," Roly calls out. "You get the mother?"

"Navan guards are on their way there now," the guy says.

"D'arcy," Roly says, "this is Detective Sergeant Padraig Fiero—" But I'm already saying, "We know each other."

Padraig Fiero is staring at me. "Mrs. D'arcy, I'm—"

"Garda D'arcy actually, now," I tell him. I turn to Roly. "The case in West Cork last summer. Detective Sergeant Fiero and I were down there at the same time."

"Ah, of course. Well, he's just joined the team and with half of our detectives tied up in that Inchicore murder, I'm glad to have him ready to go." Roly, still looking a bit surprised, nods and takes one of the suits the crime scene techs offer to him and the divisional detective and puts it on. They all go in but I know they won't be in there long. The detectives can't do much until the techs have processed the scene, but as an investigator, you always want to at least take a look.

"So you did your training, yeah?" Padraig Fiero asks me. Now I see that he's got his sunglasses tucked in his shirt pocket under his jacket, even though the weak October sun is buried behind the gray clouds that have rolled in over the last hour. When I first met him in West Cork last summer, I found him cocky and full of hyper-masculine bravado. Nothing that happened changed my opinion much. He was working a drug smuggling case that intersected with two homicides on the remote peninsula where I was spending the summer with my daughter, Lilly, and my boyfriend, Conor, and his son. Fiero got a solve on his case and my friend, Detective Sergeant Katya "Griz" Grzeskiewicz, got a win, too.

"Yup," I say. "I've been on community patrol for a couple of months now."

He frowns as though he doesn't approve, then says, "I've been onto the lads in Navan. They're sending the FLO but Jade's sister says they don't have Laurel. They'll make sure, of course, but it looks like she's missing. Victim's mother says the little girl's full name is Laurel Roxie Maguire. She's almost two, birthday in a few days, so not a baby. She's not insulin dependent. She has no other chronic health conditions. Eileen Elliott seemed confused on the phone. Officer who spoke with her said he thought she might have some dementia or something. She kept asking where Laurel was, kept asking what was happening to her." He runs a hand over his buzz cut. "Officer said it was brutal. They're waiting until they get there to tell her that her daughter's dead."

Roly comes out again and Fiero updates him on the situation in Navan. Roly blanches. He's got four kids, two girls and two boys, and I know that, like me, he's imagining a toddler now, old enough to know something's wrong. She must be terrified. I force myself not to think about what might be happening to her.

"Get the alert started, Pat," Roly barks at Fiero, who nods and steps outside to start working his phone. *"Fuck!"* He runs a hand through his hair and then looks back at me. "Well-spotted though, D'arcy. It might have taken hours to realize the kid was missing. Anyone find her phone in there?"

"Yeah," one of the techs calls out. "But it's got a password, no fingerprint access. I tried the usuals. No dice." They'll take the phone back to the lab and try to get into it.

I knock on the door of Unit 204 and introduce Roly to Gail Roden and her husband, who she says is named Phil. "Who else have we got on the floor?" Roly asks them.

She points to 202. "That's the Phillipses. They're an older couple and they travel a lot. They might be out of town. And that's Denise over there in 203. She's a single girl. Works a lot."

"They're not home. Do you have numbers for them?"

When she says she'll go check, Roly turns to me and Jason. "They need crowd control outside. Can you two help secure the scene? We need to do this area before it gets contaminated any further. And someone needs to locate the CCTV." He tells the property manager to take him to his office for the footage and we all troop outside again, passing Fiero, who's working his phone in the parking lot. I feel a small, hard knot of resentment start in my gut. I'll be stringing up crime scene tape while he gets to work the case.

The residents of Canal Landing have realized something is going on now. Jason and the other uniforms and I get control of the scene, ushering them away from the entrance to the block and telling them to go to their own apartments. A woman in a bright pink ski jacket is filming us on her phone and when we tell her to go inside, she starts screaming about her rights. "I was going to post that on my Insta!"

"Get inside now," Jason tells her patiently. "You wouldn't want your phone taken away."

"You can't do that!" she throws back at him. "That's my legal property."

The Garda Technical Bureau van is pulled up close to the entrance, and just as we get the woman through the door, an ambulance arrives for when they're ready to release Jade's body.

Someone from the bureau is organizing a search of the canal and a door-to-door canvass. They'll need to start combing the parking lot and streets outside for evidence. For Laurel Maguire's body.

I feel the familiar rhythms of a case beginning, everything still to be discovered, every pathway as yet unexplored.

But it's not a case, not for me anyway. I'm just here to secure the scene, to guard the detectives who are doing the real work. Then they'll run with it and I'll be back to rescuing ducks from sewers tomorrow. I try not to let it get me down. This posting is a step on the path to a job on one of the detective teams, maybe a job as a divisional detective. I've known that for a while. While I have a long career as a homicide investigator behind me in the US, I have to prove myself all over again in Ireland. Nothing has changed because I happened to respond to a suspicious death on my patch. I smooth my dark hair back into its neat ponytail, straighten my uniform, and find a piece of mint gum in my pocket to take the sour taste out of my mouth.

Roly comes out of the property manager's office and into the parking lot. Dense, gray clouds have swept in from the west. It's four P.M. now and I predict it will be raining any minute, just like Jason said.

"D'arcy," Roly calls out to me when he's off the phone, waving me over with his hand. I cross the pavement, conscious that all the other uniforms are watching me.

"Yeah, anything on the CCTV?" I try to keep my voice casual, but Roly knows how invested I feel already.

He smiles, just a little, not so anyone who doesn't know him would know, and he leans in to say, in a conspiratorial way, "Bad luck on that. We've got cameras out here." He points to a mounted camera pointed at the parking lot. "But the ones around the canal side were taken down while your man was painting the trim. Nothing obvious on the car park footage, but given the open door, I'm thinking around the other side is where the action was." He sighs. "The techs will process the apartment and we'll keep searching around here, but I don't like it. We're getting the CRI alert up right away."

"Good," I say. "I mean, I wish the baby had been with a family member, but . . . That's the right thing to do."

"I know what you meant."

He pauses. "I recognized her," he says after a long moment. "Jade Elliott. I thought I knew her from somewhere and then one of the lads said it to me, she was on one of those reality show yokes a few years ago. The girls liked it, Áine especially because it was to do with fashion or modeling or something."

"Really? Was she, like, famous?" That gives this a whole new angle. A reality TV star. A celebrity-obsessed stalker.

"I don't think so. It got canceled after a few months. Áine was mad about it."

He looks around the parking lot. We can feel all of the residents waiting in their apartments, watching from behind their windows. Do any of them know what happened to Jade? The complex feels suddenly alive to me, a breathing, living organism of human components, each one part of a bigger social structure, connected in ways we can't even imagine yet.

I think Roly's thinking about it, too, and he confirms it when he says, "Could be a crime of opportunity. Some pedo's been watching them and sees the doors open . . . But strangulation doesn't fit. Too emotional, too close. Why not just take the baby while they're sleeping or threaten her with a weapon? I don't know. Feels like it might have been someone with a connection to her."

"The father? France isn't that far. And there's that call we responded to on Saturday. What if it wasn't the TV? You need to check whether he flew back or took the train, check when he actually left." Roly hears me make an effort to use *you*.

He meets my eyes. "Look here, you know a bit about the neighborhood. You've worked on missing kiddies. Besides, I'm shorthanded with this gangland thing. Griz and half the team are tied up in that. They're short on divisional detectives to work it. I want you helping out on this. You have your investigative interview techniques training done, right?"

"Yeah." I feel my hopes swell and try to keep it out of my voice. "I've done SICC, too." Serious Incident Canvass Coordinators organize the door-to-door searches after an incident like this one. I know we'll need those skills in the next few days.

"You up for some long days? I may be able to get you off some of your patrols, but you're going to have to keep up with things, too. Everyone's shorthanded right now."

"I can do it," I say too quickly, trying not to grin.

"Okay then. I'll talk to your superintendent. You find the baby"—he says it *babby*—"and you may be able to burn that fucking uniform before the week is out, yeah? It looks like shite on you anyway." He smiles again, just a little, then puts his serious detective look back on. "The divisional lads are staying here to work the scene. You're coming up to Navan with myself and Fiero to talk to her mother. I want you to drive so we can work the phones. One of their sergeants is setting up the incident room at Kevin Street.

They'll start checking up on everyone, see if the father's got a record or anything. You've gotten used to driving on the left, yeah? You think you can get us there without killing us?" I nod and he glances back toward Jade Elliott's building. He's holding the photograph I took off the fridge, and I know it will be copied and tweeted and shared and posted and printed hundreds of times in the next twenty-four hours. I fix my eyes on Laurel Maguire's little face, her small ears and wisps of curly blond hair. I try to memorize every detail of her chin, her forehead, her determined mouth.

Roly's eyes follow mine and he studies the photograph for a second. "We've got to find this little girl."

Five

....

Conor goes quiet on the other end of the phone when I tell him what's going on and that I won't be home anytime soon. He's a father, so he reacts first as a father, taking it in for a moment before saying, "That's horrible. Do you have any idea where she is?"

"Not really. We're going up to talk to the mother of the victim in Navan now."

"Poor woman. Imagine getting that visit. Your daughter and then not knowing about your granddaughter, too."

"Can you tell Lilly? I said I'd help her with her English tonight." My daughter, Lilly, is studying for her Leaving Cert exams and I'd offered to drill her on literary terms when I get home tonight. Unlike Conor's son, Adrien, Lilly's not naturally good at taking exams. I suspect the late nights due to her nascent singing career in pubs around the city aren't helping either.

"Yeah, maybe Adrien can help her out. Keep us posted, yeah?"

I tell him I love him and not to wait up. We've been living together for over a year now, but I was at the Garda Training College for a lot of that, and he's not yet used to cohabiting with a partner who can be called away at any moment on a case. I'm alert to the flat tone of his voice when he says, "Yeah, love ya too. Good luck," and try not to read too much into it. He's been moody the last few days, stressed about his new book on Irish political history, which comes out in March. It's his first book that will be published by a mainstream publisher in Ireland, the UK, and the US simultaneously, and his first for a general, nonacademic audience. His editor told him they should start seeing early reviews and he told me he's on edge every time he checks his email. I imagine the feel of his arms around me, using it to steel me for the job ahead.

It's an hour up to Navan on the N3, and Roly and Padraig Fiero spend most of it on their phones. Fiero is in the back working on setting up the missing child alert. Roly, next to me in the front seat, is talking to someone from his team about setting up a tipline for members of the public to call, and then to the French police who are escorting Dylan Maguire to the airport in Lyon. Roly will have someone meet Maguire at Dublin Airport when he gets in tonight. I listen to him say that they need to start checking his alibi in Lyon. If there's any chance he wasn't where he said he was, or that he was at Jade's place the night Jason and I responded to the possible DV incident, we need to know now.

"Pathologist have any sense how long she's been dead?" I ask him once he's done. In the rearview mirror, I see Fiero look up at that, listening for Roly's answer.

"That's the question, isn't it? If Laurel Maguire was taken, how much of a head start does her kidnapper have?" He glances over at me as I change lanes to get in front of a slow truck. "Assistant pathologist thought last night but they won't know for sure until they get her on the table." He pauses for a minute, then says, "My thinking is point of entry was either through the complex or out that door on the canal side. Security at that place is pretty sound. If it was through the main entrance, you'd first have to get through the gate to the parking area, then you'd need a key to get in the lobby door, and then you'd need a different key to get into the flat, sorry, the *apartment.*"

Fiero speaks up from the back. "So if that was the entry point, our suspect was known to her, someone she let in or someone who lived in the complex. Maybe both."

"Or someone she gave keys to; Maguire, a boyfriend, a babysitter, a cleaner. Hopefully the mother can tell us everyone who had a key," Roly says.

"Yeah . . ." I say. "The father sounded genuinely surprised to me on the phone, but he's who I go to just right off the bat."

"I wish we'd been able to see his face when we told him," Fiero says. I catch his eyes in the rearview mirror. He looks away, but I know the words were meant for me.

I hesitate before saying, "I had to find out if she was with him. Delaying notification wasn't justified with a missing kid." It's raining in earnest now, the wiper blades sweeping across the windshield, the roadway shiny in the dwindling light. I'm hunched over the steering wheel, trying to stay completely focused on the motorway in front of me. I've been driving regularly in Ireland for more than a year now, but I still have to concentrate extra hard to stay on the left side of the road; thirty years of habit is hard to break, especially when I'm tired or it's raining.

Fiero doesn't say anything, but next to me, Roly shrugs. "She's right. But I'm pretty interested in what we get on him. We find out he was there Saturday night before you and your partner made your visit, D'arcy, or that she'd made a complaint and he's got a DV charge, things are different. Now, lads, let's say Maguire has an alibi. I think it's got to be that open door. What do you think, Fiero?"

Fiero leans forward so we can hear him. "Yeah, say she left it open.

Could have been a crime of opportunity. Someone walking by, sees them in the window, sees the door open. That railing around the terrace would be easy to get over. Or, he'd been watching 'em and he came in with a plan to kill Jade Elliott and take the little girl."

"It would be nice to know if she regularly kept that door locked," I say. "It's right there on the street, so it seems like she would have."

"Yes, it would." Roly looks out the window and then slams his hand down on the dashboard. "We've got to find that baby." Fiero's phone rings and he answers, talking in a quiet voice about monitoring motorway CCTV.

We drive in tense silence for a bit before I ask, "How'd Jade's mother take it when the guards up here told her? Have you heard?"

"Nah," Roly says. "I'm sure she's in bits. Ah, we're almost there." The approach to Navan feels familiar, the patchwork of green countryside bisected by the motorway, and the increasing residential density as you approach the town center, bland housing developments clustered around shopping centers that remind me of Long Island. I get off the motorway, and in five minutes we're pulling up outside of one of the nearly identical horseshoes of brick and beige-sided town houses. As we get out of the car a group of kids, still in their school uniforms, watches us from across a scrubby lawn. It's five o'clock now, darkness falling, and they're eking out the last bit of playtime before they're called inside. They remind me of our little crew in Portobello.

"Let me lead, yeah?" Roly says to us as we walk toward the unit where Eileen Elliott lives. "If I scratch my right ear at ya, though, it means I want youse to jump in. Fiero knows. Got it, D'arcy? Like this?" Roly reaches up and does an exaggerated scratch of his earlobe to show us.

"Sure. Right ear," I say. We grin at each other conspiratorially, a welcome release from thinking about Laurel, but when I look over at Padraig Fiero, he looks like a kid who's had his favorite toy snatched out of his hands.

A female officer lets us into Eileen Elliott's house. It's uncomfortably cluttered, too much furniture, too many things on the surfaces. The air inside is warm, too warm, and the dingy wall-to-wall carpeting emits a strong smell of cat. It's a far cry from Jade's city apartment, but there's something familiar I can't quite access. The clutter, maybe. A woman I assume is Eileen is collapsed in a recliner pushed against the wall in the small living room, dabbing at her eyes with a tissue. She has short gray hair and a puffy, swollen look to her. Her legs are covered in a woolen blanket and there's a walker next to her chair. The television sits on a table with wheels, pulled up close to the chair, and its position makes me guess it's usually on. Another woman is in the kitchen, putting tea things on a tray, and a uniformed guard—a middle-aged guy with bright red hair laced with white—is sitting across from Eileen, looking uncomfortable and distractedly patting a long-haired black-and-white cat sitting in his lap.

"Mrs. Elliott," Roly says, sitting down in the armchair next to her and placing a hand on her arm. "I'm so sorry for your loss. My name is Detective Inspector Byrne and these are my colleagues, Detective Garda Fiero and Garda D'arcy. We wish we could leave you alone to grieve in private, but we need to ask you some questions in order to investigate your daughter's death and try to find your granddaughter as quickly as we can. Do you understand?"

"We understand," says the woman in the kitchen. She lifts the tea tray, and as she steps into the light I can see a resemblance to the picture of Jade from the refrigerator. This woman is older, maybe thirty-five, and heavier, but with the same high cheekbones and small mouth. Her dirty blond hair is pulled back in a painfully tight-looking ponytail.

"I'm Jade's sister, Nicola," the woman says, putting the tray down on a low coffee table in front of the couch. "We want to do anything we can to find whoever did this. Please, ask us anything." She's focused and alert and I know what she's doing and why. It's common for the family members of murder victims to throw all of their energy into the investigation to avoid the grief that will come crashing down as soon as they let it.

"Nicola Elliott?" Roly asks. Fiero gets out a notebook, ready to write down whatever she has to say.

"I'm married. My husband is Keating, so I'm Nicola Keating."

We get her address and confirm phone numbers for her and Eileen, and Fiero asks for Laurel's date of birth. She'll be two on the thirty-first. Halloween. An image of my daughter at two flashes across my consciousness. "Mama, we go beeswim," she used to say, combining "beach" and "swim," then two of her favorite words. When Lilly was two, she had a blanket she called her "soffy" for softy and she took it everywhere with her. I wonder if Laurel Maguire has a blanket that is special to her.

"Time is of the essence here, so I'm going to just ask you: Does either of you have any idea where Laurel could be?" Roly says.

Eileen gasps and begins to cry. "No, no," she says. "If she's not with Dylan, she's . . . I don't know where she could be. You have to find her. The little dote, you should see her, smiling at her nan. You have to . . ." Her crying has an odd, performative quality to it. I see Fiero notice it, too, and frown involuntarily.

"Mrs. Keating?" Roly prompts Nicola.

Despite her resolve to help us, I can now see the impact of the last few hours on her face. Her green eyes are bloodshot. Her hands are wringing the paper napkin she's holding. "I don't have any idea," she says. "Do you know who is responsible? For Jade? Have you charged someone yet?"

"I'm sorry. Not yet. When was the last time you each saw Jade and Laurel?" Roly asks them.

"A few weeks ago," Nicola says. "I went down to Dublin to see an old school friend and I stopped in to see them. We had tea and went for a walk along the canal. It was lovely. I feel, well . . . quite grateful for that now." She inhales sharply and tears roll from her eyes.

There's a short silence before Roly prompts Eileen. "And you, Mrs. Elliott? When did you last see Jade?"

"I don't know . . . She came up to meet me, with her little girl. When was that, Nicola?"

"I think it was in July, wasn't it?"

Jade's mother only lives an hour from Dublin, and she hasn't seen her daughter and granddaughter for four months? Most grandmothers of a two-year-old would have been wearing a path in the motorway driving down to see the toddler every chance they got. I can feel Fiero and Roly both thinking it, too.

"Mam's legs are bad," Nicola says, by way of explanation. "And Jade doesn't have a car, but you had a lovely visit in July, didn't you, Mam?"

Eileen nods sadly, still slumped in the chair.

"Was Jade afraid of anyone? Had she been threatened in any way?"

"No." Nicola hesitates. "But Jade was . . . well, I don't know if you've seen a picture. She was . . . She worked as a model. She used to . . . People always . . . noticed her."

"She was so lovely," Eileen sobs. "Even as a baby."

"Who else spent time with Laurel?" Roly asks. "Is there a minder or a close friend of Jade's, a boyfriend, someone who might have cared for her who could possibly have her now?"

Nicola waits for Eileen to speak first. "She didn't work any longer, after Laurel," Eileen says. "Dylan was so kind about that. He said it was better for her to be home with the baby for now."

"She didn't have a childminder," Nicola says. "I don't think she was going out with anyone. At least she never said."

"What was her relationship with Mr. Maguire? Did they get along?"

Nicola sighs and glances at her mother, choosing her words carefully. "As you might imagine, Laurel wasn't planned. Jade and Dylan weren't together very long, but when she found out she was pregnant, they decided to try to co-parent. It wasn't . . . easy." She pauses. "Jade could be . . ." She hesitates again, and I have the sense she was about to say something negative and then remembered Jade is gone. Her eyes fill up again. She says, more deliberately, "She was very immature, very young, in some ways, and well, Dylan did right by her financially. He paid for everything. He owned the apartment and gave her an allowance. They managed to co-parent fairly well, I think."

Eileen says, "I couldn't understand why she didn't just marry him, like he wanted. He's a lovely man. But she couldn't do it just for Laurel. I don't . . ." She starts crying again. "I don't understand."

"What was their custody arrangement?" Roly asks.

"He took Laurel every other weekend, is that right, Nicola?" Eileen asks.

"Not that much," Nicola says. "He traveled quite a lot for work, so it wasn't always regular. I think he was hoping for more time with her, perhaps. They had been arguing about custody recently, maybe going to court. Jade could be . . . difficult, as I said. But . . ." She looks up at me with her eyes full of tears. "She was young, but she was a really good mother. She didn't plan it, but she loved Laurel. She would have done anything for her."

I make a note in my notebook to check up on the custody situation some more. It sounds like it could have been a source of tension between the parents. Fiero writes something in his own notebook, and I know we're probably thinking the same thing. If they handed Laurel off at the weekend, that might have been the source of a fight on Saturday night. Perhaps someone heard but then Jade denied it when Jason and I knocked on her door.

The cat meows and stands up in the guard's lap, rubbing its face against his chest. He sneezes, and through tears, Eileen says, "He likes you, I think," and we all smile, glad of a redirection. Roly scratches his right ear.

"Something I'm wondering about," I say, picking up the interview. "Did Jade have friends? Maybe from when she was on the TV show? Anyone who she might have confided in about someone who was making her uncomfortable?"

"You American?" Eileen asks suddenly, as though she's just noticed my accent.

"Yes," I say.

"And they let you work as a guard?"

"They do." I smile at her. "I'm sorry, Jade's friends?"

"Her friends were here," Eileen says grumpily. "At home."

Nicola watches her, then says delicately, "Jade hadn't been in

Dublin very long. She was modeling and did that show, but it ended after a season and then she fell pregnant. Her co-stars from the show weren't close friends. But maybe there were girls who modeled with her . . ."

"What was the show called?" Roly asks. "Something about fashion, yeah?"

Nicola frowns and looks at me. *"Ireland's Next Star Model.* I think it must have been based on your one in the States."

Someone knocks on the door and the liaison officer gets up to answer it. We hear her talking and then the door shutting again. "Did she move to Dublin for the show?" Roly asks.

Nicola sighs. "She wanted to be a model. From the time she was little. When she was twelve, we started letting her work with an agency and do a few shoots for local businesses. She did them here and there when she was still at school, but she wanted more. Mam and I tried to say that she should get some experience while still living at home, but she was impatient. She left school and found a roommate and got a job working in a café while she did some modeling jobs. She made good money. Then the show came along. She seemed happy. Then she told us she was . . . that she'd fallen pregnant." Her face does something complicated. Nicola Keating is clearly the sister who did what she was supposed to. Jade, not so much.

"Was she still working as a model?" Fiero asks. "Recently, I mean?"

Nicola shakes her head. "No, she was focused on Laurel."

I meet Roly's eyes and he gives me a tiny nod, as if to say, *Go ahead and ask.* "I hate to ask," I start. "But did Jade have any problems with addiction to alcohol or drugs?"

Nicola shakes her head. "No, she smoked cigarettes before, but

I think she'd given them up." Remembering the dish of butts out on the terrace, I wonder how well Nicola knew her sister. There's something here I can't quite put my finger on, a distance that suggests estrangement, though neither of these women is admitting to it.

"Where is she?" Eileen croaks out, the tears starting again. "Where's my granddaughter? Why haven't you found her? Did you talk to Dylan? Maybe he has her? Maybe it's all a misunderstanding."

"They said they talked to Dylan, Mam," Nicola says. "I'm sure the guards are doing all they can. They need us to stay strong so that they can find out who killed Jade." She looks up at me. "And find Laurel. That's what Jade would have wanted." Eileen nods, tears running down her face, and Nicola tenderly covers her hand with her own. Eileen's eyes are vacant. She's barely taken this in. We've gotten about as much as we can for now.

"We need some more pictures of Laurel," Roly tells them. "As soon as you can." Nicola nods and picks up her phone from the counter in the kitchen. She shows us ten photos that Jade has shared over the past month or so, then forwards them to Fiero. The one from Jade's refrigerator is there and there's a more recent one, just of Laurel, that's perfect. The little girl is sitting on a blanket and looking right into the camera. She has more curly, pale blond hair here, tucked behind her ears, wide green eyes, and a distinctively elfin-shaped chin with a dimple that ought to stick in people's minds.

"Can you tell me if there was a coat that Laurel always wore, or a toy she always carried?" I ask Nicola. "Anything that someone might remember if they saw it?"

"She had a lovely little coat," Eileen says. "Bright pink, with a little hood with fur on it. Was it real fur, do you think, Nicola?"

"I don't think so, Mam." We all catch Nicola's irritated eye roll.

"What about the changing bag we gave her?" Eileen asks.

Nicola turns to me. "She had a few different coats, I think. But my mam's right. Jade almost always carried a pink diaper bag we gave her when Laurel was born. It was pale pink, with little gray elephants on it. She kept everything in there."

Roly spends some time with the local guards before we go. They're setting up twenty-four-hour surveillance and the rotation of guards who will be at the house in case Eileen is contacted. They'll work on video surveillance, too, and a trace on the landline. It doesn't feel like there will be a ransom request, but they need to plan just in case. Nicola takes Fiero and me upstairs to show us Jade's room. "We shared until I left home," she says, leading us up the narrow stairs to one of two bedrooms on the second floor. "She was in here for five years before she left for Dublin. Mam hasn't really changed it. Honestly, she doesn't even come upstairs anymore. She sleeps in that chair most nights. I know it's not right, but . . . I have a husband and three boys at home. There's only so much I can do." She looks despondent for a moment. She's alone now, the only one to care for Eileen.

The bedroom is painted a pale yellow that might have been cheery when fresh, but now reminds me of urine stains, and the floor is covered in cheap beige carpet, fraying at the edges. There's a twin bed pushed against each side wall, one covered in a yellow floral coverlet and the other one stripped bare. Over one of the beds, magazine pages featuring nearly naked models are pinned to the wall in the form of a heart, and I notice Fiero taking an extra-long look at them, then looking embarrassed when he sees me noticing. There are two small, mismatched bureaus on the only wall with a window, and we each take one after Nicola leaves us alone to search. We put on latex gloves, but there isn't much to find, just stacks of fashion magazines from the years Jade would have been in high school and a pile of printed shots of her striking various poses, her makeup heavy and not quite expertly applied. She's wearing casual clothes in all of them and looking more closely, I can see that many of them were selfies or taken in this room right here. There's something earnest about the way she's looking at the camera, a child's idea of how a model poses. Fiero puts them in an evidence bag. He looks out of place in the feminine bedroom, too male, too large for its scale. Checking behind the bureau, he steps back and bumps into me, knocking me into one of the beds. "Jaysus, sorry. I'll go back downstairs," he says. "You do the rest up here."

While he searches the rest of the house, I check the bathroom, finding old bottles of highlighting shampoo, fake tan cream, dried-out lipsticks and mascaras, hair depilatory, boxes of soap and tampons and cold medicine. Everything's dusty and faded.

Then I go outside and wander around a little, looking for neighbors to talk to. It's nearly seven and quiet. The news hasn't gotten out yet, so there are no rubberneckers, no press, no neighbors coming over to show support. It will happen soon enough, but for now it's just a few kids playing a pickup game of soccer on the scrubby grass. "What happened in there?" one of the kids calls out to me. "Somebody die in there?"

The other kids laugh and one of them says, "Don't ask that! What if someone did?"

I walk over. "The lady who lives in there has a baby granddaughter. Did any of you ever see her?"

They shake their heads, anxious to go back to their game.

"You haven't seen anything strange, have you? Someone you don't know hanging around, looking at Mrs. Elliott's house? Anything like that?"

One of the kids says something I don't catch and they all laugh.

"Well, look, if you remember something or you see something, let your parents know to ring the guards, okay?" I tell them. "My name is Garda D'arcy. Can you remember that?" They all nod solemnly. As I walk away, I'm thinking of our little gang of kids in Portobello, of their reconnaissance around the neighborhood, and I'm thinking of my cousin Erin and myself at that age, before things went wrong between us, how we roamed the neighborhood, watching, listening, trying to figure out how to be grown-ups, trying to figure out who we were.

Six

··

Roly glances over at me once we're back in the car. "You all right to drive, D'arcy? Fiero can take over if you want."

"No, I'm fine," I say, backing up carefully and turning around. I'm aware of the extra effort my brain has to make to mirror the familiar action.

Roly studies me for a long moment before saying, "All right, I just got word that Dylan Maguire is back in Ireland and on his way to the family home in Portarlington. We'll meet him there. How long a drive, you think, Fiero? You worked out there for a bit, yeah?"

"Yeah. 'Bout an hour, little more, depending on how fast you drive." The rain has slowed. I'm starting to feel my energy wane and I lean forward, gripping the steering wheel, keeping my focus on the road.

"Make tracks, D'arcy," Roly says. "What did you two make of the family?"

"The mother's fuckin' mad, isn't she?" Fiero says breezily. "Aside from the shock. Sister seemed off to me, too."

I look up and make eye contact with him in the rearview. "I agree with you about Eileen. Maybe some early Alzheimer's there, but I thought the sister seemed okay. What do you mean she 'seemed off'?"

"Not quite sure," he says. "But I felt like she was holding something back. Something not right there. We should keep an eye on her."

I hesitate, not sure I should push back, but then I see Fiero straightening the collar of his jacket in the mirror. "I disagree," I tell Roly. "She's clearly bearing the brunt of Eileen's care, and she was just told her sister was murdered."

Roly's drumming his thumbs on the dashboard. "We'll see," he says noncommittally. "We'll ask Maguire about the sister anyway."

"Do we know how old Dylan Maguire is?" I ask.

"System says birthdate in '83," Fiero says. "So thirty-five."

That gets my attention. "She was, what, twenty-one? That's a big age difference. There may have been aspects of control in the relationship."

"But it can't be him, can it?" Fiero asks. "He was in France when she was killed."

"He *says* he was in France," I say. "Roly, you have all his social media and work details?"

"Yeah. They're working on it, and we can check his phone if we need to. Seems like the France thing would be hard to fake. We've got to get face-to-face with him, see what he can tell us."

I glance over at him, trying to read his mood. He's focused, scrolling through texts on his phone, his foot tapping against the side of the car door. We stop for coffee and motorway sandwiches in Edenderry. While we gulp them down, Roly checks in with the team, then gives us the update. "The alert is active. Still nothing from the surrounding area. Water Unit took a look but it was too dark. We'll have the divers out at first light to search the canal. But if she somehow made her way out of the apartment and was walking or crawling that way, you'd think someone would have seen her, would you not? Picked her up?"

"Unless it was the dead of night," I say. "No one around."

"My kids are older now," Fiero says. "But from what I remember, kids of that age don't just hurl themselves over walls and across roads and into canals. She'd be crying, sure, scared out of her mind. Wouldn't she be more likely to stay where she was?"

He's right. "Yeah," I say. "I don't think there's any way she left on her own. But you've got to rule it out, haven't you?"

Roly says they've had a few calls to the tipline already. "Seems like it's all shite so far though. They're working on social media and trying to get into Jade's phone and electronics. They've got the floaters viewing the CCTV right now."

"What about Maguire's residence in Dublin?" I ask when Fiero heads off to use the petrol station's restroom. "Anyone searched it?"

"We have a uniform outside," Roly says. "But unless he gives us something to go on, we'll need cause. You sure you're okay to keep driving down there? I can have Fiero do it."

"I'm fine to drive," I say, too quickly. "How'd he end up on your team anyway? He was on the drugs unit. Seemed like he was good at it, too."

He must hear something in my voice because he appraises me for a second, and then says, "I'm not sure why he wanted the transfer. Decision was made above my pay grade, but he's here because he's smart and he's a good investigator, D'arcy, and he's got experience with missing persons cases. He has a nose for 'em. Just like you. Now." He spots Fiero coming across the parking lot. "Off to Portarlington."

The sun is setting as we do the last leg down through County Offaly toward the border with Laois. I keep my eyes fixed on the road, thinking of Dylan Maguire, already in a car speeding through the gathering darkness. What does he have to tell us? Assuming he didn't do it himself, does he have any idea who killed Jade and took his daughter? And if he does, will he tell us the truth? I think again about Jade Elliott's still, silent body. *If she could just tell us who did this.*

Of course she can't. I press my foot down on the accelerator. *Of course she can't, Maggie,* I tell myself. *That's where you come in.*

Dylan Maguire's parents live in a big Georgian house at the end of a long drive just outside of town. Conor and I drove out to Portarlington for one of his cousins' weddings in September, and I got the impression of a largish market town, prosperous and maybe a bit conservative, the main street lined with businesses and pubs, lots of nice new houses on the outskirts. I brace myself for reporters, but the only other cars in the circular drive are a shiny black Citroën and a marked Garda car that must belong to whoever escorted him from the airport; no one's figured out that Dylan is the missing toddler's father yet, that this is where the child's grandparents live. It's only a matter of time, though.

A uniformed guard opens the door and whispers that Maguire's just arrived and is having a quick shower. Roly looks alarmed, but we can't haul him out and demand he not destroy evidence. We've got nothing to say he had anything to do with this.

The family liaison officer who brought him from the airport shows us into a large living room and tells us that Dylan's parents are in Geneva but will return home as soon as possible. I look around the room, seeking out pictures of Laurel, but I don't see any, just photos of an elegant older couple and one family portrait of them with five kids of various ages taken when the two oldest kids, boys, were young teens.

"So why'd he come here rather than his own gaff?" Fiero asks.

"Wouldn't you come here if you could?" Roly says, looking around at the elegant surroundings.

"There's a pool," the liaison officer whispers, her eyes wide.

Fiero cups his hands around his face and peers out the wide windows along one wall. "What about outbuildings?" he asks. "Any garages, sheds, boltholes, and so forth?"

She nods and he says, "We should have a look before we go." He seems at home in this well-appointed room, full of history and good taste, even in his ridiculous jacket, his service weapon holstered under his arm. I just feel bulky and conspicuous in my unflattering uniform—and naked without a gun. After years as a plainclothes detective, I can feel the difference in the way people perceive me, the way they keep their defenses in place when their eyes light on my vest.

Maguire joins us almost immediately. He's wearing workout clothes and his dark hair is wet from the shower. He's a good-looking guy, not quite as objectively physically stunning as Jade, but unquestionably attractive, with broad shoulders and toned arms under a gray T-shirt, a strong jaw and athlete's build. They must have made a stunning couple.

He turns to sit down and I see it at the same moment Roly and Fiero do—a long, shallow scratch down Maguire's right cheek. It looks fresh, only a day or two old, pink but not actively bleeding, only superficial. Suddenly, the room is full of tension. I know Roly's doing complex calculations. If he mentions it, Dylan Maguire will be on his guard. If he doesn't, we'll miss a chance to see him react.

"Is there anything on Laurel? Where is she?" He looks genuinely distraught, his eyes bloodshot, his mouth drawn in worry. "Do you have any idea who took her?"

"No. We're hoping you can help us find her, Mr. Maguire," Roly tells him. "I know you have a lot of questions for us, but there are some things we need to ask you immediately. The first question we have for you is whether Jade ever told you about anyone who scared her or had seemed obsessed with Laurel. Were there any incidents we should be aware of? Did she ever report anything like that?"

He looks up, running a hand through his hair. He might have been crying in the shower, I think. His eyes have that red, puffy look. "No, she never said anything. Only, there had been some break-ins in the neighborhood. One at the complex a few months ago. I don't think they ever caught them."

"Nothing else? This is very important now. Did she ever report feeling threatened or unsafe?"

He leans back against the sofa cushions, crossing one leg elegantly over the other. "No, only . . . there was a man in the neighborhood. I didn't like the way he looked at Laurel. A few times I saw him near the apartment, when I was bringing her back."

"Describe him." Fiero and I both take out our notebooks.

"Sort of middle-aged, balding. He has a limp. I only saw him a few times. I've no idea where he lives, but he . . . looked too long at Laurel, if you know what I mean. It was a bit creepy. I mentioned something to Jade and she knew who I was talking about, but she kind of laughed it off."

"She didn't know his name? Where he lived? Anything like that?"

"No, I think she saw him as harmless. Other than that, I can't remember anything."

Roly nods, leans back against the sofa cushions, keeps his voice casual. "When was the last time you saw Jade or spoke to her?"

Dylan thinks for a moment. "I picked up Laurel on Friday and I dropped her off before I left for Lyon on Sunday. So, Sunday morning, I suppose." I write that down.

"Did you know that gardaí were called to Jade's residence on Saturday night for a noise disturbance?" I ask him.

He looks surprised. "No, she didn't say anything about it."

"Where were you and Laurel Saturday night?" I ask. "Did you talk to Jade at all?"

Surprised, he glances at Fiero, then says, "Home. I watched *The Little Mermaid* with her and we had fairy cakes as a special treat. I rang Jade around eight so Laurel could say good night. We didn't really chat, but she seemed okay, said she was having a quiet night in."

"How did she seem Sunday morning?" Fiero jumps in.

Dylan shrugs. "Yeah, grand. She was happy to see Laurel. We chatted for a bit and then I left for the airport."

"Did you speak with her while you were in Lyon?" I ask.

"No. I was busy, with work."

"Was that unusual?"

He runs a hand through his hair. "Not at all. We didn't normally speak unless it was about Laurel."

Fiero and I both look to Roly to see where he wants to go next. We've got to address the scratch. After a moment Roly says, "Mr. Maguire, can you tell me about your custody arrangement?"

The liaison officer comes in with tea for all of us and Dylan seems grateful for a break. When he's got a cup in his hands, he says, "I had her every other weekend, for up to three nights, but that sometimes changed because of my work. It's hard with a baby. She wanted Jade, you see. But as she gets older, I'll take her more and more. At least that's my hope. Jade could be . . . difficult." He looks up at us, realization dawning. "Oh, God. I keep forgetting. I'll have Laurel all the time, won't I? If you . . ." He looks terrified suddenly, then guilty, realizing he was about to say, *If you find her,* and says harshly, "Where is my daughter? Why haven't you found anything? Why haven't you fucking found her?" The tea sloshes out the cup as he roughly puts it down on the table. His head drops into his hands, he gasps a few times, and then he looks up at us in despair, his eyes filled with tears, and says, "Sorry, I'm just . . . This is awful."

He may be bullshitting us, but it feels authentic to me.

"Mr. Maguire, I know this is incredibly difficult," Roly says. "But we need you to stay calm so you can help us. Can you tell us about your relationship with Jade? You never married, I assume?"

"No, I . . . well, I wanted to once she decided to go ahead with the pregnancy, but she . . . didn't want to." He casts a hurt look our way. "She was right of course. It never would have worked. I was trying to do the right thing, but we don't have much in common." He picks up the tea and takes another long sip, then inhales deeply, steadying himself.

I don't want him steadied. I ask quickly, "How long had you been seeing each other before she became pregnant?"

He looks up with a sheepish expression on his face. "We weren't even . . . You couldn't call it seeing each other. We were together a few times and then she told me she'd turned up pregnant. It was . . . not ideal, as you can imagine. She'd told me she was on birth control, that she was good about taking it." As if he can read my mind, he adds quickly, "I know that's no excuse. I should have taken precautions. But she seemed so sure."

"How did you meet?" I ask him.

Again, the sheepish look. "Look, I don't want to pretend this was anything it wasn't. I was at a club, I'd just ended a long relationship, I'd had a few jars, and I started talking to a gorgeous girl. She'd had a few as well and . . . one thing led to another."

"How old was she when you met?" Fiero asks it casually, but we know how old Jade was and we know how old Laurel is and we could figure it out ourselves. He wants to see how Dylan handles it.

Dylan grimaces. "I know how it looks. There was a big age difference. I guess she was nineteen at that point. She'd been on the show though and living on her own for a while, and she seemed much older."

"When did you find out she was only nineteen?" Roly asks.

"When she told me she was pregnant. Honestly, it was a bit of a nightmare. I assumed she'd . . . end the pregnancy, but she didn't, and I had to . . . make the best of it. It was very difficult. I'll tell you something though, when I saw my daughter for the first time it was like . . . Do you have kids? When you see your child . . . She has my nose, you see." His eyes fill with tears. "Where is she? Where the fuck is she? Who took her? Who killed Jade? Why aren't you out looking for Laurel?"

"We have many, many officers out right now looking for her," Roly says. "I'm sorry, but we need to get some more information about Jade. If we can locate the person who killed her, we can find Laurel. Who owns the apartment at Canal Landing?"

He takes a deep, raspy breath. "It's mine. I bought it ten years ago and when it became clear it wasn't going to work out between us, I moved out so she and Laurel could have it. It's a relatively safe neighborhood and . . ." He looks up in horror, realizing what he's said.

"Did she work?" I ask. I already know she didn't from Nicola and

Eileen, but I want to see what he says. "Was she still making a living as a model or doing any acting?"

"No. The show was canceled and she gave the modeling up before Laurel was born. I think she was tired of it and she wanted to focus on being a mother. I . . . don't mind supporting her while Laurel's little. You don't know what you'd get at a crèche or with a nanny. You hear stories about these places . . ." He shrugs.

There's a long silence. A radio or television is on somewhere in the house. I can hear voices filtering through the walls. "Your parents are in Geneva?" Roly asks casually.

Dylan frowns. "Yeah, they're on their way back. They should arrive later tonight."

"And you're sure they don't have any idea where Laurel could be? This couldn't be some kind of misunderstanding?" Roly says it offhandedly, like he's not taking the idea seriously, but he's watching Dylan's face.

"No," Dylan says, picking up on Roly's tone. "They've only met her once or twice. They didn't approve of Jade at all, didn't approve of her going through with the pregnancy. It's partly my fault. In the beginning, I was . . . well, frustrated. I asked my father about legal options, and I think they've never really forgiven her for ruining the experience of their first grandchild. My siblings have followed their lead. No, there's no chance she was with my family." His voice is bitter. He may have come home for some support while we look for Laurel, but I'm not sure he's going to get it.

Something passes between Roly and Fiero and I get ready for a question about the scratch. But instead, Fiero leans forward and fixes his eyes on Dylan. "Do you know anything about Jade's death and Laurel's disappearance, Mr. Maguire? I just have to ask. Did it seem like this all might be easier if Jade was gone, if you didn't have to fight for custody?"

Dylan's eyes go wide. For a second, his good looks go rabbity and shocked. "What, how could you . . . ? No! No, I don't know anything about it. I just want Laurel found."

Roly comes in fast, following the punch with an undercut. "Where'd you get that scratch on your face?"

The tension buzzes in the room. The liaison officer is wide-eyed, holding her breath.

Dylan's hand flies to his cheek. "What? You don't . . . I was putting my bag in the overhead bin on the plane and the zipper got me. It's not . . ." He stares at Roly as though he's betrayed him and then says in a low voice, "Jaysus."

Roly says, more gently, "Are you sure you don't know anything that could help us find Laurel? Is there anything else you can tell us?"

Dylan puts his head in his hands and moans before looking up again and saying, "No, if I knew something, I'd tell you. Of course I would. Look, Jade was . . . You must know by now she was beautiful, only gorgeous. A lot of people knew her from the show. There must have been some man who was obsessed with her, who figured out where she lived. It's the only thing I can think of." He drops his head again, absolutely deflated, and I know we're not getting anything else out of him tonight. They may have gone out on a limb asking him directly if he had anything to do with Jade's death and Laurel's disappearance and about the scratch, but his reaction—authentic to my eye—is good information. "I told you about the man who I saw looking at Jade and Laurel. It must be something like that."

Roly considers that. "You think you could describe him, this fella? So we can come up with a portrait to show around?"

Dylan nods. We ask him to write down the hotel where he stayed in Lyon, a timeline of where he was on Monday and Tuesday, and all of the information he has about Laurel's doctors and anyone who ever babysat her.

"Can I ask you something?" I say as we get ready to leave. "It seems like Jade didn't see her family much. What was that relationship like? Why hadn't they spent more time with Laurel?"

He sighs. "Eileen . . . Did you meet her? Jade's dad passed away, a long time ago, and Eileen never got over it, could never stand on her own. She didn't like Jade moving out of the house and leaving her. I think she punished her for it, made her feel guilty. Honestly, she's like a fucking black hole, Eileen. That sounds cruel, like, but it's true."

"What about Nicola?" I ask. Fiero looks up, interested in the answer.

Dylan's eyes narrow a little. "Nicola resented that Jade went to Dublin, left her to care for Eileen. She has a few kids of her own and she didn't want the extra work. I've always encouraged Jade to keep up with them, to take Laurel up there, but I don't think she felt very welcome."

I meet Roly's eyes. That puts a slightly different spin on things.

"One more thing," I say. "Was there a coat or something distinctive that Laurel always wore? What would she likely be wearing?"

He covers his face with his hands, overcome. Finally, he says, "She had a purple one, but I think it's still at my place. Jade had a few different ones for her. She had a changing bag, pink, with elephants. That had all her things in it and it came with her when she went between our flats. And Laurel has a blanket she keeps with her. It has a little bear stuffed toy on it, sort of part of it, if you know what I mean, just the head." I nod.

"Mr. Maguire," Fiero says. "We will be sending crime scene officers to get fingerprint impressions from you and to photograph the wound on your face. We would also like to take a look around here, out of an abundance of caution. The sooner we eliminate family members, the sooner we will be able to find Laurel. Is that all right with you?" I watch Dylan's face carefully. He looks exhausted, resigned.

He sighs. "Sure. Search anywhere you'd like. I know what you think but I don't know where she is. I wish I did."

The uniformed guard stays, to keep an eye on him and in case someone tries to contact him while they set up surveillance, and Roly gets flashlights from the car. "He didn't seem worried about us looking around," Fiero says.

Roly opens the door to the garage, finds a light switch inside. "No, he didn't. Didn't seem worried about the scratch either. If he's got Laurel, I don't think she's here," he says as an overhead fixture illuminates the inside of a very clean and organized garage and workshop, boxes and plastic crates neatly stacked against one wall.

"It'd be a good place though," I say. "It's far enough away from other houses that you wouldn't have nosy neighbors listening in." We search the garage, empty except for a well-cared-for vintage Mercedes completely covered in a cloth and a few more stacked boxes. Then we search the shed on the other side of the swimming pool. There's nothing to find, just lawn and pool care tools and supplies. But it's got me thinking. If she's still alive, she'll be in a place like this.

As we head for the car, I feel the ache that started behind my eyes on the drive down from Navan blossom into a dull throb.

I start up Roly's car, but I hesitate before pulling out.

"You okay there, D'arcy?" Roly asks.

I hesitate. "Would you mind driving?" I ask Fiero. "I'm tired. I don't think I'm up for it."

"Of course," he says, just a little too gallantly. He's delighted. No one says anything, but I feel their judgment. Roly brought me along so I could drive, and I can't even do that. We get onto the motorway, the silence suffocating me in the back seat, and we're passing Kildare and the Curragh Racecourse before Roly says, "What do you think, lads?"

"His grief seemed genuine to me," Fiero says. "But that scratch."

"He was lying about how he got it," I say. "I'm sure of it."

"I don't know," Roly says. "He came up with it awful quick."

"Of course he did," I say. "He had to know we'd ask about it. He had the whole plane ride home to come up with something. He probably saw someone whack themselves with their bag."

Roly's silent for a bit. Then he says, "Pat, I know you're half Italian and all, but how's your French?"

"*Tres bien*," Fiero says. "You want me to check up on his alibi?"

"Yeah," Roly says. "We need to definitively rule him out right away. D'arcy, what did you think about how he described the relationship?"

I lean back in the seat, my exhaustion flooding through me. It's ten. I've been up since five this morning. I don't know what I think at this point, but I come up with, "The way he talked about Jade. It wasn't a hundred percent transparent. I felt like he wanted to say something but was holding back, you know?"

"Yeah, I felt that as well," Roly says. "You think he just didn't want to speak ill of the dead?"

"It might be that. The relationship was clearly complicated."

"I think he was trying not to tell us she was a psycho who saw a fat bank account and made her plans," Fiero says. He hesitates, then says, "I don't think he's got anything to do with her murder. He didn't seem the type."

"What *type* is that?" I ask. "Because I've seen a lot of murderers who didn't seem the *type*."

"No, I know, I just . . . That was my instinct. I'll go see what they say in Lyon. But to my mind, the most interesting thing he said was about the dodgy fella in the neighborhood. We'll get on to Protective Services, will we, Roly? See who's in the neighborhood? Get the Evo-FIT, yeah?"

The Evo-FIT is a new kind of police composite sketch. I've used similar technology and it gets good results. I don't say anything.

Roly spends the rest of the drive on the phone, getting updates and giving assignments. In the parking garage, he tells us to get some rest, though I know he'll probably spend the night at the station. I yawn. It's been a long day. Tomorrow will be even longer.

"I've got you off patrol duty tomorrow and the next day, but if this gets resolved or you're not needed, I'll have to send you back," he tells me once Fiero's gone.

"I can live with that," I say. "Thanks, Roly." Then I think of something. "Will Griz be on this?" My friend Katya Grzeskiewicz is a member of Roly's team, too.

"Not unless things really go south," he says. "She's on the gangland thing and she's making some headway. Look, what I said, about Jade's life, the neighborhood, figuring out who she spent time with, worked with, yeah? I really meant that. I don't know, but I have a feeling that's how we solve this. I think she was killed and that baby was taken by someone who knew them or at least had seen them before. I think someone in the neighborhood must have seen something. But in the meantime, we've got to come at it from every single angle we've got. See you for the briefing at eight, right? Maybe we'll find something overnight. Maybe we'll get something off the tipline." He looks exhausted, and I tell him to get some coffee.

"Keep your phone close," he says. "Thanks, D'arcy. I'll see you in the morning." I know we're both thinking the same thing. It's eleven now, the air is chilled, dry leaves skipping down the pavement behind the breeze. *Where is Laurel Maguire spending the night?*

Seven

....

I smell it the second I come in the door: Conor's been baking. The scents of warm cinnamon, sugar, and fruit fill the house and lead me to the kitchen, past a curtain of plastic hanging from the ceiling and blocking the living room and hall. Yesterday our contractor, Gerry, started sledgehammering a hole in the wall separating the kitchen from the rest of the house. I love Conor's house, which he and his ex-wife bought almost twenty years ago, but its separate first-floor rooms and small bathrooms are apparently not in demand in the current real estate market and he's been advised that creating an open floor plan downstairs and a master suite upstairs will significantly increase the eventual selling price. So, we're living in a construction zone; a construction zone that will lead to opening up the house to potential buyers and then finding a new house and moving all of our stuff and . . . I try not to get overwhelmed by the prospect of it all. Conor's ex-wife finally agreed to wait to sell until both Adrien and Lilly know where they're going for university. It was a relief last year, but now the time for action is fast approaching.

I make my way around the plastic and poke my head into the kitchen. Conor sees me and says, "Hiya, I made a barmbrack. Lilly's never had it before and she's just gotten the ring in her slice."

Lilly, dressed in running clothes, her long dark hair in two braids, is at the table, her boyfriend, Alex, sitting next to her. He's visibly relishing a slice of the dark, fruit-studded bread. Conor's son, Adrien, is sitting at the table, too, working away diligently at what looks like math homework. Both Adrien and Lilly are in year six of the Irish educational system, studying for their Leaving Cert exams next spring, which will determine admission to their chosen courses of study at university. My two months in uniform, with a more regular schedule, have allowed me lots of evenings at home with them all, helping with homework, making them late night snacks. It's been nice, and though I can feel the old excitement of an investigation coming back, I also feel a flash of caution at the way things are about to change for all of us.

"What does it mean if you get the ring?" I ask Lilly.

"Good fortune!" Conor says quickly.

"I thought it means you're going to get married," Adrien calls out.

"Or good fortune," Conor says, giving Adrien a meaningful glare.

"Don't worry, nobody's getting married," Lilly says, grinning at Alex. "Alex's apartment is crap."

Alex laughs and says, "I think that's my cue to go back to my crap apartment. I have to be up early for work." He works at a coffee place off Camden Street, slinging lattes and flat whites during the day and singing with his band—and sometimes Lilly—at night.

"Oh, yeah, I'll talk to you tomorrow," Lilly says, kissing him lightly on the lips. Standing next to each other, they're a study in contrasts, Lilly dark-haired and dark-eyed and Alex fair and blue-eyed. I find myself just staring at them, Adrien too, soaking in the details of their faces and bodies and smiles, knowing my daily proximity to them is coming to a close. I can't help thinking of Jade Elliott and wondering if Eileen felt that way about her when she moved to Dublin. And

I can't help thinking of Jade and Dylan Maguire—Jade fair, Dylan dark, the inverse of my beautiful daughter and her handsome boyfriend. Was Dylan's account of their relationship accurate, or would Jade have a different take, if I could ask her? A deep weariness settles over me for a moment, and as though he can feel it, Conor's corgi, Mr. Bean, comes over and puts his paws on my foot, looking for a scratch.

"Alex, take some brack with you," Conor tells him, wrapping a few slices up in aluminum foil.

"Hey, you might not be able to walk all the way home along the canal," I tell him, following him to the door. His apartment is in a run-down house on the South Circular Road, not far from Canal Landing, I realize. He hasn't been living there very long and Lilly says it's in bad shape and that his bandmates, who share with him, aren't very good at cleaning, which is probably why he spends a lot of time at our house. "They've blocked off some of Portobello Road."

He gives me a thumbs-up and I smile at this kid who's come to feel almost like a son to me. He and Lilly started dating a year and a half ago in the summer, and after he moved to Dublin last fall, Conor and I wondered how long it would be before teenage love met the realities of school, friends, music, social lives, and for Alex, earning a living. But to our surprise, they've stayed together, providing support for each other as they've navigated their new lives. Lilly's been back to West Cork a few times to visit Alex's brother and sister-in-law and their baby, and Conor and I drove down over the summer for a week. I think of Alex's niece, Julia, only a little younger than Laurel Maguire. My stomach seizes up suddenly. She's been gone more than twenty-four hours now. The statistics on child abductions are chilling. Most abducted children are killed within three hours of their abductions. By twenty-four hours, you're looking at a tiny percentage still alive. If I'm honest with myself, I know this is likely a double homicide at this point. I shiver.

"Anything new?" Conor asks me back in the kitchen. "It was on the *Six One* news. How awful. Do they know where the little girl is?"

"No," I say, taking the thickly buttered bread from him and taking a bite. It's really good, rich with whiskey and tea and dates. "She's not even two yet. Hopefully we'll have something to go on by tomorrow. I'm wrecked. I've been to Navan and then Portarlington today."

"What happened to her?" Adrien asks with big eyes.

"Did she get taken by some child sex trafficker or something?" Lilly asks in a hushed voice. She's been listening to a lot of true crime podcasts lately, and I jump in to say we don't know anything yet and we're hopeful we'll find her safe and unharmed. She nods, yawning, and starts cleaning up her homework.

"We have to tell Maggie about our mystery," Adrien says suddenly, when Conor suggests it's time for bed.

"Oh, yeah, show her the pictures," Lilly says.

Adrien goes over to the drawer where we keep pens and pencils and paperclips and Conor explains, "Gerry found it today, when he was making the big hole. Someone had carefully hidden these photographs, wrapped in butcher paper, inside the wall out there. Behind the plaster and everything. The lads didn't find anything else, but it's really weird."

Adrien lays the paper and the photographs out on the table. There are four of them, all featuring the same young woman, dressed in a dark dress with a dropped waistline, her bobbed hair pinned to one side with a hair clip. She has a solemn expression on her face in all of the photos, formal and intense, her dark eyes looking right at the photographer. "They look like they were taken in the twenties, from the clothes and all," Adrien says. "One of them says 'Clara' on the back. We think it must be someone who lived in this house then. But the question is, why were they hidden in the wall like that?" Adrien's glasses slip down on his nose, just the way Conor's do, and he pushes them up again and scratches his cheek. He's wearing a beige sweater and a pair of Conor's wool trousers, and he looks so handsome all of a sudden, his awkward teen stage almost over, that I can't help but reach out and tousle his too-long hair. He gives me an indulgent, if quizzical, smile.

Lilly, stacking her books and papers, says, "I think there was a guy, right? And he lived in this house with his wife or something, but secretly he was in love with this Clara woman, so he had to keep the pictures hidden. Maybe they had a love child together and she died in childbirth but he never forgot her." Along with true crime, Lilly's been memorizing the lyrics of traditional Irish and Scottish ballads recently, and she seems to have internalized the drama and heartbreak.

"Or it was just his sister or something," Adrien counters. "It could have been one of those, like, time capsules."

"Well, maybe I can figure out who was living here when these were taken," Conor says, wrapping them up again and replacing them in the drawer. "When we bought the house we got some records. I think they must be filed with the mortgage documents."

I let him make me a plate of leftover pork roast and green beans and more bread and Lilly and Adrien tell me about their days. By the time the kids drift off to their rooms, it's nearly midnight.

"What do you think happened to the little girl?" Conor asks me once we're in bed. Mr. Bean is already asleep on the floor, his soft snoring a familiar accompaniment to sleep for me now.

"I don't have a good sense yet," I say. "If someone broke in to rob Jade Elliott's place, I'm not sure they would have taken the baby." I hesitate. "Could be a case of abduction and sexual abuse, though. I didn't want to say this to Lilly, but there have been some of these cases around Europe recently, trafficking of babies and toddlers, videos that get traded on the dark web. Horrible, horrible stuff."

"And you're on the case, like as an investigator?" I can hear a little bit of pride in his voice. He knows this is what I want. I thought I'd have to wait quite a bit longer to get it.

"I'm tasked to the investigation for a couple of days," I say. "No promises, though Roly said if it goes well, maybe I'll get moved up to his team or one of the others sooner than I thought."

Conor thinks for a minute, then says, "Adrien went missing once, when he was about four, for only ten minutes, but it was the longest fucking ten minutes of my life. We were on holiday and went to one of those train villages and it was quite crowded. Bláithín had him by the hand and we stopped to look at something, but when we turned around he was gone. He'd seen something and taken off, then been sort of swallowed up by the crowd. One of the employees found him crying and we got him back."

"That happened to me with Lilly once, too," I say. "At the supermarket. She went right up to the information desk and announced herself, said her mother was a police officer and that they needed to announce her whole name so I would come and get her. I heard them announce, 'Will the mother of Isabella Lillian Erin Lombardi please come to the information desk.' She'd been calling herself Isabella, after some book we read. She'd snuck it in. I almost died of relief."

"We're lucky," Conor says sleepily, turning off the lights and taking my hand. I turn toward him and throw a leg over his, taking comfort from the familiar warmth and shape of his body. "When I saw the news, I just kept thinking about how lucky I've been."

I wake up at four A.M., thinking about Laurel. Who is she with? Is she scared? Is she being hurt, assaulted, neglected? Does she know enough to know that she's in danger? *Is* she in danger? Is she even alive? I lie there in the dark running through the worst possibilities. As an investigator on Long Island, I never worked on a child sexual abuse squad or task force, but I investigated child sex abuse–adjacent murders, including the killing of a woman by an acquaintance who kidnapped her six-year-old son and took him across state lines to deliver him to a sexual predator. That one stayed with me for years, as did the murder of a couple whose fourteen-year-old daughter's older boyfriend killed them because they were preventing him from seeing the girl.

But we can't go too far down that road without additional leads. This could be a lot of other things, too: a grudge against Jade, a stalker, mistaken identity, a burglary gone wrong, one of those women who steal babies and try to pass them off as their own, though that's usually infants. I have to consider a family member, too. Her mother seems to have disapproved of Jade's lifestyle. Perhaps she thought she would do a better job raising Laurel. It's hard to believe Eileen would have had the strength to strangle her daughter, but perhaps she'd had help from Nicola. It doesn't track with my impressions of the women yesterday, but you never know.

And then there's Dylan Maguire. Maybe it's just the scratch, but I can't shake the feeling I have that he's involved. Shared custody is difficult. I should know. As Fiero pointed out to him, if he was frustrated at having to share Laurel with Jade, maybe he started thinking about how much easier his life would be if Jade wasn't in the picture, if he didn't have to pay for all of her living expenses. It doesn't seem likely he could have made it back from Lyon, but maybe he'd paid someone to do it for him.

I see the flaw in my thinking, though. Why would he have taken Laurel or had someone take her when custody was going to automatically transfer to him anyway upon Jade's death? If he hired someone to kill Jade, all he had to do was to wait for the police to show up. Why take Laurel?

My mind goes to an even darker place. He told us he didn't want to be a father, that he hadn't planned on it. What if he wanted to be free to live his life without the burden of parenthood? What if he'd killed Laurel, too, and hidden her body?

Mr. Bean has heard me in the kitchen now, and he comes in and barks twice, asking if it's time for our walk. I pour my coffee into a to-go mug and slip on my boots.

The sun is just coming up and the streets around Herbert Park are mostly empty, just a few early dog walkers and joggers. I pass the playground, now closed, and, as I do almost once a day now, the spot where, two and a half years ago, I ran into Conor while he was walking Mr. Bean on a warm day in early spring, cherry blossoms littering the path the way fallen leaves do now. It seems impossible to think of it, the way time has collapsed and lengthened to contain all the things that have happened since then: the death of my ex-husband and Lilly's father, Roly and Griz and I solving the murder of my cousin Erin, my involvement with a case with international implications last year, Lilly falling in love with Alex during our summer in West Cork.

And here I am, living in Dublin, right on the edge of a new career, everyone doing well, Conor and I stronger than we've ever been after the challenge of a long-distance relationship while I was in training last year. In some ways, my being away during the week really did make our hearts grow fonder—the weekends felt special and romantic—and I'm feeling more like a Dubliner now, especially since Lilly likes her school so much and Alex and his band have done so well in the city's music scene.

I check *The Irish Times* on my phone. The headline is GARDAÍ STEP UP INVESTIGATION INTO MISSING TODDLER over a reproduction of the picture I took from the refrigerator, and it shocks me into action. What am I doing walking the dog? I need to get moving. This is going to blow up today, with "Baby Laurel" on every phone screen and the front of every Irish newspaper. Managing the press is going to be an extra treat for us alongside the investigation. I look up a few of the tabloids. They seem to be going with a slightly different angle: BELOVED *STAR MODEL* JADE MURDER SHOCKER and MODEL JADE ATTACKED; TOT TAKEN.

Searching frantically won't work, but I need to get going calmly and with purpose. We have the briefing this morning and will find out if Roly and the team got anything overnight. Then, I need to use my time wisely and follow up on some of these threads.

As I walk back past the empty playground I think of the parents and grandparents and au pairs I've gotten used to seeing here. I'm betting they know who all the babies and kids in the neighborhood are and whether there are any sketchy guys around who linger too long by the swings or who make them feel uncomfortable.

I'm betting the parents and childminders of Portobello do, too.

Eight

....

There are a few reporters camped out by the entrance to the Garda station, but they don't bother me. They're probably waiting for Roly to come by so they can yell at him, but I slip past them and head upstairs for the case conference.

Because this is both a murder investigation and a missing persons investigation, they've taken over the two largest incident rooms, opening the sliding partitions in the center so we can all fit in. It's a crowd: divisional detectives, uniformed guards like me and Jason, crime scene techs, and bureau detectives from Roly's team. Everyone looks up when I slip in at the back. I'm still in my uniform, still no service weapon—that was part of the deal in me joining the investigation for a few days—and they're confused by my age.

Roly looks like he's been up all night. His usually crisp suit and dress shirt have devolved into a rumpled heap of expensive fabric, and he's clutching a giant paper cup full of steaming liquid like it's the only thing keeping him going. The divisional chief superintendent in charge makes some introductions and then asks Roly to brief us. I'm still learning about how incident rooms are staffed and run here, but I've been told that because everyone's so shorthanded and because of the complex nature of this case and its intersection with an urgent missing persons investigation, Roly is taking the lead on coordinating the cases. When he starts speaking, I can feel him digging deep for the energy, but by the time he's finished giving the basics of how we discovered Jade's body and realized Laurel was missing, he's looking more like himself, full of buzzing vitality and a sense of vibrating but focused action.

"Now," he says, "during the night we continued limited searches in the vicinity, and gardaí from roads policing have been out looking for Laurel Maguire. We did what we could by the canal but this morning the Water Unit returned and have set up a base of operations. They will search the area of the canal near the residence where Jade Elliott's body was found throughout the day. We've already started door-to-doors, so we need more of youse for that, and we'll need uniformed officers to provide security and crowd control around the canal. Look for those jobs, yeah?" He goes on: "The Child Rescue Alert was activated at six P.M. yesterday. We set up a dedicated tipline, and as of nine A.M. this morning, there are forty-six messages to follow up on. Detective Garda Chen will be organizing that." He nods to a young guy sitting in the front row. "And we need to continue with the door-to-doors and witness interviews and statements from the neighborhood. Someone must have seen something."

The screen at the front of the room lights up with a picture of Jade in a strapless ball gown, posing on Ha'penny Bridge. It advances to one of her in a promo shot for the reality show. Under the words *Ireland's Next Star Model,* three young women and three young men pose on a low couch. Jade is in the middle, wearing high heels and a very short skirt and mugging coquettishly for the camera.

"Now, Jade Elliott, twenty-one years of age. Born and raised in Navan. Moved to Dublin four years ago. That's a modeling photo she took when she first came to Dublin," he says. "She used it as her Twitter handle and on her Instagram page. More about that in a second. Next photo is her on a reality TV yoke called *Ireland's Next Star Model*. Some of youse may have seen it. It didn't last long.

"Almost three years ago, she had a short relationship with Dylan Maguire and fell pregnant with their daughter, Laurel Roxie Maguire. The relationship didn't last long but it seems to have been mostly amicable, though recently he had been asking for more time with Laurel and that might have been a bit contentious. We need more on that. As you know, he was in Lyon when she was killed. He's got a scratch on his cheek that we're taking a look at."

No one asks questions about Dylan or the scratch, even though everyone's dying to; we all know Roly needs to get through the basics before we start looking for more details.

"Now, electronics," Roly says. "Her phone was in the bedroom. Password was the kiddie's birthday; we got in last night. She'd only had the phone for six months and she doesn't seem to have transferred over her old texts, so not a lot there except for pictures of Laurel and a few messages, but we'll check her account for backups. There was a missed call from Dylan Maguire from Sunday morning before he dropped Laurel off on his way to the airport, and then a text letting her know he was on his way. A few other simple texts, one to the sister, arranging a lunch Nicola Keating told us about when we interviewed her yesterday evening.

"The calls were mostly to Mr. Maguire, Eileen Elliott, Nicola Keating, and a number she had in her contacts as Dr. Deeley, Laurel's pediatrician. And she had a few short phone conversations with someone at a number that's not in her contacts. No luck tracing it and we think it might be a burner. So, obviously that's something we need answers on. There's another number with a few short calls in the log. It's in her contacts as *Liz*. We're working on tracing that.

"There were a lot of text messages between her and Maguire about the baby, logistics, etc. There's one we'll want to ask him about. Five months ago, at two in the morning, she wrote the following: You up? Feeling lonely. You want to come over? There's a winky face there. He didn't respond until the next morning, when he wrote, Jade, you can't send txts like that. Remember this is my work phone. We should only be in touch about Laurel.

"Cold," someone says.

Roly shrugs. "It sounds like maybe he wanted to marry her when she became pregnant. She said no. Maybe he was hurt. But this sounds like maybe she was interested in a casual thing, and he wasn't having it. We'll have to see if there's more of that. I'm sure you're all thinking what I'm thinking. It's Maguire, right? It's got to be. Arguments over custody, romantic complications. Oldest story in the world. But . . ." He shrugs again. "He was on a business trip in Lyon when she was killed. He definitely flew there on Sunday. We've checked the plane manifests, and he didn't fly back to Dublin on Monday. But there may be other possibilities. Detective Pat Fiero flew to Lyon this morning and he'll coordinate with the police there and make sure there isn't something we're missing. Maguire says he got the scratch when his wheelie bag nicked him as he put it in the overhead bin on his way back. In any case, he struck me as shocked when we spoke with him. There wasn't any love lost between them, but I believed him. Was that your impression, too, Garda D'arcy?"

Everyone turns to look at me and I stand up, smoothing my uniform trousers. "Yeah. He seemed quite authentically in shock, grieving and so forth," I say, my voice cracking. I'm conscious of my accent, conscious of my uniform and regulation hairstyle, more severe than how I usually wear it. I don't feel like myself. "That makes me think, though. If she was lonely and Dylan Maguire wasn't interested, then she might have been out looking for companionship. Have we checked the dating sites to see if she had a profile?"

"Nothing on the phone," Roly says. "There wasn't a laptop in the apartment, only an iPad for Laurel. But she must have had one at some point. Someone get on that. Check the dating sites. See if you can match the photo or the name or anything that seems similar." Another plainclothes officer in the front row raises his hand to volunteer. Roly nods and goes on: "We're going to see what we can get from her carrier about other calls she made. That might give us something. Now, her social media." The slides advance through a series of Instagram posts of Jade in various poses, most of them fairly elaborate. She's wearing tank tops or dresses or bikinis in most of them, and pouting or staring at the camera. "It's mostly selfies," Roly says. "A few photographs from her modeling jobs before the baby was born, fewer after. We're still going through it all, but the DMs are a lot of creepy stuff from fellas she didn't know, 'Ah you're so beautiful, let me know if you ever fancy a shag,' et cetera, et cetera. You'd be surprised how many unsolicited willies she got."

"You might be, but I wouldn't," a woman in plain clothes up at the front calls out.

"Fair play." Roly smiles, just a little, and there's a round of uncomfortable laughter from the male officers in the room.

"There were a few messages that jumped out at us, extra hostile and misogynistic, like. I need a couple of youse to get out and find these fellas. You? Okay, here ya go." Roly hands a printed piece of paper off to the two uniforms who raise their hands.

"What about CCTV?" someone asks.

Roly says, "There was a camera at the gate into the complex. We're still sorting through. The angle is sort of strange. It gets anyone who rang up to be let in, but not necessarily the residents, who went in the other gate farther down the walkway. And just our fucking bad luck, the cameras on the canal side had been taken down while they painted the back of the building."

"What about CCTV from surrounding streets and buildings?" I ask. "Another camera may have caught something, especially if our killer was on foot or carrying Laurel."

"We'll get to that today," Roly says, and I hear the weariness creep back into his voice. "And we'll keep working the social media angle and her electronics. Now, on Jade, the deputy pathologist says we'll have more later, but it seems to be manual strangulation. No surprise. She was small, quite light, just a little over eight stone. Wouldn't have taken a lot of strength, she thinks. She's placing time of death sometime between three P.M. and midnight on Monday. The open door kept things cold. That's why the long window. But the autopsy should narrow things down."

There's a bit of buzz around the incident room about that. "So the baby may have been taken during what would have been a busy time outside?" someone asks. "People on their way home from work or the pub and so forth. You'd think pedestrians would have seen something or heard the baby crying. If our guy climbed over the balcony holding a baby, I'm thinking someone would have seen him."

"Yeah, that struck me, too," Roly says. "I suppose he could have gone out the door, leaving it open behind him, but none of the neighbors heard anything or saw anything. Still, we should give the media some video from along the canal there. It might tickle someone's memory. And we need to continue with the door-to-doors. Someone must have seen him taking Laurel out."

"Unless our suspect killed her, too, and carried her in a suitcase or a bag, something like that," a young guy, one of the detectives they've brought in from another station, says, a bit too jauntily.

There's a long silence. His tone was wrong, but it's a good point. Everyone considers that for a moment.

Roly says, "Okay, we need to get back to that apartment and see what else is there. But here's another angle. Dylan Maguire said that Jade had complained about a dodgy fella in the neighborhood who sometimes looked at her and Laurel too long. We've had him do the composite, and who's working with Probation Services on sex offenders in the neighborhood? Detective Chen?"

A youngish guy in the front row stands up and says, "Yeah, there are a few in the area. I've got the list and thought I'd start visiting them today. I'll let you know if I need help." Unlike in the US, information about where sex offenders are living isn't publicly available in Ireland. Gardaí would have to go through Probation Services or check the PULSE computer information system to find out about anyone with crimes against children living in the neighborhood. Now that Dylan Maguire's described the guy and they have a likeness, they'll want to see if it matches up with anyone they're already monitoring.

Roly nods. "What else? Any other ideas?"

"Drugs?" someone asks.

"Path says nothing obvious like track marks or nasal tissue damage, but we need the tox screening."

I raise my hand and say, "Nicola Keating told us she and her mother gave Jade a distinctive pink diaper bag when Laurel was born. I don't think it was in the apartment, but we should double-check.

Dylan Maguire said he brought it back to Jade's when he returned Laurel on Sunday. Assuming it's not there, I think we may want to find a photograph of it from the manufacturer and get it out to the public. It's the kind of thing someone might recognize."

"Okay, great. That's enough for the moment. We need that CCTV and we need to know if there's anything on the tiplines. And we need to talk to the neighbors again. Someone must have seen something. Garda D'arcy and I will meet our scene of crime colleague and go over what they've found. Youse keep on the door-to-doors."

Roly goes quiet then, and after a few seconds everyone stops talking or writing and focuses on him. "Look here," he says. "Laurel Maguire isn't even two years old. She doesn't know what's going on. She's scared and God knows what's been done to her. She's been missing thirty-six hours now. I don't have to tell you what the stats are on abducted kids. If we're going to find her alive, it's got to be soon. Get me a sighting. Get me something I can work with, right?"

That's it. We have things to do. Everyone nods and sets off. It's barely ten o'clock and we've got the whole day ahead of us. I've got my morning coffee coursing through my veins. It still seems possible we might find her. My elevated mood lasts until we get down to Canal Landing and the reporters descend. There must be twenty standing in front of the gate. When they see us, they come to life, like some kind of huge, multicelled organism.

"Where's baby Laurel?" one of them shouts at us. "Do you think she's still alive?"

There are more people than usual walking by the complex for this time of day, rubberneckers from the neighborhood. They've chosen this route so they can have a look at the place where the girl from *Ireland's Next Star Model* was murdered.

"Who's got the baby?" another reporter screams.

I want to turn around and shout at them, tell them to imagine they're her father, and to have a little respect. But Roly winks at me and we wait for the property manager to let us in, ignoring the questions and keeping our faces stoic and still.

Nine

....

We don boiler suits and shoe covers and gloves outside Jade's apartment and meet the crime scene tech inside. He's an older guy, balding, his blue eyes shrewd behind small glasses. "Where do you want to start?" he asks, all business.

"You tell us," Roly says.

"Wineglass in the sink then." He points to the kitchen. "First of all, she wasn't a cook. Not much in the way of kitchen utensils and so forth. She had a lot of baby food around, things she bought prepared for the little girl, biscuits and snacks. For herself, she seems to have relied on takeaway. The fridge was full of old containers. As Garda D'arcy mentioned, there was a bottle of red wine on the counter, about half empty. Only one glass in the sink, though, with one set of prints, and lipstick marks on the rim that match a lipstick in the bathroom, so if she was drinking the night she died, she was drinking alone." I feel my hopes fall. I've been counting on prints from a second glass.

"Now, let's look at the bedroom." He leads us up the stairs and points at the spot where Jason and I found Jade Elliott yesterday. There are little evidence markers all over the room, on the floor and on top of the bed. "Path and I think whoever did it didn't move her when they were done. Now, see how the bedclothes have come off the bed?"

"It started in the bed and then they rolled off and onto the floor," I say.

"That's what I'm thinking. The assailant may have started choking her on the bed and then she rolled away to escape and the assailant followed her. Once they were on the floor, the assailant finished the job." He's being careful to say "assailant" and not "him."

"Any evidence in the bed?" Roly asks impatiently.

"Yeah, but not the kind you're hoping for. No fluids at all on the bedclothes, cover on the mattress, probably because of the baby. The only hairs on the bed seem to be hers—they're all long and blond—or the little girl's. We matched it to short, curly hairs found on a pair of little girl's pajamas in the hamper and on a blanket downstairs. Seems like the little girl slept there with her rather than in the crib. I don't think anyone else was in that bed with her right before she was killed."

"So he broke in then? It wasn't someone she was sleeping with?"

"Maybe, but something else stuck out to me. There's no sediment on the carpet up here. I don't care how nicely you keep your shoes. If you've walked outside, there's going to be dirt, sand, rocks on the treads."

"Her assailant was in stocking feet. Which means maybe she knew him," Roly says.

The tech raises his eyebrows and shrugs as if to say, *That's not for me to say.*

"Now, tell me you got some good prints, John," Roly says.

"We've got some good prints, Roly," John says. "Lots of them. Up here, on the surfaces in the bathroom, and from the kitchen as well. But you know yourself, it will take us some time to put that together."

"Get it to me as soon as you have it."

"Of course. Now then." He leads us back downstairs to the living room. "We've gone through her papers. Not much to see. All her bills, including her phone, were paid directly by Dylan Maguire, though she did have a bank account in her own name. Hasn't been used in a while though. Not much in there. You'll want to take a look. And there's this." He points to a large fake leather case someone's placed on the island in the kitchen. "Her modeling portfolio, I think. We've printed it already so you can flip through."

Roly opens the portfolio. On the inside is a business card, minimalist chic with just a small line of type reading "The Delaney Agency." He lifts it up. Similarly small type on the back reads, "Fiona Creedon, principal."

I write down the number and address as he flips through the contents of the folder. The photos are about half black-and-white and half color. They mostly show Jade in full-length poses, wearing casual clothes or evening dresses, posing against a white backdrop or in various "gritty" locations around Dublin. She looks much older in the photos, mostly because she's wearing full makeup, but there are a few where she's in casual clothes and she looks so young it takes my breath away. They all have labels on the backs with photographer credits. "Can we take this?" Roly asks. "We'll need to track down all these photographers who she worked with."

"Not yet," the tech says. "But I'll have one of the lads make you a list so you can start ringing around."

Roly nods.

"Did you find a pink diaper bag, with elephants on it?" I ask. "Sorry, changing bag is what you'd call it, I guess."

"I don't think so," the tech says. "But you can look around as long as you don't touch anything."

I check the bedroom, then go out in the hall to search for "Pink elephant changing bag Ireland" on my phone. I save screenshots of the ten or so possibilities that come up. Then I dial Nicola Keating's number and when she answers, I ask her to check the photos I'm about to text her and tell me if any of them are the one she gave Jade. She texts back within seconds that it's the third one, a bag sold by an online baby shop based in Waterford.

"I've got the changing bag," I tell Roly back in the apartment.

"Great, send it to Detective Chen. He's coordinating the content for the appeal they'll do tonight."

Before we go to talk to the neighbors, I stand in the living room and look around, trying to get a better sense of Jade Elliott. Now that I've seen the house where she grew up, I find myself noticing her decorating choices with a different eye. She's painted the walls a pale gray and has a few framed photographs, including the two of her, hanging on the walls, though not quite enough of them to fill the space. The couch is expensive, but worn, so I assume it was originally Dylan's. But Jade brought in green throw pillows that brighten the room up, and the fluffy white rug under the glass coffee table feels like something she bought.

I imagine her choosing the pillows, placing them carefully on the couch when she got home from the store, plumping them every time she walked by. When Lilly and I moved into Conor's house, the house he had lived in with his ex-wife, I'd gone out and bought some new cushions and a throw blanket for the living room couch, new sheets for our bed. I'd wanted to put my stamp on the house, I suppose, and I feel like I've gotten a glimpse into Jade's personality. She wanted to assert herself here, I think. She wanted to control something.

It's Wednesday, a weekday of course, but we've asked all of the neighbors to be available to talk to us this morning and no one gave us any pushback. We start with the Rodens, and as we wait outside the door, I make a conscious effort to reserve judgment. When you're interviewing the neighbors and close contacts of a homicide victim, you're always thinking along two tracks. The first is what they might have seen or heard, and the second is what they might have done. Most homicides are a result of physical proximity, one way or the other, and so you need to think of those closest to the victim as witnesses and suspects at the same time, even if it seems far-fetched. I try to keep this in mind when Gail Roden answers the door and says, "Is there any news on Laurel? I couldn't sleep last night, thinking about her." She does indeed look like she didn't sleep, her eyes puffy and her face drawn and pale. I think she's been crying.

"No, I'm sorry," Roly tells her. "We're looking for her right now and we're hoping you may be able to help us."

Behind her is Phil Roden and—I'm surprised to see—the teenage boy from the neighborhood gang of kids. She introduces him as her son, Andy, and invites us to sit down. Her husband sits close to her on the couch, a comforting hand on her knee, and Andy Roden sulks from an armchair next to them. He's wearing his school uniform, the tie in a messy knot somewhere south of his collar. If he recognizes me, he doesn't let on. We start by taking down their full names and birthdates and phone numbers. Later, we'll get their fingerprints, mostly to rule them out since Gail Roden said they babysat for Laurel a few times. Gail is forty-eight. Her maiden name is Deeley and she tells us she works as a nurse at the Coombe Hospital. Phil Roden is forty-nine and works as a product manager for a software development firm based in London. He's a quiet, athletic-looking guy, clearly worried about his wife from the way he keeps checking on her, and he tells us he's only had the job for a few months. Andy is fifteen and goes to a school on Synge Street I've walked by many times.

Roly looks up from his notepad and says, "Could you go back to Monday afternoon and evening again. Where were you all?"

"I was working at home that day," Phil Roden says. "Had video meetings and so forth. I suppose I got off the computer around six."

Roly studies him for a long moment. "And you didn't see or hear anything? No voices from Jade's apartment, nothing out on the terrace?"

"No, I'm sorry," he says. "I was occupied of course and I had my headphones on, but I think it was quiet. There was nothing out of the ordinary."

I feel my hopes sink. The headphones mean he may not have heard the murder. By six, Jade Elliott may have already been dead and Laurel already gone.

"I was at hospital. My shift ended at six and I got home around seven," Gail Roden says when we ask her. "But like I told you the other day, I didn't hear anything. You . . . You're sure there's nothing on Laurel?"

"No, I'm sorry, Mrs. Roden. What about you, Andy? Where were you on Monday?" Roly asks gently, turning to the boy.

He looks down at his hands. "I . . . I was at school. Then I was with my friends, and then I was home."

"What time did you get home?" Roly asks.

He stammers out, "Seven, maybe." He seems very nervous, too nervous, though it may just be my uniform.

"I was starting the tea when you came in, so it must have been seven thirty," Gail says.

"And you didn't see or hear anything unusual?" I ask Andy. He shakes his head, not making eye contact. He sits hunched over, as though he wishes he could disappear into the couch.

"What about last Saturday evening?" I ask them. "Someone rang the guards to report they'd heard a fight in Jade's apartment. My partner and I responded but Jade told us it was the TV. That wasn't you who reported it to Mr. Egan, the property manager, was it?"

Gail shakes her head. "I was on an overnight shift; we have to do them once a month. You were here, weren't you, love?"

Phil nods and Andy says, "Yeah, me and Dad were here playing *Call of Duty.*"

"And you didn't hear anything?"

Phil takes a long moment to answer. "No, uh, no we didn't. But the video game was quite loud." He smiles a hesitant smile, not sure it's okay.

Gail says, "Even when this lot aren't playing, you can't really hear what's happening on that side of the complex. I'm not sure what it is. We sometimes hear Denise, who's next to us here on the parking lot side, but I've never heard anything from across the hall."

We'll have to test that out, but if it's true, that's interesting. It means that whoever made the call was on the canal side of the complex. If anyone heard anything, it's going to be the neighbors on the other side of the hallway who share a wall with Jade's place.

"How well did you know Jade?" I ask. "Did she ever talk to you about her personal life or her family?"

Gail says, "Not well. I felt sorry for her, I suppose. She was so alone and so young. We helped her with Laurel sometimes, when she didn't have childcare, but I didn't want to make it a regular thing. I didn't want her to rely on it, you see."

"But she wasn't working, was she?" I ask. "Was it just so she could get a break?"

"Perhaps sometimes, or to do the shopping. Back in the summer, she said she needed to meet with someone."

"Meet with someone? Do you think it was social or business?"

Gail says, "Business, based on the way she was dressed, but I can't be sure, of course."

Roly and I exchange a glance. We'll need to ask the modeling agency if Jade had booked any jobs recently. Dylan said she wasn't working, but if she was having business meetings, she might have been.

"What about you, Mr. Roden?" Roly asks. "Did you ever speak to Jade about work or her personal life?"

He shakes his head. "No," he says. "We'd say hello and like Gail said, we both helped her with the little girl sometimes, but . . . not much beyond that." We wait to see if he has anything else to say, but that seems to be it. He seems distracted, looking down at his phone, which is faceup on the table, and I remember it's a weekday. We asked him to delay the start of his workday so we could talk to him.

"And were you aware of Jade's social life? Did she ever have guests, other than Laurel's father? Was there anyone new visiting her recently?"

They glance at each other, unsure of who should start. Phil says, "I didn't see anyone. Maybe it's just that I often worked late, but . . ."

Gail's silence is tense, full of unexpressed meaning. She presses her lips together, starts to speak, then stops. "Mrs. Roden?" I prompt her.

"She had . . . I saw at least one man visiting her. Late at night." There's something in her voice that interests me, disapproval maybe, or resentment, but when I ask for more details, she says she doesn't know who they were, just that a few times she heard voices and looked through the peephole on her door to see a man in the hallway, ringing Jade's bell, and then Jade letting him in. "Late at night," she adds again.

"Are you sure it wasn't Dylan, Laurel's father?" I ask her. "He would have been here fairly frequently."

She looks nervous now. "I know what he looks like. He used to live here. Perhaps once or twice it was him and I couldn't see his face, but there were others, too, or at least one other one."

"Can you give me any descriptions of the man you saw?"

She looks panicked now. "Brown hair. I didn't see much more than that. The light was low in the hallway. I'm sorry."

"How well did you know Dylan, when he lived here?" Roly asks. "Were you friendly?"

Phil shakes his head. "He wasn't here much. Nice enough fella though."

Roly thanks them and says, "Please let us know if you think of anything else." They nod and we leave them to their quiet apartment, as clean and orderly as a magazine ad.

"I want the dating site angle," Roly says. "If she had fellas coming by, she must have met them online, right?"

I think for a moment. "But wouldn't there have been something on her phone?"

Roly shrugs. "Maybe she deleted the apps. Maguire paid all her bills, including her phone. He might have had access to it through the plan. And if she was trying to get back together with him, she wouldn't have wanted him to know she was dating." We look at each other. That's good. That could be it.

The neighbors on the canal side of the building who share a wall with Jade's apartment are a couple named Fern and Tim Phillips, originally from Dublin and Galway, then London. They've been back in Dublin for ten years, Fern tells us. She's sixty-seven and Tim is sixty-eight. They're fit and white-haired, oddly alike, with a pair of expensive-looking bicycles on a rack near the door. They retired and sold their house in London to move here after inheriting a lot of money from a distant relative, Tim tells us. "We got a deal on the property," he says. "Seemed like a good investment, but the management firm doesn't keep things up very well. The construction was done on the cheap. We'll still get a packet when we sell though, Dublin real estate being what it is. As long as this doesn't affect things." He grimaces, embarrassed. "Ah, that doesn't sound right, but you know what I mean." They tell us they travel frequently and haven't really gotten to know their neighbors. "I knew Jade to say hello, of course," Fern tells us. "Her little girl was sweet. But we didn't know her well. Right, darling?" Tim says yes, he didn't know Jade well, though they're horrified at what's happened.

"Were you home on Monday afternoon and evening?" Roly asks them.

"Yes, we were in. I've tried to think back. We had our dinner, watched something on the telly, and then we went to bed. Nothing seemed out of the ordinary at all."

"What about on Saturday?" I ask them. "One of Jade's neighbors said they'd heard screaming coming from her apartment, but we don't know who it was. Was that you?"

They look genuinely confused. "No," Fern says. "We were out to dinner with friends Saturday so we wouldn't have heard anything."

"Do you hear sound coming from Jade's apartment?" I ask. "Usually, I mean? We're just trying to figure out who might have rung the guards or where the sound carried."

They glance at each other. They're embarrassed about something. "We did hear . . . well, when the little girl was a baby, we heard a lot of crying. I'm sorry to say we had words about it with Jade. She was . . . I don't think she was a very experienced mother and perhaps sometimes she didn't know how to make her be quiet?" Fern takes a deep breath and then goes on. "And she would have people over sometimes. We'd hear them talking out on her terrace and we complained to her a few times about the noise and the smoke drifting over. She had a . . . man with her once, and when I called out there, asking them to be quiet, he shouted a . . . profanity back at me. Anyway, things were a bit chilly between us after that."

"Did you ever see this man?" Roly asks quickly. "We would want to trace any friends who spent time here. Of course."

"No. His voice was . . . well, rough, if you see what I mean. But we never saw him."

"Dublin accent?" Roly asks, keeping his face neutral. His own

Dublin accent ranges from the kind of rough Fern is thinking of to a modulated version he uses in most professional situations.

"Yes, I suppose," Tim says, uncomfortable now.

We get all of their information and then go to talk to the final neighbor, the one who's on the opposite side of the landing from Jade. She's a single woman named Denise Valentine, originally from Cork, though she's been in Dublin since 2008 and says she works as an accountant at a restaurant supply company. She and Jade were polite and chatted sometimes, she says, but they weren't really friends, aside from Jade asking her to keep an eye on Laurel once when Jade needed to go out to pick up a prescription. Denise is tall, dark-haired, and primly serious in a pantsuit and silk blouse. She's about thirty, and when I ask her if she was here when Dylan Maguire lived at Canal Landing, she blushes and says she did know him, and that they went out for drinks a few times.

"Was it a relationship?" Roly asks, studying her face carefully.

"No, no, just a few casual drinks. A meal. That's all." But she says it too quickly, looking down at her lap. There's something more there.

We ask her about whether she saw or heard anything on Saturday or Monday night, and she says she worked late Monday and was out with friends Saturday, and that nothing seemed out of the ordinary when she came home.

"Have you ever felt unsafe in the neighborhood?" I ask her. "Ever seen anyone hanging around or watching Jade or Laurel?"

"No. I mean there are always ould fellas near the pub and sometimes you'll get lads who've been on the drink yelling at you as you walk by, but nothing more than that."

We get her cell phone number and place of employment as well as names and numbers for the friends she said she was out with, and then we tell her we'll be back to see her soon.

"Is there anything on the little girl?" she asks hesitantly. "I haven't been able to stop thinking about her since I heard. What might be happening to her."

We say we wish we had news, and then leave her alone.

Ten

Roly and I stand outside in the parking lot for a moment, conscious of the reporters just on the other side of the gate. It's lunchtime. They must be getting hungry, but they're afraid they'll miss something. I search the crowd for my friend Stephen Hines, a crime reporter for the *Irish Independent,* but I don't see him amongst the crowd.

"I don't know," Roly says. "I don't think there's anything there, do you? The ones complaining about the baby crying couldn't have done it, yeah? That last woman though. You think she and Maguire had a relationship?"

"Maybe," I say. "Could have just been she had a thing for him. She seemed ashamed of something about the connection with him. He's a good-looking guy, has money. Let's say she fell harder than he did and he had to tell her it was just for the sex and he didn't want a relationship. That could explain it."

"That kind of thing, would it give her a motive, ya think?"

"For killing Jade? Maybe. But taking Laurel? Not unless she's a lot more psycho than she seemed. Someone looked her up to see if there are any indications of her being a psycho?"

"I told 'em to. There's so much to do and we're missing half the divisional detectives and half my team on this gangland thing. I may get a few of them back today, but . . . You can check with Geoff Chen when you get back. He's point person on all the tech stuff. He just messaged me that it's going to be a while on the prints. They just lost one of their techs in the fingerprints section. Anyway, check with him and see if Denise Valentine has a record. And we'll need to ask Maguire about her."

"I don't think it's her. If she took Laurel, where is she?"

"Yeah." Roly looks up at the flats. "Did the lad not seem a bit shifty to ya though? Andy Roden?"

"I see him around the neighborhood a bit," I say. "He's part of a little gang of kids my partner and I have been trying to get to know. He's pissed off about something and he seemed eager to establish his alibi."

"Yeah, I noticed that, too. I suppose lads that age always seem a bit shifty," Roly says. "Maybe check with his school? He said it's up on Synge Street, yeah?" He looks down at his phone. "They're ready for the postmortem. I've got to go along. I can't bring you, D'arcy. But someone needs to go along to the agency and get her employment records, or booking records or whatever you call it for modeling, and find out if there's anything there that needs to be followed up on. Did she do a job where someone got obsessed with her or with Laurel? Did she meet anyone that way? He becomes obsessed with her, stalks her. That sort o' thing. And Gail Roden thought she might have been working again recently. You up for that one?" I nod. "They might like the accent, you know. Tell 'em you're from New York. That's where all the big-time models are from, right? Do your best New York fashionista act, yeah?"

I laugh. "If Lilly heard you say that, she'd roll her eyes and say that I'd have to have a complete wardrobe overhaul for that to even be plausible. Anyway, I'll head right over. I had another thought, too. I'm going to figure out where the closest playgrounds and parks are. That's a good place to get a sense of the other parents with babies in the neighborhood. I was thinking about how you get into some pretty in-depth conversations while you're watching kids play at the playground, baring your soul to people you don't even know. It's worth a try anyway. If I find anything I'll hand it off to you for a proper interview."

Roly winks. "Sounds like a plan." And he's off, making his way expertly through the gauntlet of reporters, murmuring about how it's a sad old thing sure enough, and the guards are doing everything we can and thanks for your understanding, lads.

I look up the agency and find their website, as spare and modern as the business card, with a physical address off Camden Street. When I get there, I find a corner building with a sleek modernist exterior, metal siding painted a dark charcoal, and a discreet sign above the entrance reading THE DELANEY AGENCY.

The lobby is painted an elegant pale gray and smells wonderful, like a woman wearing expensive perfume was here and now isn't, leaving just a whisper of lemony floral scent behind. On a low, glass coffee table is a spiky arrangement of fresh flowers, birds-of-paradise and pale pink stock, color-coordinated with the geometric-patterned blouse of the attractive young woman behind the reception desk.

The woman sweeps her eyes quickly down the length of me, my uniform pants and fleece top under my vest, and says, "How can I help you?" in a voice that conveys her strong opinion that clearly I'm not here because of anything even vaguely related to the fashion business. There are three tabloid newspapers on the reception desk, each one with a picture of Laurel on the cover and a headline screaming some version of WHERE IS BABY LAUREL?

"I'm a Garda officer," I say, betting that she isn't going to notice the difference between "officer" and "detective." "I'm investigating the death of a young woman who we believe was a—I'm not sure what the word is—a client? Of your agency?"

The woman's face lights up. "Jade Elliott. We saw the news yesterday. And the little girl. It's horrible. Fiona was wondering if we should ring you up."

"Who would be the best person to talk to? I'll need to see all of her employment records and the details of any jobs she went out on."

"I'll just buzz Fiona," the woman says. "Fiona Creedon. She's the managing director." She picks up the phone on the desk next to her and pushes a button. I can hear a female voice on the other end say, "Yes?"

The receptionist turns her body away from me and whispers, "There's a guard here asking about Jade Elliott. Yeah? Okay."

She turns back to me and says, "You can go right in. Fiona's just through there." She points to a frosted glass door underneath a huge black-and-white framed photo of an androgynous-looking teenage boy with long hair, an interestingly angled face, and a spray of freckles across his nose and cheeks.

On the other side of the door is a tall, silver-haired woman in a black pantsuit and bright fuchsia blouse waiting for me. I'm betting she once worked as a fashion model herself; there's something about her rigid posture and the absolute stillness with which she holds her body that feels like long, well-ingrained habit. Behind her is an open plan office with eight desks surrounded by frosted glass partitions. Three of them are occupied by extremely thin young women who look up at me and then quickly go back to their work. "I'm Fiona Creedon," the woman says, shaking my hand. "I thought we'd go talk in my office." She points to a wall of more frosted glass, and I follow her through the door and sit down as she shuts it.

She sits down behind the desk and adjusts her hair. "We were just saying this morning that we needed to contact you. We were horrified when we heard the news. Is there anything on the baby?"

I don't answer, just take out my notebook and say, "Why did you think you needed to contact us?"

Her mouth contracts into an O. "Just because . . . well, she was a client of ours at one time."

I wait before saying, "You're the managing director of the agency? How long have you held that position?"

"We opened our doors in 2010," she says. Her metal desk is almost clear, just a silver laptop closed in the center, a single pen and pad of lined paper next to it. The walls are decorated with framed magazine pages but the space is devoid of anything personal or specific.

"You own it?"

"With my partner, Mal Delaney. My business partner." She blushes a bit and looks down at the pristine desk and I wonder why she feels the need to explain.

"And when did you first meet Jade?"

She thinks for a moment. "It was likely at an open call, but I would have to check. We do them around Ireland, to give talent outside of Dublin a chance to meet agents and launch their careers. In any case, she signed with us formally in 2011, when she was thirteen, as part of our child model division."

"Open call?" I ask. "That's like a big audition?"

"Yes, an event for talent to meet with agents. We would hold it in a central location, an arena or shopping center or large hotel, and aspiring models would come along with their portfolios and learn about the opportunities available. Sometimes clients attend to see if they see someone with the right look for a campaign. It used to be that you had to go to London to have a hope of booking shoots, really, but in the last fifteen years, we've come quite far here in Dublin."

"How would Jade have heard about the open call?" I ask.

"Oh, we advertise online, and in newspapers. If she searched for 'modeling' she might have come across one of our listings. Or sometimes it's through dance studios or hair salons. We might put up adverts there."

"Would you have met her at that open call?"

"I believe we were both there, both Mal and I, I mean." She blushes again.

"Could you get me all of the records of her time with the agency?" I ask.

She seems surprised. "Well, that would be quite a lot of pages . . . Some of it might be confidential as well. I could—"

"We need to see everything," I say. "We're investigating a death as well as an abduction. It's possible her agency records are relevant." I stare her down, making it clear I'm not going to give up.

She turns to the computer on her desk and starts tapping at the keyboard. "This is . . . Well, it's hard to filter for . . ."

"Just print everything you've got," I say.

Silently, she navigates with a wireless mouse and printed sheets start shooting out of a printer sitting against the opposite wall. When it's done, she stands up and takes them from the printer tray, tapping the stack against the table so it's neat.

"Thank you. Is Mr. Delaney around?" I ask, taking the papers and tucking them into my bag. "I'd love to talk to him as well."

She smiles. "He's in Berlin right now, but I can give you his number."

"That would be great. Where was the open casting call where you met her? Was that here in Dublin?"

She shakes her head and sits down again. "I believe it was the Town Centre in Navan. What you'd call a mall, I suppose, in the States. It's a shopping center."

I think for a moment. I need to ask about the reality show, but first I need to know if there's something obvious for us to follow up on. "Ms. Creedon, as I'm sure you can imagine, we're interested in whether Jade's killer met her or became aware of her through a modeling or acting job. Did she ever complain about someone harassing her or showing an interest outside of a professional one? Perhaps when she was on the reality show?"

"Not that I can recall," she says primly, reaching up to pat her hair as though it wasn't already sleek perfection. "I always tell our girls to report anything like that. Things are . . . well, they're much better now than they were when I was starting out, but . . . incidents still occur. I can't remember anything like that with Jade though."

I quickly scan the dates of the work Jade booked through the agency. "The last job she booked was in 2016, around the time the reality show ended. Can you tell me about the show?"

"*Ireland's Next Star Model*?" Fiona considers her words for a long moment. "She didn't obtain that opportunity through the agency, in the beginning," she says. "I think a producer or someone approached her on the street and suggested it. Those kinds of shows had been popular in the UK and the States and this was going to be Ireland's turn at it. But I knew some of the people involved and I . . . well, I didn't think it was a smart choice for her."

"Why not?"

"As a legitimate model, you want to be a . . . blank slate, in a sense. You must have personality and a unique look, yes, but that look is in service of the client's clothes, of the vision for the shoot. You don't want to be too . . . accessible, if you see what I mean."

"So, the idea was that Jade and the other contestants competed for modeling jobs? I'm sorry, I don't really watch those kinds of shows, despite my teenage daughter's best efforts."

She smiles and rolls her eyes. "I don't either, except I have to know about them. There have been a few models who have broken out after appearing on them, but not many. Yes, they create a bunch of jobs and then sort of set the models up to compete against each other for them. It's all scripted, who gets it, who doesn't, and the only thing they really care about is the drama."

"How would we locate the other contestants? To interview them?" It occurs to me that we need to talk to everyone involved with the show. It was a while ago, but she may have lasting relationships—or lasting resentments—from her time with the other contestants.

She goes back to the computer and looks something up, then writes a name and a number on a slip of pale gray paper and hands it over. "That's someone I know at the production company. She would have all the contact information."

"Thank you. Jade stopped working when she got pregnant. Was that her choice?"

"Yes." Fiona looks uncomfortable. "Well, she might have done pre-natal work . . ." She shrugs. "But she wasn't really interested anymore. I think she was more focused on the baby." She puts a hand to her mouth. "It's terrible, isn't it, thinking of her. Do you know who's got her? Are you allowed to tell me?" Her eyes are wide, too curious, hoping I'll drop something.

I ignore the question again. "What was she like? Jade? As a model? As an actor?"

"Lovely face, very fine-boned. Blond. Classic. She was a very nice girl. Professional, but . . . young. She was a bit emotionally imma-ture, I guess you might say."

"She was only thirteen when she started modeling," I say. "That's very young."

"It is," she says. "Usually girls of that age would have a mother or guardian with them, to guide them, but Jade's mother never came along. When a guardian was required, I believe her sister accompa-nied her. Or we provided one." She adds quickly, "Safety is para-mount in our child division."

I'm aware of all the thin young women on the other side of the glass wall glancing up from their desks to try to figure out what we're saying. "Did she have a successful career ahead of her?" I ask. "If she hadn't gotten pregnant, I mean."

She presses her lips together and considers her words. "I hate to . . . It's so difficult to know if someone will be, well, if the camera will *love* them," she says finally. "Jade had some headshots that were quite good, or good enough, I suppose. When she was starting out, we had a few clients that were looking for a very particular *feel* and I was able to book her based on that. But she didn't have . . . well, it's hard to explain. She didn't have the right look for where modeling is going *now,* if you see what I mean. She was a very pretty girl, as I said, but she wasn't *unique* enough. It sounds terrible to say that now, but I assume you want the truth. I think that's why she was tempted to do that show, which we advised her not to do. She may have felt it was her only option."

I smile at her. "Thank you. This seems pretty straightforward. We'll let you know if we have any more questions." Back out in the lobby, she walks me to the door. The receptionist is watching us from the desk, and she looks back down at her keyboard when I meet her eyes. Fiona starts to say something, then stammers out, "I do—I do so hope there's some news on that poor baby soon."

I say gently, "So do I, Ms. Creedon. So do I."

It's one P.M. now, and Camden Street is busy with office workers ducking out to grab lunch or coffee. I cut across the little streets between Camden Street and Heytesbury Street, then follow Kevin Street up to St. Patrick's Cathedral where the park next to the cathedral is full of people enjoying the dying sunlight. An elderly man is throwing bread from a bag to a crowd of seagulls circling overhead and a couple is kissing underneath a colorful tree. There are a few groups of office workers eating their lunches on the benches, though it's a bit chilly for that. I zip up the collar of my fleece jacket and walk over to the playground. I'm going to have to be straightforward. A middle-aged woman in uniform without a young charge, lurking in the playground and watching toddlers playing, is going to attract attention, so I open the little gate and step inside.

"Gardaí," I say to the first young woman I see, flashing my warrant card. "You've probably heard about the abduction of a two-year-old child in the neighborhood?"

"Yes," the woman says, frowning and putting a protective hand on the stroller. "My employer didn't want us to go out at first, but then she said it was okay." She has a French accent. *Au pair,* I think.

I take the picture of Jade and Laurel out of my vest pocket and hold it out. "This is a picture of the baby and her mother. Did you ever see them here?"

She studies the photograph carefully. "Maybe. I have only been in Dublin for a few weeks, but the baby looks familiar. I don't know about the mother. She is very beautiful, no?"

"She was," I say gently. "Do you come here every day? Are there other playgrounds that parents visit in the neighborhood?"

"I have only been here a few times," she says. "I have been walking all around the city, getting to know it. I have gone up to Dublin Castle a few times and let her walk on the grass."

"That's a bit of a hike though. If you lived down by the canal, this is where you'd come, I would think." She nods but she doesn't have much to offer me.

I move on to the next dyad, a woman about my age watching a toddler in a hot pink coat playing with another toddler on the wooden play structure. She says she remembers seeing Jade at the playground a few weeks ago, remembers Laurel. "The dote. I hope you'll find her. It's mad, isn't it? Gangland thing, yeah?" I don't comment on that and she goes on. "I told my daughter, maybe I'll get killed and the wee one abducted at the playground. But she says Keely needs fresh air and she needs to work, so . . ." She shrugs and I can see exhaustion and resentment on her face. She's young to be a grandmother. She must feel roped into providing childcare. When I show her the photos, she says, "Yeah, I used to see her sometimes. Hard to miss her. I assumed she was an au pair or something because she's so young. But then I saw in the *Mirror* she's the poor baby's mammy."

"When was the last time you saw her here?" I ask.

"Not for a while. Maybe three weeks ago."

"Can you write down your name and address and your daughter's as well?" She does and I see that her daughter lives on Daniel Street, a narrow lane with small bungalows, some fixed up, some not, and that her own address is in one of the new developments on Clanbrassil Street. "My name is Edel Fahey and my daughter's Amber Singamurthy." She writes it down and puts her arms out as the toddler in the hot pink jacket comes running. "Hello, love," she says, her face breaking into an unmistakably sincere smile. She may be exhausted, but she loves this child.

"Thank you," I say. "Oh, one more thing. Did she seem to have any friends she spent time with here at the playground?"

The toddler climbs up in her lap and snuggles her face into her grandmother's neck.

"She walked with another young one who I see around the neighborhood. You'd see them out with the prams sometimes."

"Any idea what her name is or where she lives?"

Edel Fahey thinks for a moment. "No, her little girl is Sarah though. I heard her calling to her a few times. Sarah and your one who was taken used to play together. Lovely little pair they were." I write that down. "Your woman, Sarah's mam, she has a green pram, very bright, sort of a neon lime green, one of the fancy ones that cost a lot. My daughter wanted one of those—she showed me a picture—but they're very dear now. It didn't seem worth the expense."

"My daughter's seventeen," I say. "Looking back, I bought way too many things that were expensive and that I only used for a few months. When I moved over here, I realized my garage was full of them."

"That's what I try to tell her." She shrugs. "Babies don't need a lot. They do need love though." I've revised my opinion of Edel Fahey. She's still snuggling the little girl when I leave her and move on to asking the other adults inside the fence if they remember Jade and Laurel. A few people say that they heard about Laurel and think that they saw her here once or twice, and a thirtyish guy with bags under his eyes, his eyes darting between his phone and a four- or five-year-old boy on the swings, says he remembers seeing Jade a few times. "She was lovely," he says apologetically. "One of the other dads told me she was on that model show, *Fashion Star,* I think it was called. You couldn't help, well, notice her, like."

I stop in at the café where Alex works, but he's not on duty. I get a coffee and sandwich anyway, scarf down the sandwich, and then head back down to Canal Landing. Another uniformed officer lets me through the cordon, and I walk along the canal, where the divers are working. Roly has uniformed officers searching the water's edge and more walking slowly and carefully along the sidewalks and street near Jade's unit, looking for evidence. I stand there for a moment, looking at Jade's terrace, trying to imagine an adult climbing over the waist-high wall while carrying a toddler and the changing bag. At four or five in the afternoon, with people on the streets, you'd be noticed right away. There's a lot of pedestrian traffic along the canal in the afternoon; I'm remembering our Donald the duck adventure and how many passersby there were to listen to the commotion.

The uniforms walk slowly, their eyes down on the ground, the water of the canal reflecting the grayish sky, crowded with clouds.

You'd want to get off the canal and the main streets as quickly as you could. In the late afternoon most days, the side streets and lanes are pretty quiet. If Laurel was crying, if she was shouting for her mother, you would have been much better off getting on to one of the side streets.

I turn the corner and start walking up Richmond Row. I wander for nearly an hour, walking slowly, my eyes on the sidewalk, looking for anything out of place, trying to access the part of my brain that used to be good at this work, once upon a time. You need to enter a sort of fugue state where your unconscious brain takes over, sorting out what should be there and what shouldn't.

I find a few paper receipts and bus tickets and so forth and I photograph them and put them into the Ziploc evidence bags I have in my pocket, but I doubt they'll be relevant. Then I walk back down toward Canal Landing, once again trying to put myself in the shoes of Laurel's abductor. Let's say I've planned this. Let's say I've been watching Jade and Laurel and I broke into Jade's apartment with the express purpose of killing her and taking Laurel. What are the possibilities? Either she let me in the front door and I exited with Laurel from the terrace. Or I came in through an unlocked terrace door—since the door was left open, not broken—and left either that way or through the front door. Either way, I would have wanted to get as far away from the apartment as I could. I discount the idea that he would have gone out Jade's front door. He could have run into anyone, could have been spotted through the peepholes in the doors.

The neighbors didn't see anyone, didn't hear anything.

So, despite the difficulties, he must have gone out the sliding glass door on the terrace.

I walk past the vacant lot next to Canal Landing again, taking in the murals and graffiti painted on the temporary wall, most of it profanities directed at Ireland's political leaders. There's a padlock on the corrugated metal doors, but despite our calls to the company that owns the lot and is supposed to be maintaining it, it's easy to squeeze past where the boards are coming away on one side. Jason and I have responded to reports of disturbances here more than a few times. Kids like to come in and smoke and drink here at night, and one corner is used as a bathroom by the few homeless people left in the neighborhood. From the graffiti inside and what look like fresh cigarette butts, I can tell that we haven't been very successful in deterring locals from hanging out here.

A bright spot of color catches my eye and I bend down to pick up a red square, rolled into a headband. The fabric is printed with a classic bandana pattern, except that the usual teardrops are little black skulls. I think it belongs to one of the teenage girls I'm always seeing, the one with the Goth style and scowl.

A bird calls overhead and when I raise my head, I'm looking right into one of Jade's bedroom windows. If you wanted to watch her, this would be a pretty perfect place to sit. The long wall around the lot on the canal side has a few places where the siding has come away, and I walk over and put my face up against the cold metal to look through to the other side.

A burst of yellow from the willow tree on the canal flashes into view, and I can see the Water Unit's staging area a bit further down the canal, the uniformed officers searching the banks, and the green dome of St. Mary Immaculate peeking through the trees. When Jason and I first started working in Portobello, I would look for the landmark whenever I got turned around, like a dial on a compass orienting me again from anywhere in the neighborhood.

Suddenly, I notice a burst of activity about two hundred yards east of where I'm standing. Someone shouts. I watch as one of the uniformed guards waves and two more come over, one reaching for her radio on her vest. One of the divers in the canal is signaling, holding up a hand. Feeling a sense of dread, I jog back through the vacant lot, slip out through the gap in the fence, and keep running toward the commotion as my radio starts going. I answer it but I don't really need to. I know the choreography in front of me.

They've found something in the canal.

Eleven

It's the diaper bag, the pink one with gray elephants on it that Nicola and Eileen gave Jade when Laurel was born. Once I'm through the cordon, I watch the divers bring it out and carefully lay it down on a tarp under the canopy, recognizing it immediately from the pictures I sent to Nicola.

The reporters are going nuts. Even though they're sectioned off at Richmond Row, they saw the same activity by the canal that I did, and they've been around investigations long enough to know what it means. I help Jason and the other uniforms push them farther up the street, creating more room for the staging area. "Did they find her?" they shout at us, desperate for a scoop. "Did they find the little girl? Garda, excuse me! Is Laurel in the canal?"

We keep our faces impassive, say please and thank you as we move them back, ignore the shouted questions. Jason and I take the far end of the line.

"How are you?" I ask him. "Sorry to abandon you yesterday. Everything okay with you?"

"Ah, it's been dire, but I've managed," he says with a wink. "We've been doing crowd control mostly, some searching and door-to-doors." He reaches up to scratch his forehead. "How about you?

They told me you've been loaned out for the investigation. Is it nice to be detecting again?"

"Yeah, I mean this case is awful, but . . . it is."

"One thing I meant to say to ya, someone's been quite interested in the situation here." He raises his eyebrows and subtly inclines his head toward the sidewalk next to the vacant lot, where a familiar dark head is just visible around the corner. It's the teenage girl with the dyed black hair and Goth aesthetic who hangs around with the neighborhood kids.

"Alannah, right?" I ask him, taking a quick sidelong look so she won't know she's been noticed. "Tina's her friend, the blonde. But that's Alannah."

"Yeah, Alannah O'Reilly. She's been haunting the place since yesterday."

"You think she saw something?"

Jason puts up a hand to warn a reporter who's trying to pretend he's not making a move on the cordon. "I don't know, but I thought I'd say it to ya."

"I found something I think belongs to her. She'll run if I try to talk to her," I say. "If you get a chance, see if you can get anything from her or the other kids. And tell her I have her bandana if she wants it back." Jason nods and we go back to crowd control as a couple of rubberneckers try to get past us to see what's happening. I scan the crowd, recognizing a few neighborhood regulars, including another familiar figure making his way around the back of the crowd, looking for a vantage point where he can see what's happening. He cranes his neck, checking out the action, pushing one of the reporters out of the way.

Cameron Murphy.

I watch him for a second. He looks worried, more than just curious. He's got something at stake here and I want to know what it is. But someone tries to break through the line and when I check the crowd again, he's gone.

The techs are in place by two P.M., another blue tent set up on the canal bank in case they find Laurel's body. Roly, who arrived not long after I did, waves me down to the staging area.

"What do you think?" I ask him while we watch the divers. "Is she in there?"

He looks up into the sun and closes his eyes, then looks back at me. "I don't know. Sometimes I get a feeling, but this time I'm not sure. Maybe he just dumped the bag after he abducted her. Maybe he killed her and was dumping evidence but buried the body somewhere else. What do you say?"

I think for a moment. "It doesn't make sense to me. You kill Jade and take Laurel. Why would you take the bag with you? You'd want to get as far away as possible. Why would you bother to take the bag and then stop to dump it so close to the scene of the crime?"

There's another flurry of activity. We wait. I watch as one of the divers surfaces and waves to the techs. I feel my stomach drop. They've found something else. But when the diver lays what he's found on the plastic drop cloths on the sidewalk, it's just a blanket, a blanket with a teddy bear attached to one corner. Roly and I tell the techs that we believe Laurel Maguire had one like it, and they bring us over to look at what they've found so far, laid out on a tarp under the tent, ready for transport back to the lab.

Next to the pink bag are three sodden diapers, a couple of white T-shirts and a pair of pink leggings, a bottle, a couple of pacifiers, and a packet of digestive biscuits, the kind Lilly likes that are dipped in chocolate.

We wait around while the divers go back into the canal. "What'd you get from the postmortem?" I ask Roly.

"No surprises. Manual strangulation. Path thinks it wouldn't have taken an adult man. Just someone with a bit of strength. She was a little slip of a thing. Healthy. Tox screens aren't back yet, but he doesn't think she was using anything regularly." He grimaces. "He confirmed no sexual activity in the previous couple of days. They did get a few hairs and carpet fibers off the body though. Maybe that'll give us something."

As it starts to get dark, the divers tell Roly they don't think she's there. He's relieved, but now he has to make the decision about whether to have them search a bigger section of the canal tomorrow.

I listen and don't offer anything until I'm asked. I don't know the budgets yet. I don't know all the implications. "What do you think?" he asks me finally. "You think there's any chance she's in there?"

I try to decide if I want to weigh in. It's his call. It feels like a no-win situation, but he's my friend and I really don't think she's there. "I don't think so," I say. "If he killed her in the apartment, he would have left her there. If she was alive when he fled, then he wanted her for something. I can't believe he would have killed her on the street with people all around or thrown her alive into the canal. It would have been easy to drop the blanket and bag in, maybe because they could be recognized or because they were weighing him down; although again, why did he take them in the first place? How did he even know where to find them? That makes me think it's someone who knew her. But I don't think she's in there."

He looks out across the stretch of water. "I'd say you're right. If she's not in this section, I don't think she's here. We'll call them off for now. It tells us which way he came, though, yeah? If he dumped the bag and the blanket here, it means he either came around the corner, walked east a bit, then dumped them in the canal. Or he came out the open door and over the wall around the terrace. Wouldn't be too hard to do. Maybe he struggled a bit getting Laurel off the terrace and holding the bag at the same time and that's why he decided to dump it. In any case, he must have been heading east. You wouldn't want to attract attention by dropping it, then stopping and going back the other way."

"Yeah," I say. "You'd want to be as smooth as possible. Especially if you were holding a toddler. But Roly, if he'd climbed over the wall holding her, wouldn't we have something? One of her hairs on the fence, a few fibers from his jacket stuck on the wall, something like that?"

"Good point. And don't you think someone would have noticed if a fella was running down the road with a screaming kid? Wouldn't she have been yelling at the top of her lungs for her mammy?"

I think for a moment. "I'm not sure," I say. "Don't you remember what it's like having a kid that age? They're constantly having meltdowns in public. Just the other day I saw a kid having an absolute fit at the market. Everyone was averting their eyes."

We both look toward the canal, imagining our guy walking along, holding Laurel, dropping the bag. "Anything from Fiero?" I ask. "It'd be nice to rule out Maguire."

Roly checks his phone. "He'll be back tomorrow morning. Sounded like the story checked out so far, though. Here, I've got a text from Geoff Chen. He's got something promising off the tipline. Why don't you go and see if there's anything in it." He looks out across the water. The ducks and swans have moved down the canal for the night. The peaceful scene of yesterday morning seems so much more sinister to me now.

"At least we didn't find her," he says. "At least she wasn't in the canal."

The incident room is busy, a big crowd of uniforms scrolling through CCTV footage and Roly's team working the phones.

I find Detective Chen and he briefs me on the call into the tipline.

"Mrs. Mary Gill. Her address is 40 Grove Park, Rathmines. Yeah, so she left the message this morning," he says. "Said she saw the photo last night on the *Six One* and recognized the little girl. She thinks she saw a man carrying her along the canal, then getting into a car. We can talk to her now."

Mrs. Gill has already been shown into the family interview room and someone's brought her tea in a paper cup. "How's the tea for you?" Geoff asks her. He's got a nice way with her. Roly told me he's been on the team for two years and has turned in some impressive work.

"Fine." Mrs. Gill is eighty-one next week, she tells us. She's wearing a whimsically fuzzy pink jacket that reminds me of one my grandmother had, but she's businesslike, focused, ready to help.

Geoff reads it and gets right down to it. "Now, you told the officer on the tipline that you saw a man carrying a child near the canal. Can you tell us your full name and where you live and exactly what you saw?"

"Yes, my name is Mary Gill and I live at 40 Grove Park. I was taking my dog for a walk and we were on the Rathmines side of the canal, by the bridge, just poking along. He likes to sniff everything so we don't get far, and I saw a man across the canal near the water. You know how far it is. I could see him fairly well. He was holding a little girl and she seemed quite unhappy, struggling and screaming and so forth, and he looked unhappy, too. I thought to myself, 'That poor man.' His wife has asked him to take the little girl to school and she's having a fit. Well, he walked quickly and then he put her in the back seat of a blue car parked along Charlemont Mall, across the bridge there. And then they drove off. I'm sorry I didn't get the reg plates, but it must have been her, mustn't it? I could kick myself. I only realized when I saw a picture of the little girl in the paper. But the little girl I saw had the blond curly hair and she was wearing a bright pink jacket, just like the story said."

"Okay, Mrs. Gill. Thank you," Geoff says. "Can you describe the man at all? What did he look like?"

"Well, he had a hood up around his face, so I don't know if he was fair or dark. He was sort of tall, I think. At least, he seemed tall."

"How old would you say he was?" I ask.

"Oh, I don't . . . not *old,* if you see. He wasn't stooped over or anything, but I couldn't really tell, and he was walking a bit funny because he was holding the little girl."

"Thank you. And the car? What can you tell us about the car?" Geoff asks her.

"It was small, not a lorry or something. I wouldn't know the make of it. I've never owned a car myself, but it was quite blue, quite a *vibrant* blue color. But one of the doors was a different color, like white, but sort of dirty. It . . . stood out, if you see what I mean."

Geoff nods. "We'll get some photographs of cars and some paint chips to help you identify the color. Can you remember which door was white? And do you think you can remember anything else about it? You said you didn't see the reg plates, but maybe the county?"

"No . . . I don't think so. I'm sorry. But the door must have been on the driver's side, musn't it, because I was looking at it from across the canal. Do you think it was her, the little girl?"

"It may very well be," Geoff says. "Thank you so much for your help."

"It was her photo that did it," she says. "When I saw the little girl's picture. But it was confusing because they said it was Monday evening, but I saw them on Tuesday morning. That's why it took me a little bit to realize."

Geoff and I both look up. "I'm sorry, Mrs. Gill," he says. "You saw them on Tuesday morning?"

"Yes, didn't I make that clear? Muffin and I were out for his morning stroll. He wakes up quite early. It was right around seven A.M. in the morning." She folds her hands in her lap. "So you must have gotten it wrong then, mustn't you? When the poor wee thing was stolen?"

"But this narrows things considerably, doesn't it?" Geoff says, once Roly's back in the incident room. "We can start looking at all the CCTV around here, all the CCTV going out of Dublin. We can pull all the blue cars. This is good."

"If it's her," I say. "She seemed pretty sure, but . . ."

Geoff nods. "If it's her. And if it's her, maybe it means Jade wasn't killed Monday night, she was killed Tuesday morning?"

Roly shakes his head. "Postmortem says no. She was definitely killed Monday. Range is three to midnight, but she was dead by Monday evening."

The realization hits us at the same time. "So where was Laurel all that time?" I ask.

"That's what I want to know. Where was she all night? Was she in the bedroom with the body?" Roly looks as horrified as I feel.

I think for a moment. "She would have been screaming. The neighbors, the ones who share a wall, they said they didn't hear anything. Maybe whoever abducted her had her somewhere close by and waited until the morning to move her."

"I matched up the list from Probation Services with Dylan Maguire's description of the man he said seemed too interested in Jade and Laurel," Geoff Chen tells us. "There's only one candidate in the neighborhood. His name is Nigel Canning, with an address on the South Circular Road." He holds out a piece of paper and Roly snatches it from his hand.

"Come on, D'arcy. We're going to go talk to this fella. The rest of youse get cracking on that car. It's a good lead, so it is." He winks at them. "That lead is solid gold."

Nigel Canning lives on the top floor of a shabby building at the corner of Stamer Street and the South Circular Road. The paint is flaking off the trim, and the bricks are crumbling. At least one window is broken and covered with plastic and there's a pile of trash in the small, rocky front garden.

"It could use a coat of paint," I say as we stand at the front door, pressing the buzzer for the top-floor apartment.

"I'd say it could," Roly says. "Won't be long before some developer comes to snap it up."

I stand back and look up at the open window. The curtain parts for a moment and then drops back into place, and a few minutes later someone yells "Come up" through the window.

We climb the stairs to the top floor and knock on the only door on the landing. It takes him what seems like a long time to get to the door, and we understand why when he opens it. He's leaning on a cane. I feel my heart sink. Unless he's faking it, it's unlikely this guy was able to kill Jade Elliott and kidnap Laurel.

Roly gave me the quick version of Nigel Canning's crimes as we walked over. In 2011, when he was thirty-six years old, he was arrested for sharing and downloading images showing the sexual abuse of very young children. He served a year in prison and had to undergo counseling and a few years of probation. During his probation, he was caught with more prohibited images, including pictures he'd surreptitiously taken of children playing at a playground. He did another few months and was set free again. Since then, he seems to have kept his nose clean.

"Any evidence he took his interests into the real world?" I ask.

"No," Roly said. "But as you know, that's a hard thing to catch. He went as far as taking pictures of kids at a playground, so who knows if it ever went further than that. He has a couple of sisters who have kids and he's not allowed to be around them anymore."

"How's he supporting himself?"

"He does some kind of computer work and he gets some disability stemming from an attack when he was in prison."

Canning shows us in and points to two armchairs positioned across from a small love seat. The apartment is neat, pleasantly fur-

nished with shabby but comfortable items. There are a few pictures
on the wall of natural landscapes, but nothing at all personal. He's
a slightly pudgy middle-aged man, nondescript, though of course
that's a cliché. He has thinning dark hair, a pinched pale face, and
an air of worry and exhaustion about him.

"You know why we're here, Mr. Canning," Roly says. "There's a
child gone missing, her mother killed, in a residence just around the
corner from you. Do you know anything about it?"

"Of course not. I only just heard the alert." The apartment con-
tains a small kitchenette and a desk with a computer on it. I'm betting there's some kind of monitoring software on it as a condition
of his probation.

"Where were you on Monday?" I ask, my pen poised over my
notebook.

He looks startled at my accent, then says, "Right here. I was
working during the day and I was home all evening."

"So you didn't go out at all?"

He thinks. "Monday? I walked up to the shops on Camden Street
around four, to buy milk and bread."

I can feel Roly sit up and take notice. The assistant pathologist
said she could have been killed anytime between three and midnight. I'm still having a hard time imagining this sad character having the strength to kill her, but he could be pretending to be more
disabled than he is.

"Anyone able to confirm that?" Roly asks.

"Girl in the shop. Maybe a few neighbors who saw me on the
street."

"Anyone in particular?"

"There's a blond lady I see out walking a lot. I nodded to her."

He looks away. "I think she lives on Lennox Street. I see her out frequently, walking."

"Does she walk alone?" I ask. "Was she alone when you saw her Monday?"

"No." The look away again. "She has children. She was out with a pram. A green one."

"Do you know her name?"

"No, but I've seen her go into a house on the street. I think she must live there."

"Was it not Jade Elliott who you saw on Monday?" Roly asks him. "This is a picture of her." I put it on the table.

He shakes his head quickly, which doesn't necessarily mean anything. Jade was noticeable. That's how beauty works. Most of the neighbors probably knew her. "I saw her around, too, though. Some of the mums in the neighborhood get together during the day. I would see them sometimes. I didn't know her name, but I recognize her." Again, the glance away. "And the little girl. I saw the picture earlier and I recognized the little girl."

"You knew we'd come to see you as soon as you saw the alert?" I ask him.

He blinks. "Yes. It's not the first time."

"Do you know where the little girl is?" Roly asks him, harshly.

He shakes his head. "I have no idea. I hope you find her safely."

"Do you mind if I just have a look in the other rooms?" I ask him.

He doesn't say anything, just sweeps his arm resignedly as if to say, *Be my guest.*

It doesn't take me long. The bathroom has only a shower stall and the one closet is full of towels. The bedroom is simple, a queen-size mattress on a low platform, neatly made and covered with a blue blanket, the small closet fitted with a hanging rod on which he's hung a few coats and pairs of trousers. Additional blankets are folded neatly on the top shelf.

"Do you have access to any other buildings we should know about?" I ask him. "Family members' houses? Outbuildings? Vacant properties?"

He shakes his head. "This is all I have," he says. "I used to visit my sister in Lucan, but I don't anymore. I don't have anything else."

As we walk back out onto the South Circular Road, Roly says, "Had to stop myself feeling sorry for the fella, you know? What a fucking sad eejit. But then you think about what he's done, and . . ."

"He *was* sad," I say. "Most sex offenders are, except for the real sociopaths."

"Yeah, I suppose. You dealt with a lot of these fuckers?"

"A few," I say. "Not as many as the cops I knew on the sex crimes squad. That's the kind of work I don't think I could do, day in and day out."

"Yeah. I have a few mates on our squad as well. Don't know how they stick it. What'd you think of our man?"

"I'd be very surprised if he had anything to do with this." There's something there though, something about him, that's bothering me.

"Yeah. I'd say the same." Roly looks out across the intersection. The streets are mostly empty now. It's one of those strange pockets of quiet in the middle of the day, after lunch, before school's out. As we walk quickly back down toward the canal, I can't help but look in all the windows, every one representing a household, a person, a hidden network of relationships.

"She could be anywhere," I tell Roly. "Look at all those windows, all those flats. She could be in any one of them. She could be right here and we just don't know where to look."

"Or she could be miles away." Roly looks up at the windows. "She may be dead, D'arcy. You know as well as I do, chances are she's dead."

I scan some more windows. From one, an older woman stares back at me.

A frigid wind comes hustling down the street. I can feel winter on the air. When I shove my hands into my jacket pockets for warmth, I feel the soft fabric of Alannah's bandana. Roly runs a hand through his hair. "D'arcy, think this through with me, the psychology, yeah? What does this tell you? What's different now?"

I say, "You know the statistics on child abductions. Most children who are abducted are killed within three hours. If Mrs. Gill is telling the truth, then Laurel was still alive yesterday morning. Her abductor kept her somewhere overnight and then he put her in a car and took her somewhere else. That's . . . There's two ways to look at it. On the one hand, taking her somewhere, that's not good. It means he needs privacy for whatever he's doing. Keeping her overnight, dumping her belongings, taking her away from the neighborhood in a car at a time when he had a lower chance of being seen . . . I don't know. I think it means he wanted to keep her for some reason."

Roly says, "Yeah. That's what I'm thinking, too. Jaysus, that poor little girl. This is a good lead. It gives us something to go on. We'll get it out to the media. Blue car, next to the canal yesterday morning. Your woman will do an artist's rendering. Okay, then. Pat Fiero will be back from Lyon in the morning. D'arcy, check in at the scene first thing and get back here by ten. Try to get some sleep tonight. It's going to be a long day tomorrow."

The house is dark when I get home at six, the only light back in Conor's study, and when I call out "hello" into the silence, I don't get an answer. The workmen have made progress. The wall between the kitchen and the living room is now completely gone and they've pulled up the flooring in the hall, leaving a trail of drop cloths that lead me to the kitchen where I pour a glass of wine, get chicken and broccoli out of the fridge, and slip off my boots. Upstairs, I change while inspecting the progress on the master bathroom, and I'm back in the kitchen chopping garlic and peeling ginger when I hear the door open and Mr. Bean comes rushing in, swirling at my feet with delight at seeing me.

"Hiya," I call out. "Nice walk?"

"Yeah, grand. Nice to get out," Conor calls back. When he comes into the kitchen, he kisses me and pops a raw broccoli floret in his mouth. His cheeks are pink from the cold, his green tweed blazer bringing out flecks of green in his eyes. His thinning dark hair is mussed from the wind and he smiles when I reach up to smooth it.

"Where are the kids?" I ask.

"Lilly had a choir practice, I think, and Adrien's studying with a friend. He should be home soon. He just texted me. Anything on your case?"

"Not really." I shrug. "Nothing I can talk about anyway."

"Right." He disappears again and I hear him opening and closing the closet door in the hall. When he comes back into the kitchen, he goes straight to the liquor cabinet and gets out a bottle of scotch, pouring himself a finger neat. He holds it in his hands for a moment, and I'm about to ask if he's okay when we hear the door and then Lilly's voice in the hall, running through vocal scales, her rich alto trilling up and down.

"Hey, songbird," I say. "How was practice?"

"Good." Her face is flushed when she comes into the kitchen, her hair wavy from the cold damp air outside. She's got her friend Ciara with her and they ask if Ciara can stay for dinner since they have an English project to work on. Adrien comes in just as I'm finishing up a stir-fried chicken and broccoli, and Conor, done with his scotch, pours two glasses of wine while the kids set the table.

While we eat, Lilly and Ciara tell us about their project, and then Adrien announces that he found out he's been accepted into a maths competition in the spring. "I get to go to Brussels," he says. "For three days."

"Can I go with him?" Lilly asks. "I want to go to Brussels."

"Maybe we'll all go," Conor says. "It's very exciting."

"I love Brussels," Ciara says. "It's so, like, *opulent*." Conor looks down at his plate to avoid meeting my eyes. He finds Ciara, with her wealthy parents and almost-American drawl, a bit much to take, and he loves to imitate her accent, which he claims is a highly specific signifier of kids from our neighborhood. It's mostly good-natured though. She's been a good friend to Lilly and I like her company. She and Lilly sing together sometimes, and she's actually a talented sketch artist and a genuinely nice person, pretentious accent aside.

"Oh, I have news for all of you," Conor says. "Gerry and his lads found another photograph of the mysterious Clara. It was hidden under a floorboard." He gets up and goes over to the drawer. "Here, look. There's an address on the back, too."

When he hands it to me, I turn it over and see someone's written "Clare, 13 Stamer Street." The photograph is similar to the others, except in this one, Clara is wearing a pale summer dress and is standing in front of a brick-faced house.

"I know right where that is," I say. "It's on my beat. I was quite near to there today. So, what's the photo doing here?"

Conor shrugs. "I don't know. There must be a family connection. You could ask at the house if they know who Clara is, couldn't you?"

I nod, chewing my chicken and broccoli.

Adrien takes the photo from me. "Maybe she grew up here and then went to live in that house or something?" he says.

"I'm telling you, secret love affair. Her lover had to hide his passion away in the wall," Lilly says, explaining to Ciara about the work crew and their find. "Come on, Mom, you of all people should be intrigued by this."

"Did Jade Elliott really get murdered?" Ciara asks me, checking my face to make sure she hasn't overstepped. "I saw it on my friend Harriet's Insta. And they kidnapped her baby?"

"Sadly, yeah," I say. "Hey, did you ever watch that show she was on? *Ireland's Next Model Star*?"

"*Ireland's Next Star Model*," Ciara corrects me. "Oh my God. That was my favorite show for a while. Jade was the best one. She was like the young one, and the quiet one, but she was fierce when anyone gave her a problem, you know? She had this whole rivalry going with this girl named Stella."

"I saw a picture of her," Lilly says suddenly. "It was on the front page of the *Mirror* or one of those papers when I went to get coffee before choir. She was sooooo pretty."

"She was quite young, wasn't she?" Conor says.

"Yeah, she was." I realize with a start that Jade was almost as young as Lilly is now when she moved to Dublin. I'm trying to imagine Lilly getting herself a place to live, working, paying her own bills. It's hard to see. I'm flooded with admiration for Jade all of a sudden.

When we're done with dinner, the girls call me into the living room. They've cued up an old episode of *Ireland's Next Star Model* from Ciara's laptop and Ciara advances through it to find Jade's scenes.

It's eerie, seeing her alive, walking and talking and interacting on the screen with the other wannabe models. She's even more beautiful in person than she was in static fashion photography, and I can see why she was Ciara's favorite member of the cast. There's something vulnerable and charming about her, and the thing that strikes me is how tiny she seems out of high heels and without the altered perspectives of fashion photography. In the episode we're watching, both Jade and another woman on the show, Stella, are vying for a photo shoot with a luxury handbag design firm. At one point, Jade is talking with the show's model coach, and she says, "Look, we all know I'm the best. I just have to make them believe it, too." She turns to the camera and winks and there's something about the gesture that opens her up for me, that gives me a sense of her as a real person, with ambition and humor, full of life.

The rest of the show is oddly stilted and hard to watch. It's clear that it's mostly scripted and the models are improvising within an already established structure, except they're not very good at improvising and they've been told to throw out cruel one-liners as often as possible. The show seems to love highlighting these moments of tension between the characters, and when one comes on, Ciara says, "Here comes a good one!"

When it's finished, she closes the laptop and the kids all drift off to do homework. Conor and I read in the living room, but what Ciara said about Jade's age keeps bothering me. Finally, I go get my laptop out of my bag and go to the *Irish Mirror*. Sure enough, there's a photograph of Jade on the front, not one I've seen before. She's wearing a skimpy dress, skintight, with a deep V in front that shows off half her breasts.

I understand why Ciara called her young. She looks grotesquely girlish in the photo, like they pasted a twelve-year-old's face on an adult woman's body. She's making what I think is supposed to be a sexy face; I find it disturbing.

I search for her Instagram page and find a grid of photos, most of them of Jade in bathing suits or skimpy dresses. They all seem to be from before Laurel was born.

Conor comes up behind me and looks over my shoulder. "Is that the victim?"

"Yeah, I was thinking about what Ciara said. She looks so young."

"She does. Although those photos are quite . . . mature, aren't they? You sure she was only a model?"

I see what he means. Most of the shots do have an overtly sexual feel to them, nothing that would cause her to run afoul of the filters, but enough to make anyone looking to buy sex go visit a website if she'd had one. I know from a presentation on sex trafficking and prostitution we got during my time at Templemore that this is how a lot of sex workers advertise, using legitimate social media sites to direct traffic to coded ads.

"I think so, but I guess we need to look into it." Conor rubs my shoulders and then leans down to kiss my neck. I turn to look up at him. "What did I do to deserve that?" I ask.

"You just look beautiful in that light," he says. Part of me wants to stand up and kiss him back, pressing my body into his, and let him lead me upstairs, but a bigger part is too antsy, too focused on the fact that Laurel Maguire is still missing, too distracted by the hundreds of questions and details and to-dos ricocheting around my head. I feel both exhausted and like I've had too much caffeine, jittery and drained.

I gently push his hand away from my shoulder and say, "I've got a bit more to do here, but I'll be up soon."

He sighs. "Okay. I'm heading up."

By the time I get into bed forty minutes later, he's already asleep. I lie there, thinking about what I need to do tomorrow, who I want to talk to. We need to stay on the neighbors, of course, and we need to follow up on the other actors from the show and track down the photographers she worked with. I need to check with Jason, to see if he has anything on Alannah and ask him to keep an eye out for Cameron Murphy, who seems just a little too interested in the investigation, for reasons I can't even begin to imagine.

All the names and faces swirl together, and it's a long time before I sink into unconsciousness.

Twelve

....

I'm at Canal Landing by nine A.M. the next morning. I want to see who's checking up on the scene and I'd like to visit with the neighbors again. But as I round Lennox Street, what I see instead is a woman leaning down to talk to a toddler strapped into a stroller.

A bright, neon green stroller. One of the fancy ones that looks like it could go airborne if only you pushed the right button.

Sometimes in this work, you get lucky breaks. You just do. Every once in a while, the piece of information you need comes across your field of vision, walks right past you, falls into your lap. I could have spent days, weeks looking for the woman whom Edel Fahey told me she saw walking with Jade Elliott, whom I'm betting is the blond woman Nigel Canning said walked with Jade. I could have tried contacting the mother of every baby named Sarah born in Dublin in the last two years and I still might not have gotten anywhere close to identifying her.

But here she is. Right in front of me. She's a good deal older than Jade was, more like early thirties, I think, with a thin, serious face devoid of makeup and dark blond hair cut in a short bob. Her down jacket is stylish, expensive. She's wearing sweatpants and running shoes and still manages to look polished and put together.

The woman smiles at the little girl, then stands up and starts pushing the pram along the walkway toward Richmond Street. I have to stop myself from sprinting up to her and grabbing the stroller.

"Excuse me, but were you friends with Jade Elliott?" I say, walking up to her. "I'm a Garda officer and someone at the playground said she had a friend she walked with. She remembered your green stroller—sorry, your pram."

The woman looks up at me, surprised, wary. The little girl in the pram—*Sarah,* I think—has bangs cut straight across her forehead and big blue eyes and she waves at me, her face freezing when I smile and wave back. "Yeah, I got it at the sales. The color's horrible, but it's the one I wanted. Sorry, yes, I knew Jade. Not well, but . . . we walked together sometimes." She gestures toward the canal. "I saw the news and I wondered if I should ring you, but I was so upset." She lowers her voice and turns away from her daughter so she can't hear. "Do they know anything? About who killed Jade? Have you arrested someone?"

"We're doing everything we can to find out," I say, taking out my notebook. "I'm sorry, your name is . . . ?"

"Elizabeth Ruane. This is Sarah."

Liz. Jade had her in her contacts. That detail might be enough to bring her in, do this in an interview room, but there's something a little fragile about her and my instinct tells me I need to see what she's got first. I don't want to scare her into silence.

A large stuffed bear is sitting in the smaller seat behind Sarah, and she points back to it and says, "Dat Bobo."

"Hello, Bobo," I say to the bear. Sarah's eyes widen at me and then her face breaks into a smile. She looks enough like Laurel Maguire to be her sister.

I close my notebook, to put Elizabeth Ruane at ease, and say, "Could I ask you a few questions about Jade? I'm desperate for a cup of tea. Maybe we could find a café?"

Elizabeth, still unsure, considers that, then glances at Sarah. "Actually, we live just down there." She points to the row of two-story houses along one side of Lennox Street. "Could you just come in to chat? I can make you a cuppa? It'll be easier with this one; she can play with her toys or watch something on the tablet and I can get her something for her breakfast. We've been out for milk." She gestures to a shopping bag hanging on the stroller.

"That sounds good," I say. "I'm Garda Maggie D'arcy, by the way."

She nods, tucks a stray piece of hair back behind her ear, and sets off. I follow her past six brightly painted doors fronting brick houses. They're not particularly fancy, but the shiny paint jobs on the doors and trim tell me they've been recently renovated. Conor and I have been looking at houses a bit lately and I know that they're probably worth a million euros or more each. I'm curious now about Elizabeth Ruane and what she might have had in common with Jade. On its surface, the friendship doesn't make sense to me.

She expertly drags Sarah and Bobo and the pram up the steps before I can help her and lets us into the house. There's a little alcove inside where she leaves the pram, unbuckling Sarah and lifting her out and onto the floor, leaving Bobo strapped in. "You sit down in there," she says to me, pointing to a sitting room through a doorway to the right. "And I'll put the water to boil. My husband's away on a work trip so I'll have to tend to this one, but I think she'll cooperate." Sarah follows her down the corridor and I look up to see a glass door at the back and a long narrow garden, shaded with trees, and a stone patio next to the house.

The living room is lovely, painted a pale blue color and decorated with original oil paintings of vaguely abstract landscapes, mostly in soothing beiges and greens and grays, but with pops of color here and there that are picked up in the cushions on the charcoal linen-upholstered sectional couch. I suddenly wonder if Jade bought the bright cushions after visiting Elizabeth and the thought makes me sad. A stack of issues of a high-end Irish lifestyle magazine called *Weave* sits on the coffee table. Morning sun streams through the windows and I look around, trying to get a feeling for Elizabeth and her family. There's a sideboard against one wall, below black-and-white family photos arranged artfully in silver frames. In the center is a professional wedding portrait of Elizabeth and a tall, fair-haired guy in a tuxedo. Her hair is longer in the photo and her wedding dress is expensive-looking, shiny silk, off the shoulder, elegant, the train gleaming behind her. She's smiling up at her husband and he's gazing adoringly at her. The portrait is surrounded by baby photos of Sarah, from a bewildered-looking, swaddled newborn to a grinning, chubby baby of six months or so, to a more recent one of her in a frilly yellow dress.

"Milk? Sugar?" Elizabeth calls from the kitchen.

"Just milk please," I call back.

She comes in holding two mugs and hands one to me. "Here you go. I gave her the tablet so she should be okay for a bit." She sits down in a chair across from me and takes a sip of her tea.

"Your house is beautiful," I say.

"Oh, thank you. We like it here." She cups her hands around the mug, soaking up the warmth.

"So, you were friends with Jade?" I prompt her. I gulp down the tea and immediately feel warmer and more awake.

"Yes, well . . . not friends exactly, but . . . we walked together," she says, with a little shrug. "After this one was born, I would be out walking and I started seeing this woman with a pram and a baby who looked just about the same age. I couldn't tell where she lived, but one day I was at the playground by St. Patrick's and I put Sarah on the grass and I saw her come in. She put Laurel down, too, and the girls started playing together—well, as much as babies *can* play together—and since they seemed to be about the same age, we started chatting, like, where did you have her, how's the sleeping going, that sort of thing."

"How close were you?" I ask. I want to get a sense of the level of questions I should ask.

She hesitates. "Not very. I suppose . . . we didn't have a lot in common. But we had the girls, and they like each other, love each other actually, as though they were sisters, and so . . ."

"When they're this age and you're in the thick of it, that's enough, isn't it? Another kid who will keep yours occupied for ten minutes so you can have a break? Someone who understands what you're going through."

She smiles sadly and meets my eyes. "That's it exactly. We walked a lot of mornings. We'd meet on the corner there." Her face crumples suddenly and I know she's realizing they'll never do it again. Tears fill her eyes and she wipes them away with the sleeve of her sweatshirt. "I haven't really cried yet."

"I'm so sorry," I say. "But did she ever talk to you about feeling unsafe? About someone who might have threatened her or shown an interest in Laurel or anything like that? Did you ever witness her or Laurel being harassed?"

Elizabeth takes a long sip of her tea. "Jade was . . . well, you've seen pictures of her. She was beautiful. She used to work as a model. And she was on some show about celebrities. I never saw it, but I'm sure you know it?" I nod. "Men bothered her, called out to her. Even just walking around the neighborhood. Though she once told me that they didn't do it as much once she'd had Laurel. It was like they were put off by her being a mother or something."

"But no one specific? What about Laurel? Was there anyone in the neighborhood who seemed obsessed with her, who made either of you uncomfortable?"

"No . . . not really." She's troubled though. There's something there I need to come back to.

I'm ready to ask about the calls and I do it quickly, not leaving any room for her to fabricate an explanation. "You rang her a few times in the last couple of months. What were those calls about?"

She answers easily. "Oh, I suppose just, 'Will we meet up this morning? I'm running a few minutes late,' that sort of thing."

"Did she talk to you about Laurel's father? Did they get on okay? What was their relationship like?"

"I didn't know him," she says carefully. "I never met him. By the time Jade and I started walking together, he had moved out and they were trying to get along for Laurel's sake. I had the sense that, well, that it never would have been anything more than a one-time thing if it hadn't been for Laurel. But they tried to make the best of it, you know? Jade was . . . well, she was young, she hadn't had many relationships. She was sometimes a bit emotional, I think. I heard her getting angry at Dylan on the phone a few times. He was very busy with work and traveled a lot. He was always in Germany or Hong Kong or somewhere, so Jade was basically on her own, though I think he paid for everything, for the apartment and an allowance for her. So, I don't know . . . It was a difficult situation. The custody situation was on their minds."

"Any reason to think he was ever violent toward her? That he hit her?" I'm thinking of the call about a woman screaming in Jade's apartment. I'm thinking of that scratch on Dylan Maguire's face.

She answers quickly, no hesitation. "No, nothing like that. She never said, anyway." Sarah comes into the room and reaches up to pull at Elizabeth's arm. I know the signs of a hungry toddler. My time is limited here. Elizabeth tries to get her involved with a book on the coffee table, but Sarah's not having any of it. "I should get her breakfast ready," Elizabeth says, hinting.

"I'll leave you, but I just have one more question. Is it possible that Jade was seeing someone? That there's a romantic partner who hasn't come forward?"

It's not true that most people have tells when they're lying; I've interviewed suspects who lied to me about every single thing I've asked them, and I would have sworn they were being truthful. Other times, I was sure someone was lying, and it turned out they were nervous because of something unrelated to the investigation and were telling the absolute truth. The one thing I'm always able to spot, though, is when someone is putting something together for the first time. It's not as obvious as a light bulb over their head, but it's unmistakable.

Elizabeth Ruane has realized something.

She looks up, her head cocked, thinking, and after a long moment, she says, "Not a romantic partner. I would have known if it had been that, but I think she was in touch with someone . . . new. Or . . . I don't know. There were a few times when we were walking and she said she had to get back because she had to talk to someone about something. But . . . I don't know. It could just have been she was going to ring her mother."

"But why wouldn't she have said?"

"I don't know. I may be imagining it."

I'm thinking about what Gail Roden said. "Any chance it was about a job?" I ask. "One of her neighbors thought she might be working again."

"Maybe." She shrugs, but looks troubled. "That could be it."

I finish my tea and put the mug back down on the coffee table. "Thank you so much for talking to me. We'll let you know if we have any more questions. In the meantime, here's my number," I say, handing over a card printed with my contact information at the station on which I've written my cell number. "Bye-bye, Sarah, have a nice breakfast now." I wave and she waves back, following her mother to the door to see me off.

I'm back on the walkway outside when Elizabeth comes after me, standing in the doorway.

"I've thought of something just now," she says, a bit awkwardly. "A conversation we had a few months ago. We were walking and talking about that model who married the footballer. I don't remember why. Maybe we'd walked past the newsagents and seen her on the cover of *The Sun* or something. But she told me that I would be surprised about some of the people who worked in her . . . industry, in modeling and television and so forth, that she had seen some illegal things."

I'm interested now. "Illegal? What did she mean?"

She glances back into the house. "I wish I could tell you more. She didn't say. Just that she'd had some experiences that would surprise me. I didn't push her."

"Did she mention anyone in particular? Was she referring to her time on the show, or the agency that represented her, or maybe someone she'd worked for?"

"Might have been. It was just a comment, like she'd seen something illegal in the course of her career." She shrugs. "I'm sorry. I know that's not much to go on, but I thought you might want to know. My dad is a retired guard. In Kilkenny. He wasn't a detective, but I know that things like this can help sometimes."

"You're right," I say. "Thank you. Every little bit helps."

"Illegal?" Roly asks me once I'm back in the incident room. "What did she mean?"

"I don't know. She doesn't know. Jade just made a statement about how she'd seen some illegal things 'in the industry.'"

"What, on that model show? Or when she was doing photo shoots?"

"Elizabeth didn't know. But she said something else that was interesting." I tell him about her sense that Jade was in touch with someone new, that maybe she was working again as a model.

"What did you think of her? She reliable? You believed her?"

"Yeah . . . She seemed very upset about Jade. And she seemed very worried. But that's natural, isn't it? She clearly cares about Laurel. She must have seen the activity down there and worried we'd found her body." I remember the anguish on Elizabeth Ruane's face, the way she cried when we talked about Jade. "Yeah, I think she's reliable. I asked her about the calls in Jade's call log and she wasn't evasive at all. Said they must have been arranging their walks. Only . . . I still feel like I don't have a good handle on how close the friendship was. I'm not sure why. We could ask the neighbors if they ever saw her visiting Jade."

"Okay," Roly says. "I want more on her phone records and that unassigned phone number. The lads are following up on all those contacts you got from the agency. They'll ring everyone involved in that show. That should give us something. They've already viewed the CCTV from out in the parking lot and all the neighbors' accounts of their movements check out. It doesn't show anyone taking Laurel out that way so it must have been through the sliding door. And—" He's about to say something else when we both look up to see Padraig Fiero coming in. He's pulling a wheelie bag, so he must have come straight from the airport. Roly chats with him quietly for a bit and then says, "Okay, lads, Pat's going to tell us about his trip. Take it away, there."

Fiero looks tired—even his buzz cut seems deflated and his jacket is rumpled and has a stain on one sleeve—but he launches into his report. "I interviewed staff at the Marriott, where Dylan Maguire stayed, and also other attendees of the conference he was at. It's a European web design association and they hold this conference every year at this time. Last year it was in Munich. It will be here in Dublin next year. His company's called Red Rocket Media Web Design and they had a booth, brought five employees along. Anyway, he arrived on Sunday, checked in at three P.M. and then attended the opening night dinner of the conference. Returned to the hotel and used his key card just before three A.M. Then he was confirmed at conference events all day Monday. He returned to the hotel to change around six and then we have him in and out of conference dinners and cocktail hours until one A.M., when he returned to his room alone. No sign of him on the security cameras, no further entries to the room via his key card, and I checked to make sure he couldn't have gone out the window or anything. He was up at six, confirmed at a conference breakfast, and then he was at events all day until Garda D'arcy rang to tell him about Jade and Laurel."

"Are we sure it was him?" I ask. "Couldn't it have been someone with his key card?"

"Yes, it could have," Fiero says, in a slightly condescending way. "Which is why I confirmed it was him with footage from the security cameras in the lobby. Now, apparently, there were groups of attendees from the conference who went out for drinks at bars near the hotel. Some of the conversation lasted quite late. That's what he told us when we spoke with him on Tuesday and it seems to check out. To be clear, there are a couple of hours there that are unaccounted for on Monday, but that wouldn't have been enough time for him to return to Dublin and get back to Lyon. I confirmed this with all area airports and train stations. He wasn't in Dublin on Monday afternoon or evening killing Jade Elliott."

"Maybe he's secretly the Flash," someone says. Everyone laughs at that. It seems as good an explanation as any for how he could have gotten back to Dublin.

"What about hiring someone to do it for him and using the business trip as his alibi?" Geoff Chen asks.

"Well, yeah," Fiero says a little sarcastically, stifling a yawn. "That's what I'd go to next. It's a possibility, 'course it is. And if he knows who killed her, if he arranged it, he must have some way of communicating with the killer."

"Okay then," Roly says. "We'll keep on that. Tonight and tomorrow, our focus is on door-to-doors. We need to figure out where Laurel Maguire was on Monday night. Whoever took her must have a connection to the neighborhood; either he lives here or there's someone who let him stay, someone he was working with. What do you want to do, Fiero?"

"Officer who's been watching his place says Dylan Maguire came back from Portarlington last night," Fiero says. "I thought I'd go chat with him, have a bit of a look around."

"Should we get a statement from him?" Roly asks him. "Do we get him in an interview room?"

Fiero shrugs. "I think we keep it casual, no hint we're looking at him. I'll tell him I'm coming and have the officer watch to see if he takes anything out to the bins, like. I want to see what his gaff looks like, if there's anything he's protective of, that sort o' thing, you know."

I listen to them toss it back and forth. We really need to get Dylan Maguire's statement on the record, but I think Fiero's probably right.

Fiero says, "If he did hire someone, they might contact him, there might be something in the apartment that links them. I just want to take a look."

"Okay, that's grand then," Roly says. "Take D'arcy with you, right?"

The look of distaste that flashes across Fiero's face is unmistakable. "Right then," he says, nodding to me. "I'll ring him and then I'll just get the car and meet you outside."

"That okay for you?" Roly asks me once he's gone. "Go along to Maguire's with Fiero."

"Sounds good. But Roly . . ." I start, then hesitate.

"Yeah?"

"It's just . . . you don't think Fiero or any other members of the team resent that you've brought me on, do you? Before I've got my detective rank?"

He looks up quickly, something I can't read in his eyes. "No, of course not. Sure, Pat's just joined the team, too. You've got specific expertise that we need on this investigation. And you've had your training. You're just waiting for a spot. It's well within my rights. Sullivan agrees." Sullivan's his superintendent.

"I know, but . . . okay."

He winks at me. "Better go meet your man there. Nervy fella like that, he won't like to be kept waiting."

Thirteen

....

Fiero and I park down the street from Dylan Maguire's apartment, the whole third floor of a newly renovated building off Camden Street. The exterior is painted bright yellow and there's a lot of understated modernism in the lobby and elevator, chrome letters in a mid-century modern font, large windows, and walls of glass. A couple of reporters are staking out the entrance, snapping to attention when they see us approaching. "Is there news on the baby?" one shouts to us. "Have you found her, guards?" The street feels dangerous suddenly, too many people walking past trying to get a look at the father of the missing child. I can't tell who's a reporter and who's a resident and who might be someone to worry about, and I can tell Fiero feels it, too.

I wonder again why my friend Stephen Hines isn't here. This kind of story seems right up his alley: high profile, a little salacious, involving a minor Irish celebrity.

Dylan Maguire is clearly expecting us; when he shows us into the sleek, open floor plan space, there's already a tea tray with three cups and a steaming pot of tea.

"I can make coffee as well," he says.

We tell him tea's fine and sit down to talk. "Is there anything? Any news?" he asks. "Detective Byrne said they think someone had

Laurel in the neighborhood the night she was taken? Do you have any idea where it was?" The last few days have left their mark. His face looks hollowed out, older, his eyes bloodshot and baggy. The scratch is now a line of darker red.

"We're working on that. Is there anything you can tell us?" Fiero asks him.

"No, I . . . I mean, I've lived in the neighborhood for years now, first at Canal Landing and then here, and my office has been here for years, so I know a lot of people, but no one who would do this."

I ask to use the bathroom and he points it out. It's new, clean gray tiles and simple design, lots of expensive-looking male grooming products that I'm not used to since Conor prides himself on having used the same brand of cheap, strong-smelling soap since he was ten. I pass what must be Laurel's room, a spare bedroom with a crib and a bookshelf filled with new books and toys. I hover there for a moment, getting a feel for it. It's a hopeful room somehow; Dylan went out and bought things that he thought she would like, but it doesn't feel lived in at all. Laurel clearly doesn't spend a lot of time here. I look into the other bedroom and see a neatly made bed and, against the far wall, a desk covered with computer equipment and chargers. There's no way I can investigate without him seeing me though.

When I get back, Fiero's asking him about the car. "Mr. Maguire, do you know anyone who has a bright blue car, medium-size sedan, the witness said?"

He looks startled, but pauses to consider. "I can't think of anyone immediately, though I must know someone with a blue car. They're fairly common, I would think. But you don't think it's someone I know, do you? I don't know anyone who would do something like this."

"Are you sure?" Fiero asks him. "You mentioned the fella in the neighborhood and we're following up on that, but there's no one who gave you a bad feeling, who maybe you didn't like to let alone with Laurel? Anything like that?"

Dylan looks a bit indignant. "I wouldn't be friends with someone like that, Detective Fiero."

Fiero gives a sympathetic smile. "Of course. And what about your family? One of our officers spoke to your mother and father when they returned from Switzerland. They said that—"

"Stepmother," Dylan cuts in. "My mother died when I was four. But they wouldn't be able to tell you anything. As I told you, they've only met Laurel twice since she was born. They didn't approve of Jade and they didn't want much to do with Laurel."

"Ah," Fiero says. "You have some siblings, half-siblings, correct?" Dylan nods. "What about them or other family? I hate to ask, but anyone who seemed . . . too interested in Laurel? Or the opposite? Someone who was hostile?" Dylan shakes his head.

"What about Laurel's custody?" I ask. "You said that you were asking for more time with her. Had you hired a lawyer? Was it a formal request?"

"No, no, I just asked Jade if I could have her more often. It wasn't formal. I didn't go to the courts or anything. I hoped we could start gradually and then I might work up to more equal time with her." He doesn't meet my eyes. "I don't know. She might have changed her mind. It wasn't . . . We weren't rowing about it or anything. I didn't want to press her." There's something here, something he doesn't want us going near. I think back to what Nicola Keating said. She seemed to think they *were* fighting about it. We need to get some more accounts of the relationship from third parties, and we need to know if any lawyers were involved on Jade's end. I think there's something he's not telling us.

"Mr. Maguire?" I ask. "Did you ever meet a woman named Elizabeth Ruane? Jade may have referred to her as Liz? She was a friend of Jade's. They walked together sometimes."

Dylan looks up at that. "Is that Sarah's mother? Laurel talked about them sometimes. I don't think they were close friends though."

"That's right," I say. "What about other friends? Did you know her when she was on the reality show?"

He puts his mug of tea down on the coffee table. "She was already off the show by the time we conceived Laurel," he says. "Of course she mentioned it to me, but I didn't know a lot about it. It was . . . Have you seen it? It was quite silly. I don't know why she wanted to do it." Like Fiona Creedon, Dylan Maguire seems to have thought *Ireland's Next Star Model* was beneath Jade.

"Was she in touch with anyone from the show, as far as you know?"

"Oh, no. It's all fake, you know. They made it out like they were lifelong friends and the competition over the jobs was tearing them apart, but in fact, she barely knew them."

"And what about with her agency? Any negative experiences there?" Fiero asks.

Maguire looks up, interested. "The agency? No, they're lovely there. She'd given all of that up by the time she had Laurel."

"She never complained about anyone there, then? Any harassment, inappropriate behavior, anything like that?"

He looks shocked. "No, nothing like that."

"I'd like to ask about her neighbors," Fiero says. "The Rodens and the Phillipses and Ms. . . . Denise Valentine. Ms. Valentine told us that you . . . were seeing each other at one time. Could she have been jealous of Jade?"

Dylan gives us a small, wry smile. "Denise? I wouldn't flatter myself. We only went out a few times. It seemed convenient, I suppose, but there wasn't much of a spark there. I doubt she's given me a second thought in all these years." He shrugs. "The other neighbors were fine. One of them complained about Laurel crying, but I can't remember which one."

Fiero puts his mug down and says gently, "We're working hard on this, Mr. Maguire, and we hope we'll have some good news for you soon. We've had quite a few tips from the appeals and we have Roads Policing out looking for the car. That's often how these cases are resolved. I know it may feel like we're not doing much, but we have hundreds of officers engaged and they are carefully and methodically working through leads and conducting searches. You're in good hands." He makes a good job of it, leaning forward and looking Dylan Maguire right in the eyes. It's the most human I've seen him act, and if I'm honest, I'm impressed.

"Thank you," Dylan says, looking up at us. Tears fill his eyes. Now I can see the pure anguish on his face. "I hope so. I don't know how much more of this I can take. The not knowing, the wondering where she is, what's happening to her, I can't . . ." He starts sobbing, and we wait for him to regain his emotional composure and then leave him alone, brushing past the reporters on our way out.

"I want to know more about the custody situation," Fiero says once we're out on the street. "What he said doesn't line up with what the sister told us." He buttons his coat against the sharp wind. Dry leaves are tumbling down the street.

"I know. Who can we ask?"

He thinks for a moment, and then he says, "I need to check in with his employees anyway, make sure there's nothing dodgy there. I'll bring it up in a nice, subtle way, like, 'Oh, he seems to have been really involved with his daughter.' See what comes of that. I already checked with Tusla and there weren't any case files for abuse or neglect opened on him there."

"What about calling around to solicitors who handle family court cases, see if she contacted anyone?"

He nods, distracted. "That's good," he says. "I'll mention it to Roly and he can get someone started on that." He watches a reporter approaching the entrance to Dylan Maguire's building and getting rebuffed by one of the uniforms. "His reaction seems authentic to me, you know."

"I don't trust him," I say. "That scratch. It's too much of a coincidence. I think he's lying about something. I'm just not sure what."

Fiero sighs. "There's no way he came back from Lyon. I don't see how he could have had anything to do with it."

"There's something we're not seeing," I say after a minute. "There's something we haven't put together yet. There must be."

Fiero watches me, barely disguised skepticism on his face. "Well, let me know when you find out what it is," he says coldly. "I'm off to his office and then I have something to check out. I'll leave the car here and catch up with you later, right?" He doesn't ask if I want to come along. He just sets off into the busy rush hour streets.

I walk down toward the canal, thinking about Dylan Maguire's assertion that there'd been nothing between him and Denise Valentine. He'd been casual, offhanded about it, but there'd been something on her face that made me think she had taken whatever the relationship had been more seriously. I wonder how it felt to her when Dylan's new girlfriend moved in and then when they had a baby.

She isn't home when I arrive at her apartment, and when I dial the number I have for her, it goes straight to voice mail. The Phillipses aren't home either, but when I knock at the Rodens', Phil Roden answers after a minute, opening the door and pointing to the phone held up to his ear, indicating with a raised finger that he'll be off in a minute. I wait by the door while he says, "Yeah, yeah, mate. I know. It's been good so far. We're making money hand over fist, so yeah . . . okay. I'll be back to you in a few days then. Thanks again."

"Sorry about that." He gestures for me to come in but doesn't ask me to sit down. His laptop is set up at the dining room table and there are file folders and stacks of papers everywhere. "Working from home today. Is there any news about the little girl?" He looks genuinely concerned as he waits for my response. "We've been terribly worried about her."

"I'm afraid not. I just wanted to ask you a couple of follow-up questions related to the ongoing investigation. Is that okay? It shouldn't take long."

"Yeah, fine. Sorry about the mess." He's distracted, glancing at the laptop and files, but he smiles and waits expectantly.

I get right to it. "Were you aware that Mr. Maguire and your neighbor across the hall, Denise Valentine, were dating at one time? This would have been before Ms. Elliott moved in. Before Laurel was born."

He rubs his chin thoughtfully. "Yeah, I think we had a sense there was something between them. Gail might have seen him coming out of her place once, early in the morning. Something like that."

"Did you have a sense of how things ended there?" I ask.

He shakes his head. "I'd say we talked about it, you know, are they together? But then I was out in the lobby there, like, with the two of them, and they didn't speak to each other at all. It was a bit awkward and I said to Gail that evening, you know, 'Oh, they must have split up.'"

"What about your son?" I ask. "Did he ever see Denise and Dylan together?"

"Andy? No, he was just a young fella then. I doubt he'd have picked up on it." He's annoyed all of a sudden. He doesn't like me asking about his son.

"How well did Andy know Jade?" I ask. "Did they ever spend time together? I'm just trying to get a sense of who might have known about her social life, who her guests were, that sort of thing."

"I don't think he knew her very well. We were neighbors, like, but he has his school and football training and so forth." He stands up and starts rearranging the stacks of paper on the table.

"Have you been working at home for a while?" I ask him. "How do you like it?"

He shrugs. "Few months. The company that hired me is renovating its offices. It's really noisy so it's handier to work from here when I can. The job is . . . Well, I work hard. You hear someone's working from home, you think he's watching telly all day, but it's not like that. I'm on the phone or the laptop most of the day. Barely have time to break for lunch, really." He smiles apologetically. He's trying to get me out of here.

I'm not going to play.

"Your wife thought Jade had people visit sometimes, at night. Men, she said. What about you? Did you ever see anyone?"

He looks embarrassed. "Look . . . I don't know for sure, but, yeah,

I think she had . . . dates over sometimes. I didn't see them, but Gail did. I know your couple next to her complained about her sitting out late at night and smoking with a fella sometimes. The Phillipses. There might have been some bad feelings there."

"'A fella,'" I repeat. "Would that be the same person or multiple people?"

"You'd have to ask them." He gestures in the direction of the Phillipses' apartment. "I never saw him."

"What about your son?" I want to see if he displays discomfort again. "Do you think he ever saw her with these men?"

He does. "No . . . no, I wouldn't think so. He's at school and then training. So . . . no." He clears his throat.

"And what about a woman with a little girl about Laurel's age? Her name is Elizabeth. Did you ever see her?"

A blank look. His phone buzzes and the computer keeps pinging with notifications. "I don't think so. I'm sorry, I should really get back to my work."

"Yes, of course. Please let us know if you or your family think of anything else. Thank you, Mr. Roden." He nods and when his phone rings, he takes it gratefully out of his pocket and tells me goodbye.

Out in the lobby, I look around at the four doors. There are no cameras here. If Denise Valentine had gone into Jade Elliott's apartment—if any of the neighbors had gone into Jade Elliott's apartment—there wouldn't be a record of it. Outside, I check the angles of the cameras again. We've gotten everything we can off of those, though. And there was nothing but normal sidewalk traffic for all of Monday and Tuesday morning. There must be some cameras around that we haven't found yet. I look around, trying to find the most likely spots.

I see Alannah before she sees me. She's in her school uniform, walking slowly along the street, lost in thought, her backpack dangling from her arm. When she reaches the gate in front of Canal Landing, I see her look up at the flats, toward Jade Elliott's, I think. She stands there for a moment, her eyes narrowed, looking worried beneath her dark bangs. Then she sees me watching her from behind the gate. "Alannah," I call out, waving. "Hang on a second. I want to give you something."

But she either doesn't hear me or pretends not to and continues walking, turning the corner and heading north.

I try to follow her at a distance, just to see where she goes, but she loses me on the dead-end streets off Kingsland Park Avenue. The sidewalks are full of kids coming back from school, parents and grandparents hurrying them along. I'm walking back along Stamer Street when I remember Clara and the photograph, so just for fun, I find number twenty-three. There's a FOR SALE sign out front and a woman in a pantsuit is coming out of the front door, a large set of keys jingling in her hand.

"Is everything okay?" she asks when she sees my uniform and obvious interest in the house. "I'm the property agent. We've just had a showing, but it's over now." The house is a little shabby looking but seems to be in good repair. The front door hasn't been painted yet, but someone has taken the time to put planters out front and the steps have been swept clean.

"Yes, everything's fine," I say. "I was just curious about the history of this house." I tell her about our renovation. "I'm wondering if you know of someone named Clara who might have lived here or had a connection to it in the 1920s."

She looks down at some papers on the clipboard in her hands.

"The seller is the son of a couple who had lived here since the fifties," she says. "They've passed away now, but the name is Crowe. I don't know if that helps. You could ask around, though there aren't many of the original families left on the street."

I thank her and then on impulse, say, "What's the asking price?" The house isn't much to look at from the outside, but it's a great location and I know from responding to an emergency at a house farther up the road that they have good-size gardens in the backs.

"Here's all the information," she says, obviously in a rush, as she hands me a pamphlet. "That's got the asking price and everything on it." I thank her and watch her get into a shiny black Range Rover. The real estate business seems to be working out well for her. As I suspected, the asking price is almost a million euros. It sounds like so much money, but once Conor and Bláithín split the proceeds from the sale of the Donnybrook house and I sell my Long Island house, we'll have the funds to buy something in that price range. It's a lot for such a modest place though. Million-euro houses are about all we've found to look at lately, though, and we haven't come to any conclusions about what neighborhoods we want to be in. Not knowing where the kids will be for university isn't helping any. If one of them ends up at university in Dublin, staying in a central neighborhood makes sense. If they both go to schools where they'll board on campus, then we could look farther afield.

Thinking about houses and university and big life decisions, I decide to walk home along the canal, veering off at Ranelagh Road and making my way around the back of the hospital. Halloween is coming and there's a festive atmosphere on the streets now, black and orange displays in shop windows along Sandford Road, little paper witch hats amongst the sausages at the butcher shop; a group of teenage girls wearing headbands with cat ears on them passes me, laughing and crowding each other.

We have a quick dinner, everyone antsy to get back to homework and email, and once I've done dishes and started a load of laundry, I call Roly, who answers on the first ring. He's still in the incident room. I know from the distracted tone in his voice and the sounds behind him. "Any developments?" I ask.

"Nah, nothing good anyway. Fiero told me about your conversation with Maguire. We'll start ringing 'round to solicitors in the morning. You got anything else?" He's pissed now. I can hear it. It's been three days and we don't have a single suspect. The car hasn't gotten us anywhere and the clock is ticking for Laurel Maguire.

I tell him about my conversation with Phil Roden. "He seemed sensitive about his son," I say. "We never checked with the school, but we should. And I think we need to follow up on this guy she smoked with out on the terrace. I want to know who he was. If they were dating or had some sort of relationship, he might have developed a fixation on Laurel. I was thinking I'd drive up to Navan tomorrow and talk to the family again. Maybe they can help us ID him. You okay with that?"

"Yeah, only do it as fast as you can and keep me in the loop," he says. "You and Fiero getting along okay?"

"Yeah, fine," I say, without going into it. "I'll check in from Navan."

I'm telling Conor about the Stamer Street house when Mr. Bean comes in and whines for his walk. "You want me to take him?" I ask. "I was about to go up to bed. I want to get an early start tomorrow since I need to drive to Navan."

Conor gets the leash and says, "No, I'll take him."

But he doesn't look at me. I wait a minute and ask, "You okay?"

"Yeah, just tired." He leans over and gives me a quick kiss. "Have a good sleep. I may stay up and get some work done."

And then he's gone, and I can feel the distance spreading and filling the room, seeping through the giant hole in the living room wall. I decide not to think about it and take myself to bed, sleep finding me so quickly and completely there isn't even space for dreams.

Fourteen

The radio hosts all want to know why we haven't found Laurel Maguire yet. I flip around on the drive, hoping to get a sense of what the public is thinking. By the time I get to Navan at ten, I have a pretty good idea. They think we're falling down on the job. "You have to wonder what it is that all these officers are doing, Mick," a guest tells one of the hosts. "I think every Irish citizen is imagining that it was their little girl missing, and confidence in the Gardaí is not high at the moment."

I turn it off as I exit the motorway, grumbling, "We're trying, for fuck's sake," to the empty car.

I start with Nicola Keating since she told me on the phone last night that she has to leave to pick up one of her sons at school. She lives on the other side of town from Eileen, but in an almost identical development, the small attached houses painted a yellowy beige color, now dingy from sitting so close to the busy road. There's a uniformed guard sitting in a car out front, and she tells me there hasn't been anything strange, no one watching the house, nothing off from Nicola or her family. Her husband, Hugh, is a plumber and the uniform says he left for work early this morning. Nicola, in jeans and a pink hoodie, her hair pulled back in a tight ponytail again, greets me at the door, says she's already put the kettle on, and leads me into a warm sitting room with a tired-looking brown corduroy couch and low coffee table. There are a few framed family photographs on the wall of Nicola and a man who must be her husband and three little boys. Portraits of other relatives. Lots of baby pictures of the three little boys. One portrait of Laurel in a pink frame with "To Aunt Nicola, Love, Laurel" written in glittery silver paint. A few updated ones show the boys as tweens.

"There haven't been any developments, I'm sorry," I say quickly. "I know how hard it is waiting for news."

She's been keeping it together, but I can see that the past couple of days have her nearly done in. She can't sit still and her foot taps out a nervous rhythm on the worn carpeting. "I just don't understand," she says, starting to cry. "Why don't we know what happened to Jade? Why haven't you arrested someone? It's been three days since you found her. How can you not have anything?"

"I know how hard this is," I say. "We're doing everything we can. But we're having trouble creating a picture of the people who she spent time with. We've located a woman in the neighborhood named Elizabeth Ruane, who seems to have been a friend of Jade's. Did you ever meet her or hear Jade talk about her?"

Nicola hesitates, then nods, wiping her eyes. "Jade told me about the little girl, Sarah, first. She said that Laurel had a little friend in the neighborhood. I think she showed me a picture of them together, said she had gotten to know Sarah's mother a bit."

"Were they close friends, do you think?" I ask.

"I really don't know. I'm sorry." She looks away and I think about what Dylan told us about Nicola's resentment when Jade moved to Dublin and the distance that grew up between them. I think about Fiero's initial impression that Nicola was hiding something from us.

I'm wondering if the distance and Nicola's anger or guilt around it is what he noticed.

"We've also heard that there was a man whom Jade may have had over sometimes. Or perhaps just once. Did she tell you about someone she was seeing, or perhaps just a friend?"

Nicola looks surprised. "I never heard about anything like that. She was quite busy with Laurel."

"Can you tell me a bit about her modeling career?" I ask. "How it started?"

She says, "She . . . I wasn't living at home then, of course. There's a ten-year age difference between us. She was only thirteen. I'd just had Darren and then Aaron came so quickly and we were so busy. But I knew Jade had been pressuring Mam to let her do it. Finally, she asked me if I'd take her down to the Town Centre to have some sort of audition. She needed an adult with her. She dressed so carefully, in a dress and jacket and everything, and she'd done her makeup." She smiles sadly, then dabs at her eyes with a tissue when the tears come again. "She looked really nice. I told her that. I guess it went well because the next thing I knew, Mam said she'd signed with an agency and then she had some catalog jobs. Here, I think I still have one of them." She gets up and goes into the other room and comes out with a stack of department store catalogs with Post-its in them. I flip through, finding Jade in a series of back-to-school ads, wearing jeans and sweaters that look like the ones I bought for Lilly five or six years ago. She looks even younger than thirteen, her cheeks still a little chubby and her hair in schoolgirl pigtails.

"Were you happy with the Delaney Agency?" I ask. "With the way they treated Jade, I guess."

"I suppose so." She doesn't say any more. "They took care of everything, giving her rides and all that. Especially since Mam didn't often go." Her eyes dart away, toward a pile of laundry at the end of the couch.

"So there wasn't anything that made Jade uncomfortable or that seemed . . . out of the ordinary?" I'm trying not to use the word illegal, but I'm not sure she takes my meaning.

"No," she says, then snaps, "but maybe you should ask some of the other models. They could probably tell you."

"Thank you, we will." I pause, giving her a chance to take a breath. "I know this is tough, Nicola, but were you at all aware of how Jade got paid when she was still a minor?"

Something flashes across Nicola's face, and she sighs heavily. "The agency gave Mam cash to cover Jade's living expenses, and then they kept the rest for her. I think she got some of it when she moved to Dublin, but I'm not certain."

"You mean they took in all of her money and then gave Eileen and Jade cash?" I try not to let my shock show on my face.

"Yes, at least that was my sense of it."

"That seems highly irregular to me. Your mother was her guardian. Shouldn't she have gotten Jade's earnings?"

Nicola purses her lips together and looks away for a moment. "I think I know why they did it that way. My mam has a . . . She's always had a compulsive spending problem. Jade must have told them that if Mam had access to the accounts, she'd just drain them. I'm sure that's why. But Mam must have signed off on it." She sighs, twisting the tissue between her fingers until it breaks.

"Ah, thank you. What did you think of Jade's wanting to model? Were you in favor of it?"

Nicola looks embarrassed. "I . . . You have to understand. I had to basically raise Jade. My dad died when I was fourteen and Jade was four. Mam completely disappeared, really. I cooked and cleaned and deposited her dole checks and paid the rent to the council, and then when I married Hugh and Jade was older, I needed to . . . separate from them a bit. Sure, I was having my own babies by then and I needed to start my own life, if you see. It was time for Jade to take some responsibility." She looks embarrassed as she says it, though her words are strong, practiced. She's had this dialogue in her head many times.

"I do," I say. "That must have been hard. It must have been a relief when Jade started making money, when she moved to Dublin. You didn't have to worry about her anymore."

She looks up quickly. "But then I had to worry about Mam. She couldn't care for herself, really. She spent all the money she got. I resented Jade, asked her to move home. She said no. When she started on the show and was making a bit of money, I asked her to help out. But she said she was saving so she could get a place of her own. And then . . . Laurel came along and now I . . . I just wish I could go back and apologize."

"It very likely has nothing to do with Jade's death, but some-one she knew informed us that Jade once said something about the agency, or about the industry in general. She'd seen illegal things, this friend said. I'm wondering if it was something to do with her finances or the way they paid her," I say.

I've tipped my hand and she looks interested. "Do you think the agency was . . . somehow involved?"

"No, we're just . . . following up on everything that might help us locate Laurel," I say.

Nicola starts to say something, then stops and looks away, suddenly evasive.

I study her profile, give her a chance to say something else. But she doesn't.

"What did you think about her being on the show?"

Nicola rolls her eyes. "It was . . . Have you seen it? It was ridiculous. It was all staged and it made out like they were all on the verge of becoming top models or something, but it was all . . . fake. We, Mam and I, watched a few episodes, but Jade acted as though she didn't even have a family. On one of the episodes, she even made fun of Navan, said she couldn't wait to get out of here. It was . . . cruel. Mam didn't want to say, but she was hurt by it."

"It seems like there was distance between you. Is that why?"

At first I think she's not going to answer. Somewhere in the house an appliance beeps. I can hear birds calling outside, traffic on the main road. Nicola's head is down and when she looks up, I can see she's sobbing. She nods and I reach out to touch her knee. "Yes," she chokes out. "God forgive me."

We're done and I know it. I pat her knee again and say, "Thank you for your help. I'm going to see your mother now. How is she holding up?"

Nicola looks up. "She's been in bad shape. I don't think it's really sunk in yet that Jade is gone, and she's quite upset about Laurel. I don't know what you'll get out of her."

"Well, I'll do my best," I say. "Thank you. I know this is difficult."

Again, she starts to say something and then stops. Suddenly, I see the full extent of her anguish. "Thank you, Detective D'arcy." I don't bother to correct her. I hate to admit that Fiero was right, but I think she's hiding something.

I have to drive right through the center of Navan to get to Eileen Elliott's, and I take a short detour to find the Town Centre where Jade had her first casting call. It's a generic, slightly run-down-looking shopping mall, and the sight of a young woman holding a baby and smoking a cigarette out front makes me so sad I have to turn away. I try to imagine Jade driving here with Nicola, hopeful, nervous, following her dream, unaware of everything that was to come.

An image of my cousin Erin comes into my mind then, and I realize that I've been thinking about her more than usual the last couple of days. Suddenly, it's obvious to me why: a young woman, arriving in Dublin, hopeful, full of plans, and then . . . violence.

I grip the steering wheel and speed past a car pulled over on the side of the road, heading for Eileen Elliott's.

I find her watching some sort of midday talk show, the uniformed guard making tea and the cat purring on Eileen's lap. She looks confused when she sees me, and I gently shut off the television and sit down opposite her with my tea while the guard says she'll leave us alone to talk.

"I'm sorry we don't have any news for you yet," I say. "But I wanted to learn a little bit more about Jade's career and recent life. Is that okay? Nicola's told me some, but I was hoping I could get your perspective as well. Can you tell me about how she got involved in modeling?"

"She always liked the magazines," Eileen says. "That's what she spent her pocket money on. And someone saw her in the street once, said, 'You should be a model,' and that was it. She was on at me to let her get photographs taken. It didn't seem . . . I didn't have time, but she kept saying it, kept asking, and finally I said she could go to something. I had to sign a paper."

"Was it the casting call?"

"I don't know. You can ask Nicola. She knew about it . . ."

"Jade met a representative of the Delaney Agency at that casting call," I say. "Do you remember her telling you about that?"

Eileen shifts in the chair, trying to get comfortable, but I can see that her legs are bothering her. "Delaney, that was one of the fellas who came to have me sign the papers, I think. Malachy. He was a nice man. The woman was the one Jade actually worked with. Fiona. But they said that I had to sign the papers so she could be paid. So I did."

"Of course. Do you have a copy of those papers?"

"I don't think . . . I don't know. Jade has them, I think." She looks confused then and claps a hand over her mouth. "Oh, I forgot." Her eyes fill with tears but when I push the tissues over to her, she ignores them.

"It's okay," I tell her. "After you signed the papers, Jade started working then? How would she get to the modeling jobs?"

"They picked her up sometimes. Fiona, usually, I think. They would drive her so they could look out for her." She reaches absent-mindedly for the remote and holds it in her lap, even though the TV is switched off.

"That's good. How did Jade feel about her work? Did she ever express any concerns? Did she feel like they treated her fairly?"

Eileen looks surprised. "She loved it. She was so happy whenever she got a new job. She absolutely loved it. That's why . . . Nicola said I shouldn't let her move to Dublin when she was only seventeen, but she wanted it and . . . what could I do?" Her eyes fill up with tears. "What could I do?"

"I'm so sorry, Eileen. I'm almost finished. What about the finances? Did the checks for Jade's work come directly to you?"

"No, I . . . well, Fiona said it was better for them to have an account for her modeling money that would be like a trust for her. They gave me cash from the account for our shopping and things."

I lean forward, writing this down in my notebook. "Nicola said that Fiona handled all of Jade's money until she was eighteen. So, you never saw the checks at all? They just gave you cash?"

"Yes, they all said it was better that way. For Jade."

"Did you get statements showing what she'd earned?"

"I don't think so. You should ask Nicola. Maybe she saw them." She looks really uncomfortable now, shifting from side to side in her chair, the pain etched on her face.

"I'm almost done, Eileen. I know this is hard. After Jade moved to Dublin, did she ever talk to you about money, about how much she was earning?"

She shakes her head. "She had Dylan to help her, didn't she? He was lovely about helping us out."

"But before that, did the agency continue to handle her money or did she do it herself?"

"I don't know. She stopped modeling, you know. She didn't need to anymore, once she had Laurel. I think Dylan didn't like her doing it. Wearing the clothes and all."

I study her carefully. I had the sense that Dylan looked down on Jade's modeling career, but I didn't think he was jealous. "Was Dylan jealous of the people she worked with on photo shoots? Do you know if that's why she stopped?"

Eileen glances toward the television again. "I don't know. She never said."

I've lost her focus. I touch her knee so she'll look at me. "Eileen, I'm sorry, but I have to ask you, was Dylan ever violent toward Jade? Was she ever scared of him?"

She looks confused now, shaking her head. "Dylan is wonderful to her," she says. "He pays for everything. I don't know why she won't marry him. He's so good to her." She grimaces and shifts again in her chair.

I'm done. I won't get anything else out of her. "Okay, I'll leave you. Is it okay to go up and look in her room again?"

"Yes." She waves, stretching her legs out on the ottoman and clutching the remote. I'm barely up the stairs before I hear the strains of an advertising jingle.

Jade and Nicola's room looks just as it did the other day, but alone now, I feel tuned into it in a way I didn't with Fiero there. The magazine pages over Jade's bed all feature models who look a bit like Jade, all of them very thin. She clearly knew her type, knew where she fit in. I look under the bed again, check the mattress, double-check all the drawers that Fiero and I searched. There's only a small closet and I sweep the top shelf, but don't find anything but old blankets and sheets and pillowcases. Pinned on the closet wall is a tattered piece of paper and I shine my flashlight on it. "Goals" it reads in a childish hand. "Lose weight and get in shape. Learn to do smokey eye. Get more profeshonal. Get better clothes." I take a picture of it and then place it into a plastic evidence sleeve. Somehow this sad, childish list tells me more about Jade Elliott than any witness has been able to.

I scan the room again, searching for hiding spots. Human beings are quite predictable when looking for places to secrete things away. I have a list of the places I search first, and it starts with under any mattresses in the subject's room. But no luck. I check the closet, behind the desk, behind the beds, then under the mattresses again.

Fiero and I searched thoroughly the other day, but I just want to be sure. So I go over the room again, looking at the bed frame, searching every desk and bureau drawer, even behind the bureaus, to make sure she didn't tape anything to the wall. I'm not sure what I'm looking for, but I'm on my way downstairs again when I see the upstairs bathroom door. I searched the drawers and closet when we were here on Tuesday, but I realize I didn't open the boxes or look behind the toilet.

Do it right, Maggie.

I put on latex gloves and check behind the tank. Nothing. The mirror pulls away from the wall and I check that, too, then start on the drawers under the sink. The boxes all hold exactly what their outsides say they do.

Next, the closet.

It's mostly old towels, folded and smelling of mildew and only faintly of laundry detergent. Nicola said her mother uses the bathroom downstairs so it's likely been a long time since anyone's used them. At the back of the closet is a stack of dusty boxes of maxi pads and soap. I check each one carefully, then move on to three faded boxes of Lemsip, a cold and flu remedy.

The first box has a couple of faded packets of powder inside.

The second one is her hiding place.

It's already been opened and taped shut, and when I look inside, I see a wad of folded euro notes. My heart beating, I take a photograph of the box in situ, then the cash in the box, and finally I take the cash out and count it.

Six thousand euros.

My heart pounding, I slip the cash and box into an evidence bag and put it in my pocket. I'll head straight back to Dublin, find Roly, and we'll get it to the tech bureau where they'll examine it, see if they can get fingerprints off it and whether the notes are traceable in any way. I'm betting they'll find Jade's prints on the bills, and not Nicola's or Eileen's but we need to check.

What were you doing, Jade?

Downstairs, the uniformed guard tells me that a nurse is coming later to help Eileen do her physical therapy. I think about asking Eileen about the envelope, but it was clearly placed there so she wouldn't see it, and I don't think she's got anything else to tell me.

"Remind me again when Jade was last here," I say. "Was that back in July?"

"Yes, I think so," she says.

"Has anyone else been upstairs recently?" I ask.

She shakes her head. "Jade was up there, getting some of her things, when she was here in July. She brought her little girl. Do you . . . have you found her?" I tell her we're doing everything we can and that we'll be in touch. A few tears fall from her eyes, but she doesn't look away from the television screen.

I'm putting my coat on when my phone rings, and I wave good-bye and step outside to take the call. The housing estate is quiet with all the kids at school. An older woman walks slowly along the edge of the parking lot, a small terrier trailing behind her. I wave at her but she ignores me.

"D'arcy." Roly's voice comes quick and panicked. I feel my stomach drop. They've found Laurel's body. *I'm sorry, Eileen. I have something to tell you.*

But instead, he says, "You still in Navan?"

"Yeah, just leaving. What's going on?"

"Good. You're not going to believe this. Laurel Maguire's been found alive. And she's there, in Navan."

Fifteen

....

I stay outside to avoid being overheard while I get the basics from Roly. He and Fiero are driving north from Dublin and I can hear Fiero talking behind him, probably on the phone with the guards who responded to the scene where Laurel was found.

"A fucking crèche, D'arcy. This fucking sicko left her at a crèche!" Roly tells me.

The Happy Fairies Crèche is a childcare center on the outskirts of Navan, located on a sparsely settled road. A fenced-in outdoor play area wraps around the back of the center and thirty minutes ago, right around lunchtime, one of the carers was watching the children at play when she saw a little girl, dressed only in a toddler diaper and brand-new pajamas and socks, standing on the outside of the fence and talking to some of the children through the chain links. The carer hadn't been working at the center long and at first she thought one of their charges had gotten out of the fence, but when none of the other staff recognized the little girl, they brought her inside, put her in a lost-and-found coat, and rang the guards. Before the officers got there, though, one of the young women who worked at the center recognized the little girl from the news reports, so that by the time the local guards arrived, they knew there was a pretty good chance it was Laurel Maguire.

"They're in the process of getting all the kids off the premises and the local guards have secured the area where she was found," Roly tells me. "But since you're on the spot, I want you to have a look around and make sure they're doing it right and see what we can get for CCTV in the area. Whoever dropped her off must have done it in a vehicle. It's a good distance out of town and there aren't many houses near. We're on our way."

He's elated, talking fast and in a register he only goes to when he's happy. She's alive. These cases almost never end this way, but this one has, and we've got a live and apparently unharmed kid.

"I should be there in twenty minutes," I tell him, keeping my voice low. "I'm still at Eileen Elliott's. We need to tell her, don't we?"

"I'd rather keep it quiet, but . . . tell ya what, I'll ring Maguire first and then them. But I'll wait 'til we're there. We need to make sure it's her and we need to make sure the news doesn't get out. In any case, we'll have to get her to hospital before they can see her. It's mad, D'arcy, leaving her at a crèche, mixing her in amongst all the other kiddies! As though we might not notice! I'd almost say our fella's messing with us, like, ya know?"

"Will we interview her?" Interviewing very young children who have been the victims of crime is tricky. Kids are highly suggestible, and one Laurel's age probably doesn't even have the words to tell us where she's been.

"We'll try, but first we'll do the exam and then we'll probably need one of those, whadyacallit, play therapists, to do it. Fuckin' puppets and so forth. It's not going to be today anyway. But it's a good outcome all right." I can hear the triumph in his voice. It wasn't our police work that found her, but no one will care about that. All they'll know is that she was found alive.

It isn't until I hang up that I realize I forgot to tell him about the cash. I lock it in the glove box of Conor's car. I'll need to get it to the tech bureau as soon as possible.

The crèche is a ten-minute drive from Eileen's. It looks like a high-quality place and it's in a semirural setting, a renovated detached house painted a sunny yellow with a large yard around it and a new-looking fence and playground equipment. No reporters yet, though I see a few cars slow on the main road, trying to figure out what the Garda presence is about. Locals know Jade Elliott was from Navan. Someone's going to start asking questions. We don't have a lot of time.

They've moved all the kids inside until they can be picked up and their parents have been sworn to secrecy. The director and the woman who found Laurel come out to meet me and show me inside. The center is freshly painted, the walls decorated with children's art and posters with the alphabet and the numbers from one to twenty, the days of the week. It smells like diapers and cleaning solution, the smell of childcare centers the world over, and suddenly I flash back to the place we sent Lilly before she was able to start pre-school, the panic when I was running late, the sharp shock of joy I always felt when she saw me and ran over to hug my legs and tell me what she'd been up to that day.

They have Laurel in a small office off the main play area, a uni-formed guard at the door. When I poke my head in, one of the teachers is sitting on the floor with Laurel and handing her dolls, but not touching her, as instructed by the responding officers. A glass of water and a plate of sliced apples and biscuits is sitting next to her, and another uniformed guard is in the room, keeping an eye on her. I remind them not to change her clothes or diaper until the techs arrive. I feel my heart catch in my throat when Laurel looks up at me, her huge green eyes curious and a little wary. I recognize her immediately from the photographs I've spent the last few days studying, and I realize I've imagined her body lifeless so many times that I can hardly believe she's here in front of me. Trying not to scare her, I crouch down on the ground and say, "Hello, Laurel. I'm so happy to see you." She peers up at me, then points to my uniform and says, "Boo?"

"Yes, my uniform is blue. It's a nice color, isn't it? And see, my vest is yellow. Do you like yellow?"

"Boo," she says, in a self-satisfied way, and goes back to the dolls. She isn't visibly injured and she has the relaxed look of a child who's been well-cared for. The thought pops into my head: Could she have been with someone she knows? But who? Everyone in her life has been accounted for the past few days. And I know that her demeanor may be misleading. Trauma has a funny way of hiding, and whatever's happened to her over the past couple of days is going to come out one way or the other. All I want to do is say, *Laurel, who had you? Who have you been with?* But I can't do that. If there's anything we can get from her about where she was, it needs to be done carefully and in a way that won't jeopardize a future prosecution.

I thank the teacher who's caring for her and ask to see the woman who spotted Laurel outside. She still can't believe it, she says, can't believe the little girl is here. "I've been following the news and then I saw her there. It's just . . . I'm still in shock," she says, leading me out through a set of doors into the play yard. It's well-kept, with a wooden jungle gym and some swings and wooden animals for the kids to climb on.

The teacher points to the long back fence that faces the road behind the center. "I was standing here, watching the kids, and I noticed two of the little girls had gone over to the fence and, it was so strange, like, I realized there was a child on the outside of the fence. It took me a minute to figure out that she was on the other side, you know how your eyes play tricks on you. I called to Kate— she's with the four-year-olds—and I asked her to watch the kids. I had to go around because there's no gate, for safety reasons. I ran through the center and around the side and she was right there, just standing there, looking through the fence at the other kids. I said, 'Where did you come from, then?' but she didn't answer. She looked scared and when I asked again, she pointed back toward the road and said something like, 'Bee.' I picked her up and walked down the road a bit, thinking maybe someone had been walking with her and had fallen or collapsed or something. But there was no one. That was when I realized she looked familiar, and I realized she must be the missing little girl. So I brought her inside. She seems okay, doesn't she? Where was she? How did she get here? The poor little thing. And her mother dead."

"Did she say anything to you to indicate who she was with?" I ask. "Anything about how she got there."

"She kept pointing to herself and saying, 'La'—for Laurel of course, though I didn't realize it until I figured out who she was. She had some other words, but I couldn't make them out. At this age, a lot of it is sounds, not fully formed words, and only caregivers who spend a lot of time with the child would be able to tell you what he or she is trying to say."

"My daughter called applesauce 'ru ru' because we always served it to her in a red bowl," I say. "We were always explaining to people that ru ru was applesauce."

"Yeah, they're funny that way, aren't they?" She smiles.

"And you didn't see anything, a car? A person running away? Anything at all?"

The teacher shakes her head. "Nothing, I'm so sorry. They may have driven away while I was coming back through the center. I should have looked, I suppose, but I just wanted to get her away from the road and . . . it was all so odd, and then once I realized who she was, I suppose I panicked."

I look through the fence at the narrow lane that runs along the back of the playground. The car must have pulled up along the fence line and the driver must have put her out and driven away. "Do you know if the crèche has CCTV back here?" I ask her.

"I think it's just around the front," she says. I check the eaves of the building anyway, but I don't see any cameras here. The roads are too small to have cameras placed.

I try not to groan. If the car dropped her off back here, it could easily have continued along the road without being caught on the camera at the front of the center. Same thing if someone walked her here. I go back through the center and around the back of the playground, standing at the side of the road for a moment, trying to imagine where there'd be evidence. The narrow road is paved but crumbling, and it hasn't rained in a few days now. They likely won't get any tire prints off the road, but there might be some other kind of evidence: a flake of paint off the car, a crumpled receipt that blew out when the door opened. I scan the roadway but don't see anything obvious.

On the other side of the road is a stand of trees and a deep trench, half filled with murky rainwater runoff. I check the surface but don't see anything other than leaves and sticks. Whoever dropped her off was taking a chance. If she'd toddled off into the trees, she might have fallen into the trench and drowned. Had her abductor watched until she'd been spotted by the fence?

A small gray car comes speeding along the road and pulls over a couple of hundred yards before the center. A young woman jumps out, holding up a phone and, I assume, taking pictures of the scene, the four marked cars and the uniformed gardái, who go to meet her and block her way.

The word is out about Laurel being found.

I make sure they cordon off the entirety of the road along the fence to preserve evidence, and I'm checking for sight lines from the center's windows when Roly, driving a pool car, pulls into the driveway. I watch as he and Fiero go inside and then come out a few minutes later.

"Where's the CCTV?" Fiero asks as soon as they reach me. He's not wearing his jacket and sunglasses today. Instead, he has a dress shirt and jacket on, the same bright navy blue as Roly's, and he's immaculately groomed, freshly shaven, his gray crew cut a precise two inches. He must have gone home and done a little self-care last night. His blue eyes sweep over me dismissively. "You got it, yeah?"

"There isn't any back here," I say. "I think he must have pulled up along the fence, gotten her out, left her here, and then driven away. He could have done it without ever going around the front where the cameras are."

"But we won't know that until we look at it, so you secured the CCTV from the front, yeah?" Fiero's voice drips with condescension.

I glare at him. "Not yet," I say. "I wanted to see if there was evidence out here." I point to the cordons. "Nothing obvious but they'll want to check."

Fiero can't hide his annoyance at me. He rolls his eyes and turns away with a dramatic sigh.

"The techs are on the way," Roly says. "Should be here in ten minutes. Pat, you go get the CCTV. See if there's anything there." Fiero nods and throws me a dark look.

"What's his problem?" I ask once he's out of earshot.

"Ah, he's fine. He thinks we'll have our fella on the CCTV. You don't think so?"

I shrug. "If he thought about it for two seconds and did any kind of reconnaissance, he'd have come along here and then continued on to the main road from this direction."

Roly thinks for a second. "You saw her?"

"Yeah, she looked healthy. And this . . ." I point to the fence, the playground, the center. "This says he wanted her to be taken care of. He found a safe place to leave her. That says to me someone who cared about her."

Back inside, Roly tells the director she'll have to close for the rest of the day and maybe a few days next week, too. "I know it will be a hardship for your families. We'll try to finish up as soon as possible. And we'll need a list of everyone who was on the premises, to see if any of them saw anything."

She nods. "I suspect a lot of our families will be holding their kids tight this evening. It's a happy outcome, but it really makes you think, doesn't it?" She looks away and then back at me. "Do they know if she's all right then? Was she . . ." She looks away. "Interfered with?"

Roly says kindly, "We can't talk about the investigation. But we're grateful you took care of her. The family asked me to thank you specifically." They didn't, but it's a harmless way to get her off the topic of whether Laurel Maguire was assaulted.

Fiero comes out of the room where they let him watch the CCTV. He shakes his head, *Nothing there,* and thanks the director, giving her a smile and flirtatious wink that I think is meant to get her on our side. She blushes a little and says that if we need anything, we should just ask.

There are a few kids in one of the rooms, waiting for their parents to pick them up. We wave at them and walk around the inside of the center, checking the sight lines from the windows while Roly goes to talk to the techs.

"Why'd he pick this place?" Fiero asks me, reaching up to tap on the glass in an empty classroom. "What does it tell us about him that this is the spot he picked?"

"Well, there's something logical about it, right? Either way."

"What do you mean?"

I gesture to the building. "If you were trying to make sure she wasn't discovered for a while, if you wanted to get away, leaving her at a childcare center was pretty smart. It's a nice day. If she'd been on the other side of the fence, mixed in with the kids, then she might have been there for thirty minutes before someone noticed her. By the time she was found, she would have been playing in the mud, touching the other kids, you know how toddlers are. So it was smart."

"What do you mean, 'either way'?"

"Well, it was smart in terms of wanting to get away, but leaving her on the other side of the fence was a bit risky, wasn't it? There's a trench with water in it on the other side of the road. Think if she'd gone down the hill and into the water. That tells me that her abductor needed to get rid of her for some reason. He was desperate. But on the other hand, he—and I'm just going with 'he' for the sake of discussion—chose a place where she was likely to get good care. That tells me that maybe he cared about her."

"Or maybe he was hoping she'd just mix in with all the other kids and wouldn't be noticed for a while. The psychology is mad, isn't it? You go to all that trouble of abducting the child, killing the mother for some purpose of your own, probably a fucking psycho pedo one, and then you just leave her. What the fuck is that about?" What I took for anger at me is actually anger at Laurel's abductor, I realize. He feels the way Roly does, that our guy is toying with us, and he's furious.

"Something happened to change his circumstances," I say. "The place he was holding her was no longer safe, he thought he was going to be found out."

"Yeah, or . . ."

"Or what?"

"Or he had second thoughts," Fiero says. "He started to feel badly about what he was doing. He couldn't go through with it."

"Yeah . . . That's good," I say, meeting his eyes. They've softened a bit. He's listening to me now. "It doesn't seem planned out. It doesn't seem organized. He needed to get rid of her for some reason."

"Who the fuck is he?" Fiero, angry again, slams his hand against the wall.

I get a drink from the child-size sink in the middle of the room, leaning over to slurp from the running faucet and then using my hands to splash cold water on my face. I need coffee and I need something to eat. The room is neatly organized, a box of toy cars and a stack of books on one of the shelves, some puppets and dress-up clothes hanging on a hook.

"Hey," I say, standing up. "I just thought of something." I step into the hall and wave over the teacher who spotted Laurel. "Do you have a kid here who's really into cars? Like, one of those kids who knows make and model and everything? There was a boy in my daughter's childcare like that. He used to stand by the window and call out, 'Ford Explorer,' 'BMW.'"

The teacher's eyes widen and she nods, smiling. "Yeah," she says. "We've got one of those. He's still here. Hang on."

Fiero looks confused and I say, "I read an article once that the reason little kids are so good at identifying cars is that we have some kind of primal survival instinct to recognize the shapes of animals. It was important to be able to tell if something was a woolly mammoth or a lion or whatever. Adults take in so much other information that we've lost touch with that ability. Adults sometimes remember color, size, the broad strokes. But kids still have the memory for details."

"I was mad for the lorries when I was little," he says, nodding. "I could identify all different kinds of tractors, excavators, all the different lorries."

The teacher is back, holding a small, wary-looking boy of about five by the hand. "This is Vincent," she says, leading him in. "Vincent, this nice guard wants to ask you a question."

I'm about to speak when Fiero leans down, looking him in the eye, and says, "Vincent, I hear you like cars."

Vincent nods solemnly. "Well," Fiero continues, "this morning, when the little girl showed up at the fence, did you see a car there?"

Vincent picks at a loose thread on his sleeve, staring at the ground.

"Did you see a car, Vincent?" the teacher prompts him. He nods. Again, Fiero jumps in before I can say anything. "What kind of car was it? Do you know?" I can hear the frustration in his voice, but his tone is too aggressive. He's scaring the kid.

Vincent stares at the floor some more.

"Vincent," I say gently. "What's your favorite car? Do you like fast cars?"

He looks up. "My dad has a Škoda," he says. "He has a white Škoda."

"That's a nice car. Is that the car you saw outside today when the little girl was at the fence?" He shakes his head. "What kind of car did you see, Vincent?"

He tugs at the teacher's pant leg and she bends down so he can whisper in her ear. She nods and smiles at him.

"He said it was a blue car. Right, Vincent? He said it was a blue . . ." She looks at him again. "A blue Opel Astra? Is that what you said?"

He nods. "Yeah, I saw blueopelastra. Blueopelastra." He runs the words together adorably and I have to stop myself from smiling. *Blue.*

"Thank you, Vincent," I say. "Was it a bright blue?" I point to the royal blue arc in a painted rainbow on the wall. "Or a dark blue? Like my trousers here?"

He points to the rainbow.

"That is so helpful, Vincent. You are such a good helper. I just have one more question. Was one of the doors white?"

He looks confused, then shakes his head. "It was blue," he says.

"If it came along by the fence, he would only have seen the passenger side," Fiero whispers, then says, "Vincent, good man, you should be a guard yourself. Thank you."

The teacher looks from Fiero to me. The triumph is all over our faces. She smiles, proud of her small part.

"Thank you so much," I tell her.

We find Roly and Griz outside, and Fiero is racing over to tell them before I can even process the fact that he's screwed me over, taking credit for my idea. Now there's no way I can say I thought of it without looking petty.

"Brilliant," Roly says. "Opel Astra, bright blue. And it confirms that sighting in Dublin. We can find witnesses and CCTV in surrounding areas and narrow it down. We'll have him tonight. I've got a good feeling. Can you organize the door-to-doors, Fiero? We're heading for the hospital and we'll be back once we're done there. Well done, you two!"

A social worker from Tusla, along with a family liaison officer, arrive with a car seat to take Laurel to a hospital in Dublin where she'll be examined and then reunited with Dylan. Roly goes along and tells us to work on the car.

The first thing is to find a blue Opel on CCTV or traffic cameras here in Navan and see if we can get a registration plate. Our guy is scared and desperate. If Fiero and I are right that he left Laurel at the crèche because the place he was keeping her was no longer safe, then that means he's on the run and it means we have a good chance of finding him. They put out the alert to Roads Policing, and back in the incident room in Dublin, Geoff Chen starts organizing the appeal to go out to the press. He'll find the manufacturer's image of the car and try to put it in front of as many people's eyes as possible, hoping someone saw it somewhere.

We get ten uniforms from the Navan Garda Station and a few of the surrounding towns and Fiero and I immediately put half of them to work going door-to-door, asking about home security footage, asking if anyone saw anything. The other half are ready as Fiero works the phones to his contacts in Roads Policing to get all of the traffic footage from a ten-mile radius. It doesn't take long; when he tells them that Laurel Maguire's been found and we're close to finding the bastard that took her, everyone moves heaven and earth to help us.

"We'll have him by tomorrow morning," Fiero says when I drop him off at his car at one A.M. We're heading home for a quick sleep before we pick it up again in the morning. The parking garage is sinister in the dark, scant lighting angling from the anemic bulbs up by the ceiling, and his face is sagging, his eyes puffy now. He smells of his herby deodorant, which has been working hard today, and stale coffee. Sitting together in my car this time of night feels uncomfortable somehow, as though there's something illicit about it.

Suddenly remembering my search of the bathroom at Eileen's, I hand over the cash, explaining how I found it, and he says he'll take possession of it and get it to the techs first thing. "So how do you think it got there?" he asks.

"I think Jade hid it there when she was visiting her mother in July," I say.

"But it could have belonged to the mother or the sister, couldn't it? We'll have to ask them."

I shrug. "It could have, but it didn't. The mother hadn't been upstairs in a year, according to Nicola. And Nicola's desperate for cash. I could tell from her house. If she'd had six thousand euros lying around, she would have been using it."

"What do you think Jade was hiding?" he asks, reaching to open his door. "You think she was on the game or dealing drugs or something?"

Tired, I say, "I don't know. We need to look into everything. I'll see you in the morning."

Driving home, I'm thinking about Erin again. When I was looking for Erin after her disappearance, I'd had the sense that she was leaving clues for me—and only me—to follow. The money in Eileen Elliott's bathroom feels that way to me, but of course that's ridiculous. I'd met Jade Elliott only once and she'd hidden that money long before the night Jason and I responded to the call about a woman screaming in Jade's apartment.

Sometimes, when you're investigating a homicide, the victim becomes alive to you, and you forget that you never knew them when they were still breathing. You forget that they weren't leaving messages for *you*, because they never knew you.

Jade isn't Erin, Maggie, I tell myself. *Don't make that mistake.*

It's two by the time I let myself into the quiet house. I called Conor earlier and let him know that Laurel Maguire had been found safe and sound.

"Thank God," he said, his voice tired, a little husky after I told him not to wait up. "Well done, my love. It's what you've been hoping for."

Now, still just a little too hyped up for sleep, I pour a glass of wine and, realizing I left my laptop at the station, wake up Conor's desktop to see if the news outlets have Laurel's rescue yet. A few do, but the bigger papers seem to be waiting for the morning. I find myself thinking of Laurel. Once they've examined her, they'll let Dylan Maguire see her and find a pediatric psychologist who's worked with the Garda before to talk with her. I feel a wave of relief at the fact that she'll be reunited with a parent, but also sadness. What is she thinking about Jade, about where she's gone? In a few years, will she even remember her? Will the trauma of seeing her mother killed, of whatever's happened to her, stay with her and haunt her for the rest of her life? Hopefully Dylan and Nicola and Eileen will show her pictures of Jade and will talk about her to keep Laurel's memories of her alive.

Now that we know Laurel's safe, I can feel Jade Elliott stepping to the forefront, asserting her personality, her history. I remember her face the day Jason and I found her, her eyes staring at the ceiling, the wisps of hair settled on her cheek. I think of her walking down the street in the scene from *Ireland's Next Star Model,* alive with anticipation, hopeful about her career.

I'm about to shut down the computer when I see the window Conor had open before he put the desktop to sleep tonight. The tab in the front is a pre-publication review for his new book. POLITICAL HISTORY AS DESTINY, the headline reads.

It starts out okay, describing him as "one of Ireland's preeminent historians," but it goes downhill after that, criticizing the book for being "overly lengthy and painfully dense, with many chapters that would only be of interest to the most dedicated scholars of Irish political history." It finishes with a snarky line about how his book could be used as a doorstop.

I sit there for a moment, resisting the urge to run upstairs and wake him up and hug him. But he didn't tell me about it. He must not have wanted me to know. If I wake him up now, he'll be exhausted tomorrow. If I bring it up, it will force him to think about it when he probably just wants to forget he ever saw it.

I leave everything the way it was and put the computer back to sleep. I'm too tired to wash my face properly or change into my pajamas, so I just strip down to a T-shirt and underwear and snuggle in next to Conor's warm body. He doesn't stir.

I sleep like the dead that night, no images of Laurel Maguire to wake me, no flashbacks to Jade Elliott's body lying on the floor of her bedroom, just the blissful nothingness of unconsciousness.

Sixteen

....

The news that Laurel Maguire is alive and well breaks overnight, and by the time I stumble into the station at seven the next morning, the reporters have formed a ring around the entrance and are shouting at anyone who enters. "How is Baby Laurel? Who took her?" I'm waiting for a question about how we let him get away, but so far they seem to be focusing on the fact that she's alive.

I catch sight of my friend Stephen Hines in the crowd and once I'm safely inside, I text him, What took you so long?

Whatever do you mean? he texts back, but with a smiley face.

Do you have anything for me?

The answer comes back quickly: I'd think it would be the other way around.

I leave him hanging and go up to the incident room.

The case meeting starts at ten. The divisional detectives make a presentation and then Roly tells us that Laurel Maguire seems to be in good health. "Doctors say they don't think she was assaulted or abused in any way. They tried a little with the therapist, but she was exhausted and her father didn't want her any more traumatized than she already is. She nodded when we asked if she went in a car and if she was at a house. She kept talking about someone named 'B' so we'll ask about that some more." I can see the frustration on Roly's face. If she was only a year or two older, she'd be able to tell him exactly what happened. "We'll give it the weekend and try again Monday."

"How did she seem when she saw her father?" I ask Roly. "Was she happy to see him?"

He turns to look at me, perplexed by the question. Then he realizes why I'm asking. "Yeah, she seemed a bit confused at first, but she called him Daddy and so forth, let him hug her. It definitely seemed like they hadn't seen each other in a while. He was pretty emotional." He shrugs. "It seemed authentic to me."

I nod. "When will she see her aunt and grandmother?"

"I think Maguire said they could come down today."

I can feel Fiero watching me. "Great," I say. "Thank God she's okay." Roly nods and sends everyone off to help with combing through the CCTV.

No one gives me an assignment, so I get my notes together and look over the news coverage. The tabloids are all leading with pictures of Laurel and the crèche, proclaiming her safe return the "Navan Miracle." The *Independent* has the pictures further down but is leading with the manhunt angle: GARDAÍ HUNT FOR KIDNAPPER; ASK PUBLIC'S HELP. There's a picture of a similar car and a plea for drivers to keep an eye out for it, maybe with a white driver's side door. I know from experience that they'll get lots of fake sightings, but if they have the manpower to vet them, they may just find the car this way.

Dylan Maguire is quoted in all of the stories, thanking us for our hard work and asking for privacy while he and Laurel adjust to normal life again. He also thanks the public for their prayers and good wishes. I study the picture of him, his perfectly trimmed hair and elegant clothes. OVERJOYED FATHER SAYS HE THOUGHT HE'D NEVER

SEE LAUREL AGAIN, one of the papers proclaims. But there's nothing about the person who killed Laurel's mother, about vowing to hunt him down. There's nothing about getting justice for Jade.

It's like he planned it this way, I can't help thinking.

I get up and go to find Geoff Chen, who's scrolling through CCTV footage at his desk. "Is there a way to search Jade Elliott's known associates for car registrations?" I ask him. "I was just thinking about some of the people around her, her friends, the people she worked with, her neighbors. If one of them, or one of *their* associates, has ever registered a bright blue Opel, well . . . our guy's got to have some connection to Jade and Laurel or to Dylan Maguire, and the sooner we figure out what that is, the sooner we'll know where to look for him."

Geoff nods. "Good idea," he says. "I imagine they've done it already, but I can check. Have they not trained you on the system yet?"

"I had the initial training but I'm not sure how to bring in the vehicle registrations."

"Ah, yeah. That can be tricky. I can try to get to it Monday for you." He yawns. I can already feel the different energy of the investigation now that Laurel is safe. The energy has shifted to the hunt for the car. It's out there, on the roads, up to other people.

"Sounds good. Thanks, Geoff."

"Oh, one other thing. I've got something," he says. "That number from her phone, the one we couldn't trace? I just got a hit for it in the system."

"What do you mean?" Roly, coming into the room, asks him. "I thought it was a burner."

"It is," Geoff says. "But it came up because it was entered as part of another investigation."

"Really? Tell me," Roly says.

"Okay, so the investigation into your man's death in Inchicore, Robby Noonan?"

That's the one Roly's team has been working on. I try to remember the details. A local business owner, one with ties to one of Dublin's criminal street gangs, was gunned down in broad daylight as he walked out of a pub.

"It's a gangland thing, yeah?" Geoff continues. "Likely the Coughlan gang, though they haven't pinned it down yet. As part of that investigation, they've been collecting the numbers of all the phones that rang the victim in the weeks and months before he was killed."

"And that number was one of them?" I ask. I know this doesn't mean much. Criminal gangs use burner phones all the time. The chances of us figuring out who was using this particular one are pretty small.

"Yup. But it's even better. Detective Sergeant Grzeskiewicz tracked it down by comparing it to known calls to an informant and intel from some other investigations."

"How do you mean?" I ask. I don't understand what he's saying.

Geoff and Roly exchange a glance. Roly nods and Geoff says, "There's an informant somewhere, a fella who has been on our radar for a while and who passes us intel from time to time. When Robby Noonan was killed, we got warrants for a lot of phone records. I'm guessing this number was on one of those other phones and Griz sort of triangulated it, using the process of elimination and what she knew about the contents of some of those calls to assign this one to a specific fella. Then she put it in the system so if it ever shows up in another investigation, if we ever pin something else on him, she might be able to lean on him for some more intel."

"So who is it?" Roly asks.

"We think that number is from a phone that was used a few times by a low-level drug dealer from Dolphin's Barn named Cameron Murphy."

I stare at him. "Holy shit," I say. "I know Cameron. He's around the neighborhood a lot. He was haunting the police cordon at Canal Landing the other day. He's seemed way too interested in what's going on down there." I'm trying to figure out how he could be involved. Then I remember. "That cash I found at Eileen's house! What if Jade was his customer? Or working for him or something like that?"

"That would explain his interest," Geoff says. "If she had his money and he wanted it back."

"The car," I say. "I don't think he owns a car, but we can search up the registrations for known associates and see if that's it. Did we get the prints back from Jade's apartment? Cameron must be in the database, yeah? I know he's got a few charges."

"They said soon," Geoff says. "I'll check, yeah?"

I'm trying to figure out how it all fits when I see the look on Roly's face. He hooks a finger toward the door. "Come on out there with me so I can talk to you," he says quietly to me.

I know what he's going to say before he says it.

"I'm sorry, D'arcy. The boss says you're to go back on patrol next week. Now that we've got the kiddie back, it's a different game. He says they've all the resources they need now. Fiero and I will stay on it, but otherwise the divisional fellas are going to work it. We'll likely have the fella in the next few days from the motorway cameras and, well, then we'll see about the homicide investigation. I may be able to bring you in to take statements and so forth, since you're trained for interviews. And if things change . . . I know you're invested. I'm sorry."

I nod. There's nothing to say. He told me the first day that they were only bringing me in because they were shorthanded. He told me it would be just to help out. I have no reason to be disappointed.

"You've been grand," he says, running a hand through his hair. "Everyone knows it. When something opens up, you'll be top of list. But uniformed guards don't grow on trees. You're to take the weekend and then you're back on the mean streets of Portobello." He's not looking directly at me, and I can tell he's uncomfortable.

"I get it, Roly," I say, to let him know I'm not holding it against him. "It makes sense. Thanks for letting me be a part of things."

"Of course. And I mean it, D'arcy, you're top of list. Now—" He starts to turn away, back to the CCTV or liaising with Roads Policing or whatever he's got to do next.

I put a hand on his arm to stop him. "I'll say it once, Roly, and then I'll leave it. I think we're missing the connection. This guy has to be linked to her in some way, some personal way, related to her family or her relationships. If we can figure that out, we can find him, rather than just waiting for the car to show up."

"You still think Dylan Maguire had something to do with it?" His pale blue eyes are bloodshot from lack of sleep, but he's focused on me now.

I shrug. "Maybe, or someone else she was intimately involved with, you know? I think the answer is out there, from people we've already talked to. If Maguire hired someone, maybe it was Cameron Murphy, or maybe someone she was dating."

"Like that film, with your one, Gwyneth Paltrow," Roly says. "*Dial M for Murder,* yeah?"

"Grace Kelly, *then* Gwyneth Paltrow. But, right. I think you should reinterview everyone, look for links, ask the neighbors if they saw him around Jade's place. And I think we need to get Dylan Maguire in and question him officially."

Roly sighs, shifts his eyes back to the incident room, where I can see Padraig Fiero watching us. "Look, D'arcy. We got to let Maguire settle in a bit. The poor kid's been through it. Take the weekend. If something comes up, I'll let you know, right? And we'll chase down Murphy as much as we can. But right now, we've to . . . let things play out. We've got to find the car. I bet we'll know more by Monday."

He pats me on the shoulder and then he's gone, and I can feel Fiero watching me as I get my things together and go.

Saturday feels like the late Octobers I remember from Long Island falls, the air cold on my nose and cheeks, a stiff wind blowing, dry leaves skittering on the driveway. It's four days before Halloween and quite a few of our neighbors have carved jack-o'-lanterns out in front of their houses or in their windows, candles glowing inside and lighting the night.

We've been invited to a dinner party, a long-planned event at the home of my friend Emer and her girlfriend, Monica, that, despite my sour mood, I'm suddenly glad I didn't have to cancel. Emer, who I first got to know when I was investigating my cousin Erin's disappearance, is a tech executive. Monica is a painter and photographer, and they had their first baby, a little girl named Carla, a year ago. We've gotten together with them a few times since she was born, taking them dinner and a bottle of wine and playing with the baby while we catch up, or staying with Carla so they can go out alone.

Tonight, though, is a festive event, a party to celebrate the opening of a major show of Monica's work. "You'll like the crowd," Emer told me when she invited us in September. "Monica's friends are much more interesting than my techie workmates, and you can see how much Carla's grown. She's walking now."

Walking over to their house in Ranelagh, Conor and I exchange details about our days. I tell him that I'm back on patrol and he checks my face to see if I'm okay.

"I understand why," I say. "Everyone's shorthanded. I don't even know who they brought in to patrol with Jason, and Roly's probably right that they'll get the guy in the next couple of days—someone's bound to recognize the car—and then the investigation's over. It's just . . . I don't know. I had things I wanted to follow up on."

He's dressed up a little, nice shirt and a fresh shave, and I turn my face up for a kiss, feeling his smooth cheek and soft lips. "I'm sorry, Maggie," he says. "I know you've loved being back on an investigation." He squeezes my hand. He's distracted and I think about mentioning the bad review. But I don't want to bring it up just as we arrive at what's supposed to be a fun event, and so I squeeze back and keep my mouth shut. I've learned not to bring up difficult topics with Conor unless we have time and space to talk them through. We both find it easier to just power through negative emotions, and we've been so busy that there hasn't been time or space to talk about anything but the most necessary logistical things in quite a few months.

It's dark at seven thirty, but the streetlights on the cold night are somehow festive, and the lamplight coming from the windows along Emer and Monica's street give everything a cozy glow.

"I meant to tell you that I walked by twenty-three Stamer Street yesterday," I say. "It's for sale and the property agent was coming out. She gave me a pamphlet about the house, but she didn't know anything about a Clara who might have lived there." I tell him about the Crowe family and the information on the pamphlet.

"The Crowe family," he says. "I'd say we should be able to find out some more about them. The house is very dear, isn't it? You think it's worth a million euros?"

"No, but someone will pay it. You know what the market's like. Remember that one we looked at in Smithfield? It's a bit like that."

Somehow I'd thought that looking for houses would be romantic, a gesture toward our new life together in Dublin, but instead it's just seemed depressing, nothing that seems like good value for money and nothing that feels like *us* yet.

I sigh. We just need to keep looking.

We're the first ones to arrive, and I take Carla and hold her while they finish getting the meal ready and Conor helps them lay everything out. Carla's a tiny, solemn, dark-haired girl who reminds me a little of Lilly at this age. I let her play with my dangly earrings and I point to household items and say their names very seriously while we walk around the first floor of the house. One of Monica's paintings that I haven't seen before is on the wall in the living room, a huge swirling canvas of red and orange and black lines weaving together and then transitioning to calmer yellows and peaches in the upper right-hand corner. It reminds me of a sunset and sunrise, the center of the painting unsettling, but the resolution ultimately soothing, satisfying.

"This is beautiful," I say. Carla points at the painting and babbles. "Yes, it is. Your mom is a good painter, Carla."

Monica comes into the room and when Carla reaches for her, she takes her from me, kissing her head and hugging her against her chest. "Thanks, Maggie. I started painting it right when we were in the thick of it all, the sleeplessness and the new baby and Emer's postnatal depression. I couldn't finish it then, but just recently, I went back to it and I was really happy with the result. It's not in the show but I wanted to hang it anyway, maybe to remind myself of what it was like, how far we've come." We both stare at it for a minute. There's something overwhelming about the colors in the center. I feel briefly panicked, swamped by emotion, as I think I'm meant to.

"It's nice to see her feeling good again," I say. "You two have really been through it. It's hard enough under the best circumstances."

"She's worked hard to get better," Monica says, as Carla starts babbling in her arms. "I've heard from so many friends who have experienced postnatal depression but never talked about it. I try to ask everyone I know who's having a baby or whose partner is, do you know the signs? Do you know how to ask for help?"

I'm remembering now the day I came over to bring Emer and Monica a meal, shortly after Carla was born. Emer seemed off to me, her anxiety ratcheted up as she fixated on whether Carla was gaining enough weight, and she admonished herself for not feeding her often enough. I exchanged a glance with Monica, who seemed unsure of whether this was something to worry about. A month later, I stopped by again and found Emer in bad shape. Monica told me that Emer hadn't slept much in more than a week and that she couldn't stop worrying about Carla. Monica was finally insisting that Emer talk to her doctor. I think there were a few bad months and then, with the help of medication and more childcare, things improved dramatically. The next time I saw them, Emer seemed more like her old self.

The other guests arrive, and the party gets underway. We drink and meet people and chat about weather and real estate. Conor knows a few of Monica's friends since his ex-wife, Bláithín, runs an art gallery in Dublin, and I lose track of him for a while, catching only fleeting glimpses of him across the room.

As I'm looking for him, I see a familiar profile in a group looking at one of Monica's paintings on the other wall. It takes me a minute to recognize him, though, he's so out of context.

It's Fiero, wearing jeans and a blazer, and when he feels me watching him and turns his head, he looks as surprised as I feel. I wave and he grins and does an exaggerated shrug. *Wait, how are we both here?* Suddenly, I'm self-conscious in my short black dress, its low back revealing more skin than I'm used to showing.

I'm on my way over to say hello when Monica and Emer, holding Carla, shout to get everyone's attention, and Emer says she wants to give a toast. She holds her glass in the air and says, "To Monica, my favorite artist, my partner in life and parenthood and all things, I'm so proud of you and all you've accomplished. Sláinte!"

Monica raises her own glass and says, "Thank you, love. I am feeling especially lucky tonight as I look around at all of our wonderful friends and family, and I'm so happy to be celebrating the show with you and Carla. Actually, we've been very sneaky here. We are celebrating the show, but we have another happy announcement to make as well. A few weeks ago, I asked Emer to marry me, and she said yes!" The room erupts in applause and congratulations and they hug and kiss each other, Carla in the middle, and then we all drink a toast before Monica announces she's taking Carla up to bed.

"I'm so happy for you," I tell Emer when she comes over to the group of people I'm standing with. "It's so exciting."

"It'll be you and Conor next," she whispers, looking around for him, but I don't see him in the crowd.

"Well, the house renovation may kill us first, so don't get your hopes up," I joke. Wanting to change the subject, I point to Fiero. "How do you know him?"

She looks. "Who? The fella who looks like a guard? I don't know him at all."

"He *is* a guard. But what's he doing here if you don't know him?" We both watch as he bends down to say something to the red-haired woman standing next to him. She laughs.

"Oh, he must be Jenny's date," Emer says. "She works with me. She split up with her husband last year and she's been doing online dating. I think she said she was excited about someone she'd met. That must be him. You work with him?"

"Yeah, he's coming over. Pretend we weren't just talking about them."

"Maggie," Fiero says as he approaches us. I introduce him to Emer, and she introduces us to the woman standing next to me— she's a painter—and tells her we're both guards who have been working on the Laurel Maguire case.

"It's mad, isn't it?" the painter says. "That someone could just kill her mother, take her out of the apartment, and escape with no one seeing them. Then drop her off and get away? I mean, we're not that large a country. He couldn't have made it onto a ferry or something, could he?"

I push down a little bit of irritation. It sounds like criticism of the guards, though she's absolutely right. It *is* mad no one saw him. It *is* mad we haven't caught him yet. The scowl on Fiero's face tells me he's annoyed, too.

"I've worked with Dylan Maguire a bit," one of the men says. "Talented fella." He turns to his wife, who works with Emer at a software company with a fancy office in the Docklands area of the city. "He did a website for Donna's business. Remember? She was quite happy, I think. Poor man, it must have been terrifying."

I resist the urge to say that Dylan seems to be fine. I'm conscious of my dislike of him, but of course I have no good reason for it. He *has* been through something terrible. By all accounts he was overjoyed to be reunited with Laurel. Roly told me that he couldn't stop crying and thanking them over and over when they told him she was safe.

"I couldn't believe it when I realized that poor girl was the one from that *Star Model* show," the guy who worked with Dylan says. "I had no idea he had a baby with her. How did *that* happen, I wonder?"

"I never watched it, but my little sister was really into it," the painter says. "She decided *she* was going to be a model, too. I think Jade was her favorite. It's drivel, of course. She insisted on showing me clips from it. It was always just the girls saying shite about each other and dramatic camera angles."

"Jade Elliott, she was lovely though," Emer says. "I saw some of her shots in the papers. Reza, did you ever meet her or work with her?" I remember she said that the English guy standing next to me now is a photographer.

"Nah, I don't think she did the kind of jobs I do," he says diplomatically. I know what he's saying, though: *Jade wasn't a high-class model like the ones I work with.*

"Have you ever met anyone from the Delaney Agency?" Fiero asks him, interested now. "They represented her."

The photographer hesitates. "Not directly, but I know who they are."

Something in his voice makes me ask, "What do you think of them?"

"Eh . . ." He pauses, then says, "I've heard of them refusing to pay photographers a few times. I don't know anything specific." He thinks a moment. "I was warned off working with them, when I first came to Ireland. I can't remember who it was. Have you met them?"

I'm conscious of Fiero listening. I don't answer his question. "What do you mean that they refused to pay photographers?" I'm thinking now of the financial arrangement the agency seems to have had with Jade.

"Just a rumor," he says. "A friend of mine did some portfolio work for them and they refused to pay. I can't remember the details." He hesitates. "I met Delaney once. Struck me as a bit of a grifter, if I'm honest. The modeling industry in Ireland is fairly new, so there's room for bad behavior. Not a lot of competition. But word gets around. You don't think they had anything to do with the murder and the abduction of the little girl, do you?"

"We're just looking at everyone she knew," Fiero says, a bit too forcefully.

Conor comes over and when I introduce him to Fiero, he says, "I think we met down in West Cork," before Fiero's date whisks him away to a different conversation.

"When is your book coming out, Conor?" Emer asks. "Have there been any reviews yet?"

Conor blanches and says, "March. Yeah, they're just starting to come in," but before anyone can ask him anything more about it, I say, "We've had a mystery at our house," and tell them about the photographs of Clara hidden in the wall.

"It must be someone who lived in your house," Monica says. "But why would they have hidden them in the wall?"

"That's the question, isn't it?" Conor says. "Maggie's daughter thinks there was an illicit love affair. Whoever hid the photos had to keep their passion for Clara a secret for some reason."

"How intriguing," Monica says. "So you don't know anything about her?"

I say, "Well, one of the photos has an address on Stamer Street written on it, so we're thinking she may have lived there at some point. It's funny, the house is for sale now so I got some more information about it from the property agent. It looks like the family that's selling has owned it for a long time. Their name was Crowe, but she didn't think there was a Clara."

"I was raised around there," says the guy who came with Monica's painter friend. "There was a market called Crowe's on the corner, I think. I'll have to ask my brothers. May be the same one."

"Who knows what else you'll find as they're working on the house," Emer says.

"I hope photographs are the extent of it," Conor says. "The job's already going pretty slowly."

I'm coming out of the bathroom later when I run into Fiero outside Emer and Monica's bedroom holding what I presume is his date's coat and purse.

"You getting out of here?" I ask, enjoying the way he blushes and nods and then looks away.

"What'd you think about what that photographer said?" he asks, his eyes flicking up to look for his date, who is standing near the door looking antsy.

"It's worth looking into," I tell him. "The financial stuff with the agency, it's weird. I feel like there's something there. But I'm off the investigation, so . . ." I shrug.

"Right," he says. "Well, maybe we'll get that car tomorrow." He studies me for a long moment, and I have the sense he wants to say something else. Finally, he nods. "Good night then."

I watch him go, handing the coat and purse to his date as she smiles up at him flirtatiously. She says something that makes him smile and put his hand on her waist, running it down over her hip, and then they're gone. Feeling off-kilter now, I go to find Conor.

We stay to help clean up and the conversation turns to the uncertain timelines of construction projects, and then to what seems to be a perennial conversation topic at dinner parties these days: the intricacies of Dublin's out-of-control real estate market. I think again about the job ahead of Conor and me, finding something we like, making the sales, lining up the financing, moving, getting to know a new neighborhood. I feel an immediate wave of exhaustion.

Emer, glowing from the wine she's had and, I think, the success of the party, talks about her work and how crazy it's been since she went back after her maternity leave. "I like being back but I'm so fucking tired all the time," she says. "Carla never sleeps, but she's so lovely I can't ever be mad at her. It's good to be back though, get my brain working again, and our nanny's perfect, Silvia. She's teaching Carla Spanish." She smiles broadly and I can see the relief on Monica's face as she reaches over and rubs Emer's shoulder, smiling at her and then brushing a piece of hair from her cheek. I think about Jade Elliott suddenly, what it must have been like going through those early months with financial support from Dylan but not the love and emotional support you really need when you're making the adjustment to being a parent.

"I just think about that poor woman," Emer says, nodding to me. "She must have been trying to protect her baby, keep it from being taken. And they killed her. It's really horrible. I didn't want to take Carla to the playground the last few days, you know?"

"Well," Monica says. "I've been going to the gym again, so if anyone tries anything on us, I will come out swinging. I'm protecting my family!" Emer smiles and reaches out to squeeze her shoulder.

"You'd do anything for them, wouldn't you?" Conor says quietly.

"They tell you that, but you don't really understand it until you're there," Monica says, putting her arm around Emer. When I first met Monica, I wasn't sure I liked her, whereas Conor clicked with her right away. She has an artist's moodiness, extroverted one minute, disappearing into herself the next, and I worried that Emer was more invested in the relationship than she was. But since Carla was born, during Emer's struggles, Monica's shown such fierce and steadfast love for her and Carla that I've done a 180-degree turn in my opinion of her.

Somewhere, deep inside my brain, something thrums, an insistent pull at an idea that's been brewing there but is still just out of reach. What was it that Nicola Keating said? *She didn't plan it, but she loved Laurel. She would have done anything for her.*

Is that why Jade Elliott died? Because she was willing to do anything to protect her child?

Conor's quiet on the walk home. I battle with myself for a bit, and then I squeeze his hand and say, "When I got home last night I saw the review on your computer. I wasn't sure if you'd want me to say anything, but I can't not say anything, you know?"

He looks over, surprised, and then smiles sadly. "I was hoping it would be a good one. This book is . . . It took so long to write, and I thought it might be the one that really took off. It's not about the money or the sales figures or anything like that. It's just that . . . Everyone I know will see that review. When I go out to talk about it, everyone will have read it."

"I know. But they're going to read the book and then they'll see how amazing it is. And they'll see how wrong that reviewer is. Fuck the reviewers. The book is terrific." I lean in, hugging him awkwardly while we walk.

"Thank you, Maggie." But he's still distracted and of course, it doesn't matter what I think. I'm just a cop. What do I know about writing books?

"Nice party," he says after a bit. "I'm happy for Emer and Monica."

"Me too." I smile up at him in the darkness. But it suddenly feels like there's a universe of unspoken words between us. I think about Emer's comment about Conor and I getting engaged soon. We've tried to stay in the moment, to get Lilly and me settled in Dublin and ease Conor and Adrien into sharing their house, and we haven't talked much about the future. But renovating the house in preparation for selling it means we need to buy something else. Buying something else raises all kinds of questions about whether we'll buy it together and how that will work and what we're doing here anyway . . . I can feel my heart start to race. Seeing Fiero and talking about the case didn't help any. I'm suddenly swamped by anxiety.

We walk home in silence.

Seventeen

The driver of the blue car, whoever they are, lies low through the weekend.

We go for a walk in Wicklow on Sunday, driving down to Blessington with Lilly, Alex, and Adrien and hiking around the lakes in the chilled air, warming up with a pub lunch on the way home. I read the papers while Conor makes dinner. There haven't been any developments, except for nine possible sightings of a man with a toddler driving a blue car in various locations around the country in the days before Laurel was returned. I figure most of them are bullshit, but I think of Roly and Fiero and the team, running them down, searching the registration details if they have them, trying to see if any of them are solid.

Conor's making dinner when my phone rings and I see my friend Griz's number on the screen. I take my wine out into the back garden so I can talk without being overheard. "Griz, how are you?" I ask. "You got a break on your case?"

I hear her sigh. "I wish," she says. "I'm actually in Spain right now, looking into someone. This one is horrible though, Maggie. We know exactly who did it, we just can't prove it. We still haven't turned up the gun and no one is talking to us."

"Well, your investigation gave us a hit," I tell her, updating her on the phone number in Jade Elliott's calls.

"That's why I'm calling actually. Geoff told me about the number. You got anything on Cameron Murphy? I'm looking for leverage I can use to get him to talk. We think he might know something."

A bird alights on a tree next to me and calls a short sharp warning. I wave my hand to quiet it. "He wrapped up in your homicide?" A gangland hit seems above Cameron's pay grade to me.

"No, but he might know who is. Any chance he's your guy?"

"I don't see how he could have had the kid." I tell her about the blue car. "And he's been around the neighborhood the last few days. But there's obviously some connection between them we haven't uncovered yet. You'll have to ask Roly about it though. I'm back on patrol tomorrow."

I think I've managed to keep the resentment out of my voice, but she says, "Sorry, I know it feels crap. But you'll be up with us in no time, right? Sounds like you're doing well. Listen, I've got to go. But I'll talk to you soon, yeah?"

There's good news Monday morning.

A Roads Policing unit officer was heading eastbound on the M7 yesterday when he saw a bright blue Opel Astra with a white driver's side door driving too fast in the westbound lane. He wasn't able to get a registration plate by the time it passed but he thought there was a single male occupant of the car. He found a turnaround and tried to follow, but by the time he was able to reverse directions, the car had exited the motorway and was nowhere to be found. Other units in the area also tried to find it but had no luck. They're busy looking at CCTV footage though, and they're hoping they can find it somewhere else and get a clear picture of the registration plate.

My shift starts at three and I take the car in since Conor doesn't teach today.

I'm heading into the locker room when Geoff Chen calls out to me and hands me a manila envelope. "I ran those searches on known associates yesterday," he says. "No blue cars, but I thought you might want to see what I found anyway. Nothing that jumped out at me, but . . ." He shrugs. "Roly said you're back on patrol but that I should give you a copy anyway."

"That's great. Thanks, Geoff," I say. "I'll have a look later. Anything new on the car?"

"Not yet, but they've got a lot of images to look at, so . . . fingers crossed."

"And the prints?"

"Yeah, they came back the way we thought they would, lots of hers, lots of Laurel's, the sister's, a few from the neighbors who minded Laurel for her. A few we haven't been able to identify, too, so we'll match them against prints in the system."

I thank him and tell him good luck.

Jason and I catch up as we walk our familiar routes. He updates me on what's been happening in the neighborhood, recounts some gossip, and I tell him about the kids and our day in Wicklow.

I can tell he's happy to see me again, and after sparring with Padraig Fiero over the last few days, my easy camaraderie with Jason is a welcome relief.

"Did you miss me?" I ask him as we walk down Longwood Avenue, past one of my favorite street murals.

"Oh, yeah," he says, grinning. "It's been dire."

"Sorry to leave you in the lurch."

"No problem. It's wonderful, isn't it, the little girl being found alive?" He doesn't ask if I know who had her and what was done to her, the way a civilian would.

"It is," I say. "That's almost never the outcome, so it really is wonderful, and sort of a miracle." I tell him what I can about the investigation.

"I saw Alannah O'Reilly the other day," I say as we turn onto the South Circular Road. "She was looking up at Jade Elliott's apartment. At least I think she was. Maybe she's just curious, but I've had the feeling she knows something, you know? Like you said."

"Sorry to disappoint, but I think I've sussed why she's been hanging around the flats."

"Yeah? Why's that?"

"I do believe she's carrying a torch for the young fella, Andy Roden."

I picture Alannah's face, the dark makeup and perpetually pissed-off expression. "How would you know?"

"Overheard her talking to her friend, the Tina one. The blonde. They were walking along from school and I happened to be behind them, minding my own business, thought I'd see what they had to say, and I heard Tina say, 'Have you told Andy you fancy him?' Alannah nearly smacked her, she was that embarrassed. But finally she said, no, she wasn't going to tell him. He only thought of her as a friend, like."

"You were eavesdropping on teenage girls, Jason? I don't know if that's shameful or ingenious."

He grins. "Well, I have sisters, like. I learned a lot listening to them chatting to their mates. Anyway, Tina said maybe she'd tell Andy, and Alannah said, 'Do that and I'll murder ya' and it went on like that for a bit until they went into the chipper."

I have a sudden flashback to my own crushes at that age, the way I would hold the secret until I couldn't anymore, and the rush of humiliation and fear when one of my friends or my cousin Erin mentioned it or threatened to tell.

"Interesting," I say. "If she has a crush on Andy Roden, she may have been hanging around Canal Landing more than we realized. She may have seen something or known Jade better than she let on."

"Yeah." Jason thinks for a moment. "Did I tell you I was patrolling with an older fella, was on this beat a few years ago. Said he knows Alannah's da. He's a bad one, in and out of jail for drug offenses, beating up her mother. Mother's had her own run-ins with the Gardaí. Poor kid. It makes sense why she's so distrustful of us. Will we not have a wander up to the school at three?" he asks me, a little smile on his face. "We can see if she's in a talkative mood."

"Sounds good." But we get involved in helping an elderly man find his way back to his daughter's house, and by the time we've made sure she's home and he's safe, it's after four.

We walk down Richmond Street to Camden Street, keeping an eye out for purse snatchers. There have been quite a few lately, teenagers jostling older women in shops and then yanking their bags away and taking off toward the city center. We have a few of them on CCTV and we have a pretty good sense of who's doing it, but no one's been able to catch them so far. We stop in at the shops where they seem to like to work, making ourselves visible, checking in with the shopkeepers about anything they've seen.

On the racks outside a newsagent, I see the screaming headlines:

BABY LAUREL ALIVE. GARDA INVESTIGATION CONTINUES. The more low-brow publications speculate about who had her, with headlines like PEDO NIGHTMARE? HOW WILL THEY FIND HER KIDNAPPER?

Out on the street, a misty rain is hovering, not sure yet if it wants to fall or not.

We walk the whole neighborhood, stopping for sandwiches at eight, and then get back at it, walking past the pubs that are the usual sources of trouble, checking in with the waiters to see if they need any help. And then we're passing a pub on Camden Street when Cameron Murphy comes running out, swearing loudly, standing by the door for a moment as though he's trying to decide whether to go back in.

"Everything all right then, Cameron?" Jason asks him.

He whips around. "Ah, yeah, guards. Just having a jar with some friends in there. Me mate was talking shite, but I'm going to let it go. That's the way, isn't it? *Let it go, let it go.*"

"You a fan of Disney musicals, Cameron?"

"Love 'em," he says, winking at me. The Sylvester and Tweety Bird tattoo is so incongruous with the rest of his persona that I have to try not to laugh at him.

Jason nods toward the door of the pub, an unspoken direction to me to check inside and make sure there's no more trouble while he talks to Cameron. "Now, Cameron, tell me all about it," he says gently. "Your friend was giving you a hard time, yeah?"

At the bar, I nod to one of the barmen and lean over to ask, "Cameron behaving himself?" Jason and I have helped him out a few times and he's returned the favor by giving us some tips on guys he thinks are dealing drugs, including Cameron.

"Ah, yeah," he says. "They were arguing about a video game, I think. He did well to take himself out of it. He didn't seem like himself tonight."

"How do you mean?"

"He was a bit maudlin, like. The other lads were giving out to him about it."

"Good." I'm about to leave when I think of something. "You know this murder we're looking at, right? You ever see Jade Elliott in here? She ever come in with anyone?"

"Few times. I only knew who she was from that show. It would have been a year or so ago though. Not recently. That lot gave her a hard time and she left on her own." He gestures to the group of guys Cameron was with.

"Okay, thanks." I nod toward the door. "Let us know if he comes back and starts making trouble. We won't be far."

Jason's alone once I get outside, and when I ask where Cameron went, he says they had a chat and that he's now off home. We hang around for a bit, just to make sure he doesn't come back and then walk down toward the canal. Without revealing anything about Griz's investigation or the number on Jade's phone, I ask him if he thinks Cameron could have been connected to Jade Elliott.

"Romantically, like?" he asks incredulously. I understand the reaction. The image of lovely Jade and scrawny, seedy Cameron is kind of funny.

"I don't know." I raise my eyebrows. "Or maybe a business relationship?"

"Well, he didn't take the little girl," he says. "He's been around the neighborhood more than usual lately. Seems he's there every time I turn around."

"Maybe she bought drugs from him."

"You find any among her belongings?" he asks. "If she was buying from Cameron Murphy, she must have been fairly far down that road."

"No." I can't tell him about the cash. "She might have been working for him, though."

"Maybe." Jason shrugs, but even as I say it, it doesn't feel likely to me. We cross Lennox Street and head north and he says, "So they think this fella in Navan, your one in the blue car, was just some pedo?"

"Yeah. I guess. We won't know for sure until we get him, but it does seem that way."

"It's awful to think of it, isn't it, some disturbed fella, walking around, watching for little girls."

An image of Nigel Canning flashes into my mind and I shiver. I wonder if anyone's thought to check to make sure he doesn't have a blue Opel Astra.

Jason hesitates, then says, "Do you know anything about Saturday night, when we responded? Do they think we missed something when we were there? I've been stewing over it a bit."

I turn to him and catch his guilty downcast expression. He's probably been worrying about this since we found Jade's body. "Don't worry about that, Jason. We did the best we could with what we had, and we haven't even found the person who reported it. It *was* just the TV probably. In fact, maybe we'll head over to Canal Landing and ask the property manager if he's remembered anything else about it." I shouldn't be questioning witnesses, but we could have a casual conversation and see if anything comes of it.

We're heading that way when a call comes in on the radio for assistance at the pub down the street. We leg it down there but by the time we arrive, the source of the trouble is already gone.

"Let me guess, Cameron Murphy?" Jason asks.

The barman is an old guy who's worked there forever. Jason remembers him from his own childhood and they have a good rapport. "That's right. He was on a right tear about something, ranting and raving to that fella over there." He points to another young guy drinking in the corner. "Real aggro, like, even for Cam."

"You spent a lot of time in there as a kid?" I ask Jason once we've told the barman to call it in if Cameron comes back.

"Fair bit. I'd go with my da and he'd let me sit and listen while he talked with his friends. Learned just as much that way as I did listening to my sisters and their friends."

I scan the houses and shops along the street. "Hey," I say. "You remember a market in the neighborhood owned by a family named Crowe?"

Jason thinks for a moment. "Yeah, though I think it had closed by the time I was born. But it was painted on the side of the building, like. Crowe's Grocer, I think. It must have been down around Richmond Street. We're nearly there, aren't we? I'll show you." We walk up to Richmond Street, relatively quiet on a Monday night. "I think it was just along . . . Ah, yeah, look, there it is. Funny how things sort of disappear into the background, isn't it? I hadn't seen that in a while."

Jason points up to the side of a brick building where faded white letters spell out J. CROWE GROCER. They're so faint I wouldn't have noticed them if he hadn't pointed them out. The building now houses an Argentinian restaurant and, on the second and third floors, flats. I take a picture with my phone so I can show Conor and we head back out on patrol.

Bobby Egan has a small studio apartment on the first floor of Canal Landing, and when he answers the door, an expression of alarm crosses his face. "Don't worry, nothing else has happened," I say. "We just want to ask if you've remembered anything about the tenant who knocked on your door to report they'd heard a woman screaming."

He doesn't ask us in but he nods and says, "I really haven't. There's not much to remember. Like I told you, I was having my meal and someone knocked on the door and yelled out, 'Hey, the lady in 201 is screaming her head off. Call the guards.' By the time I opened the door there wasn't anyone there. I rang you lot. That's it."

"You said you couldn't tell if the voice was male or female. Is that still true?"

"Yeah, it was deep, like, but still . . . I couldn't say to ya if it was male or female. I know that sounds strange, but . . ." He shrugs and we thank him and go back out the car park.

"Does that ring true to you?" I ask Jason. "That he couldn't tell?"

"Maybe. I mean, it could have been someone disguising their voice, right?"

"Or kids pretending," I say. "The one thing we haven't considered is that it was kids playing a joke on him."

"Oh, god," Jason says. "You think they were messing? That's all it was?"

"Maybe."

We're rounding the corner by Canal Landing when Jason takes my arm and points to the top of the wall around the vacant lot. A thin stream of smoke curls above the wall and he raises his eyebrows and leads the way to the gap in the corrugated metal where I slipped in the last time I was here.

Cameron Murphy, Alannah, Tina, Andy Roden, and a few other teens I've seen around the neighborhood are standing against the wall, smoking and laughing. Until they look up and see us, that is.

"Uh, hello, guards," Cameron calls out sheepishly. "Just having the chats here."

"Cameron," Jason calls out. "Did you not tell me you were going home? What happened?"

Cameron throws us a little-boy-caught-with-his-hand-in-the-cookie-jar smile. "I remembered there was a fella I had to see about something in there, so I just stopped for one. No harm done, though, guards. Then I stopped for a smoke with this lot."

"This lot are all minors. Will you go home now? If you keep this up, we have no objection to charging you tonight." Jason manages to make it sound threatening and a bit nurturing at the same time.

"Okay, I will, guard," Cameron says a bit sadly. "It's cold in my flat though. I just thought a jar or two would help me sleep." The look I give him makes him put his hands up again. "Okay, okay, I'm going."

I follow him out of the vacant lot and stop him as he turns toward the canal. "Hang on," I say. "I just want to ask you something. The woman who was killed last week, Jade Elliott. You knew her from around the neighborhood?"

He looks up. He's less drunk than he'd seemed at first and I think he's calculating, making decisions about how much to tell me. "Yeah, a little," he says. "Used to see her around. Have a chat and a smoke."

He looks down at the ground, shakes his head, furiously sucking on the cigarette.

"What was your relationship with her, Cameron?"

"I told you. I saw her around sometimes. We'd say hello." He drops the butt on the ground and doesn't bother stamping it out.

"That was it?" I ask.

His face clouds. "You know what *she* looked like. You've got me right in front of you. Yeah, *that was it,* guard." And he stumbles off along the canal, heading west back to Dolphin's Barn, his shoulders down, his body language pure defeat.

Back in the vacant lot, Jason is telling the teens that it's private property. "Stay out of here and stay away from Cameron Murphy. He'll be no help to you, right? Nothing but trouble from that one."

They all nod. Tina flashes us a big, insincere smile and says, "Sorry, guards. We'll go now," and they all start to shuffle toward the entrance, Alannah and Andy at the back.

"Hey," I say. "Before you go, maybe you could help us out a bit. We're still looking for whoever killed the woman who lived up there. Jade." I nod toward Jade's bedroom windows. In the darkness, they reflect the ghostly trees above the canal and the tops of the buildings in Rathmines. "Someone reported that they heard a woman screaming a couple of days before she was killed. Anyone know anything about that?" I ask.

Andy Roden hesitates, then shakes his head and turns his body to slide past me, casting a last look at Alannah and Tina as he leaves the lot.

"Sorry, guards," Tina says.

"Yeah," one of the other boys says. "Sorry." Alannah starts to follow but I say, "Alannah, hang on a minute, will you? I found something of yours."

The other kids file out and go off in different directions, but Alannah, trapped between me and Jason, doesn't have a choice but to wait. She throws us a dirty look and says, "I need to go, too."

"You're in the flats up on Bride Street, aren't you, Alannah?" Jason says kindly. "Sure, we're walking up that way as well. We'll see you home. It's getting late."

She looks horrified. "You don't have to," she says. "I can get home on my own."

"No trouble at all." Jason gestures for her to go first and she reluctantly goes, ducking out of the vacant lot.

I take the bandana out of my vest pocket and hand it over to her. "That's yours, isn't it?" She takes it, nodding, and I follow up with, "I found it in there. You spend a lot of time in there, don't you?"

Her eyes are barely visible behind her dark bangs. "I don't have to tell you," she says. "I know my rights."

"Ah, sure, we just want to know if you've seen anything while you're in there," Jason says. "It looks right up at Jade Elliott's window."

She glances up at him and I think she's going to tell us something, but then she shakes her head and keeps walking, a few steps ahead of us, her shoulders and head down. She's wearing black fishnet stockings under her skirt and one of them has a large rip in the right calf.

The walk up to the Bride Street flats takes ten minutes, a straight shot up to the older social housing complexes that now sit like islands in the middle of all the new developments, a throwback to an older Dublin. As we get closer, I can see the few residents still out on the streets watching us approach. Alannah doesn't want to be seen with us and I'm willing to make her sweat a bit. If she thinks Jason and I might come back and embarrass her some more until she tells us what she knows, she might tell us a bit quicker.

Alannah's block is the one closest to the Garda station. Someone's spray-painted "Locals Only" on the side of a wall, and just outside the entrance to the first block of flats, someone else has written "Fuck the Police."

"Lovely," Jason says. "Very nice."

"Don't take it personally, like," she says, pointing to the sign. "It's from a rap song."

"Ah, yeah," Jason says. "Thanks."

"Alannah," I start. "Did you know Jade Elliott?"

She scowls and nods. "I saw her around, like. With her baby. She was a slag, wasn't she? No offense since she's dead and all." She looks at me. "You know what a slag is? Americans have slags over there, too?"

"Yes. I do. Why do you say that? What makes you use that word?"

Now she looks embarrassed. "Only, she had that baby with your man, the computer fella. Then she kicked him out and she had other fellas over, too."

Jason throws me a meaningful glance.

"Like who?" I ask.

She looks down at the ground, doesn't say anything.

"Did you know Dylan Maguire?" I ask her. "'The computer fella'?"

"No, I just saw his picture online." She looks up at the flats. A woman is watching us from a balcony on the third floor. She's holding a glass in one hand and a phone in the other and she's wearing a pink, fuzzy bathrobe and slippers. She looks furious. "Alannah," she calls out. "Get up here now!"

"Alannah, what aren't you telling us?" I ask.

When her eyes flash up to meet mine, wide and lined all the way around with black eyeliner, I can see that she's scared. "I have to go," she mutters.

I lower my voice. "A woman was killed, Alannah. If you know something, you need to tell us." I can hear the desperation in my voice. "There could be someone out there who's dangerous. If you're afraid of someone, if you're afraid of Cameron or someone else, we can protect you."

"I have to go." She hesitates, though, hovering there for a second before hoisting the backpack onto her shoulder and walking quickly toward the entrance, her head down and her shoulders hunched, as though that will stop her neighbors from recognizing her. I can't help thinking about Cameron Murphy, about how Jade's death has rippled out, causing trouble for him and for Alannah, for reasons I haven't figured out yet.

That's your job, Maggie. Figuring that out is your job.

Eighteen

....

It rains in the night but has mostly stopped by the time I wake up at seven, leaving the trees around the house dripping and the streets a shiny dark gray.

Today marks four days since Laurel Maguire was dropped at the Happy Fairies Crèche and a week since the discovery of Jade's body. The newspapers are starting to ask why we haven't found the man in the blue Opel yet.

GARDÁI STYMIED IN BABY LAUREL MANHUNT, a headline reads. WHERE IS HE? LOCALS ASK.

My shift doesn't start until three, so after the kids and Conor—downcast and snapping at Adrien and Lilly for leaving dishes in the sink—are out of the house, I clean up a bit and then drink my coffee at the kitchen table while I check my email. Gerry and his crew arrive at nine, so I take my laptop and bag and coffee into Conor's study and close the door, putting on headphones to drown out the sounds of drills and saws.

I have a message from Uncle Danny about his Christmas visit; he and his girlfriend, Eileen, have bought plane tickets and he's making lists of things he wants to make sure to do while they're here. I write him back and then I'm looking through my computer bag when I find the folder Geoff Chen gave me with the searches for all of the

KAs, or known associates, of Jade Elliott, cross-referenced with car registrations, plus the background searches the floaters did right after Jade's body was found. I have nothing else to read so I take a look, finding the names of Jade's neighbors, her family members, Dylan Maguire's coworkers, and his family members as well.

As Geoff said, nothing jumps out. None of them have registered a blue Opel. I flip through the background research. The Rodens don't have any notable encounters with the law amongst them, though Andy Roden has been disciplined at school a few times, the file notes, for poor attendance and mouthing off to teachers. Phil Roden worked for a city software firm until recently, had a clean employment record, and then more recently took a job with a different company, a software start-up. I recognize the name of the new company as one that was recently featured in *The Irish Times* for securing a huge round of funding. Whoever did the legwork got his salary details and it's twice what either Conor or I make. Gail Roden is a well-respected nurse at the Coombe Hospital. It sounds like they're moving up in the world.

And their kid is skipping school and cursing out teachers.

The Phillipses seem to be clean, too, though they were once sued by a builder working on their apartment for nonpayment.

Denise Valentine has been working as an accountant for ten years. Just before she got the job, she was at fault in a bad car accident that paralyzed a young woman from Navan, I'm interested to see. She wasn't prosecuted in the end, though. But . . . it's there. Navan.

Also in the file are details about Dylan Maguire's parents. He has four siblings, a brother from his father's first marriage to Dylan's mother named Colm Maguire, no record, and then three half-siblings—Cliona, Jane, and Nora, no records there—who are all in their twenties. Dylan's not in our system and has never been charged with a crime.

Nicola Keating's husband, Hugh, works as an electrician and their boys are twelve, ten, and eight. His parents are no longer alive and he has a younger brother and two half sisters, from his father's second marriage. I read the names: Alan Keating, Jenny Keating, Alice Keating, none of them with criminal records or anything of note.

I go back to Dylan Maguire. He studied computer science and design at a university in France and worked for a few large technology companies with Irish headquarters before starting a company called DM Design, which then became Red Rocket Media in 2009, right in the midst of the recession.

Despite his timing, he seems to have been very successful; Red Rocket Media won numerous European design awards and is on some list of "Top 100 Irish Web Design Companies."

Roly told me that Fiero checked in with all of Dylan Maguire's employees and that there weren't any inconsistencies in his story. The people who worked for him all said that he seemed to be a devoted father, if frustrated that he didn't get more time with Laurel. He had brought her into the office a few times and they'd all loved meeting her. When he asked them about Jade, they said they didn't really know her, and that Dylan didn't talk about her much. It seems pretty straightforward.

A morning news digest comes through on my phone, with a breaking news alert at the top: *Gardaí are involved in an operation in Kildare this morning. Sources say it may be related to the abduction of a Dublin child.* I get up and turn on the radio. The RTÉ announcer is saying, "No word yet on whether this operation by the Garda Roads

Policing Unit is connected to the abduction of Laurel Maguire, the Dublin toddler who was found safe on Friday after being taken from the scene of her mother's death last week."

I text Roly. Something happening? but he doesn't text back. A few of the online news sites have the same story. Nothing else.

I get more coffee and get out my case notes and scan through them to distract myself, then take out the records from the Delaney Agency to see if I can find an account of what Jade was paid for the show. We need to get a full picture of her finances and where all of the money in her account came from. Fiona Creedon printed two things for me: a list of all of the modeling jobs that Jade did when she was represented by the agency, and then a record of all of the money she earned and what was paid out to her.

I settle down with the stacks of paper and see evidence of what Nicola Keating told me about how they handled Jade's earnings. From the very beginning of Jade's modeling career, the Delaney Agency advanced payments to her and Eileen, fifty euros here, fifty euros there, more as the years went on, all with the notation, "AD-VANCE." Eileen seems to have used Jade's modeling career as her own personal ATM.

When I look at the dates of the jobs she took on, they end, just as Fiona Creedon said, in February of 2016, right when she would have discovered she was pregnant with Laurel. There's nothing else until July 10 of this year, when there's a notation in the record reading "Agency agreement terminated."

Fiona said that Jade just stopped working when she got pregnant. But why did she formally terminate the agreement this past summer? There's nothing to explain it in the list of her last few bookings before Laurel was born, as far as I can see. But then I think about what Elizabeth Ruane said. Jade was possibly having business meetings around the time she ended her business relationship with the Delaney Agency. In order to work with another agency or to take on modeling jobs without giving a cut to Fiona Creedon and her partner, she had to be contractually free.

Suddenly, I remember the money at Eileen's house. Jade was there in July.

July. She ended her agreement with the agency and then she hid six thousand euros in Eileen's bathroom.

Is there a connection there?

I go into the kitchen to get another cup of coffee, dodging Gerry and his workmen and returning to Conor's office with my warm mug. I need to go back to the agency and find out why Jade terminated her contract.

I text Roly the outlines of what I'm thinking and by the time I'm dressed and out of the shower, he's texted me back: Jaysus. Incident room 1 hour. I can practically hear the sigh coming through my phone.

Gerry, wielding an electric drill in the living room, is the only person who sees my gigantic grin.

The incident room is buzzing by the time I get there. Even if I hadn't seen the news alert, I would have known there's been a development. Roly sees me and waves me over. He and Fiero are sitting in front of a large monitor, looking at CCTV footage, traffic at a roundabout, it looks like. Fiero nods at me, but I can't tell if he's going to acknowledge running into each other outside of work, so I don't say anything about it.

"What's going on?" I ask them. "I heard something on the radio about an operation in Kildare?"

"They got the car," Fiero says. His eyes are shining and he's got the unmistakable look of a cop who's caught a break. I can't help wondering if his night with Emer's coworker is contributing to his good mood, too. "They caught it on a camera on an M7 roundabout and got the reg plate. It had a white door that had been replaced but not painted yet. Name on the reg is Mark Hanlon, from Navan. An armed response unit went over this morning, but get this: the house was empty. Turns out Mark Hanlon is dead."

"What?"

"Yeah. He was eighty-fucking-three years old. The door was because he was getting wobbly and sideswiped another car not long before he died. But they tracked his son down through the neighbors. His name is Michael Hanlon and he lives in Canada. Toronto. He's a plumber over there and he hasn't been in Ireland since his father died in May. He had to get back for work and didn't have time to deal with the house, so it's been empty, the car in the drive and the keys neatly hung on a hook in the kitchen."

I see it right away. "Someone knew the house was empty and used the car to take Laurel. Is that where she was? At the house?"

"They think so," Roly says, sighing. "They're processing it right now. No sign of the car though. Fiero's going to start checking Hanlon's friends and contacts, try to figure out who knew the house was empty. Now, what's this about the money?"

I tell them about the fact that Jade had formally ended her

relationship with the agency. "She may have been planning on working again," I say. "Did she need to end her agreement with the Delaney Agency because she was going to work for someone else?" As I ask the question, I'm aware of how unimportant it sounds, especially in light of the news about the Hanlons and the empty house. I want to explain to them the feeling I got when I found the money at Eileen's, the same feeling I had looking over the records from the agency, the sense I have that Jade was somehow desperate, that she needed money for something.

Fiero leans back against a desk, discounting my words with a quick wave of his hand. "And? I don't see what you're getting at."

"Why was she doing it secretly?" I ask them. "We don't know what she did to get the cash, but she seemed to be trying to raise more, right? Elizabeth Ruane said she thought Jade might be having business meetings. If she was going out on interviews, maybe she was trying to start modeling again, right? All of that seems to me to indicate she was raising money . . . for something. Dylan was supporting her, so was it for something she didn't want him to know about? We need to know what it was."

"For what?" Fiero screws up his face in an expression of sarcastic disbelief. "What does this have to do with anything? We have our fella! He's driving all over Ireland right now in a blue Opel Astra with a white door!"

"Now, now," Roly says, putting up a hand. "Hear her out there, Pat. What do you think she was raising money for, D'arcy?"

"Maybe it's related to the custody situation," I say. "She was raising money for a solicitor. It would provide a motive. Dylan Maguire found out she was going to try to prevent him from spending more time with Laurel."

"Why would she do that?" Roly asks. "Everyone we talked to said he was a good father."

"Maybe there's something they don't know about." My voice is too loud. I sound desperate to come up with something.

"Maybe she didn't want him to get custody because then she'd lose her cash pipeline!" Fiero says angrily.

I force myself not to react to that. "Someone was going to call around to solicitors in the city to see if she'd been trying to hire any of them. Did anything come of that?" I ask.

"I don't think so, but I'll check, D'arcy."

"And what about the prints they got from the apartment? Geoff said there were some they couldn't assign. Have you got them?" I'm angry, frustrated, and it comes through in the question.

Roly looks a little hurt by my tone. "Not yet. Geoff was checking on that, but I don't think so. What do you think, Fiero?"

Fiero makes a snorting sound. "We don't have any indication that Dylan Maguire is a suspect here. If anything, he seems like a decent enough fella to me. He cares about his daughter and he was in France when Jade was killed. I just don't see it. And we've got the car. Somehow, somewhere, there's a connection between that car and Jade Elliott and her friends and family. That's where all our energy should go, not on fucking Dylan Maguire."

This time I can't keep the rage from rising in my throat. "Why? Because he doesn't seem the type? Because guys like him don't kill women they're involved with?" I don't realize I'm standing up and pointing at him until I see Roly's face and I step back and put my hands down at my side.

Fiero blanches. "Jaysus. No. Because you don't have any evidence that he's done anything wrong. I don't know why you have such a thing about him. I was in Lyon. I talked to everyone at that conference. There is no possible way that he came back to Ireland to kill Jade and take his daughter."

"He could have hired someone!" I almost shout. "He could have paid someone else to do it! This guy, the guy in the Opel, it may be someone who Dylan Maguire hired to kill Jade and take Laurel. It tracks, Fiero, you know it does. Dropping her off at the crèche like that? It's exactly what Maguire would have had the guy do if it was him."

"D'arcy." Roly glares at me. "That's enough." He runs a hand through his hair and thinks for a minute, and then he says, "She's got something there though. Go talk to the agency. Fiero, you go with her while we wait for news on the car. Get some more information about why she terminated her contract and see if they know anything. If we need to bring them in and take a statement, we will. That's it though. Come right back after and check in with me."

I'm still so angry at Fiero I can only nod. We walk out together without saying a word.

This time, there are two people waiting on the elegant velvet sofas in the reception area of the Delaney Agency. A young woman, model thin and heavily made up, looks up as we come in and, when she gets a look at Fiero in his jacket, she straightens her shoulders and sticks out her chest. The guy sitting next to her gives us a nod and then goes back to the glossy magazine he's reading.

"Can I help you?" It's the same receptionist who was working the other day.

"We need to talk to Ms. Creedon and Mr. Delaney," I tell her.

The receptionist, wearing a black dress with sleeves shaped like ornamental gourds, looks panicked. "Well, I think Ms. Creedon is in a meeting."

"This is very important," I say. "We'll just go through. It won't take long."

"But . . ." she says weakly. I'm already through the door, though, and the last thing I see is the guy's startled face above the model on the magazine cover. Fiero follows me.

In fact, Fiona is not on the phone and when she sees us, an unmistakable look of panic crosses her face. "Detective D'arcy. Is everything okay?" she asks, standing up.

I don't bother to correct her. "Hi. This is my colleague, Detective Fiero," I tell her. "We're still investigating Jade's death and a few things have come up in our investigations that we need to ask you about." I sit down in the chair across from her desk and get out the records she printed for me. Fiero stands and it makes her nervous; she's not sure if she should stand or sit. "You told me that Jade stopped modeling when she got pregnant. But it indicates here that she actually terminated her agreement with the agency on July tenth of this year. Is that correct?"

She's flustered, but she finally sits down and says, "I said she hadn't worked with us since she became a mother."

"But this is very different. Why did she end the contract? Was there a disagreement?"

"No, I . . . As I told you, she just wasn't interested in working once she had a child." A quick glance down at the desk.

I point to the paper. "But that doesn't make sense. If that was the case, she would have just let it go. Said no to jobs, ignored your calls. Why would she end the relationship formally?"

Fiona looks down at the page, scanning it as though she'll find an answer there. "To be honest, I don't know exactly. But sometimes, there are ... certain disputes and it makes sense, for everyone's sake, to formally end the relationship."

Fiero speaks up. "What kind of disputes?"

"Well, financial sometimes." Her gaze lingers on him for a second and I find myself hoping he's smart enough to notice and use it.

He is. He leans forward and pitches his voice down to a sympathetic purr. "What do you mean, Ms. Creedon?"

She makes eye contact with him. "Mal met with her, so I don't know exactly, but I believe she started questioning some of the accounting for her previous work. Her claims were ... unfair. She became upset when Mal didn't apologize, I think. She was angry and terminated the contract."

Time for bad cop. "Why didn't you tell me this the other day?" I ask her.

She tears her eyes away from Fiero. "It didn't seem relevant. Her death is terrible and of course we are so relieved you found her little girl safe, but it doesn't have anything to do with us or her former career."

I stare at her for a second. "I'd like to know more about what she was claiming."

We both hear voices outside her office, and when we look up, the receptionist is standing there with a man who I take to be Mal Delaney. He's sixty or so, much too tan for Ireland in October, dressed in skinny jeans and dress shoes and an untucked floral-printed shirt. His brown hair is too dark not to be dyed.

"You must be Mr. Delaney," I say. "Is that right? I'm Garda Maggie D'arcy and this is Detective Fiero. We're investigating Jade Elliott's death, and we need to get some more information from you about her work with your agency and why she ended her relationship with you."

He looks worried but pastes on what I think is supposed to be a charming, but somber, smile. "Of course. We are happy to help in any way we can. Terrible thing, terrible, terrible thing."

Fiona says, "They're asking about Jade's termination of her contract with the agency. They seem to think we were doing something wrong in managing Jade's earnings."

Mal Delaney smiles sadly. "I think you'll find that, if anything, we were on the losing side of that financial proposition. I don't like to say it, but Jade never made very much, and her mother was incapable of handling what little she did bring in. We were constantly forwarding funds so they could do the shopping. I sometimes say that doing this work is a bit like being a social worker, but this was . . . a bit over the top."

"So why did Jade Elliott terminate her arrangement with your agency?" I ask him. "If you'd been so helpful to her?"

"I don't know, exactly," he says, his gaze shifting from Fiero and then back to me. "She came in, claiming we owed her money, that there was some sort of problem with the accounting. It was ridiculous. We showed her everything, showed her that it was all in order." He glances away and straightens his shirt. His tongue flicks quickly over his lips, almost too quick to see.

Fiona looks annoyed. "I wasn't here, but Mal told me about the conversation. She said we hadn't looked out for her, that she'd been exploited, but it was her choice to stop modeling. Her career was basically over. She'd stopped working when she had the baby. Perhaps she wanted to model again but thought she'd do better somewhere else. It's not unusual for models to switch agencies, you know."

"One of her neighbors thought maybe she had gone back to work."

Fiona says, "As I told you, we hadn't booked anything for her since shortly before she gave birth to her daughter. So it wasn't with us. And, as you pointed out, she terminated her agreement with us, so perhaps she was out looking for work on her own."

Fiero leans forward. "Would she have signed with another agency?"

Mal Delaney seems to really see him for the first time. "We would have heard if that was the case. Dublin is small. So, no, I don't believe so."

Fiero goes on. "But it's possible she could have booked directly with a client or worked with a photographer, right?"

Fiona presses her lips together. "Of course. We would have no knowledge or control over what she did in her own time. That's true for any client and especially for ones we begin representing when they're younger. Sometimes they take . . . different directions."

"Now," Mal says. "If that's all you—"

I hold up a hand. "We're not finished. If she was looking for work, where would she go? Without an agency looking on her behalf, how would she go about it?"

Fiona hesitates. "I'm sorry to say she might have found herself in a, well, in a different part of the industry," she finally says.

"Porn?" I ask.

"Well, yes." Fiona looks away. "You would know better than we how to get in touch with . . . those people."

Fiero's ready to let them go, but looking around at the photographs of the agency's other clients, I start wondering if Jade is the only one who ever questioned their accounting practices, who ever wondered if she had some money coming from them. I turn to Fiona. "We'll let you go, but can you get me that list of other clients who you represented around the same time as Jade? We talked about it the other day."

"What?" Mal Delaney sputters. "That would be confidential information. We can't just hand out client files."

"I'm not asking for their files," I say. "I'm just asking for a list of other clients from the time that Jade started working with you. Contact details, too, but I can probably find it on my own. I'm happy to pick it up later today."

"This is ridiculous. Everything was in order with Jade and with all of our clients. I don't know what you're implying, but I don't like it," Mal Delaney spits out before Fiona can say anything. His face is red, though, and his voice isn't quite as forceful as it was. He's nervous.

It's his nervousness that makes me reckless. I look at him and say, "So why did you give her the cash, Mr. Delaney? If everything was in order, why did you give Jade the cash when she came to tell you she didn't want to be represented by you anymore?"

It was only a stab in the dark, but I know immediately that I've guessed correctly. His whole body sort of buckles and he sways against the desk. I can feel Fiero's surprise.

And Fiona's.

"Mal?" she says. "What's she talking about?"

He puts his shoulders up and turns away, as though I'm physically threatening him, and says, "It was nothing. I did her a kindness is all, gave her a thousand euros to get her out of my office. She's clearly had a rough go of it, and she was someone who we once worked with, who we cared for, and I . . . honestly, she was a bit unhinged and she was making accusations and I had potential clients in. I didn't want them to hear."

Fiero is focused now, alert. He looms over Mal and asks, "That's all you gave her? A thousand euros, Mr. Delaney?"

"Yes . . ." Mal looks confused.

"What was she accusing you of?"

"I don't even remember. Honestly, she seemed a bit unbalanced." He glances guiltily at Fiona.

She's subdued now, her back and shoulders rounded under her perfect clothes, her glossy pink lips pressed together. She says quietly, "I'm glad we could clear that up for you." I almost feel sorry for her.

Taking our win, we thank them and say we'll need to speak to them again. Out in the lobby, the huge, framed photographs of models on the walls seem to watch us as we go.

Nineteen

"Well, that was interesting," Fiero says once we're out on the street, taking his sunglasses out of his shirt pocket and putting them on, even though it's still overcast, the rain clouds threatening again from the east. "Nice guess there about the money. It was a guess, wasn't it?"

"Yeah, a big one." I grin. "Sorry, it was a risk I shouldn't have taken, but I was feeling it."

"Hey, it's not a risk if it works out, right?" He winks at me. "So, she was accusing Mal Delaney of something and he gave her a thousand euros. The question is, what was the accusation?"

"That they mishandled her money, right?"

"Yeah." But he doesn't sound completely sure.

"What?" I watch the foot traffic for a moment. "You think it was something else, like maybe he made a move on her?"

He rolls his eyes and does an imitation of my accent. "*Made a move!* She was a minor. It would have been abuse, yeah?"

"Yeah." We step out of the way of someone on the street. "I don't know what to think. They're hiding something, but I'm not sure what it is. And why would Delaney have given Jade a thousand euros if there wasn't anything in it?"

"What did you think about your woman's suggestion she'd started doing porn?"

I say, "I mean, you look at her Instagram and it's one step up from that." Fiero nods, agreeing with me. "How would we find out about that? I had some cases related to prostitution, escort agencies on Long Island, but I never really had to learn about porn production."

"I've a few contacts," Fiero says, thinking. "From my days on the drugs unit. I can make a couple calls." He turns his wrist and his flashy silver watch catches the light. "We need to get back and see if there's anything on the car."

I gesture to the other side of Camden Street. "Yeah, I need a coffee though. Remember Alex Sadowksi? He works in a café just there," I say. "You want one, too?"

"Yeah, go on then." We cross the street and head north. "He still seeing your daughter?" Fiero worked the case in West Cork where Lilly met Alex, when Alex's brother was suspected in a murder and drugs case that got Fiero what will likely be one of the big wins of his career.

"Still going strong."

"The sister must know more than she told you about all of this," he says after a moment. "She was there. It seems highly irregular that she'd just stand by while the money was handled in that way. Didn't she wonder about it?"

"Nicola? I think she was so overwhelmed by her life at that point that she didn't pay attention to much of anything."

He snorts. "Bollocks. She has to have wondered where all the money was going. But even if they had some kind of major scam going or he was a royal perv, I can't quite see what it has to do with Laurel and our man in the Opel, you know?"

Alex is behind the counter, running the huge, fancy espresso machine, and when he sees me, he grins and waves me over to the counter. "What do you want, Maggie?" he asks, leaning over to give me a kiss on the cheek.

"Latte, please," I say. "Do you remember Detective Fiero?"

"Ah, yeah. Hiya," Alex says, suddenly wary. Fiero was pretty aggressive with him and his brother, and the memory has clearly stuck with him. "What do you want?"

"Double espresso," Fiero says. "Thanks."

"You been busy today?" I ask him while he makes the coffees. I know he and Lilly have been practicing a lot with his band to get ready for a gig coming up this weekend.

"Yeah, it's been mad. I'm off in twenty minutes, though. Lilly told me you found the little girl. That's great. Is she okay?" He hands us our drinks, mouthing, *On the house.*

"Thanks. Yeah, it is great," I say, sidestepping the question. Everyone wants to know if she's okay, by which they mean, *Was she assaulted?* "We're feeling pretty thankful."

"You and Conor coming to the show?"

"We're going to try." I can feel the couple waiting impatiently behind me. "But we'll see you soon, yeah?"

Walking back to the station, Fiero says, "Nice lad. Glad things have worked out for him. My eldest boy is eighteen and it's a dicey time."

"I didn't know you had kids until you said the other day," I say carefully.

"Two. I've a girl who's sixteen this year. About the same as yours. They're with their mother in Athlone, though, so I don't see them as much as I'd like." There's a note of bitterness there and I wonder what the circumstances are.

"How long have you been divorced?"

"Six years," he says quickly. "I've only just started the whole on-line dating thing, though, so I don't want you to think . . . The other night was, well, we've just been out a few times."

He's obviously uncomfortable. I'm not sure what to say, so I settle on, "It was a lovely party, wasn't it? Emer said she's really great. She enjoys working with her."

Fiero mumbles something about liking to keep his private life private, and then clears his throat. "Assuming there's nothing on the car when we get back, what do you want to work on?"

"I'm not supposed to be working on anything," I say. "And I'm on patrol tonight. But if it's okay with Roly, I want to see if I can find out some more about the agency. Maybe talk to some of the neighbors again. We need to identify the guy or guys who visited her."

Fiero drains his espresso cup and tosses it into a garbage bin along the street. "I'll make that call to my contact, see about whether she'd been doing porn. And Roly wants me to work on Hanlon, the guy in Toronto whose father owned the house and car. He should have a list for us later today, of everyone who might have known the house was empty. There's got to be something there."

There's no news on the car when we get back, but Roly says I can keep looking into the agency. He's at peak antsy, which for Roly looks like his whole body vibrating with anticipation as he roams the incident room, picking up pens and staplers and interrogating everyone else about what they're working on. The divisional detectives seem to take it in stride, but Fiero, who hasn't worked with Roly before, is trying to figure out what the hell is going on. I know to just put my head down and ignore him.

No one's compiled a background file for either Mal Delaney or Fiona Creedon, so I have to start from scratch. Neither has any criminal charges or civil actions recorded in the system, and nothing comes up related to Revenue investigations or anything else financial. All the hits I get from searching the news archives are related to industry events or fashion stories. If they were cheating their clients out of their earnings, then they've managed to keep anyone from finding out about it.

Which makes me wonder about whether Fiero's right and Mal Delaney gave Jade the money because she was accusing him of something else.

I know I can go back to the agency and demand that they turn over the list of their clients immediately, but there's probably an easier way. Sure enough, when I click on the "Clients" tab on their website, I find a directory of their models that still includes Jade Elliott; it hasn't been updated in a while.

I make a list of their other child models and use the Garda system to get updated contact information for all ten of them. The next thing is to get in touch and see whether any of them had a bad experience with Mal Delaney. I check the wall clock. I've only got thirty minutes before I need to head down to the locker room, but I can get through a couple of them.

I've just started dialing the first number when Fiero calls out, "I got something!" from across the room. "Look at this!"

Roly and I both go over. There's a document open on the computer monitor on the desk—the list of names Michael Hanlon compiled and sent us, I realize.

Fiero jabs a finger at the screen. Roly's leaning over the desk and I can't see what he's pointing at.

"Hugh Keating," Fiero announces.

"What? The sister's husband?" Roly's peering at the screen.

Fiero nods. "He knew the Hanlons. He dated Mark Hanlon's niece. He knew Michael Hanlon. They went to school together. The families lived fairly close at one time. But listen, after we got the reg plates, I asked her if the name was familiar, and she said no. She said she didn't remember them. According to the guard I just talked to in Navan, that's a load of bollocks. The two families knew each other well. She fucking lied."

I stare at him. "Nicola?"

"I knew it! I knew she was keeping something back." Fiero's delighted, puffing his chest out, a triumphant grin on his face.

"So . . . what?" I'm trying to figure out how this fits, what it means. "She couldn't have taken Laurel. Her husband either. We've had uniforms on their house."

"I know, but she lied to us. I'm going up there to talk to her right now." He glances at me and then at Roly. "You want to come along?"

"She's on patrol," Roly says. "And we might get something on the car any minute. You go, Fiero. Let me know what you find, okay?"

He hurries out of the incident room and I try to push down the wave of envy I feel as he goes.

"Ah, don't give me that face," Roly says, watching me. "I told you that you have to keep up with the patrols, didn't I? What are you thinking?"

I tell him about Mal Delaney and our suspicions about why he gave Jade the money.

"You think he's a kiddie fiddler? He was paying her off so she wouldn't report him?"

"Maybe. Maybe not. But it shows she was looking for money. I was thinking that maybe she was getting ready to hire a solicitor to fight Dylan Maguire's custody request, but . . . I don't know. Anyway, I need to check in with these other clients and see if there's anything there, and I thought I might ask her friend in the neighborhood, Elizabeth Ruane, about whether she thinks Mal Delaney behaving inappropriately could have been the 'illegal' thing she was referring to. It'll all have to wait until later though." I check the clock again and stand up, getting my things together. I'm trying not to be obvious about it, but Roly can feel my disappointment.

I can see him wrestling with himself. "Look, I'm dealing with a whole system here and like I said, they're shorthanded, just like the rest of us. I'll see what I can do to get you off patrol tomorrow, yeah? And see here, by then we should have this fella." He picks up a pen someone's left on the edge of the desk, twirls it around in his fingers like a tiny baton. "If he's out and about, the cameras will find him."

Jason and I have a mostly uneventful patrol. We do the perimeter of our beat, chitchatting about our regulars and what they've been up to. I know he wants to ask about the investigation but also knows I can't tell him much.

We take a dinner break at six and we're talking to an elderly woman walking her dog on Lennox Street when I see Elizabeth Ruane pushing the now-familiar green pram, Sarah and Bobo strapped into the seats. She has a shopping bag hanging from her wrist and she's chatting to Sarah, probably explaining that they're going home to put the shopping away. Pushing the huge pram, she looks small and bereft; but of course she is. Her friend just died. It's only been a few days. She's probably still grieving.

"You ever see her around the neighborhood?" I ask Jason, pointing out Elizabeth and Sarah once the elderly lady has moved along. "She walked with Jade sometimes. They were friends."

Jason squints to make her out across the street. "Maybe. She has two little girls, yeah?"

"Just the one."

"Oh, yeah. You think she knows something?" He peers at my face. "You look like something's bothering you."

"I don't know. It's probably nothing."

But once we've finished our shift and I've changed out of my uniform, I realize what it is. When Nigel Canning talked about seeing Elizabeth Ruane around the neighborhood, he also referred to her having "children." Which means that she sometimes had Laurel in the pram, too, that maybe they had playdates at Elizabeth's house. There's nothing wrong with that of course—she didn't say she'd never had Laurel over for a playdate—but it suggests a different and more intimate friendship than what Elizabeth described to me when I interviewed her. You don't let just anyone take your kid. I'm wondering if Jade may have confided in her about Mal Delaney or about why she was trying to get money together in the months before she died.

Jade didn't have many friends. But she had Elizabeth. I try Roly's phone, but it goes to voice mail. I should wait until tomorrow, but if she knows anything about the Delaney Agency and Jade's accusations, we need to know as soon as possible.

It's nine P.M. by the time I knock at the house on Lennox Street. The curtain in the window next to the door twitches, and it's nearly a full minute before the door opens and she says, "Sorry, I'm on my own and I'm not used to having visitors at night." She's dressed in sweatpants and a thermal top and she's holding a glass half full of red wine. "Took an hour to get Sarah to sleep," she says, gesturing with the wine.

I smile, remembering the bedtime battle and the relief when it was finally over. "I'm so sorry to bother you, but I wanted to make sure you heard that Laurel is okay. She's back with her father. I just finished my shift and thought I'd stop by."

Still wary, she says, "Yes, I saw the news. I'm so relieved. And she's okay?" Her eyes are puffy. She's clutching the wineglass and she doesn't look relieved at all.

"Yeah, it seems like it."

She doesn't ask if Laurel was "interfered with," which is a nice change. There's an awkward silence and then she says, "Was there anything else . . . ?"

"Actually, would you have just a minute? There's something I wanted to ask you, as part of the investigation."

She hesitates, glancing over her shoulder, and I wonder for a moment if she's got someone here, but finally she says, "Of course," and leads me into the living room, which is empty and a good deal more disordered than it was the other day. "I'm sorry for the mess," she says. "My husband's away and . . . Would you like a glass of wine?" There's a half-empty bottle on the coffee table.

"No thanks." I let the silence settle over us and then, seeing how uncomfortable she is, I say, "I bet Laurel would love to have a play-date once things settle down a bit."

"Yes, Sarah would like that," she says. "Is there . . . Do you know who killed Jade yet? The news said you're still investigating, but . . ."

"We're still working on it." The disappointment on her face makes me say, "Do you have any thoughts about who it could be?"

She brushes a strand of hair away from her cheek and takes a sip of her wine. I can see her calculating. Finally, she says, "I really don't. They always say that it's someone close to the person, don't they?"

"Yes, statistically it's likely to be an intimate partner or family member."

"But the paper said that Laurel's father—Dylan—was out of the country. So it can't be him." Her face is troubled and she seems to be about to say something before hesitating and then holding her tongue. "Laurel's really okay then? You saw her?"

"Yes," I say. "She seemed fine. I'm sure there will be trauma though. We don't know what she's been through."

"Well, anything I can do to help. The girls love each other and I can take . . . I mean, if Dylan wants me to take her, I could." She glances down at her wineglass, then puts it on the coffee table, out of reach.

"You were closer friends than you let on," I say quietly. "She trusted you with Laurel. I don't know why you lied about that, but you did. Why?"

She's scared. Now she's twisting her wedding ring around and around and she won't look at me.

The house is absolutely silent, whatever expensive windows they put in blocking out all the sounds of traffic from outside. "I don't know what you want me to tell you." A tear squeezes from each eye and she reaches up to wipe them away.

"I just want you to tell me the truth," I say.

Her head and neck are rigid.

Suddenly, I can't control my anger. "We're investigating a murder here and you haven't been honest with us. I just don't understand why."

The tears keep coming.

"Elizabeth?"

Finally, she sighs and picks up the wine again, taking a long sip. "I didn't know how to tell you without telling you *how* we became friends, and . . ."

I wait for a long moment then ask, "How did you become friends?"

She's silent for a long time. "I'm . . . I was a social worker, before Sarah was born," she says slowly. "I loved it, loved the work, but Colin, my husband, he travels so much and it just didn't . . . I couldn't think how to make it work once I had a baby. And we could afford it, for me to stop working and stay home with Sarah. Colin's doing really well, making packets of money. We thought we'd have another baby quickly. I . . . I didn't realize how lonely I'd be.

"We're both from Dublin, but not Portobello, and we bought this place because it seemed like a good investment. We did a big renovation. We don't know anyone though, and so . . ." She shrugs. "I was really alone."

She stops talking for a minute and I think maybe this is it. Maybe she's going to say, *I was grateful to have someone to walk with* and that will be it.

But instead, she takes a deep breath and goes on.

"After Sarah was born, I waited to feel . . . well, what they tell you you're supposed to feel," she says. "It had been a hard birth, three days of labor and then a Caesarean, and they told me I should be alert for signs of postnatal depression. They told Colin, too. But he didn't know, I didn't know."

I hold my breath, waiting. I'm thinking of Emer, the way she described to me the feeling of being behind a see-through curtain, everything quieter and duller and farther away than it should be.

"I didn't . . . Even though they'd told me, I didn't realize that that was what was happening. I just thought there was something wrong with me. I thought it was just that I wasn't meant to be a mother. Colin, he didn't understand. We'd worked so hard, for so many years, to be ready. We'd saved and saved to buy the house and then we'd saved and saved enough so that I could be home once the baby came, and she was healthy and perfect and he couldn't understand why I wasn't happy. His job was taking so much of his energy; he'd taken on a managerial role so he'd have a higher salary and he was working long hours, traveling all the time. He's making so much money, but I was alone, with Sarah, every day, for hours and hours. I started to . . . I started to have terrible thoughts. I thought, 'Well, I'm so bad at this, it would be better for Sarah if I left Colin to take care of her.' It made perfect sense to me, perfect, logical sense. That's what . . . I think most people don't understand."

She touches the couch, rubbing a finger over the upholstery seam, and looks at me. "I was going to do it. I had pills, ones they'd given me for the pain in the hospital. I did my research and I had saved enough to go to sleep and not wake up. I had a plan. I was going to do it in the bathtub. I thought that would be lovely. Just going to sleep in the bathtub, early one morning before Colin and Sarah got up, and never waking up."

"What stopped you?" I ask.

She smiles a small, sad smile. "Jade stopped me. Essentially. The day before I planned to do it, I took Sarah out for a walk, to the playground. I wanted her to remember me doing fun things with her, playing, if she could remember anything. Which she probably couldn't. And Jade was there with Laurel. The girls started playing together and we started talking. Jade was . . . It was like she saw through my mask and she saw that I was in trouble and she didn't want to let me go. She said, 'I'm so tired, all the time. Do you get tired?' We talked and talked that first day, and then she said, 'I'll meet you here tomorrow morning, right? I'll bring the tea.'

"When I got home, I said to myself, 'It can't hurt to wait a day. If I'm not there, she'll have to come looking for me and she doesn't know where I live . . .'" She smiles, broadly this time. "My thinking . . . I was in a bad way, but that made sense to me. So I went and we walked and I decided to wait another day and then we walked again and . . . again, and finally I told her how I was feeling. I couldn't say it to anyone else, but Jade, maybe because she wasn't in my world, she was so different to me, I didn't feel she would judge. She said I should go to the doctor and get antidepressants. She said she'd read an article about how difficult births, for some women, could make you sad. I was still . . . keeping my secret, about what I wanted to do, but she kept after me and she kept asking, and so finally I went and the doctor gave me medication. It helped, a lot, but also, Jade expected me and Sarah, every day. She told me that our walks and our trips to the playground were what kept her going, too. That she needed me to meet her to keep *her* going. I felt responsible for her, because she was younger, though I think she planned it that way. I was lucky."

"You were both lucky," I say.

"Yes, we were so different. I'm twelve years older than she is. I was a social worker, a social work manager, before Sarah was born. I've never watched a reality show in my life. We come from very different backgrounds, but somehow, we became friends, and, yes, you're right, we told each other a lot of things about our lives. I'm sorry I didn't tell you. My husband doesn't know about . . . how sick I was. I didn't want to have to tell him."

I wait a moment, to give her time to recover from telling the story. When people finally reveal the things they've been hiding, they often seem exhausted but euphoric, grateful to be rid of the burden they've been carrying. Elizabeth is still sitting rigidly on the couch, though, her fingers nervously rubbing the stem of her wineglass. I ask, "Did she ever talk to you about when she was working as a child model? About the agency she worked for?" My phone buzzes in my lap and I ignore it. Elizabeth doesn't say anything so I go on. "Sorry. Did she ever talk to you about someone named Mal Delaney? He was her agent and—"

She opens her mouth, about to say something, but my phone buzzes again.

I look at the screen. Fiero. I say to Elizabeth, "Sorry, let me just take this and make sure it's not an emergency. Hang on just a second."

I answer in the foyer. "Yeah, what is it? I'm in the middle of—"

"Maggie?" I can hear it in his voice. Something's happened. *The car.* "Maggie, we got him! A checkpoint in Kildare spotted the car about thirty minutes ago. When they tried to pull it over, the driver took off and led them on a six-kilometer chase. He finally crashed through a barrier near Cherryville and the car went airborne. He was unconscious when they got to the wreck, and he's got some broken bones, but they think he's going to be okay. He's at hospital. Roly says for you to get here as soon as you can. Naas General Hospital, right?"

I apologize to Elizabeth and let Conor know what's happening, and then I drive as fast as I can, trying to put it together, trying to find good reasons for all the lies we've been told.

I see Stephen Hines first thing as I force my way through the scrum of reporters outside the hospital. "Detective D'arcy," he calls to me. "Do you have anything on the identity of the man brought here by gardaí just now? Is he the same man who kidnapped Laurel Maguire and killed Jade Elliott?"

I give him a wink but ignore his question. The other reporters keep shouting but let me pass. My uniform gets me through the layers of security on the ward and I spot Fiero and Roly conferring outside one of the rooms. As I pass an open door, I can see an elderly woman inside wearing a hospital gown and looking perplexed by the crowds and noise. A nurse is helping her eat from the tray next to her bed.

"Don't let anyone near him," Roly's instructing the officer standing guard.

"He's awake," Roly says when he sees me. "They're transporting him back to Dublin for surgery later this evening. He injured his right leg in the accident, and he's in a lot of pain, so I didn't get much from him, but he's about to be out of commission for a while and I told the doctor I needed to speak to him, to make sure he didn't have an accomplice who's out there and who might be a danger to the public."

Fiero's drinking a can of caffeinated soda and looking like it's Christmas morning. He nods to me and grins as though we were in his favorite pub rather than a hospital. "We got him," he says. "We fucking got him. I knew it!"

"Who?" I whisper, conscious of the nurses and the reporters and the old lady eating her meal.

"You didn't get word?" Fiero asks. "Sorry, I thought someone told you. Nicola Keating's brother-in-law. That's who it was. Probably a fucking pedophile. He killed Jade and took Laurel. That fucker in there is named Alan Keating."

Twenty

....

"What?" I'm staring at him, trying to take in the words. "Nicola's brother-in-law?"

"Yeah. I was right about her!" Fiero says. "She must have known something. I drove up to talk to her this evening and she was cagey as fuck, clearly worried about what I was asking and her excuse for why she hadn't told us she knew Hanlon was shite. She said she was so emotional she forgot. I couldn't get anything more out of her, but this changes things.

"I just confirmed with Michael Hanlon that Alan Keating was at the pub after his father's wake, that he was sitting at the table when Michael was talking about the house. Alan Keating knew the house was empty. We're bringing Nicola Keating in. She must have known it was her brother-in-law. She must have been protecting him. Otherwise, why would she have lied?"

I feel a wave of nausea come over me. "What did he say? Keating? Did he have Laurel all this time? Did he say what he did to her?"

Fiero takes a swig from the soda can. He keeps his voice low so no one will overhear. "We asked if he had taken Laurel Maguire and he nodded. No verbal confirmation. Roly tried to get more out of him, but he kept asking if Laurel was okay. He seemed relieved when we said yes."

"I didn't know what to fuckin' think," Roly says, shaking his head.

A reporter has somehow made his way onto the ward and we all look up at the commotion as the uniforms escort him out.

"That's not uncommon," I tell them. "Pedophiles often express a sense of love and concern for their victims. You know that."

Roly sighs. "The techs got us some of the details. We asked him if he could tell us about what happened while he had Laurel, and he kept shaking his head. He was in a bad way. Nothing he told me is going to be useful anyway. I said to him, 'Did you kill Jade?' but he just kept shaking his head. And then, as we were leaving, he started crying and he said, 'Tell them I'm sorry.'"

"For killing Jade? Or for Laurel?" I ask. "Or both?"

"I assume. I don't know." Fiero looks back toward the room where Alan Keating is being prepped for the move to Dublin. "What else could he be talking about?"

Roly's buzzing like he's had twenty cups of coffee. "What the fuck? You think the sister was in on it?" he asks us.

"Or she realized it was him and was protecting him for some reason."

"Whatever it was, she lied to us," Fiero says. "And the prize for that is an invitation to come down and answer some questions in one of our lovely interview rooms. I knew she was lying. I knew it. Good to know I've still got the instinct."

A doctor comes out of the room and tells Roly that they're ready to move him. Roly says he'll come along. I know what he's thinking. If Alan Keating says something, anything, then he wants to be there for it. He can't use it, but he wants to hear it. "It should be simple now, but there's something I don't like about it," Roly says. "We'll need to bring Nicola Keating and her husband in officially tomorrow, question them, find out why they lied, and the two of you need to start contacting Alan Keating's known associates. Doctor said we may not be able to properly interview him for a couple of days, so I want as much supporting evidence as we can get. We need it all lined up so when I go in there, he's got no choice but to make a full confession. I don't want any of this, *Oh, it was an accident, officer, I didn't mean to kill her. I'm a sick man, officer,* nonsense. I want it all wrapped up so his only choice is to tell me everything. Got it? If she was protecting him, I want her on the record before he wakes up, yeah?"

They come out with a stretcher, Alan Keating a long shape under white blankets, an IV stand and various other pieces of machinery trailing along behind. I get a quick glimpse of his face as they pass. He's just a boy, barely twenty-two or -three from the looks of him. Pale and terrified looking, his arms lying over the blankets at his sides, he stares ahead, flinching when the stretcher hits the corner of the wall as they pass by.

Night has come on outside the hospital by the time Fiero and I are ready to go. We wait until we're in the car park and away from the reporters to talk about the case. Somewhere south of us, Roly is meeting Nicola at the city hospital where Alan Keating will have surgery. He'll be watching her, listening to what she says, trying to figure out what she knows, how she's wrapped up in this. Tomorrow, we'll bring her in for questioning.

Fiero runs a hand over his crew cut and I see him stifle a yawn. I've been going on adrenaline since his phone call, but now I'm starting to crash. He clicks his key fob and the headlights of a Ford on the other side of the lot come on.

"You happy then?" he asks.

I hesitate before saying, "I don't understand what Nicola had to do with it. Was she covering for him? Did she know he was planning on taking Laurel?"

"If she knew and didn't say anything . . . that's mad," Fiero says. "Fucking sick, that is. Your own niece. But we've got him anyway. We'll find out tomorrow exactly how it happened, but we've got him. It's over." But he doesn't look like it's over. He's still agitated, still on alert. I think of Elizabeth Ruane and how she should have been relieved, but wasn't, after she told me the truth about her friendship with Jade.

The sky over the car park is a dull gray, a huge, square-shaped cloud reflecting light from somewhere below. I turn back to Fiero. "Did Roly say that Alan Keating said to say sorry to *them*?"

"Yeah, I think so."

"What did he mean, *them*?"

"Her and her husband. The family, like, right?"

"What if that's not what he meant?"

"What are you talking about?" His eyes look strange and glittery, reflecting the dim light of the energy-saving car park lights.

"Elizabeth Ruane," I tell him. "She never asked about Laurel. The first time I talked to her, she was desperate to know if we'd arrested someone in Jade's death. She wanted to know if we knew what had happened. But she never asked about Laurel. And remember, when we first went up to Eileen Elliott's and—"

"Same thing with Nicola Keating," he cuts in. "She asked about

Jade's killer, she asked why we hadn't arrested someone, but she didn't ask about Laurel."

"Because she knew where Laurel was. Because she knew Laurel was safe," I say.

Fiero runs his hands over his head, his eyes wide and disbelieving. "What the fuck? They were in it together?"

"It doesn't make sense," I say. "But it's there . . . We need to get them in interview rooms. Do you want to tell Roly or should I?"

"I'll do it," he says. He starts to turn away, then puts his hands out and gestures wildly, saying, "What the fuck, Maggie? Her *sister*?"

I sigh, exhausted now. You can get used to all the ways human beings destroy each other's hearts in this line of work. But every once in a while, something breaks through. For some reason I can't quite identify, I feel sorry for Fiero. "I know. I'll see you tomorrow."

"You okay to drive?"

I smile. "Yeah, I think I can make it."

As I pull out of the car park and onto the main road, my headlights catch an animal on the road, something small and scurrying as it crosses the asphalt and disappears into the grass on the verge.

I'm home at eleven and I collapse into bed next to a sleeping Conor. When I plug my phone in before falling asleep, I have a text from Stephen Hines: This is getting interesting.

Twenty-one

....

"Detective Inspector Roland Byrne, Detective Garda Padraig Fiero, and Garda Maggie D'arcy commencing interview with Nicola Keating at 9:13 A.M.," Roly says for the tape.

We're in the largest interview room, the three of us on one side of the table and Nicola on the other. The interview room is too cold. They always are. It's a good way to inject some urgency into your questioning, to make your subject even more appreciative of the hot tea or coffee you'll bring them if they can just help you out, if they can just tell you what you need to know. Nicola is holding a cup of tea between her hands to warm herself, and even if it's only subconsciously, she's grateful to us for giving it to her.

I've got three shots of espresso in me and I'm energized in the way you can only be energized when a case is breaking, when something happens to crack it open so you can look at it, so you can finally see it for what it is.

"Now, Mrs. Keating, if you could just state for the record your full name and your address." She does, and Roly thanks her and says, "Alan Keating is your husband's younger brother, is that right?"

"Yes." She's wearing an oddly formal outfit, a chiffon blouse and black blazer and pants, as though she's come for a job interview. Despite the jacket and nice blouse, she looks unkempt. Her face is pale, her eyes tired, but she's made an effort: blush, mascara, lipstick. Her hair is tortured into a tight ponytail. I wonder why.

"When did you first meet him?"

She looks surprised at the question and says, "Hugh and I started seeing each other just after I left school, so I suppose I was seventeen, something like that. Alan was only a little boy then."

"Did he and Jade know each other?"

"Well, yes, they were family, so of course they knew each other." The tone is a classic: *Are you an idiot, detective?*

"How well?" Fiero asks.

"They were family, like I said. But they didn't know each other well." She's annoyed with us, annoyed at having to be here, and her attitude is all wrong. She should be asking us questions. *How did this happen? How did I not know?* She should be incredulous, in shock that her husband's brother could have done something like this.

Or at least pretending to be.

But she's not. She's too together. Her rigid posture, the clothes, the makeup. It's almost as though she's preparing herself for a performance.

"Nicola," I say. "Did Jade ever express discomfort with Alan? Was he ever inappropriate with her or Laurel in any way?"

"No. He wasn't. They barely knew each other," she says.

We wait for a long moment to see if she fills the silence. She doesn't.

Fiero says, "What about your husband? We'll be speaking with him, of course, but did he ever notice anything off in the way Alan acted toward Jade?"

"No," she says impatiently.

"So you never saw anything that gave you cause for concern?"

"I said I hadn't." She looks down at her hands, which are laced together on top of the table.

Fiero and Roly exchange a glance. I know what they're thinking. *Jaysus. It's like pulling teeth.*

"Mrs. Keating," Roly says, hunching down a little to try to make eye contact with her. "Were you surprised when we rang you to say Alan had been in an accident and that we were taking him into custody?"

She starts to say something, then stops, glances up at the recording device sitting on a shelf on the wall, and settles on a simple "no."

"I don't understand. You didn't know of anything strange about your brother-in-law, and yet you weren't surprised when we told you he'd been holding Laurel?"

She snatches a tissue from the box on the table and dabs at her eyes. When she's done, she looks up at me and says, "I need to use the toilet. You said I'm free to go at any time. Can I go?"

Roly says, "Why don't we keep going here and then we'll take a break."

"I really need the toilet," she gasps. Her whole mood has shifted and she suddenly seems on the verge of breaking down.

"All right." Roly looks up at the recorder. "Interview terminated 9:28 A.M. Nicola Keating, Detective Inspector Roland Byrne, Detective Garda Padraig Fiero, and Garda Maggie D'arcy leaving the interview room." We call for a uniform to come and take her to the ladies'.

"There's something fucking odd about this," Roly says out in the hallway. "She's being evasive. I'm not going mad here, am I?" He's furious, his whole body rigid, a vein popping at his temple.

I shake my head. "No, she's stalling. She's waiting for something. I just don't know what it is."

"Do you not think she's just trying to avoid implicating him?" Fiero asks.

"Why would she? He killed her sister. I don't care if he was her husband's brother, she should want him locked up, shouldn't she? So why is she protecting him?" Roly is jittery, hyped up, transferring his weight from one foot to the other, drumming his thumbs on his black leather belt.

Back in the interview room, Roly says our names for the tape again. Nicola's on edge and when he starts by asking again about Alan Keating, she freezes up. He takes the hint and shifts the line of questioning. "Did Jade ever express discomfort about anyone who spent time with Laurel?" he asks. "Any of her childminders or the neighbors?"

"She didn't have childminders."

"Well, what I mean is—"

"You're the guards? Can't you figure out—can't you do your own investigating? Jaysus! It should be obvious—" She catches herself and folds her arms in front of her chest, turning away like a petulant child.

I see Roly's eyes widen. He doesn't understand. None of us do. This is so irregular. Usually, if an interview suspect is hiding something, they come across meek, terrified.

"What should be obvious, Mrs. Keating? What is it that should be obvious to us?"

She stares at us. I shiver, the cold air working its way through my uniform. We're almost there. Next to me, Fiero is sitting forward in his uncomfortable chair, waiting for it. I can feel his energy along my arm. Roly keeps eye contact with her.

And then she dissolves in tears, her shoulders shaking as we look at each other in confusion. "I want a solicitor," she says into her hands. "I'll tell you what I know, but I want a solicitor and I want you to promise you won't go after Alan."

"I think we should try talking to Elizabeth Ruane," I say back in the incident room. "She may be able to give us some details about Alan Keating's interactions with Jade and Laurel that we can use to ferret out whatever it is Nicola knows and doesn't want to tell us. She must be protecting him, though for the life of me, I can't imagine why. Now that she'll have a solicitor, she's going to say as little as possible." Roly nods, agreeing, and I go on. "I told you about my conversation with her. They were much better friends than she initially let on. I don't know why, but she lied about it. Maybe she knows something about Alan Keating."

"All right," Roly says. "None of it makes any sense, but let's give it a go."

Elizabeth is dressed in jeans and a sweater and raincoat, her lank hair in a ponytail. They sent a uniform to her house at two A.M. to tell her she needed to come in and make a statement today, but I'm betting she didn't sleep at all after I left her. The officers who brought her in an hour ago said that her mother has come to watch Sarah, that her husband is returning from his business trip as soon as he can. She looks utterly terrified.

I meet her eyes and give her a sympathetic smile. *You okay?* I mouth to her. She nods, looking away.

"Elizabeth," Roly says after we've identified ourselves for the tape and gotten her full name and address. "Do you know someone named Alan Keating?"

She looks up at him and shakes her head. "Not really. Just by . . . by name. He was Jade's sister's husband's brother, I think."

Fiero launches right in. "Did she ever talk about him? Did he ever do anything to make Jade uncomfortable?"

She shakes her head. "No. No, she never said anything to me."

"We believe that Alan Keating is the man who killed Jade and took Laurel," Fiero says to her. "Is that surprising to you?"

She starts to say something, hesitates, then settles on a slightly sarcastic, "The whole thing is surprising, I . . . I think."

"If you don't mind my saying, though, you don't seem very surprised." Fiero leans forward and looks right at her. Her eyes dart away under his gaze.

"No, of course, I am. It's . . . just. I don't know. I'm sorry." She's twisting the hem of her jacket nervously now and refusing to look at us.

"So, just to confirm, Jade never said anything to you about Alan Keating?" Roly asks.

"No, no she never did. I suppose, only, she said *his name,* you know, 'Oh, my sister, Nicola, had a little brother-in-law who was a lot younger.' But she never said anything *else* about him."

I watch her face and make a calculation. We need to move away from the line of questioning that's making her tense. We need to make her think we're just looking for help, that we don't really think there's anything here. She may be too anxious already, but I need to try. "Let's leave Alan aside for a moment," I say. "When I was at your house last night, I asked you about the Delaney Agency and whether anything had happened there that made Jade uncomfortable. I'd started to ask you about Mal Delaney and whether she ever talked about him to you."

Elizabeth doesn't say anything.

Fiero picks it up. "Well, was there anything there? Did she ever talk about Mal Delaney?"

She shrugs, the way Lilly does when she isn't interested in talking to me. "Maybe, I couldn't really say."

I can feel Fiero's frustration. We've been trying to come around to it in a way that will build trust, that will ease her into telling us the truth, but he's had enough. "What *can* you say? Have you and Nicola Keating been in touch since Laurel was kidnapped? Can you say that? How much did the two of you know about what Alan was up to?"

Her eyes dart up, guilty. He's onto something and he sees it. Roly does, too. "Answer the question please, Mrs. Ruane," Roly says quietly. "We think Alan Keating killed Jade and took Laurel, and we think you and Nicola know more about it than you're letting on, but we don't understand why, and we need to understand if we're going to build a case against him for prosecution."

Her eyes flash and she takes a deep breath, as though she's trying to stop herself from snapping at me. "I thought that the guards have all kinds of ways of figuring out who committed a murder, DNA and phone records and fingerprints and that sort of thing. You should know who killed her. You should *know*."

Fiero brings a hand down on the table. "We're trying, but we need your help!"

I lean forward, make her look at me. "Elizabeth," I say. "The first time I talked to you, you asked me if I knew who killed Jade. You didn't ask me if I knew where Laurel was. Was that because you knew where Laurel was? Because you knew she was safe?"

Elizabeth's face freezes and then she starts to cry, the tears squeezing out of her eyes and rolling down her cheeks. She nods, almost imperceptibly, her defenses crumbling now.

I'm remembering seeing her yesterday, pushing the pram along, looking small and forlorn. And that's when I realize. The pram. Sarah and Bobo sitting in the pram.

Sarah and Laurel sitting in the pram.

Roly's drumming on the table, Fiero's leaning forward, his foot tapping out a frenzied rhythm. And I think I know what happened, but there's too much noise in here, too many people, as I try to put it together.

"Elizabeth, when was the last time you saw Jade Elliott and her daughter?" I ask her.

She glances at the recording device. "The day she died," she says. "We went for a walk that morning."

Roly hands her a tissue, but she still doesn't use it.

I focus on her, the pieces coming together. "When we spoke last night, Elizabeth, you told me that you and Jade were closer than we originally thought. We talked about that, we talked about why. We talked about how you sometimes took care of Laurel for her, because the girls were such good friends. Can you tell me about your last conversation with her?"

Fiero and Roly are watching me, unsure of where this is going.

She glances up at me and then away. "I . . . don't remember."

"Your friend died and you don't remember the last time you spoke to her?" Fiero asks.

"No, only, I couldn't remember the *last time*."

I step in. "You went for a walk with Jade on Monday morning. Would that have been the last conversation?"

"Yes, it must have been. Of course."

"And you told me that you didn't see her after that. Is that right?"

The eyes darting away, the hands busy on the hem of her shirt. Elizabeth Ruane is nervous. When she looks up at me, she blinks a few times and then says, "Yes, I guess I . . . yes."

"You went for a walk and . . ." I keep my voice low and gentle, trying to move her along.

But Roly stands up suddenly, his chair clattering back and nearly toppling. Fiero and I start, and Elizabeth gasps and sits up in her own chair. "Ms. Ruane," Roly says to her. "You don't strike me as someone who is trying to help us with our investigation. You strike me as someone with something to hide. Now why would that be? I don't understand it. Help me understand, Ms. Ruane. Help me understand!"

I put out a hand to stop him, waving him away. Fiero is watching me, trying to figure out what's happening. "Elizabeth," I say gently. "You had Laurel that day, didn't you? You had both girls in the pram. I think you had Laurel when you found Jade's body. That's why you didn't ask me if Laurel was safe. You knew where she was. You knew she was safe with Alan Keating."

The room is silent. She stares straight ahead, still crying, still not wiping the tears away, not looking at me. "I want a solicitor," she whispers. "I want you to call my husband and ask him to send our solicitor."

Twenty-two

By the time Nicola's and Elizabeth's solicitors have arrived and they've conferred privately, it's early afternoon. Outside the windows of the station, the sky has opened in a blossom of blue, the clouds pushed to the edges of the horizon. Inside, time has stopped; if not for the pangs of hunger in my stomach and the clock in the hall outside the interview rooms, I don't think I'd know what time it is at all.

We identify ourselves for the tape and I sit down to study Elizabeth's solicitor. He's the real deal, a middle-aged guy in a nice suit with a good bit of experience under his belt.

We agreed beforehand that I'll start.

"Elizabeth," I say. "We were talking about the day of Jade's death." She nods, nervous now. "I just want to establish something. Did you ever take Laurel for Jade, to give her a break? Did you ever babysit, or mind Laurel, for her?"

She nods. "Yes."

"That's something good friends do for each other," I say. "I have a daughter. I know. You don't do that with just anybody. You have to trust someone to leave your child with them. And you and Jade trusted each other. You told me about your friendship."

"You helped her," Roly says, his voice like butter, but she doesn't trust him. She's still remembering him losing his patience, so she keeps her eyes on me.

"Well, yes, we helped each other." She gulps. "My husband travels all the time and she was on her own, so . . ." She glances at me. "As I told Garda D'arcy, she helped me when I was depressed, after my daughter was born. She came over here a lot and we would talk while the girls played."

"Of course." Roly smiles. "What about the day she died? Did you help her out that day?"

Elizabeth meets my eyes and looks away. When she looks back, there are tears in her eyes. I want to comfort her, to reach out and touch her arm, but we need her uncomfortable, we need her anxious. Finally, she nods and puts her head in her hands, crying for real.

We let her, giving her time. After a minute, she sighs, takes a long sip of the tea we've brought her, and then glances at the solicitor. He nods and she says, "Jade and I went for our . . . our usual morning walk. It was quite a cold morning, so we didn't walk all the way to the playground, just around the neighborhood and down to the canal to see the ducks. As I left her, she asked if I could take Laurel for a few hours that afternoon, maybe take the girls to the park once it warmed up. She said she needed to meet with someone at her apartment, it was important, and she didn't want Laurel there."

"But she didn't say who it was she was meeting?"

"No. I . . . Well, I asked and she just said it was something she had to do, some business she had to attend to." She waits to see if we're going to ask anything else, and when Fiero nods to her, she goes on. "I told her of course I would. I offered to come up and get Laurel at three, but Jade said she'd bring her down and meet me by the canal.

She came down at three and she kissed Laurel and got her settled in my pram with Sarah. She gave me the changing bag in case I needed it. I had . . ." She sobs suddenly. "I had a bad feeling. I don't know why. There was something on her face. She was determined, but she seemed so vulnerable and young . . ." Fiero hands her a tissue and she wipes her eyes and takes another sip of her tea.

"How was she dressed?" I ask. "Like she was having a meeting?"

"No. T-shirt. Jeans. I guess she hadn't gotten dressed yet."

Fiero nods. "So, what did you and the girls do?"

"We went to the playground and they had fun, pretending to have a tea party." She smiles. "Then I needed a few things at the shops. Jade had said she would be done at five, so I walked back with the girls a bit after that. They had both fallen asleep in the pram and I didn't want to wake them, so we went around to the terrace on the canal side. I used to do that, go around to the back and lift the girls over the wall and text her. Jade would open the sliding doors and just let us in. It was much easier than going through the main gate and the door and all." She takes a deep breath and I see the trauma flash across her face. "But my phone had died so I couldn't text her and then I—I noticed the sliding doors were open, but she wasn't out on the terrace."

"Was that usual?"

"No, there had been break-ins and the people at the complex, the neighbors and the property manager, like, they were always after her to keep it closed and locked. It was strange. I stepped over that railing around the terrace and called out to her. I was going to ask Jade if she wanted me to wake Laurel up or if she wanted me to carry her in and put her down. She didn't come and the girls had woken up by then, so I lifted them over onto the terrace and we went in and I called out for her. It was . . . it was so quiet in there."

She stops talking, her arms wrapped around her body as though she's trying to hold her feelings in. When she goes on, her voice is a little surer, a little stronger. "I went to the bottom of the stairs and I . . . had a feeling. I went up. She was . . . I knew she was dead. She was so still. I have CPR training and I felt for a pulse and . . . I didn't know what to do. The girls. I didn't want them to see and I . . . and I . . . I wasn't thinking clearly. I wanted to get them out of there, so I went out with them again. I was in shock, I think. I said, 'Come on, girls, Laurel's mummy isn't here. We'll get back in the pram,' and I took them to our house and I just . . . sat there. With them still strapped into the pram."

We stare at her. It doesn't make sense. The property manager's office was right there, just outside the entrance. She could have told him. She had her phone. She could have called it in without the girls knowing, been home by the time we arrived.

She starts crying again. "I didn't think about it. I just did it. I thought I would get the girls to a safe place and then I would ring the guards. But I just sat there. I . . . her body. Seeing it like that. It was horrible."

Roly's been listening, but now he takes a turn. "What did you do then, Elizabeth? Once you were back at your house?"

"I got the girls a snack and put on a movie and then I . . . I called Nicola," she says. "I called Nicola. Jade had given me the number once when I was minding Laurel for her. I . . . ." She's sobbing now, her whole body racked with grief. It feels like we're seeing her realize that Jade is gone, that she isn't coming back. "I need to take a break," she sobs. "Please. I need a break."

Her solicitor puts an arm around her, lets her sob. "We need a break," he says.

"Please, Elizabeth," I say. "We need to know what happened."

"I'm sorry. I just need . . ." Her head is in her hands, her thin shoulders shaking.

"Okay, ten minutes," Roly says. "Detective Inspector Byrne, Detective Garda Fiero, and Garda D'arcy leaving the room at 1:56 P.M."

"Jaysus," Fiero says out in the hallway. "What the fuck is going on here? What did they do?"

Roly swears, too. "How do we play this?"

They're looking at me expectantly.

"Let's talk to Nicola," I say. "Whatever this is, she's a part of it, too."

Twenty-three

Nicola's solicitor is a young woman, nervous and uncertain, the ink barely dry on her law degree, I'm betting, and she pats Nicola's shoulder as we come into the room. "Mrs. Keating is willing to tell you what she knows, but she would like some assurances for her brother-in-law," she says primly.

"We can't give any assurances until we know what we're dealing with," Roly says quickly. We talked about this beforehand. We don't have to give her anything. The fact that her brother-in-law is in the ICU is a kind of leverage.

"We want to hear your story," I say. "Your cooperation will be part of the record."

The solicitor nods and Nicola says, "Where should I start?"

"Elizabeth told us that when she discovered Jade's body, she rang you once she got back to her house with the girls," I say. "Why don't you start there. With her phone call."

She exhales and begins, "Yes. She rang me. We'd never met, but I knew she and Jade were friends. The last time I saw Jade, she told me about Elizabeth, that they had become close mates. That they . . . confided in each other. That Elizabeth minded Laurel sometimes. Elizabeth told me she had Laurel with her and she told me about finding Jade. I . . . I was so upset. I didn't know what to do, so I told her to keep Laurel for the moment. To keep her away from the apartment. She'd made the right decision. It would have been traumatic for Laurel to see guards there. To possibly see her mother's body. And also . . . well, I told Elizabeth that I would ring the guards and then I would have to come and get Laurel from her. We didn't know if anyone knew about her friendship with Jade, if they'd come looking for Laurel. I . . . sat there for a while. I had a drink. I almost never drink. But I poured a glass from this old bottle of Bushmills my husband had and I started thinking and then I . . . And then I . . . You know this. I didn't ring the guards." She looks up, her eyes set in determination. "It's my fault. It's all my fault. I asked Alan to hide her. I just wanted him to keep her for a little bit until, well, until it was safe."

Fiero starts to ask her what she means, but I move my hand toward his on the table to say, *Wait,* and he lets her go on.

"I knew that I needed to deal with Mam and I knew someone was going to start looking for Laurel. I knew that once they found her, you would be coming to Navan, and so I knew I couldn't keep her there. I told Elizabeth to wait and that I would make a plan." She puts her face in her hands. "I didn't think it out. I thought someone would report it sooner and maybe it would all be . . . settled. But you didn't even find her until the next day." There's an accusation in her voice. I don't understand it, but she's blaming us somehow.

She takes a deep breath.

"Alan happened to be at the house. Hugh wasn't there. My husband, Hugh, doesn't know anything. I want that on the record, yeah? He knows nothing about any of this. But Alan . . . he could see something was wrong and I . . . I told him. I told him everything. I didn't know what else to do. I was crying, like. I couldn't hide it. I knew it might take some time to . . . I asked if he could help."

"You asked if he could take Laurel," Fiero says. "If he could go get her from Elizabeth."

She nods. "He said he had a friend, a plumber like himself, who was living in Canada now, but he'd come home after his father passed and Alan and some of their mates had taken him out for a few jars, after the wake. Alan overheard him say how his parents' house was empty since they'd passed. There was a car there, this fella said, and he was going to come back in the summer and try to sell everything. Alan knew where the house was. He'd stopped a few times to fix things for this fella's parents, since this fella—his name was Michael—was in Canada. Alan knew where they kept a spare key and he said there weren't any neighbors. He could use the car and he could get Laurel from Elizabeth and could take care of Laurel there for a bit until we figured out what to do. We thought it would be a day, maybe two.

"I drove him to the house and made sure the car keys were there. I gave him an old car seat and told him to buy supplies and then drive down to Dublin early in the morning before anyone was up. He went around the back of Elizabeth's house, where there aren't any cameras. Elizabeth said she knew it would be safe because they'd had a break-in and there hadn't been anything from that side, only from the street. She brought Laurel down and Alan took her and walked with her and put her in the car and took her to his mate's parents' house. Then Elizabeth went and threw Laurel's changing bag in the canal because Alan had forgotten it. She knew you might find her and come to her house. Alan drove back to Navan with Laurel. The poor wee thing. She must have been so confused. I hated thinking of it. But . . . I knew Alan would be kind to her. He was only a boy himself when his mother died, and then Hugh's father remarried and they had two more kids. Alan took care of them, changed their nappies, everything. He was lovely. I knew she'd be safe with him, but I worried so. It was awful. Pretending. I rang Elizabeth and she told me it was done but I couldn't call Alan because I'd told him to turn off his phone, just in case. We tried to give you clues, like, but we couldn't say too much. Elizabeth said if we tried too hard, you'd get suspicious."

Roly's sitting on his hands, forcing himself to keep quiet and let her finish, but I can see the confusion on his face.

"I don't know why he took her to the crèche—someone must have been after coming to the house and he was worried they'd be found. He must have thought she'd be safe there. He's such a good boy. I don't . . . He has to be okay." She begins to cry, then gets ahold of herself. "He has to be."

The room is silent for a long moment.

"Alan said to tell you he's sorry," Roly says finally. "In hospital. He said something about a car that kept driving by. He must have been worried they'd been spotted. Bringing her to the crèche, that was his way of making sure she'd be safe. He wanted to be sure of that, too."

She sobs once, puts her face in her hands.

It's Fiero who finally breaks the silence and says, "I don't understand. Why did you do this, Mrs. Keating? Why did you keep Laurel hidden? All you had to do was ring the guards."

She looks up at us, incredulous. She can barely believe we've asked the question. "Because of Dylan," she says. "Because of Dylan, of course. Because I knew, when Elizabeth rang me, I just *knew* that he'd killed Jade and I needed to keep Laurel from him until you arrested him. Because of what I knew about him. I couldn't let him get her. But she would have gone to him, wouldn't she? You would have given her to him. I thought if we kept Laurel for a day or two, you'd arrest him right away. I thought you'd see. Isn't it always the husband, when this happens? I thought he'd be charged that evening and we could just say that we'd been caring for Laurel, that it had been a misunderstanding, a miscommunication!" She's angry now, her voice rising, her eyes narrowed. "I thought it would be all settled!

"You came to Navan," she says, looking at me, her eyes burning into mine. "And I kept waiting for you to say that he'd been arrested for killing Jade. And then you told me that he was in France. It seemed . . . impossible. I . . . I didn't know what to do. I didn't understand. We couldn't tell you then, could we? We'd already taken her. And besides, we didn't want her to go with him. I tried to hint to you . . . I tried to say that you should ask some of her model friends. I thought maybe she'd told them. I tried to put you on the right trail!"

We're all staring at her in disbelief, even the solicitor.

"Do you have any evidence that it was Mr. Maguire?" I ask.

"No, but he did it, of course he did," she says. She puts up a hand. "I know you say he was in France when she was killed, but I am absolutely convinced he's responsible for her death. I don't know how you'll find out, but you've got to. For Laurel. She's with him now and we can't let her stay there. You have to prove he murdered her! You have to!"

Fiero starts to speak, but she looks up at her solicitor. "Is there any word on Alan?" she asks. "I need a break now."

Twenty-four

....

"I told you that Jade and I became close friends on our walks," Elizabeth says, back in the other interview room. Her blond hair is tucked behind her ears and she looks very young suddenly, checking with the solicitor to make sure she's doing it right. "And that was true. We did. She told me a lot about her life and about how she came to have Laurel and everything. I wondered about Dylan, about how they'd ended up together. I knew he was much older than she was, and I knew they weren't together any longer, but it wasn't the kind of thing I could just come right out and ask her, you know?

"But then, a couple of months after I met her, she invited me back to her apartment to let the girls play for a bit and she made a comment about how she'd only been eighteen when she fell pregnant, and how she and Dylan split up after that."

"Split up?" I ask. "According to Dylan they were never really together."

Elizabeth raises her eyebrows. "That's not completely true, but . . . well, you'll see. It wasn't until a few weeks later that the story started to come out. I think telling me . . . opened it up for her, if you see. That's not uncommon with trauma. You let a bit out and then it comes sort of rushing.

"Jade told me she actually met Dylan when she was thirteen. He came up to Navan with her agency, or what would become her agency. They were looking for child models or something and he told her she would make a great model, that he needed models for the websites he designed, and he would hire her.

"It took her another two months to tell me the whole thing," she says. "At first it was just, like, he gave her advice, he was kind to her, bought her clothes, and he encouraged her to move to Dublin, paid for a place to live." She looks up. "*That* got my attention, but I didn't want to push her. But then, well, sometimes we would have a glass of wine while the girls played, and one time, I said something about how she was lucky that Dylan was so supportive, even though they weren't together anymore. And she said, 'You know, the reason he's so nice to me and pays my rent is that he's worried I'll tell people.' Of course I said, 'Tell people what?' and it took some time for her to tell me all of it. She would make little comments and I would ask questions to try to get her to look at it in a different way." She looks up at us. "I told you I was a social worker? I studied this, for my degree, how girls, children, are groomed, how it's like Stockholm syndrome, where they think it was their idea, where they feel sorry for their abusers, blame themselves, you know."

She takes a deep breath.

"When she told me what he'd done, it was absolutely textbook: *Oh, you're so special, none of the boys your age can see how beautiful and smart you are, let's write each other letters.* After he met her the first time, he gave her his email and said they should start emailing each other. He would come up to Navan and take her for treats, after school. It's incredible, to think of it. Right under everyone's noses. Then he started asking her to send him pictures, dressed at first, and then not. So he had that over her, told her if anyone found out her career would be over. He gave her money, he made her feel special. He started a sexual relationship with her when she was fifteen, but he didn't actually have intercourse with her until she was eighteen. He knew the law. His father was a judge, you see, and he said that he had friends everywhere, that Jade wouldn't find anyone to listen to her in Ireland. He knew exactly how to keep himself out of trouble. Although, he wasn't as smart as he thought. And that's why I think he had to kill Jade."

Stunned, we all sit there in silence for a little bit until finally Fiero says, in a quiet voice, "What do you mean? What do you mean he wasn't as smart as he thought?"

Elizabeth looks up at us. "He had pictures on a laptop," she says. "Jade saw them this past summer, by accident, when she went to his apartment to pick up Laurel. Pictures of girls—eleven, twelve, thirteen, even younger. That's why she was so upset and why she decided she had to get full custody of Laurel. Because she'd seen the photos and she was sure that Dylan would abuse Laurel if he got to keep her."

"We should have seen it," I say back in the incident room while a liaison officer brings the women more coffee and tea and lets them confer with their solicitors. "The age difference, the fact that he was supporting her even though he didn't get to see Laurel much. We should have asked why. We should have figured it out!" I slam my hand down on the desk. "We knew he was lying!"

"What the fuck are we going to do?" Roly asks us. "If we ask Maguire about this, he's just going to deny it. You heard them, he was extremely careful to get rid of all evidence. They have no proof. I don't know if you noticed, but there was nothing there that wasn't the secondhand claims of a dead woman. Not one single thing. And he's got an alibi. His alibi is airtight. He wasn't even in the country!"

But he believes it. I can see that he does.

"His alibi can't be airtight. Fiero must have missed something."

Fiero's been quiet, but now he steps forward and says, "I went over every inch of it. I'll ring them back. I'll check it again, but I'm telling you. I went over every inch of it."

There's a long silence. Then Roly says, "Later, when this is all over, we'll do whatever we can to get him on the illegal relationship, but right now we're investigating a homicide, and there is no way that Dylan Maguire could have killed Jade Elliott."

"Then he hired someone," I say. "It's got to be that. He hired someone to kill her because he thought she was about to go public. That's why we don't have evidence from the killer, because whoever it was knew how to do it without leaving any! If we can find evidence of the illegal relationship, maybe he'll give up whoever he hired."

They both nod. "How are we going to prove it though?" Roly asks. "If he's as careful as they say?"

Fiero thinks for a moment and says, "Even the pedos who are really careful about leaving a digital trail slip up sometimes. I'd like to know how Jade sent him the pictures Elizabeth referenced. He was probably smart enough not to have her email them, but he could have had a second address he only checked from one computer, something like that. Or he may have had her save them on a thumb drive or an external hard drive he gave her. We'll get the cybercrimes lads onto him."

"Let's see if Nicola has anything else for us," Roly says finally. "Maybe she has a way we can get him. I think that's our next move."

Back in the other interview room, Fiero asks Nicola, "Were you and your mother aware that Jade knew Dylan before she moved to Dublin?"

"Not until recently," Nicola says after a moment. She shakes her head. "I can't believe we missed it. I'll never forgive myself. She was working with that agency and I knew she met people that way, but the first time we actually heard Dylan's name was when she rang us up to tell us she was pregnant and that she was going to live with the baby's father. She was only delighted. Said they were in love and she was so happy." The sarcasm drips from her voice.

I say, "It didn't last long, did it?"

"No," Nicola says. "She had the baby, and the next thing we knew he had moved out. But he paid all her expenses and he seemed to take good care of her, so if anything, Mam and I decided that she was probably in the wrong. Jade could be . . . childish, immature. She was desperate when he moved out, trying to get him back. That was why we didn't see it. It always seemed like *she* was chasing *him*."

"So you didn't know they'd known each other before? That they'd had a relationship before she moved to Dublin?"

"I had no idea," Nicola says. "You have to understand, the modeling thing, the television thing, it was so strange for us. She had money sometimes, new clothes, but she was booking jobs here and there and I just assumed . . . The truth is that I was having babies and Mam had no idea what was going on with Jade. We both missed what should have been obvious."

"When did you find out?" I ask Nicola.

She makes a little sobbing sound. "She asked me for money. In August. It . . . I was furious. From what I could see, she was living in the lap of luxury. She didn't have to work, Dylan paid for everything. She was home with her baby. My husband and I have struggled. I have to pay for things for Mam. And Jade was asking *me* for money! I said something cruel, about how she had made her bed and it was a very nice one and she could lie in it. She said I was right, but she needed the money for Laurel. I didn't know what she meant. I said that Laurel's father seemed to have quite a lot of money and maybe she could ask him."

"What happened?"

"Nothing. I didn't hear from her for a few weeks. Then, I was feeling guilty, and I had to be in Dublin, so I asked if I could stop in and see Laurel. I apologized and she . . . she told me. All of it. She seemed desperate and she told me about her contact with him, how it had started when she was thirteen, how he'd picked her out at the open call, the one I dropped her off at in her nice clothes!" She puts her head down for a second, getting hold of herself. "She told me how he'd given her presents and money, made her take pictures of herself, with a phone he gave her, about how he'd convinced her to move to Dublin, how he'd paid for everything but told her she had to pretend she was getting the money from her modeling if anyone asked.

"Then she got on that show. He didn't want her to do it. I think he was jealous. He was probably worried she'd make friends. But she was about to turn eighteen and someone stopped her on the street to ask her if she wanted to do it. She was proud of it, proud of doing it on her own, thought it would lead to lots of work. But then when it was canceled she was right back where she started, and I think Dylan wormed his way back into her life, started giving her money again.

"Of course, when she got pregnant, he tried to convince her to terminate the pregnancy. She didn't want to and he had to be cautious, because of what she would tell people. He had been very, very careful from what I can tell, switching out her phone and erasing everything on it, never leaving anything for her to keep as evidence. But the pregnancy meant he couldn't deny the relationship, and even though she wasn't underage anymore, he didn't want her talking. So he let her live in his place and he paid for everything."

Fiero fixes his eyes on Nicola.

"He told us that he wanted to marry her, but she said no. Is that true?"

Nicola snorts. "No. As soon as she got pregnant, he went off her, didn't he? No more pretending she was thirteen then! She said she was heartbroken, until she realized why."

"When did she see his laptop?"

"I think she said it was over the summer. May or June. Laurel was staying with him and she had a fever. Jade went over to his flat to bring some baby paracetamol and he'd left the laptop out. He went to take a work call and she . . . saw something that made her suspicious. She looked around a bit and saw the photos in a folder. She didn't think he knew she'd seen them, and she knew she couldn't let him spend time with Laurel anymore. But she also knew that he has money, connections, and if she tried to go to court to get full custody, he'd fight her and probably win. He always told her that his father knew every judge in Ireland, that he'd win any custody case she might bring."

Because we need it on the tape, I say, "What did she find on his laptop?"

Nicola spits it out. "Photographs of young girls, children. She said he'd made her do things she didn't want to do when she was the age of the girls in the pictures. He took pictures of her, with him, threatened to send them to us if she told. Some of the girls he had pictures and videos of were seven or eight."

Roly, horrified, asks her, "What did you say when she told you all this?"

"I felt terrible. I apologized to her—I'm so glad I had the chance to apologize—and I said I would try to help her. We had no extra money, but she said she'd gotten some from Elizabeth and from some other people she knew, and she said she had a plan for the rest of it. She was going to get a solicitor, a good solicitor, who would know where to look, who would know how to get him. She'd read an article in a magazine about a woman who specialized in these kinds of cases, revenge porn and so forth. She'd always believed him about his father, but this article gave her hope."

"Why didn't she report it to us?" Fiero asks. "If she had evidence he was a pedophile?"

Nicola looks up at us. "She didn't have evidence. That was the thing. She'd seen the photos once, but she knew they'd be gone if she looked again. I asked her the same thing and she said that I didn't know Dylan, that he was good at keeping things hidden, that he always made her erase things, and he used hard drives you couldn't open and that his father was a judge and had all kinds of connections. He'd once told her that he had everything organized so that no one would ever be able to find any of his pictures, but that if she ever told, he'd send her mother the ones of her."

"'Hard drives you couldn't open'? Did she tell you where he might have kept them?" Fiero asks her.

"No, but she said he knew how to keep them from being found. He was good at computers, you see. It was his business. She knew that if we went to the guards he'd just lie and he'd know how to twist things around so it looked like she was in the wrong."

"What do you think she meant, that she had a plan to get the money?" Roly asks.

"I don't know. I'm sorry. I just don't know." Her face sags. She's exhausted now, the secret out of her, all of the energy she's been using to keep it gone, too.

"Nicola, is there anything else you have to tell us?"

"Only that I'm sorry and that it's not Alan's fault. All he wanted was to help me keep her safe. He took good care of Laurel."

In the other interview room, after we've confirmed that she gave Jade a thousand euros, that Jade also told her about the plan, Elizabeth Ruane says the same thing. "It seemed like the right thing at the time. It seemed like the right thing for Laurel. It seemed like the only way to keep her safe. And then it just . . . got away from us."

Twenty-five

Roly's frustration bubbles up and over once we're back in the incident room again. "This is a fucking disaster, this is! I've got hundreds of reporters out front. Someone's going to have Alan Keating's name any minute. They're going to make the connection with Nicola. What do we do with . . . *this,* this fucking Russian novel here? What do we do with it?"

No one says anything. I take a deep breath and ask, "Well, what if they do?"

"What do you mean?"

"What if they do get Alan Keating's name? What if we let them think what they want? If Maguire thinks we're about to charge Alan Keating, then he might let his guard down. We should talk to him and tell him it's all over, that we just want to ask him about how he thinks Alan became obsessed with Jade. If we can catch him in the lie about when he and Jade met, we'll have grounds to search his electronics. He must have been communicating with the killer while he was in France. We know he was careful, but maybe there's something . . ."

Fiero's been quiet, but now he says, "I'll get on to my contacts in Lyon. We looked at all the calls from the phone in his room, but maybe there's something else."

Roly scowls, shouts, "And those women! We're going to have to charge them with something, you know. What they did, it was crazy! And that fella, letting himself get wrapped up in it. What was he thinking? Do you know how many laws they've broken?"

The room is silent until Fiero clears his throat. "You were right, Maggie. About Maguire."

I study him for a moment. "You didn't think Maguire was the type to commit a murder. Did you think he was the type to groom thirteen-year-old girls?"

"I got a feeling off him, but . . . in Lyon, it was so clear he couldn't have done it. There's no way he flew back to Dublin, like. Though . . ." He trails off.

"What?" Roly asks him.

Fiero hesitates, then says, "There's three hours I couldn't account for on Monday. The time's not right, but . . . One of the cops over there was going to look into it some more for me. I haven't followed up with her because once we had the car, it didn't seem like a priority, but maybe . . ."

"Go give her a ring," Roly says.

He nods and goes off to make the calls.

Roly's eyes grow wide and he breaks into a grin. "Well, well. Look at that. You and Fiero, making friends. I knew it'd happen someday."

I give him my most sarcastic look and he waggles his eyebrows at me.

"Now, we're going in to talk to Maguire. He's going to be wanting some information about what happened in Kildare. He has to know we've got someone in custody, and I want to see what his reaction is. Geoff and the rest of youse, take a look at the evidence from the scene again, go over everything. There's got to be something we didn't see the first time. Someone find it!"

The incident room is quiet, everyone getting ready for the next stage of this.

"What do we do about Laurel?" I ask. "Now that we know this, we shouldn't leave her with him, but if we tip our hand, it gives him time to hide evidence."

Nausea sweeps over me, thinking about Dylan, under pressure now, alone with Laurel.

Roly's face is grim. He's thinking about it, too. "We have to get him fast then. All right, we'll bring him in, and in the meantime, everybody get out there and find the evidence we need to charge that fucking bastard and get that little girl away from him."

Dylan Maguire doesn't have a solicitor, which is either a bluff or hubris.

We apologize for keeping him waiting, and when he asks, "Is there any news about the man who was driving the car? Do we know who he was?" Roly tells him he needs to do the routine for the tape and then we'll tell him what we can. I watch his face while he waits. He seems calm, composed, expectantly waiting for the news.

"How's Laurel doing?" I ask him. To try and throw him a little, I take a stack of papers out of my bag, some notes and Jade's records from the agency. I neaten the edges and look down at them as though they're important, as though there's something there that I know that he doesn't.

He shakes his head sadly. "I suppose she's as well as can be expected. She's with one of my designers, Emma. Emma likes children and she's watched Laurel for me before. Laurel asked about Jade last night. I told her that her mummy's in heaven. She seemed upset about it. But . . . she seems better today."

I nod and Roly makes a little sympathetic sound.

When neither of us says anything more, Dylan fills the silence. "So, you were going to tell me about the man who you think had Laurel?" He's intensely interested but he's trying to seem casual about it.

Roly crosses his legs and leans back in his chair. "Yes, the man who was driving the car and who seems to have had Laurel is named Alan Keating. He's Nicola Keating's brother-in-law. Have you ever met him?"

Dylan Maguire's face freezes, and then his expression breaks open in confusion. He's utterly shocked. It doesn't make sense to him. "Alan? But, why? I don't understand. Do Nicola and Eileen know?"

I can see the thoughts flit across his face. What could this have to do with him? Did Jade's family know about their relationship? He knows this must have *something* to do with him, but he doesn't know how or why.

"Did you know Mr. Keating?" Fiero asks.

He shakes his head. "Barely. I met him once, right after Laurel was born. One of Nicola's kids had a birthday and there was a family party. But that was it, as far as I know." I can see the thoughts still crossing his face. Why Alan Keating? It wasn't what he was expecting.

"Did Jade ever mention anything to you about him? Did she ever talk about Alan behaving inappropriately or making her uncomfortable?" He shakes his head slowly, so I follow up with, "Perhaps when she was a minor? We're wondering if he had some kind of obsession with her, dating back to when she was only a girl."

He keeps his face still, but I can see the discomfort in his eyes. He wants to look away, but he can't. "No, nothing like that. I don't remember her ever mentioning him at all, actually." He hesitates. "So, you've . . . charged him, have you? Do you think he . . ." He lowers his voice. "Killed Jade?"

"Our investigation is still ongoing," Roly says quickly, but he does something with his face to tell Dylan that yeah, that's what we believe, we just have to tie up some loose ends.

"So, when would be the first time you heard Jade mention Alan Keating?" I ask.

He leans back in his chair, casts his eyes up to the ceiling. "I don't know. I remember her saying Nicola had some brothers-in-law and sisters-in-law, some of them from her husband's father's second marriage. My own mother died when I was quite young and my father remarried." Here he scowls. "And had some more kids with my stepmother, so she may have brought up the similarity in our families."

"So that would have been . . . ?" I prompt him.

"A good few years—" he starts to answer, then catches himself. "Well, I suppose around the time she became pregnant with Laurel."

I wait a minute, then say, "Did Jade talk to you about her modeling career at all? How did she get on with the Delaney Agency? Did she have confidence in them?" I'm wondering if he knew that she terminated her agreement with them in July.

"I think so. You understand, she wasn't doing it anymore, so I don't imagine she had much to do with them lately, but . . ." Again, he catches himself. "I didn't know her during that part of her life, of

course, but from what she told me, she was quite happy with them."
I can't help noticing that a few beads of sweat have appeared on his
upper lip.

"So she never said anything about her financial arrangements
with them? She never complained about them . . . withholding
payments or anything like that?" I lean forward, watching his face
carefully. He's surprised by the line of questioning. He wasn't expecting this. Which is good. If we can trick him into thinking we're
interested in Mal and Fiona, we can get him to admit he knew Jade
when she started her career.

"No, nothing like that. I believe . . . from what she said they
were actually quite kind to her. Her mother, well, I told you about
Eileen. They helped them . . . I mean, I think Jade said that the
Delaney Agency actually managed their money for them, helped
them budget."

"Hmmm. You work in the industry," I say. "That seems like it's a
bit above and beyond the call of duty, doesn't it?"

Roly murmurs that it does seem like they were very kind to Jade.
"I imagine they'd want to make sure she was taken care of, looked
out for, isn't that right?"

"Yes, of course," Dylan agrees.

"You hear stories," Roly muses. "Young people are so vulnerable.
It was lucky she had them to look out for her, wasn't it?" He keeps
it casual, conversational, no meaning behind it at all.

Dylan cuts his losses and just nods. No smile. He's looking uncomfortable now, rearranging himself in the chair and smoothing
the front of his shirt.

"This agency," Roly says slowly. "Did you find them reliable to
deal with? Financially sound, all of that?"

Dylan looks surprised. "I'm sorry, did I find them reliable? In what way?"

"They told us you hired them a few times. I just wondered. It sounds like they were quite good, but sometimes . . . a firsthand account is best."

Dylan looks down at his lap to compose himself. "Oh, well. I would have to ask our chief operating officer, I suppose. I know Fiona and Mal of course. Dublin's quite small. But other . . . team members would have been the ones to have those . . . relationships."

"Ah, I see." Roly lets the silence sit around us. I put my head down and flip through Jade's client records, reading the names, and when I look up, Dylan is glancing at them, curious about what they are, but trying not to show it.

"They a good operation?" Roly asks casually. I look down at the papers again.

I was more focused on the dates when I looked through them before and I missed it, the reference to a client Jade did a shoot for in 2012, not long after she signed with the Delaney Agency. I make a note next to it and slide the paper over, tilting the top edge up, and point to it so Roly will read it.

"I'm sorry?" Dylan's confused now, not sure what we're doing with the papers, not sure what we're talking about.

Roly smoothly takes the records from me and gives a tiny imperceptible nod. *Got it.* Looking right at Dylan, he says, "The Delaney Agency, Mr. Maguire. They a good yoke, reliable, like?"

He glances from Roly to me and back again, trying to figure out what's going on. "Ah, yes, I suppose they're . . . highly regarded."

I let it get uncomfortable before I say, "You told us you met Jade in 2015, shortly after she moved to Dublin. Is that correct?"

"Yes." He looks from Roly to me. "I believe that's what I told you."

"You met her for the *first time* in 2015?" I stare at him placidly. He blinks and I can see him working to hide his surprise.

But he's smooth and he smiles and says, "I believe so, though of course I've met many people and Dublin's a small city, really. It's entirely possible we met briefly or were in the same place at the same time at some point, of course. Why do you ask?"

Roly carefully places the records from the Delaney Agency on the table in front of Dylan. "It looks like you were actually the commissioning client for a photo shoot in 2012. Jade was hired for a photo spread for a children's clothing company website, it looks like here. That's you there, right? DM Design? My colleague has noted that that was the earlier name of your company."

"Oh, well, yes, I suppose it's possible. Honestly, I don't remember. But yes, if you say so. Detective, with all due respect, I don't understand why—"

Roly's right there. "So you and Jade had no contact at that shoot?"

"Not that I remember. Many of these shoots would have twenty or more models. I would hardly remember one person with so many. Usually I just check to make sure that the vision for the shoot is being carried out. I wouldn't have much direct contact with the talent. Can I ask you why you're concerned about this? What am I meant to have done?"

"I should think it would be obvious, Mr. Maguire," Roly says serenely. "If you started having a relationship with Jade when she was a minor, that would have been against the law."

Dylan sighs and runs a hand through his hair, as though he's been through this with us fifty times already. "As I told you before, Jade and I met up in a nightclub in late 2015. Had we met before? It's possible, but I don't remember. She lied about her age, but she was definitely eighteen at that point. So I'm not sure what else to tell you. I love my daughter. I have tried to see her as the diamond emerging from a frankly terrible situation, but if I had it to do over again, I wouldn't go anywhere near Jade. Why are you asking me about this when you've found the man who killed my daughter's mother and kidnapped my daughter?" He's angry, frustrated, exhausted.

And he's right. It's entirely possible that he met Jade when she was a child and then met her later and didn't remember.

If we didn't know what we know, I can see us buying it.

"I'm sorry, Mr. Maguire," Roly says. "We're just trying to clear up some remaining questions. I'm sure you can understand that."

"Of course. But what about Alan? Are you charging him?"

"We can't share that yet," I say. And then, without thinking about it much, I say, "One other question. Do you know a man named Cameron Murphy?"

He looks from me to Roly. "Murphy? I don't think so. It's not familiar."

"You're sure?" I study him. He's got a little tic next to his right eye, but I can't tell if it's from before or if it's from the mention of Cameron's name.

"Yes." He gives us what I think is supposed to be a sad, charming smile, but just seems demonic to me, only a few clicks from Cameron's tattoo. "Now, then. I should get back to Laurel. I can go, can't I?" He gives it a sarcastic little twist. "You did say I'm free to leave at any time."

"Oh yes, of course, of course." Roly rubs his hands together. "Well, we'll keep you in the loop. You'll do the same, yeah? If you think of anything, please give us a ring. Any detail at all."

"You mean about Alan?"

"Yes, of course, or anything else."

"Yes, I will. Of course."

"Oh, and we wanted to let you know that we've arranged some security for you. We'll have a Garda officer posted outside your home for the time being. Once the reporters get ahold of this, they'll be all over you."

"That's really not necessary, detective," Dylan says. "I have quite good security there."

"We insist," Roly says, standing up. "Besides, until we finish our investigations, there are lots of possibilities here, and we want to make sure you and Laurel are well looked after."

Dylan stands and nods weakly.

I try to make my voice cheery and casual. "Goodbye, Mr. Maguire. We'll be in touch."

Twenty-six

When a case is breaking, it always feels like time should bend and change to make for longer days of work. But the clock is what it is, and even when a case is hurtling toward the finish line, you have to eat and you have to sleep and you have to take a break.

Fiero comes back and says he's got calls in to all of his contacts in France and hopes to hear something in the morning. We head down to the canteen for some coffee and nourishment. It's four o'clock now, the trees we can see through the windows at the back of the station barely moving in the stillness of the cold, clear afternoon. It'll be dark soon, I realize. Halloween night. I remember suddenly that it's Laurel Maguire's second birthday and I feel an overwhelming sense of sadness.

"He ought to be good and itchy now," Roly says, demolishing a cheese toasty and hot tea. "I'll get the uniform on his place ASAP. At least we'll know if he makes any dodgy moves, tries to throw out any computers, like Fiero said."

"I'd say he'll sit tight for a bit. It's Laurel's birthday." I wonder what they'll do for her birthday. I hope he's thought to get her a cake and some presents. I doubt he'll let Nicola join the celebration.

"Ah, fuck," Roly says. "Poor wee thing."

I drink my own coffee and I'm munching my packet of crisps and surveying the canteen when I see Jason come in. He's preoccupied, walking quickly past the food and going straight for the tea.

"You get my message?" he asks when I go over to meet him.

Something in his voice puts me on alert. "No, I've been in interview rooms all day. What's up?"

"Alannah O'Reilly didn't come home last night," he says.

Alarm rushes through me. "Really? Did her mother report it?"

"Eventually. But not until the school rang her to say Alannah wasn't there. She admitted to them that she hadn't been home last night, and they called it in as a possible misper." He looks worried and I feel a wave of guilt. I'm his partner. A kid from our beat is missing. I should be helping him.

"How long since her mother last saw her?"

"She said when she left for school yesterday morning."

"Shit. You checked with Tina?"

"Yeah. She claims she has no idea where Alannah is. I'm going to go down and check with Andy Roden in a bit. His father said he wasn't home from school yet."

Someone drops a plate in the kitchen and we both start at the sound. "I'm sorry I'm not there to help," I say.

"No worries. Her mother said they'd had a row about her mouthing off and not helping out. She probably stayed with a friend last night and bunked off school, ya know? It's just, well, with everything going on and having seen her around with Cameron Murphy. You're not thinking he's got anything to do with all this, are you?"

"It's still developing. Let me know what you find out from Andy Roden, yeah? I don't know what's going to happen tomorrow with our investigation, but I'll do whatever I can to help find her."

"Thanks, Maggie. If I had to wager, I'd say she's having a ciggie in that vacant lot and she'll be home for her tea." He smiles, trying to put me at ease, but his eyes are troubled.

Conor's just finishing making dinner when I come in the door at seven. "You're home," he says, kissing me and handing me a glass of red wine. "Lilly's rehearsing and Adrien's at his study group, so it's just us. You've saved me from eating my dinner over the sink." I help him set the table and we sit down to eat the salad and lamb chops he's made.

"Happy Halloween," he says, raising his glass. "So, is that it? Have you charged the fella who was in the accident last night?" I try not to read too much into the hopefulness I hear in his voice. He hasn't said my involvement in this case is wearing on him, but I know it must be. I've barely been home the past week.

"Not yet," I say. "There's still a lot to figure out." Hearing my defeated tone, I try to sound cheerier and add, "But we're getting closer."

"Mmm." He cuts his meat into precise squares, Mr. Bean sitting at attention next to his chair.

"How was your day?" I ask.

"Grand, I suppose. Nothing too eventful."

I hesitate, not sure if I should ask, then decide to go for it. It feels like we've been tiptoeing around each other lately and I don't want to do it anymore. "No more reviews?"

His tone is chilly when he says, "No. None that I know of anyway." He spears the last piece of lamb on his plate, pops it into his mouth, and stands up abruptly, dropping his plate in the sink and calling out to Mr. Bean that it's time for his walk.

I stand up, too. "Conor, I'm sorry. I didn't mean to bring it up."

He doesn't look at me. "It's okay. Only, there's nothing I can do, and it just feels like this whole thing is slipping through my fucking fingers." He takes Mr. Bean's leash from the hook on the wall. "I'm going to get some air."

I put my plate in the sink on top of his. "Can I come for a walk with you and Mr. Bean?"

"Of course." He hesitates. "I'm sorry, Maggie. I didn't mean to snap at you."

"I know." I hug him, holding on for an extra few seconds and breathing in the scent of him, wool and soap and butter. I want to soak up his pain, take it away like I pretended to when Lilly skinned her knee or scraped her arm as a child, letting a hand hover over the hurt and then tossing it into the air to disappear.

The streets are full of people, and I'm confused until I remember it's Halloween. We make our way past the park and dodge the families leading little witches and superheroes and Disney princesses along the streets, the trees skeletal and bare against the cloudy-dark sky. Mr. Bean is confused by the masks and strange clothes, and he stops to stare at the kids going by. Somewhere in the distance, I hear the sound of fireworks, but when I look I can't find them lighting up the sky.

"I know you can't talk about your case, Maggie," he says, taking my hand and lacing his fingers through mine. "But, are you okay? When you came in you looked like it was bad news."

I squeeze his hand. "I'm . . . I'll be okay, but I feel like I've failed her, Jade Elliott. We think we know what happened to her, but we can't prove it, and—you can't breathe a word of this to anyone—the little girl's not safe where she is and there's nothing I can do, no matter how much I want to save her. My whole job is keeping people safe and I can't keep this little girl from harm no matter how much

I want to and that's . . . really fucking unfair." I can't tell him why she's not safe, but even if I could, I'm wary of venturing into that territory. Conor has his own history of childhood trauma and abuse and hearing about this case might be hard for him.

"I'm sorry," he says. "I guess neither of us is very good at not being in control."

"I guess not. And . . ." I take a deep breath, driven by the same feeling I had earlier, of not wanting to ignore things anymore, of not wanting to tiptoe around his feelings. "The construction, the house, it's . . . discombobulating, you know? It feels like we'll never just have peace again."

"The estate agent said—"

"I know what the estate agent said," I snap. "I have no doubts you'll get more for it, but it's been hard to live like this, Conor. It feels like . . ." I search for the words to describe how I'm feeling. "Like we have no home. Like it isn't ours. Or isn't mine. But I guess it never has been."

As soon as I've said it I wish I could take it back. But I know it's true.

He doesn't look at me. "We've tried to make it feel like your home, too," he says, hurt. "But you know that Bláithín wants me to sell it and I don't really have any choice. It's not my fault that she needs the cash to get something in Paris."

We walk in tense silence for a bit, and then he says, "Besides, we said we'd look for something smaller, something that would be better for us, that would be *ours*. Yeah, the market's bad right now. I know we haven't had any luck, but something's bound to turn up."

"I know," I say. "But, Conor, we've been looking at places but we haven't even talked about what it means. About what *this* means.

Should I sell my house on Long Island? Are we going to buy this place in Dublin together? Will we co-own it? We're not even—" I stop talking abruptly when I realize what I was about to say.

"Married?" He stops walking and turns to look at me. His face is in shadow, barely recognizable. "Is that what you were going to say?"

"No . . . maybe. I'm not saying I want to get married, Conor. I just want to *know* what we're doing, what this is leading to." As soon as I say it though, it sounds wrong, not what I meant at all. It's something else I'm trying to express, something I haven't even articulated to myself yet.

He looks bewildered. "What do you mean what it's *leading* to? I thought this was what you wanted, to see how things go with us all living together, to get the kids into university. I thought we were planning on finding a place in Dublin once we know where they'll be and—"

"That *is* what I want, it's not . . ." I say, stumbling over the words. "I'm sorry. That came out all wrong. This case, it's got me feeling so . . . out of control, like you said. There's so much that's up in the air for us right now, but I feel good about us. I do. I love you."

"I love you, too," he says. "And if you want to get—"

"No, no, that's not what I mean," I say quickly. "I'm not trying to trick you into a proposal. That's not what I'm doing at all. I think it's these houses, selling them, buying them, it feels like such a huge thing and like you said, there are all these unknowns."

Now he stops walking and turns to look at me, taking me by the shoulders. His eyes are serious, and I feel a surge of love for him, for his hands on my shoulders and his eyes intent on mine, which keep me from looking away. "We don't have to buy a house right away, you know. We could rent and see what happens, take our time looking."

"Yeah, I know." I sigh. "Maybe the first thing is to let Gerry finish and hope he doesn't find any bodies in the walls." I smile up at him. The humor feels like an offering.

"That's all we need," Conor says, taking it the way I intended, laughing and kissing the top of my head. I meant it as a joke, but the thought still makes me shiver in the cold night air.

"The thing is," I say, not sure where I'm going until I get there. "I can't get rid of this feeling that the other shoe is going to drop at any moment. You know?"

He nods. "Mmmm, that's the trauma speaking."

"It is?" I turn my head to look at him.

"That's what they tell me," he says. "People like you and me, who have experienced trauma, we're always waiting for something to go wrong. Different things can trigger it, but that feeling of waiting for the other shoe to drop, of not trusting it when things are good, that's classic trauma response right there."

"Thank you, Dr. Kearney." I bump my hip against his. "Jade," I say suddenly. "It reminds me of Erin. I think that's why it's bothering me so much that I can't keep Laurel safe. Jade was trying to protect Laurel. She was trying to get them out. She was going to finally tell the truth, but she was killed before she could do it, just like Erin." I've said too much, given him details I shouldn't have given him, but strangely, it feels good, another offering, a gesture of trust.

"You're going to solve this, Maggie," Conor says, putting an arm around me and hugging me to him. It feels so good, so safe, like his love is making my bones and muscles stronger. "I know you're going to do this. I know it's going to be okay."

And we keep walking through the night, all the unknowns and *maybes* and *whens* and *hows* following us like ghosts as we smile at the trick-or-treaters and make our way home.

Twenty-seven

While I sleep fitfully next to Conor, Alannah's failure to come home becomes a full-blown missing persons case, and by the time I wake up at six, I have a message from Jason updating me on the search and two from Roly telling me to get in as soon as I can. There's been no sign of her for thirty-six hours now and, according to her mother and Tina, her phone is going straight to voice mail.

Walking into the incident room at seven thirty, I can feel the team's panic. I can feel their sense of urgency. We have nothing to say that Alannah's disappearance has anything to do with Jade Elliott, but the press, starved for fresh information, is going to pick up on the neighborhood link.

And I don't like it. The last time I talked to Alannah, I was sure she was hiding something. What if what she was hiding was that she knew who killed Jade Elliott? What if the person who killed Jade found out Alannah had seen something or heard something around the neighborhood?

And then there's Laurel. My dreams were about her last night, fragmented nightmares about babies falling through holes and drowning in pools.

Fiero, freshly shaven, dressed in a sharp black blazer this morning, comes in a little bit after me. "You heard from France yet?" Roly asks him.

"Nah, but I should this morning."

"Any word from the fingerprints section?" I ask. "If they can identify those unknown partials, maybe we can use that to get Dylan Maguire to talk."

"I don't see how. His prints were all over the place," Fiero says. "As you'd expect them to be. We already knew that."

"I know, but I'm thinking about the unknown ones. Maybe they're someone with a connection to him and a record."

Geoff Chen's been listening and he says, "They promised me they'd have it this morning. I'm going to go see if John's got it." Geoff heads off to make the call. The incident room is busy, the uniforms double-checking CCTV and going over the tipline calls again.

Fiero takes a phone call out to the corridor, doing an exaggerated crossed fingers as he goes.

"Anything from your partner on this girl?" Roly asks me.

"No, they're looking for her though."

Roly watches me for a second. "You okay?"

I've got an itch on my nose and I reach up to scratch it. "I feel guilty leaving him alone on this. It feels personal, you know? A girl we knew, one we were trying to help. We walked her home the other night and I thought she was going to tell me something. I think she was scared. I just wonder if . . ."

"If she's connected to all of this?"

"Yeah. She was around the neighborhood all the time," I say. "She was probably around when Jade was killed. Maybe she saw something, knew something. Maybe she was a danger to Cameron or whoever it was who killed Jade for Maguire."

Roly doesn't have to say a word. His dismay is all over his face.

Fiero comes back into the incident room, looking shaken.

"You okay?" I ask him. Roly and the rest of the team look up.

"I've just spoken to my contact in Lyon," he says. "She's been working this and she finally found a taxi driver who took Dylan Maguire to Lyon's red light district on Monday night. Says he saw him get out of the taxi and go over to talk to a guy known for providing young girls to johns there. Maguire told him to wait around the corner. Guy agreed to do it because Maguire said he'd pay him double."

"That's where he was," Roly says. "That's where he was during the three hours."

"Yeah, and the driver, once she'd put some pressure on him, said that when Maguire got back in the taxi, he had a new scratch on his face."

We all take that in, each of us imagining how he got it.

"Jesus," I say. "Any chance we can find the girl he was with? Any chance she'd testify?" The looks they give me are withering. The chance of that is about as close to zero as you can get. "I know, I know. Sorry."

"Where do you think he's got those pictures?" Roly asks me. "If we could just find where he's got them, we could at least tie him up in some kiddie porn charges, get a temporary custody order on the basis of that."

"We looked around at his business and at his apartment," Fiero says. "But it'd be on a spare computer or a hard drive or something, wouldn't it? So . . ."

"Hang on," Roly says. He's thinking. "We ever hear a good explanation for why he went to the parents' house when he got home, rather than his own, I mean?"

"To be with family?" I say. "Only, they didn't arrive until later. And from what he said, it didn't sound like they were going to be very sympathetic."

A phone rings somewhere. We all look at each other. "The garage was full of boxes. Any one of them could have had computers or hard drives in them. He went there to take care of something, hide it or get rid of it, because he knew we were going to be all over him," Fiero says, slamming a hand against the desk. "Jaysus. He must keep the incriminating stuff at his parents'."

"But cybercrimes can't search without a warrant and we don't have enough for one," I say. "We need someone who's got firsthand knowledge of rapes of minor girls."

Fiero says, "Look here. I just remembered something. Maggie, we were asking them at the agency about other younger clients who might have been working the same time as Jade. These fucking fellas who do this sort of thing, well, it's rarely just once is it? Maybe Maguire made someone else uncomfortable or did the same thing to another girl, right? And remember what Nicola Keating said? That we should talk to some of the other models she knew?"

"I forgot!" I say. I jump up and go over to grab my bag, explaining, "I made a list and then with Alan Keating and everything I never got around to ringing them up." I get my laptop out and bring up the list I made. "There are six of them." I turn to Fiero. "You take three and I'll take the other three. If we can get even one of them to tell us that Dylan behaved inappropriately, maybe cybercrimes can start looking around."

"Maybe," Fiero says. "Let's see what we get." We take my laptop into an empty incident room and drag chairs over.

I call the first two on my list with no results. The first girl—now woman, of course—no longer lives at home, but her mother says that they were happy with the way the agency treated them and that her daughter didn't model for very long. "It was just a mad idea she had. In the end, she found it quite boring."

The next family says much the same thing: their daughter's interest didn't last. They had no complaints about the Delaney Agency or anything that happened in the course of modeling.

I can hear Fiero talking to someone. "And this was when?" he asks, which sounds hopeful to me, and I resist the urge to stop calling. I dial the final number on the list and am surprised when an actual woman, who seems to be the right age, answers. When I ask if she's Stephanie Clarke, she says yes. "You modeled when you were about thirteen and were represented by the Delaney Agency, correct?" I ask her.

There's a short hesitation and then she says, "This is about Jade Elliott, isn't it?"

"It is," I say. "Can you confirm for me that you were represented by the agency?"

"Yes, I didn't really know Jade though. I saw the news and I tried to remember back to when I was doing those shoots. We might have done one or two together, but I can't be sure." She hesitates and I can hear the sound of a radio or television behind her. "Do you . . . do you know who killed her?"

"I'm sure you can understand that we can't talk about it. I'm wondering if you were happy with the agency, with how they represented you and managed your earnings. If they protected you."

There's a short silence, and then, "I suppose so. I only modeled for a couple of years and I never earned much money, but I don't think that was their fault. I wasn't very good at it."

"Why did you stop doing it?"

"I got a bit chubby and they stopped asking me," she says. I try to detect a note of hurt in her voice but she sounds breezy instead. "It was a relief, to be honest."

"So you don't have any complaints about the way Fiona or Mal represented you? Your parents didn't either?"

"No," she says.

"What about the clients?"

More silence. "What about them?"

"Anyone who behaved inappropriately, who made you uncomfortable?" Nothing. I take a deep breath and then prompt her, "Ms. Clarke?"

I can hear the panic in her voice. "I'm sorry," she says. "I don't think I want to talk about this." She hangs up before I can give her my name so she can call back if she changes her mind.

I turn my chair around to tell Fiero. "Holy shit," I say. "I think there's something there. We'll have to get back to—" I stop talking when I see his face. "You got something."

He looks stunned. "Yeah. Her name's Anna Finley. I came right out and asked if she'd ever worked with Dylan Maguire and she said she had, and then I asked her if he'd ever been inappropriate with her. She laughed and said she wasn't sure inappropriate was the word but that yeah, she had some stuff she could tell me. She wants to do it in person though, and she didn't feel comfortable coming in. She's in Bray and she said we could come down and meet her at the place where she works in an hour."

"Oh my God." We stare at each other, almost smiling, horrified. I hold my hand up and he gives me a high five.

"We'll get him, D'arcy. We'll get him," he says. He runs a hand over his head and jumps up, throwing on his black army jacket and striding through the station corridors and down the endless flights of stairs to the car park. I have to run to keep up with him.

It's getting colder outside, a stiff wind chasing us south, my hair blowing across my face when I get out of the pool car in Bray. Anna Finley meets us at the bookshop where she works on Bray's main drag and says we can walk over to a Starbucks to talk. We cross the river that leads out to the sea over a stone bridge and get our coffees to go, standing next to the water and watching the swans below while she tells her story. She's not who I'd pick out on the street for a modeling career; she's not very tall and her face is round rather than angular, cute rather than elegant, but once she starts talking I can see why she might have been picked out as a child. Her freckles and reddish hair and even features are classic, and I imagine she was able to model children's clothes even after she was no longer a child.

Like Jade, she was obsessed with modeling and acting, and when she saw an ad for an open call in Wexford, where she grew up, she begged her parents to go. "My mother once wanted to be a model and so she went along with it for a while, but then the driving got to be too much. By then I didn't want to do it anymore anyway. It had been ruined for me," she says, sipping her coffee and looking out toward the sea.

Dylan approached her in the same way he approached Jade. "At first it was emails, telling me how cute I was, how talented, and then it was 'take this picture for me, take that picture for me.' And then, he said he'd take me shopping, because I deserved it, only I had to tell my parents it was Fiona taking me. And after we went shopping, of course we had to go back to his place so I could try the clothes on for him."

"He had sexual contact with you?"

"Oh, yes." She takes another long sip to steady herself. At some point, if she's willing, we'll need to have her tell the whole story for the recording, with dates and details and everything. But for right now, we don't need to ask for the specific details.

"Did Fiona know about it?"

"I don't know, maybe not, but Mal did. He made a comment once, about me being Dylan's special friend. I wanted to throw up." She grimaces, the memory sudden and unwelcome.

"Was he violent with you, Anna?" I need to know if she thinks Dylan might have it in him to have Jade killed.

She really thinks about it, going back, trying to remember, though I know every moment she recalls is a twist of the knife a little deeper. "No . . . I don't think he ever was," she says. "In fact, I don't think Dylan ever even . . . delivered bad news, like. When he was finished with me, because I'd really started to develop, he had Mal tell me that he was going to be busy and couldn't see me anymore." She looks up, her eyes clouded with pain, and I can see the words send chills down Fiero's spine, just as they do down mine. "No, Dylan got other people to do his dirty work for him."

Twenty-eight

The incident room is buzzing with energy when we get back. Geoff's gotten the fingerprint analysis back and there's news: Cameron Murphy's prints are on the glass door in Jade's apartment.

He's in the system because of his prior charges and convictions, and Geoff tells us that the techs found five good prints on the glass, inside and outside, clear evidence that he'd been inside. "We've got his prints on one of those chairs out on her little terrace, too," he says. "The rest of them were what we expected, hers and the kid's, Nicola's, Maguire's, the property manager's, the neighbors who babysat for her—all three Rodens and Denise Valentine—and a few more unidentified ones."

Roly's already moving. "Okay, someone get all known addresses for Cameron Murphy, and D'arcy, you and your partner can start visiting them since you know the neighborhood. Meanwhile, we'll get as many units as we can find out looking for him and for the girl, too."

It's already starting to get dark when Jason and I check at the address on file for Cameron, a cottage on Clarence Mangan Road, a couple kilometers from Canal Landing. An elderly woman dressed in a nightgown answers our knock and tells us she hasn't seen him in a while. When we ask what relation she is to him, she says it's none of our fucking business and shuts the door in our faces.

"They call this area The Tenters," Jason tells me. "Did you know that? There's a pub with the name and all. Because they used to tent their linens to dry over frames behind the houses. I heard someone call it that the other day, and it brought it back. My mother had some aunts who lived over here. That was old Dublin there." He points to the parade of FOR SALE signs up and down the road. "I'd say it's turning quickly though. Nice big houses down some of these streets. They're already using it as a selling point, 'Come live in the historic Tenters.'" He laughs.

"Who do you think that was at the house?" I ask.

"I'm betting that was Cameron's nan," Jason says. "He probably stays with her sometimes, when he doesn't have a place to go. Sally Murphy, I think her name is. One of her sons is in prison for stabbing a man in the neck with a fork a few years back. That was when I was posted in Offaly so I don't remember all the details. Not sure if that's Cameron's da or not, the stabber, but I'd say it's a good bet."

"You think Cameron has it in him to strangle Jade Elliott?" I ask Jason. "For money or otherwise?"

"If he was desperate maybe, but it doesn't quite fit for me," Jason says. "He's got a temper on him all right and poor impulse control, but I'd say most of his crimes have been ones where he didn't have to get up close and personal with the violence, if you know what I mean."

We head back into the heart of Portobello, passing most of Cameron's usual haunts, walking every street and keeping an eye out for Alannah, Andy, and Cameron.

It's mostly dark by five, and we grab a quick sandwich and then keep looking, the neighborhood settling into its night rhythms, people heading into the pubs or home from work, lights coming on in the flats and shops along the street.

We're talking to a restaurant owner who says he saw Cameron yesterday when my radio crackles and the dispatcher asks for our location. We give it and he says that an officer spotted Cameron on Camden Street thirty minutes ago but that he went down an alleyway and disappeared and he hasn't been able to locate him again. "Responding officer thought he was talking to a teenage girl matching the description of Alannah O'Reilly," the dispatcher tells us. "Approach with caution."

We race up to the spot where he was sighted and check the alleyway, but Cameron and Alannah aren't there. So we head back down along Camden Street and onto Richmond Street, cutting across on Lennox and checking some of the places we've seen Alannah and her friends hanging out. There's no sign of them, but we're walking back along the canal when Jason nudges me and I look up to see a familiar form, standing by the water under the willow tree, almost obscured by its branches, the glow of a cigarette just barely lighting the darkness. I radio it in and we approach him slowly. There's no sign of Alannah, but if she's nearby we need to make sure Cameron hasn't hurt her. I scan the street and the canal bank.

"Hiya, Cameron," Jason says softly. "Nice night. Just step out of there where we can see you, please."

Cameron turns with a start and steps into the pool of illumination from the streetlight, his eyes searching for an out, his hands up. I can see how scared he is, how tired. Even Tweety Bird looks tired tonight, his expression somehow downcast and dejected. "Just had to leg it from one of yours. Why the fuck are youse looking for me?" he asks, his eyes wild. "I've done nothing."

"Cameron, where's Alannah?" I ask him. "That's all we care about right now, making sure Alannah's safe."

He looks up, surprised. "The Goth one, like? Is that why you're harassing me?"

"She's missing and you were seen with her on Camden Street not too long ago. We need to know where she is."

"She didn't tell me she was missing. We was just chatting, like, and then she went off and I saw this guard looking at me funny and getting out his radio. So I legged it out of there. Look here, I just saw her—she's not missing anymore, so can you leave me the fuck alone, yeah?" He's emotional now, on the verge of tears, I think, and I remember what the barman said after he ejected Cameron last week, that he'd been out of sorts for a few days. Ever since Jade was killed.

"Cameron," I say. "You need to be honest with us. We have evidence you were in Jade Elliott's home. This is your chance to explain it to us. We're looking into who killed her. You said the two of you were mates, that you liked to have a chat sometimes." I go for a lie, following my instinct, betting he likes seeing himself as a protector of beautiful women. "A few people told us that you were really good to her, helped her out. Is that true?"

He looks up at me, looks away, then takes a long drag of the cigarette. "I knew her a little. Around the neighborhood, like I said."

"So what were you doing in her apartment?" I ask him, nodding toward Canal Landing.

"I wasn't in her—"

"Don't lie to us. We know you were."

He doesn't say anything.

"Come on, Cameron. We know you were there."

He looks up guiltily. "We were mates," he says. "I know you don't believe a one like her would be mates with me, but we were. We talked, like. About life, that kind of shite."

Jason nods. "How did you meet her, Cameron?"

He shakes his head. "I don't have to tell you."

I look out across the dark water, frosted here and there by reflected light. "No, you don't have to tell us, Cameron, but I know for a fact that you're on the radar for that Inchicore shooting and I can put in a good word for you, get them to lay off."

"I had nothing to do with that," he says.

I touch his arm, make him look at me. "I know you didn't. But I also know that if the guys who did do it see you talking to us, they won't care about anything but keeping you quiet. So let's do this quickly and we won't have to bother you again."

Cameron checks in both directions along the canal. When he looks up at us, I feel a surge of worry for him. I'm using his possible knowledge of the Inchicore shooting as leverage but it *does* make him vulnerable. "I saw her around like, in the pub once or twice. She came out to smoke on her terrace when her baby was asleep because she didn't want her to breathe it in, yeah? One night I was walking by and I needed a light. She was sitting out there, staring into space, and I saw the smoke and I went over and asked her could I have a light. She gave it to me and we started talking."

"Just talking?" I ask.

"See, that's what everyone woulda thought! That's why I kept it quiet, right? I went by again a few days later and there she was. We talked some more. She said to come over the wall around the terrace and sit down and talk properly, like. So I did. It was our thing. Few times last winter I came to her door and we sat inside. Sometimes she gave me a glass of wine." He smiles a small, shy smile. "That was nice." I remember Gail Roden's statement. Cameron must have been the man she saw at Jade's door, late at night. Last winter wouldn't have still been on the CCTV footage we got from Canal Landing, which is why we didn't see Cameron there.

"What did you talk about, Cameron?"

"Life, just, like I said. What we wanted, what our, you know, dreams were."

"What were her dreams, Cameron?"

"She wanted to be a proper model, for luxury brands, like, handbags and fancy dresses." His voice gets hoarse. "She would have been, too. She was lovely and really good at what she did."

"And you're telling us you never tried it on with her?" Jason asks. "She *was* lovely."

"She was lovely, but we were mates," Cameron says. "She trusted me."

"That's heartwarming," I say. But when he looks hurt at the tone in my voice, I shrug and say, "It actually is, Cameron. What about Laurel's father? I just need to know if you know anything about him. Did Jade talk about him?"

He considers for a moment. Then he says, "One time. She said he wasn't actually a very nice fella, said I'd be surprised if I knew what he was really like. I asked if she wanted me to sort him and she said no. She didn't really mention him again, maybe 'cause she thought I'd hurt him." He draws himself up to his full height. "I probably would have, too."

"Cameron, we think Jade was trying to get together some money just before she died, to get a solicitor and make sure she had full custody of Laurel. Do you know anything about that?"

He doesn't say anything.

"Cameron, we're investigating Jade's death. I'm not the drugs squad. I don't care about that. If you were friends with Jade, you care about her killer getting caught, yeah? If you know something, tell us."

He stays silent. I can feel him thinking, calculating.

"Did Jade ever do drugs, Cameron?" Jason asks.

The answer comes quickly. "No, never. Because of her daughter. She liked her wine and she smoked more than she should. But she only did it when Laurel was asleep." There's something tender about the way he talks about her.

"Come on, Cameron," I say gently. "Do you know anything about the money?"

"She was upset, back in the summer," he says. "She wouldn't tell me why, but she said she needed money, at least ten thousand euros and she didn't want your man to know about it. I told her I'd get it for her," he says suddenly. "I could have gotten it for her no problem, but she said she had to do it herself. Back in the summer, yeah, she said she had a plan. She was going to ask some guy she used to work with or something. She had something on him, I don't know what. But then he only gave her a thousand. She was going to try to get some modeling jobs, but she went on a couple interviews, like, and they said she didn't have the right look anymore. Anyway, she got a few more off a friend of hers but she was still short. I came up with three thousand euros for her, but I couldn't risk taking any more out of my . . . savings right then." He looks up. "She didn't want to take it, but finally she did—I made her—and she said she had a plan to get the rest of it."

We wait for him to go on.

"I'd been over there having the chats the day before she was killed," he says. "And she told me she had a plan. There was some fella and he was coming over and she was going to get the cash out of him. I didn't like it. I know how people get when you ask them for money. I thought I'd just keep an eye on things, you know."

"This was on Monday?" He nods. "What time was that?" I ask him.

"She was meeting the fella at three, she said. So I just sat here, looking out for trouble. She came and opened the terrace door but didn't come out. I didn't hear anything. Nothing happened. Nobody came out. I assumed everything was okay, so I took off around four. Didn't want her to think I was creeping like."

Nothing happened. Nobody came out.

"Who was she going to ask? Who was the fella?" Jason asks him.

"I don't know. I swear to God. But that must be the fella that killed her, right?"

"You had nothing to do with her death? You swear?" I ask him.

"On my mother," he says. His voice gets husky, laced with fury. "I swear I don't know who done her. If I did, he'd be in bits."

"How did you find out she was dead, Cameron?" I ask softly.

"From an ould fella on the street. I heard the sirens like, and he told me someone was dead. I went to that lot, where you can see in the windows, and I realized it was Jade when I saw youse in there." He stops talking, listening to a siren sounding in the distance. He looks up at me and there are tears in his eyes. "I waited until they brought her out. Hours it was. I stood there in the rain until they put her in the van, like a last goodbye."

"Thank you, Cameron," I say. "What were you and Alannah

chatting about when you saw her? She hasn't been home since yesterday morning and we're pretty worried about her."

"She was asking me if I'd seen that fella. Andy, yeah? The one with the awful spots, poor eejit? That one. I told her I saw him in the lot next to the flats, Jade's flats. He was in there earlier, smoking and looking like he wanted to take someone's head off. Some of those other kids were in there, too, but he was raging, like."

"When was he there?"

"Coupla hours ago."

"Thanks, Cameron." Jason turns and starts walking away. I'm about to follow, but instead I turn back and say, "I'm sorry, about your friend. About Jade." He nods and goes back to sucking on the cigarette and looking out at the water.

"I don't think he knows anything more," I say to Jason once we're away from the canal and we've called off the search for Cameron. "I think for once in his life, Cameron Murphy was being honest with us."

"Yeah," Jason says. There's something preoccupied in his voice.

"What?"

He stops walking and turns to look at me. "Maggie, look. I was thinking about something the other day, now," he says tentatively. "About the kids and Cameron and the vacant lot. I should have rung you, like, but then they got the fella in the blue car and . . ."

"Yeah, what about them?"

"Well," Jason says after a moment. His face is thoughtful as he reaches up and moves a few of the longer pieces of hair across his bald patch. I feel a little surge of affection for him, a sense of how much I'm going to miss him if I make it onto one of the investigative teams. "I was thinking about when we were called out to Canal Landing. The first time."

"Yeah?"

"The manager fella, he said someone yelled through his door. We assumed it was one of the other tenants who heard the television, thought it was someone screaming, right?"

"Yeah?" I still don't see where he's going with it.

"Well, look, I had to go in that vacant lot the other day. That ould fella with the rucksack, the homeless one, was pissing in there. I saw him go in, poor fella, and I hated to do it, but the development company's been complaining about trespassers. So I chased him off and then I looked up at her apartment again and I was thinking to myself, let's say it wasn't the television, then what could it have been? I started playing a game with myself, like."

I join in. "It could have been someone actually assaulting Jade and Jade lying to us."

"Yeah, that's probably the most likely, right? But she really did seem surprised, didn't she, when we showed up? She didn't seem scared or upset, more just . . . surprised."

"A little embarrassed," I say, remembering her face as she'd said that no, she didn't know what the caller had heard, but maybe it was her television.

Jason starts to say something, then hesitates before following through. "Let's say someone made it up. Let's say there was no disturbance at all."

"Why would they do that?"

"Well, that's the thing. I had the thought, like, but I couldn't think of a reason *why* someone would do it. And then this ould one called in, she was worried there was a dead swan in the canal, but it wasn't dead at all, it was sleeping only, and I forgot about it. But just now, talking to Cameron, I was thinking to myself, let's say there wasn't any screaming, then why would someone do it? What would getting us here achieve, right? What's that saying? Who benefits?"

"Cui bono?"

"Yeah, that's the one. Who benefited from that call?"

I think. "Well, we showed up. I don't know how anybody benefited from that. We bothered the neighbors, we bothered Jade. We interrupted her evening."

"Exactly, we interrupted all of their evenings. Jade was home, Laurel was at Dylan's. What if Jade had a date?"

"Okay?" We slowly start walking.

"Yeah. Imagine. Saturday night, right? You're hanging out in that vacant lot and you see someone in Jade's bedroom. You see something happening that you want to interrupt, yeah? Coulda been it was something violent going on, some guy assaulting Jade. Maybe you're afraid to go in, but you want someone to intervene. But what if it wasn't violent at all? What if Jade had a date? And someone wanted to interrupt it. Someone carrying a torch for whoever the date was."

"Alannah," I say, stopping to look at him. "She looked up and she saw Andy Roden in Jade's apartment. She wanted to get him out of there, so she called us to scare him off."

Jason shrugs. "That's what I was thinking. She's always hanging out there."

"You think Andy Roden might have killed Jade?" I ask.

"I don't know, but he was right there, wasn't he? We never saw anyone going in on the CCTV, and maybe that's why. He was already inside. Cameron said she was going to try to get the rest of the money off someone. His family has money. Maybe she was trying to get him to take money from his parents, something like that. He's a big lad, no trouble strangling a little wisp of a girl like Jade."

"Cameron said no one went in and no one came out. Andy's parents seemed desperate to protect him." Suddenly, I remember. "Alannah was looking for him."

Jason nods. "We'd better try to find her," he says.

Twenty-nine

....

She's in the vacant lot, sitting alone on the ground, smoking, staring up at the sky. It's cold and she's only wearing a thin jumper. I can see her shivering.

"Aren't you freezing out here, Alannah?" Jason asks her. "It's Baltic."

She doesn't say anything, doesn't acknowledge us. Her black hair is falling in front of her face and she drops the cigarette to the ground and turns away from us, her hands in long fingerless gloves, gripping her knees.

"Your mother's worried about you," I tell her. "Everyone's worried about you. I'm just going to radio to control and let them know you're all right, okay?" She keeps ignoring us, looking toward the canal, pretending we're not even there.

When I get back, Jason whispers, "She's waiting for Andy Roden, she says. I asked if he's okay and she said he isn't, that he had to go do something, but he wouldn't let her go with him. I think we'd better check on him."

A little buzz of anxiety starts at the base of my neck.

"Alannah, we need to talk to you," I say. "We think maybe you told Mr. Egan to call in the disturbance at Jade Elliott's apartment the Saturday night before she died. Was that you?"

She starts to get up, but Jason puts a hand out and says, "Don't go. We're not mad at you. We just need to know. To help Andy."

She stays where she is but presses her lips together and shakes her head.

"If Andy hurt Jade," I say, "he needs help. If he was seeing her and something happened, maybe it was an accident. Maybe he didn't mean for her to get hurt and he needs help. Is that why you wanted us to come?"

Now she's looking up at us, confused. Her dark eyes are wide beneath the heavy bangs. "It wasn't Andy," she says, incredulous. "He would never go with that slag."

"Alannah," I say. "This is very important. I think you saw something one time when you were in the vacant lot. I think you saw someone in Jade's window. If you look up from here, you can just see into her bedroom. What did you see? Who did you see?" My breath forms a little cloud in front of me. It's getting colder by the minute.

"Alannah?" Jason prompts her.

And then I see it. "It was Andy's dad, wasn't it, Alannah?"

I got it. She looks up.

She's angry still, angry at all the ways we adults have failed her, angry at how small and sad her world seems, at the way promises have been made and broken. But she nods.

"She was kissing Andy's da," she says. "He was in her *bedroom*. I didn't want Andy to know. I know what that feels like, your parents splitting up. I thought if I made that weird fella who works at the flats call the guards, said I'd heard someone screaming, and you came, they would get scared and they'd stop doing it, maybe she'd leave him alone. Andy showed me how to get in through the gate with a credit card once. He knew how to do it because he forgets his keys sometimes. I went in and I knocked on that fella's door and made my voice sound low. I saw youse go in to talk to her and I went back to watch what happened. They'd gone downstairs, I think, but then Andy's da ran up to the bedroom and I could see him waiting there until you went away."

I try to keep my voice even, but she hears my desperation when I ask her, "Alannah, what about that Monday? Did you see anyone go into Jade's place the day she was killed?"

She shakes her head.

"Were you with Andy?"

She shakes her head again. "He said he had something he had to do. So I went home."

I remember Elizabeth Ruane's account: *She said she needed to meet with someone at her apartment.*

And then Cameron: *There was some fella and he was coming over and she was going to get the cash out of him.*

Alannah says, "I couldn't tell anyone about Andy's da and Jade because I knew it would wreck his life." She looks up, defiant. "I love him, Andy. We're going to go away together. He just has to tell his da what a fucking bastard he is and get some money off him."

"Does Andy know about Jade and his dad?" I ask her.

"Not until I told him today," she says. "I just wanted them to stop. But then . . ."

"Thank you," I tell her, my mind churning. "You're being a good friend to him by telling us. Thank you."

Jason's radio crackles.

"I have a request for assistance at Canal Landing," the dispatcher says. "Woman says her son has a knife and has become violent. Number 204."

Jason and I look at each other. Number 204.

Alannah is up and running before we can stop her and we follow, running as fast as we can. The gate's open and she's already in the hallway outside the flats by the time we get there.

"Andy," she's calling out. "Andy!"

I can hear shouting from the half-open door and I push Alannah against the opposite wall. "Stay there or I'll put you in handcuffs," I say to her.

Jason's already inside the Rodens' apartment, racing across the entryway, and the first thing I see once I'm through the door is Andy, his face red, tears streaming down his face. He's holding a large kitchen knife and he's screaming at his father, who's trapped at the table in the corner of the living room. Gail's holding her phone and when she sees us, she cries out, "Come on, Andy, put the knife down. The guards are here now. Come on, love. We can work this out."

"Ask him, ask him!" he shouts at her. "Ask him about Jade."

"Andy, just put it down, love. Put the knife down." Gail Roden is sobbing, still clutching her phone. There's a radio or a television on in one of the back rooms and the periodic explosions of laughter and applause are disturbing, giving the whole scene a surreal quality.

"Ask him, you fucking cow," Andy shouts at her.

She finally looks at her husband. "What's he talking about, Phil?"

Phil Roden just sits there at the table, his head in his hands. His stacks of papers and manuals, the laptop and file folders, are all over the ground, the papers sullied by muddy bootprints.

"Tell her!" Andy shouts. He's barely aware that we're in the room. "All your shite about working hard and being a man, sticking to your word. It's all fucking lies. You're a cheater. You're a liar. I hate you!" He's holding the knife more loosely now, the point angled down and I think I might be able to get it away from him. I take a step closer but he seems to sense me there and grips it harder. His face is flushed, a bead of sweat on his temple, and his eyes are fixed on his father and full of hatred.

"Andy, what are you talking about?" Gail says.

"Tell her," Andy says to Phil and Phil collapses, his head down on the table, like a little kid who can't stand to face what he's done.

Gail looks from Andy to Phil and back again. She's holding a dish towel and she clutches it to her chest as though it's armor. "Phil, what is he talking about?"

"He was sleeping with Jade," Andy yells at his mother. "Did you know?"

"Phil?" Gail is pale, horrified. She takes a step toward her husband. "What's he talking about?"

Phil Roden makes a low, guttural moan. I've heard the sound so many times before, the sound of the human psyche breaking, the sound of a person's sense of who they are, the part they show the world, colliding with the part they've tried to keep hidden. "It was an accident," he says. His head is still down on the table. We can barely hear him. "I didn't mean for it to happen." An explosion of transmitted laughter from the back of the duplex makes us all turn toward its source. Jason's edging closer and closer to Andy, his baton out. I try to meet his eyes, to signal he should wait, but he doesn't look over at me.

"What happened, Mr. Roden?" I ask quietly.

He moans again.

And then Gail says, "What are you . . . what are you talking about, Phil? You didn't have anything to do with Jade's death. *We* didn't have anything to do with Jade's death. What are you saying, Andy?" She's still pressing the dish towel to her body, her eyes searching her husband's. She's breaking apart in this moment, too, her whole world and everything about it she thought she knew crumbling to dust.

Andy spits out, "He slept with her. My friend saw them, in her bedroom."

"I didn't . . . mean. I didn't . . ." Phil is crying now, rubbing at his eyes with his sleeve. "It was an accident. When I got there, she was already half undressed. I thought . . . but she was talking about how she wouldn't want to have to tell you. She kept asking for money. She kept saying she'd do whatever she had to, for Laurel. I just wanted . . ." He looks up and it's Gail he's appealing to. "I just wanted to go back to the way things were before. I said I must have gotten things the wrong way 'round. I said I was sorry, but she didn't care. Oh, God forgive me, Gail. I just wanted to make her stop saying she'd tell you. I just wanted her to stop. And then she was . . . and then it was over."

Gail is staring at him. "Did you take Laurel?" she asks. "Was that you?"

"No. God, no. I'd never hurt a child." He's sobbing. "I was shocked when I heard . . . about Laurel. I still don't understand. No, I'd never hurt anyone."

His eyes widen and we all see him realizing it all over again, that he *has* hurt someone, that he's killed someone, that nothing will ever be the same.

"I don't understand," Gail says, looking to me. "Who had Laurel?"

"That was someone else, Mrs. Roden," I say. "Phil's telling the truth about that."

And then Alannah's there, forcing her way in, and that's what makes Andy drop the knife and stride across the room to her. As it clatters to the floor, Alannah takes him in her arms, holding him gently, lovingly, telling him it's going to be okay, until I get him in handcuffs, while Jason cuffs Phil Roden and takes him out into the frigid night.

We take Phil's statement at eleven, once they get a solicitor for him and the solicitor says he wants to cooperate. It's just me and Roly because Fiero is still in Portarlington at the Maguires, searching through those boxes we saw in the garage and outbuildings the day we were there.

"I did it," Phil says as soon as we come into the room, as cold as always, the night black and cold outside the walls of the station. "I did it, and I want to tell you everything so you don't have to talk to Gail or Andy. I want you to leave them alone, you hear? I'll tell you whatever you want to know."

Roly gets the caution and the paperwork out of the way and the story falls out of Phil, a waterfall of confession, about how he was lonely working at home during the days, how a few times Jade asked him to come over and keep an eye on a napping Laurel while she went to the shops, how they got to chatting.

"I didn't mean for . . . I didn't mean for anything to happen," he says. "I swear to you. She . . . One day, back in the summer, she was really upset. I could tell and I asked her what was wrong and she said her life had gone to pieces or something, she was crying, like.

Something made me hug her and . . . I swear I didn't mean for it to happen."

"You had sex with her?" I ask, for the tape. "We need you to say exactly what happened."

"Yeah." He's got his head in his hands now.

"Where?" Roly asks. "In her apartment?"

"Yeah, God forgive me."

"Did it happen again?" Roly asks him. "Or just the once?"

He looks up and I can see the surprise, the confusion there. "I couldn't believe it when she said—when she said she wanted me again, a few weeks later," he says. "I should have said no, but I . . . I couldn't. And then, last week a couple days before . . . a couple of days before, she said she needed money and I saw what . . . what she was doing. What she had done. We were talking about it and then you came. I ran upstairs. Someone called in a noise disturbance. When you left her I told her I couldn't give her money, that I had to get out of there. But then she said I had to, that she needed four thousand euros or she would tell Gail and Andy. She was . . . businesslike. She said I was making good money. I could afford it. It would be nothing to me. I didn't understand. I asked her is that why she slept with me. She tried to say that it wasn't, that she was lonely, but . . ."

He tells us that he thought he could reason with her when he ran into her outside on the street Monday morning, as she was heading out for her walk, and told her he wanted to talk that afternoon. She said she'd have someone watch Laurel, and he went over before Gail and Andy got home.

"She said she was desperate," he says. "That she needed the money and she was going to get it and that if she had to tell Gail, to get it from her, she would. I don't even remember . . ." He looks up, his eyes hollow. "I think I . . . I wanted to scare her. But she ran upstairs and . . ."

"You strangled her, because she wouldn't see reason," I say. "Because you couldn't stop her. She was determined."

He nods, sobbing now. "God help me," he says. "God help me. I deserve everything that's coming."

It starts raining on my way home, the streetlights splashing fragments of light onto the pavement. I get home to a silent house at two A.M. and let Mr. Bean out for a pee. I don't feel the heady triumph I usually feel when a case is done. I just feel depleted and sad, for Jade, for Laurel, for Gail and Andy. And yes, for Phil, though I know I shouldn't waste my sympathy on him.

When I come into the kitchen, there's a piece of paper on the counter, a block of text circled in red pen. I pick it up and read a few lines before I realize what it is and I'm up the stairs and flinging open the bedroom door before I realize Conor's already asleep. But I don't care. I kick off my shoes and turn on the light and jump onto the bed, reading aloud:

> Kearney's comprehensive history of 20th century Irish political history is a joy to read and an invaluable resource for the serious student and the casual observer. A masterpiece of accessible recent history and timely political insight, the prose soars as the research grounds us firmly and completely. Highly recommended.

He opens his eyes and as I read the rest, he can't keep the smile off his face.

"It's a great review," I say, holding the paper up and snuggling into his chest. "I'm so proud of you. It really couldn't be better."

"Yeah, it's pretty good, isn't it?" he says, a shy smile on his face, his eyes unfocused without his glasses.

"We got the guy," I whisper. "We got the guy."

"I knew you would," he says sleepily. "I knew you'd do it."

Thirty

....

"Jade was desperate," I tell Roly and Fiero the next day, after they've charged Phil Roden and gotten further details about how he killed Jade. "She went to the agency and Mal Delaney gave her a thousand euros to get her to stop accusing him of facilitating Dylan's abuse of her, but she didn't have any real proof that Mal was involved, and she knew she wasn't going to get any more out of him. With Dylan, it was complicated. She knew that if she tried to blackmail him, he'd stop paying her and Laurel's bills and I think she knew he was smart enough not to leave evidence anywhere she could find it. Elizabeth gave her another thousand—it was all she could take without making her husband suspicious—and Cameron found her three thousand euros. Knowing who he works for, he was probably taking his life in his hands doing it."

"So how did she land on Phil Roden?" Fiero asks.

"The Rodens had started spending a lot of money recently," I say. "Gail must have mentioned to her that Phil had a new job and was making good money. Gail worked a lot of late shifts."

"Jade was playing a nasty game," Roly says, a hint of scorn in his voice. "Sleeping with him and then blackmailing him."

I turn on him. "It was a game she'd been taught to play by Dylan Maguire. From the time she was thirteen. She was desperate, Roly.

She'd seen those photos. She had to do anything she could to prevent Dylan having access to Laurel. She was just trying to protect her kid."

"Fucking hell," Fiero says. "He was right there the whole time. His fingerprints were in the apartment but we didn't think anything of it because we knew he and Gail had minded Laurel. Cameron and the CCTV didn't see him going in because he lived there. And the girl knew all along. We should have asked her."

"I don't think she'd have told us," I say. "She's in love with Andy. He was all she cared about. What about Dylan Maguire?" I ask. "What did you find, Fiero?"

Fiero tells us that he got back from Portarlington late last night, after we'd already brought Phil Roden in. "We were right about him using external hard drives. We got a warrant for the garage and found forty of them. They're encrypted, but we'll try to get into them. Most importantly, we can now search all the computers at his office, all of his email accounts. And Anna Finley found an old email. It's not signed—he was too smart for that—but the lads at cybercrimes think they might be able to get something from the address. They can start working on his phone and his call records, too."

"What about Laurel?" I ask Roly. "What are they going to do about her?"

Roly sighs. "The Solicitors Division thinks we've got enough to get an order for temporary custody for Nicola. She and her husband have said they'll take Laurel. Dylan will get visits most likely, but they'll be supervised. And who knows what will happen with his case. If Fiero gets the goods, then he'll be going to jail."

"What's going to happen to Alan Keating? And Nicola and Elizabeth?" I ask. "Alan could be charged twenty times over with kidnapping and who knows what else. And as for Nicola and Elizabeth, they lied to Garda detectives, obstructed an investigation, there's probably a conspiracy charge in there, too."

Roly takes a deep breath. "We'll just have to see. I'd be very surprised if the DPP decides to prosecute, but you know we're just the cops, so we'll have to let them decide. It's a fucking sad one, all the way around, but you two did good work on this. D'arcy, you're in Sullivan's sights for a spot on the team now, you know."

"Yeah," Fiero says, a little awkwardly. "Well done." His blue eyes are kind. He means it, I think. He holds his gaze on me a little too long, then looks away, straightening the pockets of his jacket and I have the urge to make a joke about how he must keep snacks in them, there are so many of them.

I don't. "You too," I say. "Thanks for everything."

When I look back at Roly, he's smiling, just a little, and when I roll my eyes at him, he says, "I knew you'd be a good team, even if you hated each other in the beginning. It's what they call managerial intuition."

"Is that what they call it?" Fiero asks. But he's smiling, too, and when we all start laughing, it feels good; it feels like success.

Thirty-one

November comes in damp and dreary, the days short, the street-lights bravely lighting the dim evenings as I finish up my last few shifts with Jason.

On Thanksgiving Day, we work an eight to three, getting off easy with a few purse snatchers and a couple of home security check-ins, then a chat with the neighborhood kids about the whereabouts of Donald the duck. I stop at the butchers on my way home and I'm back in Donnybrook by five. I've picked up lamb chops at the butchers, and by the time Conor gets home at six, they're sizzling in a pan on the stove. Once they're nice and brown, I take them out and add garlic and rosemary, then deglaze the pan with red wine.

He kisses me, takes his stuff into his office, and then comes back in, holding a wrapped present behind his back.

"What's that you're hiding?"

"Nothing." He grins and puts it on the table. "It's for later." Then he inhales the air and looks around at the progress in the kitchen. Gerry has done everything but the final stage, which is to rip out the flooring and all our appliances and put in an entirely new kitchen that will be more to the taste of the hypothetical millionaires who will buy the house. After our Thanksgiving feast this weekend, to which we've invited all of the Americans Conor knows at Trinity, plus

Emer and Monica and Carla and a few other friends, we'll be eating takeout for at least a few weeks. This is my last hurrah for a bit.

"What's that smell?" Lilly calls out. She makes her way past the plastic curtain and pours herself a glass of water. "That smells amazing."

"Lamb chops," I say. "We're celebrating another good review for Conor. And my new job. And also, it's Thanksgiving. Happy Thanksgiving, sweetie. We'll have our big turkey thing this weekend, but I thought we should at least do something today."

"Happy Turkey Day," Lilly says, kissing me on the cheek. "It's weird, you know. Not having Uncle Danny over, not walking down to the beach after dinner. I think because we went to Paris last year I didn't realize how weird it would feel."

"We'll see him for Christmas. And we can go back for Thanksgiving next year if we want. I even found a can of cranberry sauce, so our feast will be complete."

Conor pours me a glass of wine and we all sit down as soon as Adrien gets home, talking about our days and the plans for the weekend.

We finish eating and Conor says, "I brought Maggie a present. Well, it's really for all of us, but I'll let Maggie open it."

The package is flat and hard, about the size of a piece of printer paper, but thicker.

I tear the paper off and find myself looking at a framed photograph of a couple, standing in front of a house that I recognize immediately. "It's Clara," I say. "In front of our house. This house. But who's the guy?"

"There has to be some benefit to having a historian in the family," Conor says. "Once you figured out that Clara was connected with the Crowe family in Portobello, I did a bit of searching and was able to figure out that she was likely Clara Gurwitz. She was born in Dublin in 1903 and grew up in the Jewish community in Portobello. Her family were quite prominent, and they lived on the South Circular Road for most of her life. She married Harry Crowe, the son of the grocers, and they had a nice long life together. I don't think anyone made too much of a fuss about the mixed marriage. Their first house was on Stamer Street. Which you know about. They had three sons and a daughter and then eventually moved to Rathmines. Harry started a home supply company and did very well, passed it on to the oldest son, and when their fortunes were good, they bought this place. Clara died in the late eighties and Harry lived until 1990, leaving the house in the family. They sold this place and bought something smaller. The people we bought it off were named Hanley, so I didn't recognize it, but that was their daughter."

"Where did you get this?" I ask him, holding the photograph and studying Clara's smiling face, tall, handsome Harry's arm around her waist. I like the feel of them together, the way they're leaning toward each other, the look on her face, like he's just made her laugh.

"I rang up the grandson—a colleague figured out who he was for me—and he loaned me the original photograph so I could make a print. I thought we should have them hanging in their old house, now. What do you say?"

"That's it?" Lilly asks. "They had a nice long life. No love child? No hidden passion? Why were the photos hidden in the wall?"

"The grandson said that Harry Crowe had dementia for the last few years of his life, after Clara died. The grandson remembered some work being done on the house during those years and he thinks maybe his grandfather thought someone was trying to take them.

They were prized possessions, a record of their early years together, and he wanted to keep them safe. The grandson thinks that maybe in his addled state, he squirreled them away, to preserve them, to keep his family history secure. I made copies for us and gave him back the originals."

"It was like a time capsule," Adrien says. "Except no one else knew he was doing it."

We all go out into the living room. The walls aren't finished—they've been primed but not yet painted—but Conor finds a nail in the jumble of Gerry's tools and hammers it into the center of the wall, then hangs the framed photograph there. Clara and Harry smile out at us.

"Sure, we'll take it to our new house, wherever that turns out to be," he says, turning to me. "It got me thinking, about how a house is just a house. We'll find something good, I promise."

"When you do, I'll take a picture of you out front," Lilly says. "Then we can hide it in the wall."

She and Adrien disappear upstairs to study, but Conor and I stand there for a long moment, looking at Clara and Harry, before we go to clear the table.

The next morning, I go for a walk with Jason. The canal is gray, dead leaves floating on the surface. There's a touch of frost in the air; Jason and I stand on the bank, watching the swans making lazy circles on the surface.

"Where do they go in the winter?" I ask him.

"I don't think they go anywhere," he says. "I suppose their feathers keep them warm."

"I suppose so."

"It'll be spring before you know it," he says. "You'll be all settled in on the new team by then. When do you start?"

"Two weeks," I say.

"And that fella Fiero is going to be your partner?" I nod. "Does he know what he's in for?"

I laugh. "I think he's got an idea. What about you, Jason? You did good work on this case. Shall I put in a word for you? You have any interest in being a detective?"

"You know, I don't," he says. "I like helping people in the moment, I think, doing what needs to be done. I don't want to know so much about the terrible things they do to each other. Do you know what I mean?"

"I do. You've got a knack for this. I think I'm better suited to the terrible things."

"Besides," he says. "This lot here." He points to the swans, the pairs of ducks floating silently on the still canal. "They're always getting into trouble. Someone needs to be there for the ducks. Donald now, he's quite vulnerable."

We stand there for a few minutes watching the swans circling slowly and then, without a look back, moving along the glittering surface of the water until they're gone from sight.

Acknowledgments

Thanks to everyone in Dublin who helped make my Portobello research rambles possible and fruitful. I'm grateful to Paula McLoughlin, Rachel Hegarty, and all the residents who talked to me about the neighborhood.

I'm also grateful to the Garda officers and detectives who have answered my questions, including big thanks to Chief Superintendent Liam Quinn. All mistakes, as well as willful alterations to Garda hierarchies, procedures, and assignment protocols for the purposes of story and character development are mine and mine alone!

Big thanks to Gillian Fallon, for her sharp eyes and her "Irish edit," and for helping me keep my flats and apartments and my mams and mums straight.

I am indebted to the lovely folks at Minotaur Books. Thank you to my editor, Kelley Ragland, who always knows how to make the manuscript better, and to Madeline Houpt, Sarah Melnyk, Allison Ziegler, David Baldeosingh Rotstein, and Jennifer Rohrbach, for getting my books out into the world and making them look good.

Thank you also to my agent, Esmond Harmsworth, for his stellar editing and advocating, and to everyone at Aevitas Creative Management.

As always, I send so many hugs and kisses to my family. I couldn't do it without you.